# THE
# STOLEN
# BABY

DINEY COSTELOE is the author of 23 novels,
several short stories, and many articles and poems.
She has three children and seven grandchildren,
so when she isn't writing, she's busy with family.
She and her husband divide their time between
Somerset and West Cork.

## Also by Diney Costeloe

*The Throwaway Children*
*The Lost Soldier*
*The Runaway Family*
*The Girl with No Name*
*The Sisters of St Croix*
*The New Neighbours*
*The Married Girls*
*Miss Mary's Daughter*
*Children of the Siege*
*The French Wife*

# THE
# STOLEN
# BABY

## Diney Costeloe

An Aria Book

First published in the UK in 2021 by Head of Zeus Ltd
This paperback edition first published in 2022 by Head of Zeus Ltd,
part of Bloomsbury Publishing Plc

9 7 5 3 2 4 6 8

A catalogue record for this book is available
from the British Library.

ISBN (PB): 9781789543353
ISBN (E): 9781789543322

Typeset by Divaddict Publishing Solutions Ltd

Printed and bound in Great Britain by
CPI Group (UK) Ltd, Croydon CRo 4YY

Head of Zeus Ltd
First Floor East
5–8 Hardwick Street
London EC1R 4RG
WWW.HEADOFZEUS.COM

*For Pat and Terry Brookshaw,*
*with much affection and many thanks for everything.*

# Prologue

Maggie had held him for only a few minutes, a tiny creature with screwed up eyes, a fuzz of soft hair and his face a faded shade of blue. The midwife had taken one look at him and almost snatched him from her arms. Her Roger, so longed for, ached for, so beloved at only five minutes old, taken from her arms and carried away, leaving her in the delivery room attended by an elderly nurse who would not catch her eye as she busied about clearing away bloodied linen.

'No!' Her cry was the wail of desolation, forcing the nurse to return to her bedside.

'Now then, now then, what's all this fuss about?' she murmured to the distraught mother. 'Sister will bring him back soon as he's weighed, washed and clean. You'll see!'

'I want my baby,' came the whispered reply. 'I want my Roger.'

'And you'll have him,' soothed the nurse, 'soon as Doctor's seen him. Now you have a nice little rest.'

'Where's Colin?' Maggie demanded; but the strength was going from her voice. It had been a long and difficult birth and she was wearied beyond expression. All she wanted was to sleep, holding her newborn son in her arms, to feel the softness of his tiny body warm against her own and to share the moment, the long-awaited moment, of being a parent with her husband.

Beyond the delivery room, the doctor looked at the baby and sighed. The child was nowhere near term, only seven months, and the birth had taken too long. The mother had struggled and when they had finally used the forceps the baby had been starved of oxygen. There was a flurry of activity, instructions given, resuscitation tried, the tiny body fighting for life but eventually unable to cope with the outside world, a gentle conceding of defeat. A life cut short after a few hours; before it had even begun.

Maggie, unknowing, sank into the sleep of exhaustion. When she awoke it was to find her husband Colin at her bedside, his face a pale mask of pain as he waited to break the news, news that she steadfastly refused to believe.

'No,' she said firmly, 'not Roger. He's alive. I held him in my arms and he was alive and warm.'

'I'm sorry, dearest, but he was starved of oxygen. He didn't make it.'

'I don't believe you,' she cried. 'Somebody else's baby died, not mine. I want my baby!' She started to push back the bedclothes, struggling to get out of bed. 'I want my baby. Where is he?' Colin reached out to take her hands, to restrain her as she swung her legs out of bed, but her determination gave her strength and her feet touched the floor, before her legs refused to hold her, and her head spun as she collapsed into her husband's arms.

# I

The sound of the siren swooped and wailed, cutting through the peaceful darkness of the night sky. Yet another raid. For a split second the inhabitants of Plymouth held a collective breath before they began to react. Air-raid warden David Shawbrook, already out patrolling the streets, hurried to the wardens' post. His wife, Nancy, and their young children were at home, the little ones in bed, but Nancy knew the drill and as soon as the first wail of the siren ripped the sky, she would gather them up and hurry them along the two hundred yards to the shelter at the end of the street. They had an Anderson shelter in their backyard, but with seven of them and the baby it was a crush when they were all within. Angela, aged only seven, was particularly scared of going inside, crying hysterically if her mother insisted she must, so now, if there was enough warning, they had taken to joining their neighbours in the Parham Road public shelter.

Tonight, hurried by their mother, they crawled, bleary-eyed, out of bed and poured into the street, scurrying along with only a fitful moon to guide them. When they reached the shelter, folk from the surrounding streets were already crowding inside and they had to push their way in through the crush.

The only one of the family missing was Vera. Too young to train as a nurse like her elder sister Muriel, or join up like her brother Tony, the Shawbrooks' eighteen-year-old daughter worked as a waitress at the Lord Howard pub, and tonight she had stayed on when the bar closed for an extra drink with Charlie, the barman.

Dad will be out on duty, Vera had thought, and Mam'll be in bed by the time I get home. She won't realise how late it was. And even if she does, Vera gave a shiver of anticipation, it'll be worth it to have a drink with Charlie.

She had been looking forward to it all evening, longing for George the boss to call time and shut the doors. Then, then, she'd be with Charlie. He had such lovely brown eyes, and his smile...

As the siren split the night air, Charlie grabbed Vera by the hand and pulling her off the bar stool, hurried her out into the street, running for cover.

'Come on!' he urged as they ran along the road. They heard the distant sound of approaching aircraft, saw searchlights already sweeping above them. Charlie scanned the sky anxiously and knew there was not much time. 'Come *on*, Vera!'

'I can't go any faster,' wailed Vera as she tried to run in her high-heeled shoes. They were her pride and joy and she'd put them on specially for her evening out, but they were useless for running in. 'My shoes!'

'For God's sake, take 'em off then,' cried Charlie.

Hopping from one foot to the other, Vera did as she was told, but bare feet weren't much better on the chilly cobbles of the narrow lane that led to the Parham Road shelter and safety.

Followed by the roar of the incoming aircraft they flung themselves down the steps and into the shelter, where her mother was already settling the younger children. 'Vera!' Nancy stared at her daughter as the realisation hit her. In her anxiety for her younger children she hadn't realised that Vera had been not been with them.

In a voice sharp with anger she cried, 'Where have you been? You should have been home hours ago!' Charlie melted into the background, leaving Vera to face her mother's anger, but even as she spoke Nancy Shawbrook saw him slide away and suddenly realised that Vera must have come straight from the pub. She stared at her daughter in horror and whispered, 'Where's Freddie?'

Freddie? What did Mam mean? 'Where's Freddie'?

'With you,' cried the girl.

'No!' cried her mother. 'You always bring him!'

In the well-rehearsed evacuation of the house when the siren sounded, Vera would grab Freddie from his cot and carry him to the shelter, leaving her mother free to shepherd the other children to safety. Freddie was Vera's responsibility.

Apart from Vera herself, only her parents and her older siblings, Muriel and Tony, knew the truth: that Freddie was Vera's son. When she had come home one winter's day and confessed that she'd let a good-looking sailor on leave sweet-talk her into bed, and that she was now expecting his child, her parents had stood by her in place of the vanished father and adopted the baby as their own. The neighbours guessed the true situation, but no comments were made. It wouldn't be the first, nor the last, time that a grandparent stood in for a parent, and the younger members of the family had simply accepted that on a warm July afternoon, Mam had had another baby, a boy called Freddie.

One day, perhaps, thought Nancy as she'd held the tiny scrap of humanity only hours old in her arms, we may tell him the truth, but not until he's grown up.

However, in her own way she had prepared for that day, insisting that Vera did more than her share of the looking after, and when she'd got her job at the pub, Nancy took five shillings a week from Vera's wages to help with his keep. Recently, as the number of air-raid warnings had increased, and nights of broken sleep had continued, Nancy had made it Vera's responsibility to catch up Freddie from his cot and carry him to the safety of the shelter at the end of the road.

Tonight Vera had not been at home when the sirens began their lament, and along with everyone else from the pub she had made a dash for the shelter, knowing that Mam would bring the other children from the house. Only she hadn't, not all of them. She hadn't brought Freddie... and nor had Vera. The baby, nine months old and the darling of all their hearts, was not with them in the shelter. He was still at home, alone in his cot.

With a panic-stricken shriek, Vera exploded from the shelter and set off, running barefoot along the road back to the house, with her mother's cries of, 'Take him into the Anderson!' echoing in her ears.

The enemy aircraft were overhead now, deafening as they opened their bomb bays and their deadly load came cascading down on the city below. Vera continued to run in the nightmare of the raid, heedless of the pain in her chest and the agony of her bare feet on the pavement. Flame bloomed about her as incendiary bombs began spreading fire, but she continued to run. Freddie, she must get to Freddie! It was her final thought as, caught out in the street, the world exploded around her and she knew nothing more.

Back in the shelter Nancy waited, terrified for Vera, yet impotent, knowing that there was nothing she could do. Vera was alone out there in peril on the street, and Nancy could only pray that she would get to Freddie in time and take him into the safety of the Anderson shelter in the backyard. Beyond the shelter she could hear the battle raging in the skies above and she clutched Winnie and Angela, the two youngest children, against her, as if her arms could protect them from the deadly onslaught. The two older boys sat side by side, listening to the thundering engines overhead and trying to distinguish friend from foe. It was a game they always played, making the reality of the situation into a challenge.

'Mamma, I don't like it in here,' whispered Angela. 'I don't like the bombs!'

'I don't like them either,' whispered back Nancy. 'But we have to be brave and wait for the planes to go away again. They will, you know.'

'Promise?' returned the small voice.

'Promise. Now come and sit on my lap and we'll sing a song. What would you like to sing?'

'"Old MacDonald",' cried Winnie, as she went to snuggle up with her mother and Angela.

'Well, I asked Angel first,' Nancy pointed out, 'so we'll sing "MacDonald" second. What about you, Angel? What would you like to sing?'

'I like "Row the Boat",' said Angela.

'That's a baby song!' scoffed Winnie.

'It's the one we're going to sing first,' Nancy said. 'Ready?'

With the noise of the raid as an accompaniment, the three of them began to sing, and gradually others sitting in the shelter with them began to join in. 'MacDonald' followed and then other favourites; singing until the raid would be over as Nancy had promised. As they ran out of songs, Nancy's promise was kept. The planes finally flew away, back over the sea to their base in France, leaving behind an annihilated city, ruined and in flames, buildings flattened, reduced to rubble or leaning drunkenly in their fight to remain upright. As the bombers departed, roaring away into the night, one made a final pass over the city, sending bombs hurtling downwards. A final gesture of bravado from a young pilot, pulverising shops, offices, houses... and the Parham Road air-raid shelter.

When the all-clear finally sounded and people began to emerge from their underground shelters, those who lived in the centre of the city found that it no longer existed in any form they could recognise.

David Shawbrook had been at the wardens' post throughout the raid. The pounding from the sky had discouraged patrols, and it was only now that the wardens were making a sweep of their patches. The rescue services had been in action throughout the raid, trying to douse the fires started by the cascade of incendiaries which left the city a beacon for the next wave of bombers. They searched frantically for survivors among the debris of the stricken buildings devastated by the wholesale destruction of the city centre. Partially demolished houses leaned at impossible angles, with masonry threatening to collapse, or giving up the struggle and rumbling to the ground in clouds of dust and rubble. The collapse of such buildings added to the chaos, further endangering those who risked their lives searching for the trapped and the injured... those who were now beyond help; like those who had sheltered in the Parham Road shelter and had been obliterated by a direct hit, leaving the rescuers nothing to find.

## 2

When the sirens had sounded, eleven-year-old Ernie Drake had taken shelter with his mother, Jane, in the cupboard under the stairs. They had nowhere else and Jane felt they were safer there than running through the streets to the nearest public shelter. They sat together in the darkness and listened to the pounding of the anti-aircraft guns, the throbbing drone of the incoming aircraft, the explosions as their deadly cargo rained down on the city below. The raid seemed to last all night, but it was only midnight when at last the all-clear sounded and Jane and Ernie crept out into the narrow hallway. Jane made them some cocoa and then by the light of her torch, they went back to their beds in the hope of another few hours' sleep before it was time to face the day. Leaving Ernie to crawl under his blankets, Jane had returned to her own bed, set her alarm, pulled the covers over her head and slept.

It was some time before Ernie fell asleep. For a while he lay in the darkness of the blacked-out room, but he was wide awake, his mind alive with the happenings of the night. There had been raids before, but none as long and as heavy as this one had seemed. In the understairs cupboard the house had shaken above them as they had been bombarded with sound, aircraft overhead, anti-aircraft guns, explosions. It was quieter now, and at last Ernie drifted into an uneasy sleep, but the sounds beyond the window invaded his dreams and it wasn't long before he was awake again and aware of activity outside in the streets; people shouting, distant crashes, unexplained rumbling, the bells of fire engines; the chaos left by the bombers. It was no use trying to go back to sleep again now, Ernie decided, and getting out of bed he padded across to the window, drew aside the blackout curtains and peered out into the street. The sight that met his eyes made him gasp. Though the dawn was yet some way off, the sky was alight with the flicker of flames and a dense orange smoke. He pushed up the sash and leaned out of the window, craning his neck to see along the road. Two of the houses further down on the other side had fallen prey to the bombers. One gaped roofless at the early morning sky, the other had been reduced to rubble, leaving the street strewn with debris and broken glass. And there was fire. Fire flickering everywhere; figures moving among the ruins, silhouetted against the glow as they fought to quench the flames.

For a long moment Ernie stared out into the street, both fear and excitement growing inside him. He couldn't possibly stay in bed now; he wanted to be out there. He and his pals were keen collectors of shrapnel and other trophies of war. Surely there would be a load to find today after a raid like last night's. Surely he'd be one jump ahead of Joe and Sidney if he went out looking now. You never knew what you might find, there'd be swaps to be made and he'd have the best collection in his class.

Silently Ernie got dressed and crept out onto the landing. He paused outside his mother's half-open door, listening for a moment to her steady breathing. He didn't think she'd be awake again until her alarm went off and he would be back home well before that. He tiptoed past her door and down the stairs, avoiding the second from the bottom which he knew, to his cost, creaked loudly. As he reached the tiny hallway below he listened again and, reassured by the silence from above, he unlocked the front door and let himself out. Although it was still very early there were plenty of people about. At one end of the street, firefighters with stirrup pumps struggled to contain and control a fire burning brightly in the shell of the roofless house, at the other people were emerging from shelters, dazed as they stared in disbelief at the damage sustained by their homes. A few brave souls tore at the rubble of the collapsed house, frantically searching for anyone or anything that miraculously might have survived; and all was lit by the eerie glow of the fire-stained sky.

The small terrace of houses in Haversham Road in which Ernie lived seemed relatively undamaged, but as he made his way down the street and his feet crunched on broken glass, he realised that here there had been blast damage. His stretch of Haversham Road was still standing but further along the houses had not fared as well. Here the houses were semi-detached and as he approached them he saw that the damage they had sustained was even worse than it had looked from a distance. Several houses, battered but defiant, leaned tipsily together, as if liable to collapse at any moment; another on the corner, its side sliced off as if by a knife, revealed its interior on both floors to public view. Ernie saw a warden peering into one of the damaged houses, heard him calling to see if there was anyone trapped amongst the debris. Ernie ducked away, knowing he'd be in trouble if he were seen, and turned into the next street. There were fewer people here, though here too a house had been reduced to rubble and several others seemed to lean against each other for mutual support. Ernie could see a fire engine further down the street where a group of firemen were playing a jet of water on the smouldering remains of the Lord Howard pub. Ernie watched from a safe distance, knowing he would be chased away by the fire crew if he went any closer. It was certainly too dangerous to go looking for trophies yet.

He watched the water beginning to quench the flames, sending dark smoke spiralling into the sky. The Lord Howard, his dad's favourite pub, had been reduced to a blackened shell. What would Dad say when he got home on leave and he found the Howard gone?

Ernie was about to retrace his steps home, but it was as he paused outside one of the half-ruined houses that he heard something; the wailing cry of a baby. He turned sharply and peered into the remains of the house. Its front door had been blown in and the glass from its shattered windows lay in shards on the pavement outside. Ernie could see into the hallway, a dark passage leading towards the back of the house and a staircase clinging to a wall, leading to the floor above. The whole house seemed to be leaning at an alarming angle, threatening to fold in on itself. Ernie walked to the front door and cocked his head, listening. Yes, there it was again, a baby crying somewhere inside the house. He took another step closer, straining his ears to hear.

Suddenly there was a heavy hand on his shoulder and a gruff voice said, 'Now then, young'un, what are you up to?'

Ernie spun round and found himself face to face with a large policeman.

'N-Nothing!' he stammered.

'Just thought you'd do a bit of looting, did you?'

'No, course not,' replied Ernie hotly. He knew about looters and what could happen to them if they were caught. 'I weren't doing nothing!'

'Looked to me as if you were about to go inside this house,' began the policeman.

'No I wasn't, honest,' cried Ernie. 'I thought I heard someone in there, that's all.'

'Did you now?' Police Sergeant Colin Peterson had to give the lad full marks for quick thinking. 'Well, I don't hear—' And then he stopped, for he did hear it... the cry of a baby. Not just one cry now, but an increasingly loud bellow, as the child concerned gathered its strength to express its anger at being hungry and cold.

'See?' said Ernie smugly. 'Told you!'

Colin Peterson was still gripping the boy's shoulder. He pulled him away from the house and said, 'Wait here. Don't come any closer. I'm going to look.'

Ernie looked at him. 'You goin' inside?'

'If there's a baby alive in there, I've got to fetch it out.'

Ernie looked further along the road to where the firemen were still pouring water into what had been the Lord Howard.

'What about them?' he said. 'You could get them to come and help.'

'They've got enough on their hands,' snapped Colin. 'I need to get this baby out and fast. The whole house could collapse at any time. Now,' he gave Ernie a shake, 'you stay out here and you don't come into the house whatever happens, right?'

Looking at him wide-eyed, Ernie nodded.

'And,' Colin went on, 'if the worst happens and it does collapse on us, you can run for help to pull us out. Got it?'

'Yeah, I got it,' said Ernie, adding in a small voice, 'You will be careful, won't you?'

'Don't worry, lad, I'll be fine. I'll be in and out of there like greased lightning.' Colin gave Ernie a little push. 'Now you go and stand over there and stay well clear, eh?'

Obediently Ernie took a step back and waited on the far side of the road.

As if to remind the policeman that time was running out, some tiles slid off the sagging roof and crashed to the ground in a cloud of dust.

'Careful, mister,' cried Ernie, taking another hasty step back.

The baby's cries had escalated into a continuous bellow of rage now, spurring Colin on.

'I'm coming,' he murmured, and looking up at the disintegrating building, he took a deep breath and stepped over the threshold. It was now or never.

Ernie held his breath, watching from a safe distance. He saw the copper walk in through the open front door and disappear. He glanced down the street to the fire crew who were now rolling their hoses up onto the fire engine, leaving the blackened shell of the pub, smoke drifting from its roofless walls, and making ready to move off to the next fire. They'd be gone before they would be of any use to the cop who'd gone inside.

Colin edged his way into the hallway and looked at the stairs. The bottom few looked sturdy enough, it was the ones nearer the upper floor that were hanging perilously off the wall. They might take his weight, he supposed. But then again they might not. Perhaps he should have let the lad run to the firemen at the end of the street. They might have got a ladder up to the first-floor window and brought the child out that way, without having to risk using the staircase. Still, too late now. Colin knew that the building was extremely unsafe and there was not a moment to be lost.

Slowly he edged his way forward and gripping the handrail that ran up the wall as a banister, placed his foot on the bottom stair. It didn't move and he trod gingerly onto the next step. The baby was still wailing on the floor above and looking up towards the landing, Colin moved with careful tread up the hanging stairs. When he reached the landing he found much of it was unsupported, sloping away from him where an interior wall had partially collapsed. He sidestepped along the edge and grabbed at the doorframe of the first bedroom. It was the room that looked out over the road and contained a double bed, a single bed and a cot. Standing up in the cot, gripping the rails and still crying, its face crimson with effort, stood a baby.

'All right, little'un, all right,' Colin soothed. 'I'm coming to get you. Uncle Colin's coming.'

He looked across the room, surveying the floor between the door and the cot. It looked firm enough, but even so he stepped softly around the beds, testing each step before he trusted his full weight to the floor. As he reached the side of the cot the baby's legs seemed to give way and it sat down with a bump and stared at him through the bars of the cot.

'All right, little'un,' he said again, gently, and reaching into the cot, he scooped the child up into his arms. The baby relaxed against him, its hot, wet cheeks pressed against his neck. Colin could feel the dampness of its clothes and realised its nappy must be absolutely sodden. A quick glance round the room showed him older children's clothes on a chair, but no sign of clean nappies.

Never mind nappies, he thought, we've got to get out of here, fast.

As if to encourage him, there was the rumble of something falling. He turned back towards the door and as he did so he caught sight of a bedraggled panda bear wearing a purple ribbon round its neck propped up in the cot. He reached in and snatched it up before turning to make his way back to the staircase. As he reached the top of the stairs he heard a voice from below.

''Ere, mister?' Ernie had ventured back to the house and was standing in the doorway. 'You all right?'

'Get out,' shouted Colin. 'Get right away!'

He saw the flash of fear on the boy's face as he vanished from the doorway, and then concentrated on getting himself and the baby in his arms safely out of the house before it collapsed on top of them. As he put his foot on the top step the whole staircase seemed to shudder and grabbing the handrail in the hope of taking some of his weight off the treads, Colin almost ran down the stairs, bursting out through the front door into the street, where a wide-eyed Ernie waited for him. As he reached the safety of the opposite pavement he dropped the panda. Ernie reached down and picked it up.

'Said there was a baby in there,' he remarked as he dusted down the toy and held it out to the child. ''Ere you are, mate.' But the baby had exhausted itself with crying and had simply fallen asleep in the policeman's arms.

'Here,' Colin said, 'give that to me.' He took the bear and stuffed it into his pocket. 'What's your name?' he asked the boy.

'Ernie Drake,' replied Ernie.

'Well, I don't know what you were doing alone out here so soon after a raid, Ernie Drake,' said Colin, 'but you were a brave lad to get help for this baby. I think it owes its life to you.'

'And to you,' Ernie replied stoutly. 'You was ever so brave going into that house. It's falling down.' As if to prove him right another shower of tiles cascaded from the roof.

'Yes, it is,' agreed Colin, 'and you must never go into a damaged building like that. It could collapse on you.'

'What you gonna do with it?' asked Ernie, nodding at the sleeping baby.

'I'll take it to the rescue centre,' replied Colin. 'They'll look after it. Someone may well come looking for it.'

'Nah,' said the boy. 'If there was someone to look after it, it wouldn't 'ave been in that 'ouse, would it? Stands to reason.'

Colin rather agreed with him, and he said, 'Well, if not, it'll be taken into a children's home. But we have to report that we've found it, in case someone does come forward to claim it.' He glanced down at the baby. He had no idea how old it was, but it was getting heavy in his arms. 'Don't even know yet whether it's a boy or a girl! I'll take it to the rescue centre and tell them which house it was found in.' He glanced up at the house. 'Can you see a number?'

Ernie looked back at the house and saw the number 21 painted on the doorpost.

'Number twenty-one,' he said. 'Twenty-one Suffolk Place.'

'Right,' said Colin, and repeated the address to himself before looking back at Ernie and adding in his policeman's voice, 'Better be getting along now, lad. You shouldn't be out here... and without your gas mask! Get along home, sharpish, before the warden sees you. Your ma'll be wondering where you've got to.'

As if on cue, a nearby church clock struck six and Ernie realised that he should indeed be home now, before his mother woke up and realised he'd been out.

'All right, mister,' he said and with a brief wave he scampered off up the road.

'Well done, young'un,' called Colin, but the boy had gone and didn't hear him.

Colin shifted the baby to rest more comfortably against him. The child snuffled into his neck, and sighed in its sleep.

For a long moment Colin stood, holding the child. He knew he really should take it to the rescue centre, but he hesitated. The raid had been long and heavy, there'd be casualties everywhere. From what he could see, it had been a blanket raid, the entire city being pounded by the Luftwaffe, leaving swathes of destruction behind them. The rescue centres would be overwhelmed with people who had been made suddenly homeless, who had lost everything they had in the world. There would be those who'd been injured and in need of medical care. Everyone in shock. Colin knew he should take the baby to safety at once and then get on with helping the wardens as they searched the ruins for survivors, but here was he with a survivor in his arms. The child didn't seem injured, just cold, wet, probably hungry and definitely in need of a clean nappy. Those manning the rescue centres would be run off their feet, helping all those who had nowhere else to turn, but this survivor did have somewhere else to turn. Colin could take the child home and Maggie would be there to look after it. It would be far better off in the peace and quiet of a normal home rather than being dumped into a creche somewhere with other lost or unclaimed children. *Someone may come looking for this baby* – the thought nagged him. Someone who had left it alone in the house while everyone else had taken shelter. How could anyone leave a baby in its cot during an air raid? He'd report finding the child tomorrow when perhaps things had settled down a bit. The poor kid had already been through enough. Today the child would be far better looked after by a caring woman, someone like his Maggie.

His decision made, Colin turned quickly and walked away from the ruined house, moving purposefully through the streets, back to his own home where Maggie, as always, would be waiting for him.

She'd never wanted to come to Plymouth, he knew, but he'd applied for a transfer, hoping a fresh start would help her move on.

'It's a great chance, Maggie,' he insisted. 'And promotion goes with it. I shall be a sergeant. Goodbye, Constable Peterson... hello, Sergeant.'

Maggie had managed a small smile at that, but she still did not want to make the effort to pack up and move.

What finally persuaded her to go was the legacy. Colin's godmother, an old friend of his mother's, had died and left him £500... a fortune.

'We'll be able to buy a house,' he told Maggie excitedly. 'Imagine, a house of our own. We couldn't afford London prices, but in Plymouth I'm sure we'll find something.'

So, he had accepted the job and they had moved. It had been a waste of time; Maggie had carried the tragedy with her, never allowing herself to move on. Once, when they had been arguing about the move, Colin had accused her of wallowing in her grief and pointed out that it was his grief too. She hadn't spoken to him for days afterwards, and even then there had remained an underlying distance between them.

He knew she would be at home now. Knowing no one, Maggie hardly ventured out at all these days, and seemed more withdrawn than ever. Leaving London had done nothing to help her, indeed the move seemed to have had the opposite effect. They moved into their new home, where she went through the motions of housekeeping, but never went further than the parade of shops at the end of the street. She never spoke to any of her new neighbours, and made no effort to be friendly if they met in a shop, and having been ignored or rebuffed more than once, the neighbourhood seemed to have made a collective decision to leave the newcomers to their own devices.

'That Sergeant Peterson seems a nice enough man,' Elsie Jefferson remarked to her friend, Stella Todd, as they queued at the butcher's in the hope of some kidney or a nice piece of liver off the ration. 'Passes the time of day in the street, but that wife of his, she's a stuck-up thing. You never get so much as a "how do" out of her.'

'I did hear,' Stella murmured behind her hand, 'that she lost someone in a raid in London. Someone close... her brother, was it? Turned her in on herself, made her odd? You know?'

'Well lots of people have lost someone,' pointed out Elsie. 'My Paul's sister's husband who was in the merchant, he was lost at sea a couple of months ago, but she didn't go into a decline. Just gritted her teeth and got on with it!'

'Well,' said Stella, 'things like that take people in different ways, don't they?' Then her attention had been caught by Mr Grant the butcher and was given to deciding on sausages or liver, and the strange, reclusive Mrs Peterson was forgotten as she bargained for off the ration meat.

# 3

It had been the worst raid on the city so far. There had been others, but none with the ferocity of this night's attack. As before, the first wave of bombers had brought incendiaries and flares, raining fire on the streets below.

Stupid to worry about a badly adjusted curtain, David Shawbrook had thought as he grabbed a shovel and began smothering one of the fizzing bombs with sand before it had a chance to do any damage. The trouble was that there were too many incendiaries and not enough water, stirrup pumps, shovels or sand to deal with them. When the heavy bombers followed – the target for their high explosive bombs the docks at Devonport and the railway lines – he'd taken cover at the wardens' post. Being out on the streets as the Luftwaffe tried to destroy the dockyard and flatten the city would be suicidal.

When the German aircraft finally roared back to their base in France and the all-clear sounded, rescue work began in earnest. David and the other emergency services continued to work through the night until dawn, in the chaos the Luftwaffe had left behind. As a hazy sun crept into the smoke-filled sky, fires were still burning fiercely all over the city. Daylight gradually revealed the extent of the damage, and with the coming of morning, as more and more people emerged onto the streets, the rescue work began in earnest. Frantic searches were made for people who might still be alive, buried beneath the rubble of their homes. Survivors were pulled out, some almost unscathed, others needing immediate hospital attention. Temporary mortuaries were set up in church halls where the dead could be laid out for identification and burial. The rescue centres and the wardens' posts were dealing with hundreds of shocked survivors, many of whom were now homeless.

David, weary beyond exhaustion, was just grabbing a mug of life-sustaining tea before returning to the streets when he heard about the Parham Road shelter. The news was brought in by two men who had just pulled out an injured woman from under the remains of her house, and had come to report her name and hospital destination to the rescue centre.

'Direct hit,' he heard one of them say.

'Didn't stand a chance,' agreed the other. 'Almost nothing to find.'

'Where was that?' asked Ruby Manson, one of the women who were logging the information coming into the rescue centre.

'Parham Road,' came the reply. 'Must have been about sixty people in there, and as far as we can tell there are no survivors.'

David froze. Surely he hadn't heard what he thought he'd heard. He spun round and grabbed one of the men by the arm.

'What did you say?' he whispered, then repeating it loudly, 'What did you say? About Parham Road?'

The man looked at him in alarm. 'I said, it was a direct hit.'

'What was?' cried David, still clutching the man's arm and shaking him furiously. 'What was hit?'

'Steady on, mate,' protested the man.

David released him and anguished, asked again, 'What was hit?'

'The Parham Road shelter,' replied the man.

David gave an agonised cry, half man, half animal, and ran from the centre.

The two men looked at each other. Neither man knew for certain why the warden disappeared so suddenly, but they could both guess. They looked at Ruby sitting with her ledger open in front of her and she sighed.

'That's David Shawbrook. He lives not far from the Parham Road shelter...' She faltered into silence, but she didn't need to say any more.

As David burst out into the street he cannoned into Paul Jefferson, one of the firefighters coming in for a ten minute break.

'Hey, Dave,' Paul cried, grabbing his arm as he realised who it was who had nearly flattened him. 'What's the hurry, mate?'

For a moment David didn't recognise his old friend, and tried to pull away from his grasp, muttering incoherently.

Paul, who had now seen the sheer panic on David's face, held him firmly and asked again, 'What is it? What's happened?'

'Parham Road shelter!'

'What about it? What's happened?'

'Direct hit!' He pointed back into the rescue centre. 'They said it was a direct hit. Nancy! And the kids!'

Hearing the anguish in his friend's voice, Paul's heart plummeted. He knew that David Shawbrook's family regularly took refuge in the Parham Road public shelter.

David pulled himself free. 'Let me go, I've got to go and find them.'

'Not on your own, mate,' Paul told him and together the two men hurried through the war-torn streets to the corner of Parham Road and Kelsall Avenue, the site of the large communal shelter. A small crowd had gathered and as David pushed his way through he came to an abrupt halt. Where the shelter had been, half buried underground, reinforced with concrete, there was now a huge crater. There was nothing recognisable, simply chunks of concrete, twisted metal and broken timber, tossed aside as if by a giant hand. Earth and debris so widespread it covered the surrounding ground. David stared down at the immense hole in the ground and knew it was true: no one could have survived such an explosion. Others who had come to look for survivors turned away, shaken and pale.

A cry went up and a man pointed into the crater. 'There,' he shouted, 'look there! There's a hand. Somebody is buried down there.' Before anyone could stop him, he slithered down in to the gaping hole and grabbed for the hand that was reaching out from the earth, reaching for help. The man grasped it, and then gave a shriek as he fell back clasping a severed hand. There was a collective gasp from the watching crowd as he staggered, letting go of the hand and turning away to vomit into the earth.

Paul turned away from the sight, but saw David was staring down into the crater, mesmerised by what he saw. Paul came up beside him and once again took his arm.

'Do you think that's Nancy's hand?' David asked bleakly. 'It could be. It was a woman's hand, wasn't it? It could be Nancy's.'

'Come away, Dave,' said Paul gently. 'There's nothing for you here. If they were in there, they're gone, mate.'

David suddenly clutched at Paul's shoulder and said, 'But perhaps they weren't there. Perhaps they went into the Anderson. They may not have had enough time to come here. The planes came hard on the heels of the sirens, didn't they?' His voice was pleading. 'I mean, Nancy probably thought it was too dangerous to come here with the planes overhead. She took them into the Anderson, this time. Sure to have...' He gave one more glance at the horror that lay before them and then turned away, hurrying the few hundred yards to Suffolk Place. He rounded the corner from Haversham Road and saw the group of damaged houses further down the street. He broke into a run, his feet crushing broken glass, pounding the debris-strewn pavement. Paul followed and they both stopped outside the two sets of semis, and stared at them.

'They might still be in the Anderson,' David cried. 'That's where they'll be!' Without a backward glance, he set off round the side of the house to the back garden. Ignoring the house, he rushed over to the Anderson shelter and ducked his head inside. It was empty and there was no sign that anyone had been in there for some time. There were two bunk beds crammed in, one on each side, and some bedding rolled up and stowed on one of the bottom bunks. The place smelt damp and musty, there was no warmth from the small oil stove. David climbed down into the shelter even though there was no doubt that the family had not taken refuge there.

He stood for a long moment in the half-light that filtered through the doorway, saw the biscuit tin still on the shelf, the primus stove and the kettle, both unused and cold, then he turned on his heel and stumbled back out into the crisp morning air.

Paul was waiting for him by the house. There was nothing he could say that would do any good, so he simply clasped David by the hand for a moment before they walked back out into the street.

Standing on the pavement David looked back at the ruin of his home, the house he and Nancy had lived in for twenty-five years, all their married life. He fought back the tears that threatened to overwhelm him. Perhaps there were things he could retrieve from the house. They had few valuables, but there would be things that had sentimental value to him.

'I'm going inside,' he said suddenly and before Paul could stop him, he marched up to the front door and into the house. For a moment he paused in the hallway, then he headed towards the back, to the kitchen which had been the heart of the home. Standing at its door, he looked round the familiar room. The window was cracked right across, but held together with the black tape he had stretched across it to help prevent shattering. The sink had a pile of plates stacked on the draining board ready for washing; there was a saucepan sitting on the cold gas stove and one of the chairs by the table had tipped over as if someone had leaped up from the table in a hurry.

And so they must have, thought David. The sirens went at about seven o'clock, just the time that Nancy and the older children would be finishing their supper. There was nothing for him there, but as he turned to go he saw the old tea caddy standing on a shelf, the tea caddy that held, not tea, but money for the gas and the rent. David picked it up and emptying the coins into his pocket, walked out into the hall.

'Dave!' Paul called anxiously from the street. 'Time to come out of there, mate. The whole place could collapse.'

'Won't be long,' David called back. 'Just going upstairs.'

'Stupid bugger!' came the cry from outside. 'You'll kill yourself.'

'Don't really care, mate,' David answered and set his foot on the bottom step of the staircase.

Like Colin Peterson an hour earlier, he went gingerly up the stairs, testing each with his weight before trusting it beneath him. When he reached the top, he saw that the only room he could get into was the younger children's room. He stepped inside and stood looking at the beds and the cot. The little ones, his little ones, were gone. Blown to pieces by a German bomb. Tears he could not stem streamed down his cheeks as he thought of his two eldest children – Tony, somewhere in North Africa, Muriel nursing in Portsmouth. Tony and Mu. He had to stay strong for them; they were all he had left of his family. He dragged a handkerchief from his pocket, scrubbed at his cheeks and blew his nose.

He was about to turn away and retreat downstairs when he noticed them, a trail of footprints in the thick dust on the bedroom floor. He stopped dead and looked at them. The footprints must have been made since the bombing. David felt cold fury grip him as he realised what these footprints meant. Someone had already been into the house. Some bastard looking for valuables! Looting! Free to enter the room where his young children should have been peacefully asleep; the home of a family already blasted to pieces and never coming back.

If ever he discovered the thieving bastard who'd crept into his house while others were out in the streets fighting fires and searching for survivors buried in rubble, David knew he would not be answerable for his actions. With this knowledge seared into his brain he turned and made his way downstairs. As he passed through the hall he saw one of Nancy's scarves hanging on a peg, moving gently in the draught from the destroyed front door. He reached for it and for a moment buried his face in the soft wool, catching a trace of the scent of her, before winding it round his neck and going outside to a very relieved Paul waiting for him in the street. David gave one more backward glance at the disintegrating house and then turned away. He'd find somewhere to get some sleep and then he'd come back and see if there was anything else to be done.

# 4

No one had paid any attention to the policeman striding through the streets carrying a sleeping infant in his arms. Everyone was more concerned with the aftermath of the raid, as the extent of the destruction was revealed. Fires continued to burn and people stared in dumb despair at what was left of their city. Colin hurried back home, and even as he passed more ruined houses, blackened shells and tumbled walls, he realised that his own home might have gone as well. The thought made him hasten his step but as he rounded the corner, he knew a profound relief when he saw that it was not only standing, but seemed to be undamaged. He noticed broken glass further down the road, and realised that some of the houses were blast damaged, but his home was as he'd left it the evening before when he'd gone out on patrol. Approaching the house, he paused as he always did and for a moment looked with pleasure at what they had managed to buy. It was a three-storey terraced house in a row of almost identical terraced houses, its front door and windows painted dark green and the walls a pale grey. At some point it had been converted into two flats. He and

Maggie now lived in the ground-floor flat with its cellar; the flat above, on the first floor, included the attic. This was let to a childless middle-aged couple, the Clays, giving the Petersons' welcome extra income. Occasionally they met in the shared hallway, but most of the time neither couple really noticed the other. 'I like to keep myself to myself,' Mrs Clay confided to a neighbour, 'and we never see her.'

Home! Maggie would be waiting for him in the cellar as she always was after a raid. Nothing would have made her leave the house when the Luftwaffe were overhead. The moment she heard the siren she always went down into the cellar which she had furnished with a tilley lamp in case the electricity failed, an old sofa, and a primus stove. There she could boil a kettle to make tea, and there she would remain long after the all-clear had sounded, often asleep on the couch, waiting for Colin to come home.

'The cellar's deep,' she insisted when Colin tried to make her go into the Anderson shelter he'd built in the back garden. 'I hate that shelter, it's cold and dank. I'll be far safer here. Certainly safer than you, out on the streets with the bombers over your head!'

'You could go with the Clays to the public shelter,' he suggested tentatively.

'No, thank you!' exclaimed Maggie. 'You know I don't like being shut in. No, I'll stay in our cellar and take the risk.' And Colin had given in.

As he crossed the road, the baby woke up and began to grizzle. Colin looked down at it anxiously and hurrying up the front step, let himself in through his own front door.

'Maggie, I'm home,' he called. 'Here I am. You can come

out now.' It was the way he always announced he was home. At the sound of his voice the door to the cellar opened and Maggie peered out at him.

'Colin! Thank God you're back,' she cried. 'It sounded awful out there. Even down in the cellar—' She broke off abruptly as she caught sight of the baby in his arms. 'Colin? What's that? Who's that? Let me see!'

Colin gently detached the baby's fingers from the collar of his coat and passed it over to his wife, saying as he did so, 'As you see, it's a baby, but as to who it is I don't know. I don't even know if it's a girl or a boy!'

Maggie held the child close against her and then sniffed. 'Poof! Whoever it is, is in need of a clean nappy. Let's go into the kitchen where it's a bit warmer and see what we can do.' So saying, she led the way through into the kitchen before handing the baby back to Colin. 'Here,' she said, 'you hold it while I find an old towel I can use as a nappy.'

Colin did as he was asked, but the baby did not like the transfer and began to wail again. Not knowing what else to do, he jigged the damp bundle up and down in his arms, muttering, 'There, there,' as if that might comfort it.

Maggie found the towel and ripped it into four pieces, then laying the child on the draining board she unwrapped it from its sodden clothes.

'Oh, you poor darling,' she cried as she stripped away the filthy nappy to reveal that the child was a boy. 'Let's get you clean and dry.'

Colin sat down at the kitchen table and watched his wife minister to the wee boy who had emerged from the damp clothes. He saw her face as she looked at the child and for the first time since they had lost their own boy, he saw Maggie smile, a genuine smile of love. Gently but efficiently, she lowered the baby into the sink filled with warm water and washed every inch of him before sitting down on a kitchen chair, gathering him into another towel and patting him dry. Using one of the torn pieces of towel, she fashioned a nappy and pinned it into place.

'I'll get rid of that,' Colin said and got to his feet to remove the soiled nappy.

'Leave it,' instructed Maggie as she cuddled the now clean and dry baby against her, resting her chin on the softness of the auburn down that covered his head. 'I'll wash it through later, we're going to need to use that one again.'

'Really?' Colin looked at it with distaste and she nodded emphatically.

'Of course, otherwise we shan't have enough for tomorrow.'

'Tomorrow?' queried Colin. 'I shall have to take him to the rescue centre tomorrow. I brought him here today because after last night's raid the rescue centres will all be snowed under and I thought he'd be better here.'

'You were quite right,' Maggie told him, treating him to a smile from the Maggie he knew of old. 'Poor little scrap, he'd have got lost in the system and dumped into some children's home. No, Colin, he's far better here with us. We can look after him properly.' She turned her attention to the baby and said, 'Now then, little one, let's find you something to eat. You must be starving, poor pet.' Settling the boy onto her hip, she reached into the cold safe outside the kitchen window and retrieved a jug of milk. 'Will you light the gas, Colin, and we can warm him up some milk.'

'But we haven't got a bottle,' objected Colin.

'No, we haven't, but I think he's probably able to take milk from a cup if we take it slowly. Perhaps we could dip a little piece of bread in it, and he can have that with a spoon. After all, he's nearly nine months.'

Colin looked across at her. 'What do you mean? I mean, well, how do you know?'

Maggie gave a laugh. 'How do I know?' she repeated. 'How do you think I know? I'm hardly likely to forget when my son was born, am I?'

'Your son?' Colin was startled.

'Our son,' amended Maggie with a smile, a real Maggie smile, as she cuddled the baby.

Colin ignored her comment as he handed her the warm milk and softened breadcrumbs. The baby wasn't hers but he was bringing her such comfort, he couldn't bring himself to spoil the moment. It was as if someone had suddenly waved a magic wand and his Maggie had been returned to him. The faded husk of a woman, left behind after the birth and death of her son, had vanished as she sat with this child on her lap, warm and comforting, and cooed to him while spooning the bread and milk into his mouth. Clearly he was very hungry and Colin wondered when he'd last had a feed. His thoughts chimed with Maggie's as she said, 'He was very hungry, poor little mite.' She lifted the baby onto her shoulder, patting his back gently until he brought up wind, and then held him close against her, murmuring to him until he fell asleep in her arms.

'Shall I fetch a drawer from the chest in the box room?' suggested Colin. 'He could sleep in that for tonight.'

'Good idea,' agreed Maggie, unwilling to let go of the sleeping infant. 'Bring one in here and a blanket from our bed and we can make him very comfortable for now. We can find something better tomorrow.'

Her words echoed in his mind as he went to find the drawer and a blanket. *He's nearly nine months...when my son was born...* Roger, had he lived, would have been rising nine months, but this wasn't Roger. Roger had died.

Had he, he wondered, made a mistake, bringing the child home to Maggie? Surely she would understand that he must report his find to the proper authorities and the child would be taken into care. He'd leave it for now, he decided, but he would have to make that clear in the morning. In the meantime, his original reason for bringing the baby home with him still stood. The rescue centres would be completely overwhelmed after such a heavy raid, as they tried to help those who had been bombed out, those looking for loved ones, those who had only the clothes they stood up in. They'd be grateful if someone like Maggie was able to look after a lost baby for a little while. Having talked himself into believing this, Colin took the drawer and the blanket back to where Maggie still sat, nursing the foundling. Once he had fallen asleep, she tucked him up in the drawer and began to consider what she would need for his care. She thought of the trunk they had brought with them, until now forgotten in a corner of the cellar. She couldn't remember exactly what was in it, but when Colin went back on duty this evening, Maggie decided that she would go down and find out.

Colin went to bed to catch a few hours' sleep. He would be out on the streets again that night, and he'd need to have his wits about him. It wasn't just the Luftwaffe who was attacking the city, there were sneak thieves and looters roaming in the darkness, ready to slip into the ruins of someone else's home and take anything of value they happened to 'find' amongst the debris. Very often the things they found had very little monetary value, but were of inestimable sentimental value to those who had lost them. Indeed, he had thought that lad, Ernie, was one such and had been dismayed to find one so young out on such an expedition, but Ernie had without doubt helped save the baby boy's life. True, it was Colin who had risked himself to rescue the baby from the crumbling house, but if that lad hadn't heard the child crying, nor might anyone else as the aftermath of the raid lingered with thumps, crashes and explosions.

Will the bombers be back tonight? he wondered. The city still glowed with uncontrolled fires, an easy target for the incoming planes. Probably, he thought, but until the sirens sound, under cover of darkness there could be easy pickings for thieves and he, Colin, would be on the lookout for such criminals.

As darkness fell and Colin set out for his beat, Maggie went back down into the cellar and pulled out the trunk that was stored there. It had come from London with their other luggage when they had moved, but she had never expected to open it again. After Roger's birth she had been told by the doctors that she would probably not be able to bear another child. Her uterus was malformed, they said. It had been a miracle that Roger had ever been born at all. It accounted for the two miscarriages she'd had before she carried him to a viable seven months. Now, after a moment's hesitation, she unlocked it and threw back the lid. For a moment she stared at the contents and then she began to pull them out, nappies, baby clothes and other things she had bought in preparation for the birth of her baby, her Roger. She shook out each tiny garment and looked at it. They were all too small for the baby now asleep in a drawer beside her, but there was a cot blanket, six terry towelling nappies, a baby's bottle, a rattle and a teddy bear. Those she set aside, ready for Roger to use. Maggie had already named the foundling baby; Roger, the name of her son. In the brief hours she had been looking after him, he had become her Roger, Roger Peterson. She put the small clothes back into the case, closed and locked it and then gathering together the other items, she went back to the kitchen. As she washed up and put away the supper dishes, she found she was humming to herself.

When the sirens went again, she and Roger were soon safely ensconced in the cellar. She looked at the panda bear Colin had brought with the child. It was grubby, covered in dust, the faded purple ribbon knotted untidily about its neck. Maggie sniffed it and wrinkled her nose. It was kind of Colin to think of bringing it with him, she thought with a smile, but really it was too dirty to put in the cot beside a baby. She would throw it away when the raid was over and she could go back up to the flat. She set it aside on top of the bookcase and carefully laid the teddy she had taken from that case in the drawer, where baby Roger slept, entirely unaware of the air raid ripping out the heart of the city.

As Maggie sat there, also unconcerned about the enemy aircraft overhead, she planned Roger's nursery. She would clear the little box room and set him up in there. She could make him some clothes. One of Colin's shirts, one of her skirts, they could easily be cut down and made into rompers and shirts for Roger to wear. He wouldn't look out of place, everyone was doing the same thing, and it should be possible to buy him a few new things. It was the food ration that might be a problem, but she and Colin could give up some of their rations to ensure that their new baby had what he needed, until she could get him his own ration book.

While the raid raged in the skies outside, Maggie gave Roger another feed and changed his nappy. He was a strong baby and when she sat him down on the floor with a cushion behind him in case he toppled backwards, he soon turned over and crawled across to the sofa. She had crawled after him and he'd gurgled with delight as they had played peep-bo round the side of the couch. She had watched anxiously as with great determination, he had pulled himself up and stood on wobbling legs before sitting back down with a bump, laughing. Later she had put him down in the comfort of his drawer, but as she tucked him in under the blanket she realised that it wouldn't be long before he'd be too big to fit into this makeshift bed and decided to speak to Colin when he came in about finding a proper cot for him.

It was dawn, long after the all-clear had sounded, when Colin finally returned home. Maggie had fallen asleep on the sofa in the cellar with Roger in his drawer beside her. It was the sound of Colin coming in through the front door that woke her and she went up to the kitchen to greet him. She had given him little thought whilst she was playing with the baby; Roger had had her complete attention.

'It sounded bad,' she said as she took in his exhausted state.

'Worse than the first one,' Colin said as he flung himself down in his armchair. 'They came back again to finish what they started the night before. The city is burning and though everyone who can is fighting the fires, there are too many, and little we can do to put them out.'

'You must be exhausted,' Maggie said. 'I'll make you some tea, and then you must go to bed and get some sleep.'

She went into the kitchen and put the kettle on, but by the time she had made the tea and carried it back into the living room, Colin was sprawled, fast asleep, in his chair.

# 5

David Shawbrook had spent the day in Paul and Elsie Jefferson's spare bedroom. He had nowhere else to go and Paul had insisted that he come home with him and get some sleep.

'We both need to get a bit of shut-eye,' he said, 'cos you can be sure the buggers'll be back again tonight to finish the job.'

'No, Paul, really,' David shook his head. 'Thanks all the same. I'll find a place in one of the community centres.'

'Don't be daft,' exclaimed Paul. 'We've got a perfectly good spare room going begging. Let's face it, Dave, you haven't got anywhere else to go just now, have you? Come on, mate. Come back to mine. Elsie'll be pleased to have you, I know she will.'

David wasn't so sure about that. He and Paul's wife Elsie didn't really get on. It was as if she were jealous of his friendship with Paul, which went further back than their marriage.

The two men had been together through the final months of the last war, comrades in the same battalion, but it was the night that David wriggled out into no-man's land and brought Paul safely back behind the lines, wounded but alive, which had cemented their friendship. Paul never forgot that if David Shawbrook had not risked his life to crawl through a sea of mud to the shell hole where he lay injured, he would not have survived to come back home to Plymouth, to meet and marry Elsie.

Their friendship had continued despite Elsie's lack of enthusiasm, though David's wife Nancy hadn't really taken to Elsie, either.

'Don't know what's the matter with her,' she'd remarked after the four of them had spent a rather uncomfortable evening together. 'She's forever sniping at you.'

'Just a clash of personalities, I suppose,' shrugged David.

'No,' said Nancy, 'it's more than that. You'd think she'd be grateful to you. If it hadn't been for you, she'd never've met Paul, would she?'

'Some people don't like to be beholden,' David replied. 'They get tired of saying thank you.'

'I'm not asking her to keep on thanking you,' returned Nancy. 'Just for a little civility.'

After that, Paul and David used to meet up for a pint after work sometimes, or spend an afternoon together at Home Park cheering on Plymouth Argyle, but they seldom went out as a foursome again.

Now, David was reluctant to arrive unexpectedly on Elsie's doorstep, but he allowed himself to be persuaded. Paul was right, he didn't have anywhere else to go and he needed somewhere quiet, to be alone, to take in what had happened to his family.

'Thanks, Paul,' he said. 'Just for today, eh? Then I'll need to find somewhere.'

Paul didn't argue with this, he knew his friend was still in shock and probably would be for the foreseeable future. He also knew that after a raid such as the one they had just survived, hundreds would find their homes bombed to rubble and shelter of any sort was going to be at a premium. People would be expected to take in friends and relatives who had been left homeless. He and Elsie had no children and Paul could hardly imagine what David was going through, losing not only a wife he had obviously adored, but also six of his children in one appalling night.

When Elsie opened the door to them, David knew he had been right, she was not pleased to see him on the step beside Paul, but she twisted her lips into a smile and said, 'David. What brings you here?'

'Dave's been bombed out,' Paul said quickly, a frown warning Elsie not to ask any more. 'He's coming to stay in our spare room for now. We're both exhausted, doll. We need something to eat and then some sleep.'

'Oh, well, fine,' Elsie said and stood aside to let them in. 'But first things first. You're filthy, both of you. A good scrub is what you need before you eat. There's hot water in the kettle. You get cleaned up while I go and make up the spare bed.'

She disappeared up the stairs and Paul led David into the kitchen at the back of the house. Catching sight of his grimy face in the mirror, Paul knew Elsie was right. He went to the sink and, pouring hot water into the bowl, washed his hands and face, scrubbing at the layer of dust and grime that covered his skin, sluicing the filth of the devastated streets down the drain. He looked across at David, still standing irresolute in the doorway, as begrimed as he had been.

'Come on, mate,' he said gently, 'come and give yourself a scrub.'

Meekly, David followed him to the sink and did as he was bid, watching as the filthy water swirled round the plughole and drained away.

'Sit down, mate. Take the weight off,' Paul said as he refilled the kettle and lit the gas.

Lucky enough still to have gas, he thought, remembering all the fires flaming from broken gas mains they'd seen in the city. Plenty of folks'll be without.

David sat down at the table and watched Paul as he found cups and took milk from the cold safe outside the window. The kitchen was warm and David realised that the oven must be on, with something cooking, a meal for Paul when he got home from fire-watching. For a moment the thought almost overcame him. Never again would he go home to his own kitchen, warm from the oven, and find Nancy and the kids waiting to eat with him. For a moment the cold and blackened kitchen he'd just left flashed into his mind and it was all he could do to fight back the tears.

When Elsie came back downstairs, Paul had not only made the tea, but had pulled the potato pie from the oven and was sharing it out onto three plates. Elsie eyed the small portions of the pie she had made to serve two not three, but at a fierce glance from Paul, she made no comment. She watched David push the pie round his plate, unable to face food, until at last he pushed it away with only a few mouthfuls eaten.

Paul got to his feet immediately. 'Come on, Dave, mate,' he said cheerfully, 'an' I'll show you where you're sleeping.'

The two men left the kitchen and quickly Elsie picked up

David's plate. After a moment's hesitation, she scraped the uneaten pie onto her own and Paul's plates. 'No point in wasting good food,' she muttered to herself in justification as she put Paul's plate back into the oven before making short work of her share of the discarded pie.

Paul saw David into the spare room, where Elsie had made up the bed and laid out a towel.

'Bathroom next door,' he said. 'Try and get some sleep...' His words trailed off without the unspoken *things'll look better when you wake*, because they both knew that they wouldn't.

It was a relief to David when Paul shut the bedroom door behind him and went back downstairs to Elsie.

If he could have heard the conversation between husband and wife he wouldn't have been surprised.

'How long's he going to be staying?' Elsie demanded as Paul rejoined her at the table and began polishing off the rest of David's share of the pie.

'Don't know, love, but it don't matter. The poor bloke's just discovered that his entire family has been wiped out. His house is a ruin and he's lost everything.'

'Yes, Paul, I understand that,' replied Elsie. 'An' of course he can stay with us for a few days till he finds somewhere else. Can hardly leave him out on the street, can we? But—'

'There, love, I knew you'd understand,' interposed Paul with a smile, 'and it isn't as if we haven't got the space, is it? The whole east end of the city has been bombed or burned to bits, so I reckon they're going to be asking everybody with a spare room to take in someone homeless, and I'd rather it was someone we knew, wouldn't you?'

'Yes, of course,' Elsie sighed. 'But if he's staying for any time, I'm going to have to have his ration book. We won't have enough with another mouth to feed.'

Ignoring this comment Paul pushed his plate aside and said, 'Can you squeeze another cup out of that pot, Else? Then I'll get some shut-eye, too. I'm bushed.'

Upstairs, David went into the bathroom and stared into the mirror. The man that stared back at him was almost unrecognisable, even to himself. Grey with exhaustion, his chin shadowed with dark stubble and his eyes red-rimmed with fatigue, he seemed to have aged ten years in as many hours. Ten hours that had robbed him of his wife and most of his children. Blown to pieces. Nancy and his children, blown to bits, leaving nothing to find.

Nancy's gone, he thought, struck with a physical pain in his chest, and the children. Blown to bits!

David could hear voices downstairs, louder as the kitchen door opened and Paul emerged, and he hurried back into the spare room, shutting the door. He didn't want to see anyone, not even his kind-hearted friend.

Crossing to the window David stared out across the desolation of the city below. Stricken buildings stood in stark silhouette against an angry sky, shot with red from unquenched fires that still threatened to engulf their remains. He looked in the direction of his own street, his own house, not quite visible from here, and his vision blurred as tears streamed unchecked down his cheeks, and he turned away to let them fall.

Later, as he lay on the bed exhausted and now dry-eyed, he finally fell asleep and didn't wake again until the light began to fade. He awoke with the knowledge that he must tell his daughter Muriel what had happened. Perhaps he could phone her at the nurses' home in Portsmouth, and tell her, but how could he break news like that in a three minute phone call? He couldn't. It would be bad enough to write to Tony, somewhere in North Africa, to tell him of his immense loss, but for him there was no other way. But Mu? Well, he could travel over to Portsmouth and meet her when she came off shift. Not tonight, that was too short notice for the wardens' post, but tomorrow, surely someone could be found to cover for him. With some form of action planned, David felt slightly more comfortable. He got up and went to the bathroom where he scrubbed himself all over, borrowed Paul's razor and felt a little more human than he had before he'd slept.

Evening was creeping into an early dusk when the two men set out for their various posts within the city. As they paused before going their separate ways, Paul put a hand on David's arm and said, 'Now, don't forget we're expecting you back home in the morning, right?'

'Not sure,' David said slowly.

'For Christ's sake, man,' exclaimed Paul in frustration at his friend's reluctance. 'Where else have you got to go?'

'Portsmouth,' replied David. 'I have to go to Portsmouth… to tell Mu.'

'Oh!' Paul ran a hand over his eyes. 'Sorry, mate, course you have. Take no notice of me, Dave, I haven't got my brain into gear yet.' He looked away in embarrassment. 'D'you know where to find her?'

'She works at the Royal Hospital, I'm sure I can find that, and she lives in the nurses' home. If she's not at the hospital someone will be able to tell me where that is.'

'It's a long way to go,' Paul said. 'How will you get there?'

'On the train. Probably leave when we come off shift tomorrow morning,' David said, 'but if it's all right with you and Elsie, perhaps I could come back to you for a couple of days after, till I find digs somewhere.'

'*Course* it's all right,' Paul assured him in relief. 'Pleased to have you.' He grasped David's hand and shook it vigorously before the two men set off in opposite directions.

Paul had been right. That evening the Luftwaffe were back, and back with a vengeance. The incoming aircraft droned over the city, dropping incendiaries to reignite the previous raid's fires, followed by high explosive bombs to wreak further havoc on the ruined centre of the city. The raid continued for nearly four hours without respite and in the streets below David and Paul were amongst the courageous band of civil defence volunteers fighting to save the city. Amid the chaos created, they worked untiringly to put out the fires and rescue those who could be saved, but it was only with the coming daylight that they were able to take in the devastation left by the bombers and the real work of search and rescue began. People streamed into the first-aid posts for treatment, and those who were able set about smothering smouldering fires and clearing debris, rubble and broken glass, searching for survivors.

David had realised straight away that he couldn't leave his wardens' post and go to find Mu in Portsmouth as he'd planned. He was needed here as they struggled to help those who had lost their homes. As he covered his area, his way took him back into his own street and there he was greeted with more devastation. Where his house had stood, battered and broken from the first raid, was now a pile of rubble and ragged timber and broken glass, with debris strewn into the street. The neighbouring houses had met the same fate and the whole of one side of the street lay in ruins. Everything familiar had been obliterated, blasted away, and David found himself looking at a grey and dust-shrouded wasteland, all that was left of his home. For several moments he simply stared, his mind refusing to believe, before with silent resignation, he turned his back on the ruins of his life and returned to the wardens' post. He would still have to tell Mu what had happened, but at present he was needed here. He could leave her in ignorance of her loss for a few more days.

# 6

Nurse Muriel Shawbrook and Sub Lieutenant Patrick Davenham walked arm in arm through the windy Portsmouth streets on their way to have a meal and a drink in one of their favourite haunts. The Starfish was a pub tucked away in a back street not far from the Royal Hospital where Muriel was a nurse. Patrick ordered a couple of pink gins and they carried them over to a corner of the snug where they settled down beside the smouldering log fire to spend a quiet evening together. They made a handsome couple as they sat with their heads close, talking softly. Patrick, having come straight off duty, was in uniform. Good-looking in an angular way, he had dark hair and dark eyes above a mobile mouth and determined chin; Muriel was the complete opposite, pale-skinned with a dusting of freckles across her nose, her eyes, almost emerald green, dancing in the firelight, the sweep of her copper hair, normally confined by her nurse's cap, now simply tied back to frame her face. So completely absorbed were they in each other's company that they were not aware of the faint drone of faraway aircraft until the sirens began wailing and the landlord, Mark Carter, called everyone to leave immediately or take refuge in the pub's backyard shelter. Most of his customers had opted to head for home to their loved ones, but Patrick and Mu had only each other. With no actual homes to go to, they decided for the latter and hurried through the public bar into the yard behind. The Starfish's shelter, a brick-built structure, half sunk into the ground, was a half cylinder with a rounded roof and wooden benches running along the walls. A heavy black curtain covered the doorway, but inside light was provided by oil lamps set in niches at intervals along the walls. As they settled themselves on one of the benches and tried to get comfortable, Patrick put his arm round Mu and inwardly sighed. He'd planned this evening so carefully. A drink and a bite to eat in the comfortable familiarity of the Starfish, and then in that quiet corner of the snug, he would ask the question he'd been wanting to ask almost from the first moment he'd seen her.

Four weeks earlier he had been at the hospital visiting a shipmate who had been injured in an air raid, and there was Muriel, slim and beautiful despite the stiff uniform she was wearing, her glorious red hair confined by her starched cap, her green eyes bright with compassion as she moved from bed to bed, speaking to the men in her care.

'Hello,' she'd said with a smile when Patrick walked into the ward at visiting time. 'Who've you come to see?'

Patrick, almost struck dumb by her smile, managed to name his friend, Malcolm Frith, and Muriel had directed him to a bed in the corner.

'Not too long, now,' she'd warned. 'He's had a tough time. You mustn't tire him.'

Patrick had promised not to, but he had been back to visit Malcolm every evening since and was always greeted by the green-eyed nurse with the heart-stopping smile.

'They're letting me out tomorrow,' Malcolm told him one evening a week or so later. He grinned at Patrick and added, 'You won't have to track up here every night to see me. I'm going home to my parents for a couple of weeks to convalesce before coming back on duty.'

'Well, that's good news, Malc,' Patrick replied, but his eyes flicked to the desk in the corner of the ward where the nurse was writing notes.

'Last chance to ask her out, you know,' Malcolm said, following his eyes. 'You'll be all right, I've told her all about you.'

Patrick scowled at him and retorted, 'Time you minded your own business!'

'Oh, but it *is* my business,' replied Malcom cheerfully. 'Sadly, she's not interested in me, so I'll stand aside and let you in. Just don't waste your opportunity.'

Patrick realised Malcolm was right and though he knew almost nothing about this nurse, he decided he must take his chance. As he passed the nurses' station on his way out, he paused and diffidently asked Muriel whether she would like to go to the cinema with him one evening.

'Whenever suits you, of course. We're on a refit,' he explained, 'so I'm ashore for a while.'

Mu, who had watched for him to come into the ward every evening, felt herself blush as she answered that she had the night off on Friday, before she reverted to a day shift.

'Friday it is,' Patrick had beamed. 'Where shall I pick you up?'

'Not the nurses' home,' Mu had said. 'Too many nosy parkers. I'll meet you outside the Gaumont.'

'Seven o'clock, Friday,' repeated Patrick, and then added, 'Sorry, it's ridiculous but I don't even know your name.'

'It's Muriel Shawbrook,' she'd replied, 'but my friends call me Mu.'

'Mu,' Patrick repeated. 'I like that. I'm Patrick Davenham.'

'I know,' Mu smiled. 'I know all about you,' she glanced across to the bed in the corner, 'from your friend, Malcolm.'

Patrick followed her glance and saw Malcolm sitting in a chair beside his bed, grinning and giving him the thumbs up.

And so it began, and now four weeks later Patrick had heard that he was going back to sea. The ship's refit was finished; four days of sea trials had been completed. They now had three more days in port and the promise of forty-eight hours' leave at the weekend before they returned to the war. Tonight, Patrick had come prepared. He had a ring in his pocket, and all he had to do was hold his nerve and propose.

The air raid having put paid to their cosy dinner, they were now huddled in a backyard shelter, but they were together, and that was all that mattered to either of them.

There were others seated on the wooden benches, but somehow Patrick and Mu were in a bubble of their own and no one intruded on their closeness.

'I've something to tell you,' Patrick murmured and then paused.

'Good or bad?' Mu asked.

'A bit of both, I suppose,' he replied. 'I've got a forty-eight this weekend. Can you get some time off, so we can spend it together?'

'This weekend?' Mu looked doubtful. 'I shouldn't think so.'

'Starting Saturday,' replied Patrick.

Mu shrugged. 'It'll be very difficult,' she sighed. 'When do you sail?'

'We don't know the exact details, just that it's soon, but there'll be no leave after this weekend, no shore leave in the evenings.'

For a long moment silence lapsed round them and then Patrick reached for her hands. It was now or never.

'Mu, dearest Mu,' he said gently, 'you do know how I feel about you, don't you?'

Muriel looked up at him and saw his deep-set eyes, brown and anxious, searching her face. At first she made no reply but as his grip tightened on her hands, she nodded. 'Yes,' she whispered. 'Yes, I think so.'

'"Think so" isn't enough, Mu,' he said. 'I want you to be sure, to have no doubts at all.' Again he paused before going on, her hands still captured in his. 'I want you to be sure, certain-sure, how much I love you, Mu. I love you more than I have ever loved anyone, more than I could *imagine* loving anyone. I can't imagine going through the rest of my life without you at my side; I can't imagine wanting anyone else to be the mother of my children. My darling girl, I'd planned to propose to you romantically, at the fireside in the Starfish, not in a dark and dank air-raid shelter, but the bloody Luftwaffe has ruined that. I told you that I'm going back to sea, but I can't leave without knowing if you'll be waiting for me when I come back, without knowing that when I come home, I'll be coming home to you. Darling Mu, will you marry me?'

Mu carried his hands to her lips and very gently kissed them. 'Yes, Patrick,' she replied. 'Please.'

He stared at her, unable for a moment to take in her simple answer. 'Yes, you'll marry me? Really?'

Mu pulled her hands free and slid her arms round his neck, raising her face to be kissed as she repeated, 'Yes, Patrick.'

Patrick gathered her to him, holding her as if he would never let her go. His kiss was deep and stirring, and as she returned it, Mu knew she could never love anyone else. At last he released her a little, and taking the ring box from his pocket, opened it. Gently he slipped the ring on her finger and as he did so, the whole shelter erupted with a cheer and a round of applause. Mu and Patrick broke apart and looked about them in astonishment. So wrapped up had they been in each other, they'd been unaware of the others who had crowded into the shelter behind them.

'Well done, mate,' came a call from the far end. 'Looks like you got a good'un there.'

Mu felt the colour rising in her cheeks as she realised that they had become the centre of attention, a cabaret for everyone seated on the wooden benches waiting for the all-clear. Patrick's face broke into a huge grin. He was going to marry his beloved Mu and he didn't care who knew it.

At that moment the all-clear sounded; the alert was over and they were safe again... for now. There was a scramble to get out of the musty shelter, and back into the freshness of the April night. Several people disappeared into the darkness, but others headed back to the Starfish and the pints they had left on the bar. There had been no raid, it was simply an alert. For the second night, the planes they'd heard had passed them by; somewhere else was receiving the attention of the Luftwaffe, some other city was the target for bombardment.

Patrick and Mu went into the Starfish for one last drink before Mu had to be back at the nurses' home. They returned to the fireside corner of the snug and began to make plans.

'I've got the forty-eight hours' leave this weekend,' Patrick said. 'If you can get a day off, we could go to see your parents and I could speak to your father.'

Mu laughed. 'It's a bit late for that,' she said. 'You've asked me and I've accepted you, the ring's on my finger.' She stretched out her hand to admire the ring with its tiny, single diamond. 'So you can't wriggle out of it now, you know.'

'Wriggle out of it?' Patrick pulled her into his arms, holding her close. 'My darling girl, I'd marry you tomorrow if I could.'

'Can't we?' murmured Mu from deep within his embrace. 'Can't we get married before you go?'

Patrick shook his head reluctantly. 'Afraid not, but we'll be back again soon and I'll have organised a licence by then. Then we can get married at once.'

'My sisters'll want to be bridesmaids,' Mu said.

'Of course they will. We're going to have a real family wedding. My brother Neil will be my best man; that's if he can get leave as well.'

'And your parents? What about them? Will they be pleased?'

'Course they will,' Patrick assured her. 'They'll love you. It's a pity Glasgow's so far away and I can't take you to meet them, but I'll book a call with trunks as soon as I can to give them our news.'

As Patrick kissed her goodnight outside the nurses' home, Mu clung to him. 'I do love you, Patrick Davenham,' she whispered. 'Muriel Davenham sounds good, don't you think?'

'It sounds perfect,' said Patrick and bent his head for a final kiss.

'Just in time, Nurse Shawbrook,' remarked Sister Roderick, as Mu made it through the front door one minute before it was locked for the night.

'Yes, Sister. Good night, Sister,' said Muriel, still beaming as she headed upstairs to her room.

She's very perky, thought the night sister. Wonder what she's been up to. No good, I'll be bound.

Mu's room-mate, Jean, was already asleep when Mu crept into their room, but she was too excited to go to sleep herself. As she lay in bed listening to Jean's rhythmical breathing, Mu relived her evening, filled with a wondrous happiness.

Patrick had proposed to her and she had accepted him. Patrick was truly hers, and Mu was the happiest girl alive. She snuggled back under the covers, knowing she could allow herself a lazy morning. She was transferring back to the night shift that evening, and though these shifts were easier in the ward on a quiet night, they were a very different matter if there was an alert. Then patients well enough were moved to the shelter and those unable to leave their beds were covered with blankets from head to toe to protect them from flying glass and other debris from bomb blast.

57

She would be on nights for the next few weeks. Could she arrange a swap with someone to give her and Patrick the chance to go to Plymouth and break the exciting news to her family? Perhaps Jean, whom she knew was off on Saturday, might agree to take her place, just for the one night she'd need to go home.

How pleased Mam'll be, Mu thought, smiling in the darkness.

Mam had been hinting for some time now that she thought it was about time Mu should be settling down.

'You're twenty-two,' she had said. 'By the time I was your age I'd been married three years and had Tony, with you on the way.'

'I know, Mam, but things aren't the same now and with the war...'

'We had a war as well, you know,' her mother reminded her, 'and though your father wasn't called up until 1917, life wasn't easy.'

'Well, I have met someone,' Mu spoke tentatively, 'from the naval base.'

'A naval officer?'

'Sub Lieutenant, RNVR.'

'So surely he must soon be going to sea?' Nancy sounded concerned.

'He's ashore for a while,' Mu said. 'His ship's been in for a refit, but anyway, Mam, I haven't known him long, so don't get too excited. And don't tell Dad. I don't want him demanding to know what Patrick's intentions are!'

'That's his name is it? Patrick?'

'Yes, Patrick Davenham.'

'Well, I'll keep your secret for now, pet, but even if he

knew, your dad could hardly ask about his intentions when he's here and this Patrick is in Portsmouth!'

I'll be able to tell them all now, Mu thought, her smile broadening as she imagined their delight. And Dad can't complain. At least it's clear that Patrick's intentions were always entirely honourable!

At last she dozed off, wondering as she did so if it was so wrong to be relieved, pleased even, that it had been someone else's turn to bear the attack from the air tonight. That this time, at least, unlike so many other nights, they had been left in peace.

# 7

Maggie Peterson had not wasted her time while Colin had been asleep and dead to the world during the day. With an energy she had not had since they'd moved to Plymouth, she began to make some of the things she would need while caring for Roger. She looked at the blanket that they had used the previous night and fetching her cutting-out shears, she carefully divided it into four. One quarter she stitched round three sides, turning it into a small sleeping bag, so that he should always be warm in his bed. Another she hemmed round the edges to make a cot-sized blanket. The other half of the blanket she set aside for other uses later on. She set her sewing machine up in the cellar where it had been stored since their arrival, ready to sew the shirts and rompers she had cut out from Colin's blue 'holiday' shirt.

He won't need it for a while, she reasoned; we won't be going anywhere on holiday with this bloody war on.

When Colin awoke in the early evening Maggie showed him what she had been doing. 'You see,' she said, her eyes bright with fulfilment, 'I've begun to make the things we'll need as Roger gets older. We certainly need to find something bigger and better for him to sleep in, he's almost outgrown the drawer already. And then I'll need some sort of pushchair to take him out for fresh air. Perhaps we could find those things...'

'Maggie, Maggie, slow down.' Colin put a placatory hand on hers. 'We don't have to find those things. In a few days we shall have to take him into a rescue centre so that he can be looked after properly.'

'Properly!' Maggie pounced on the word with a shriek. 'What do you mean, properly? Are you saying that I can't look after him properly?'

'No, no, of course not.' Colin immediately regretted his choice of words. 'Of course you're looking after him very well, but you know we can't keep him, and—'

'Why not?' Maggie interrupted him sharply. 'Why can't we keep him? He hasn't got anyone else.'

'We don't know that,' Colin pointed out. 'Not for sure, and you have to accept that much as you want to keep him, he's not ours. There may be a family out there absolutely devastated because they think he's dead.'

'They left him to die,' Maggie said flatly. 'They don't deserve to have him back.'

'We don't know that they did,' replied Colin patiently. 'Anything might have happened to prevent them getting to him.'

'He was left alone in that house.'

'Maggie,' Colin grasped her hands in his, 'you have to accept that he isn't our baby...'

'He is now,' insisted Maggie. 'If you take him to the rescue centre they'll just put him in a children's home and then what sort of life will he have? An orphan. Belonging nowhere?'

'I know what you're saying,' Colin said soothingly, 'but legally we must report the fact that we've found him and he's safely with us. Then if someone is searching for him, they'll be put in touch with us.'

'And then they'll take him away,' snapped Maggie. 'A family that were stupid enough to lose him in the first place.'

'Maggie, dearest girl, think how *you* would feel if he really were ours and we'd lost him and then someone who had found him kept him themselves instead of telling us he was safe.'

'We wouldn't have lost him in the first place,' Maggie broke in fiercely.

'We would be breaking our hearts over him,' Colin went on, undeterred. 'His family may be doing the same, now. We have to report finding him.'

'No! No! NO!'

'Listen, dearest,' Colin held up his hand as she began to interrupt him. 'No, Maggie, you must listen to me. When I go in this evening I shall go to the rescue centre and tell them we've got him. I'll have to tell them the address of the house in Suffolk Place where I found him, but I'll tell them we are perfectly happy to continue looking after him, rather than have him put in a children's home.'

'Supposing they say we have to give him up,' cried Maggie, getting up and beginning to pace the room. 'Supposing they—'

'They won't, dearest, I'm sure they won't,' interposed Colin. 'The children's homes will be crammed with kids who really have nowhere else to go. They'll welcome us as foster parents with open arms.'

'Foster parents? I don't want to be a foster parent who

has to give him up the minute somebody tells me to.' She spun round on her heel and glared at him. 'His family are probably dead anyway, killed in the raid. I hope they are!'

'Maggie, how can you say such a thing?' Colin was horrified.

'Well, I do.'

'Maggie, please don't say such things. You don't wish them dead.'

Maggie didn't back down, she didn't reply at all. She simply picked up the sleeping child and, holding him tightly in her arms, stalked out of the room and into their bedroom, slamming the door behind her and turning the key.

Colin sighed and flopped down into a chair. He would have to leave for duty at the police station before long, and he hated leaving Maggie in such a state. It was hard for her, he knew, and with the benefit of hindsight he realised that he should never have brought the baby home. He should have taken him to the rescue centre first, should have had him logged in with the date and where he had been found... then, perhaps, brought him home. Surely, if he had been left by accident someone would have come searching for him. Maybe they had. Maybe they still were.

'Oh God,' he sighed. 'What a mess.'

He went into the kitchen and made himself a cheese sandwich whilst heating up some soup that Maggie had made earlier. As he sat alone at the table and ate this scratch meal, he wondered if he'd be able to persuade the authorities to let them keep the child, at least for now. Perhaps Maggie was right and there was no family; they might be able to adopt him at some time in the future, but now was not the time to hide him. Feeling a little more cheerful, he finished his soup and put the dishes in the sink. Then he went and knocked on their bedroom door. At first there was no reply from within, but when he knocked again, more loudly this time, Maggie called out, 'Go away!'

'Maggie, I've got to go or I'll be late.' This was greeted with silence and he said again, 'Maggie, I've got to go.'

'Good,' came the sharp answer, 'and don't come back!'

'Maggie, don't be silly. I'll be back in the morning and we'll talk about all this again then.'

'If you tell them we've got Roger here, Colin, I'll never speak to you again. D'you hear me?'

'Yes, I hear you,' sighed Colin. 'We'll talk about it again when I get home, all right?'

There was no reply from the bedroom, and reluctantly Colin turned away, pausing once more as he reached the front door to call, 'Bye, then. See you in the morning.'

Not long after, when the sirens began their warning, Maggie gathered up baby Roger and carried him down into the cellar. She had come out of the bedroom soon after Colin had left. She was still angry with him, and some of that anger was because a tiny part of her had to admit he was probably right. What was she going to say to him if he came home tomorrow morning, already having told the authorities about Roger? Supposing some nosy person from the community centre did come and demand that she hand him back? Well, she decided, she'd deal with that if the time came. In the meantime she had to prepare herself and Roger for another night in the cellar. She would move down there straight away, so that she didn't have to wake Roger by moving him if there were a raid in the middle of the night. It was where she felt safe.

Roger had already had his last feed for the night and she slipped him into his new sleeping bag and sat down on the cellar sofa, cuddling him against her until, with his head heavy on her shoulder, he fell asleep. Gently she laid him in his makeshift cradle, then turning down the lamp she made herself comfortable on the couch and joined him in slumber.

Outside the house, the raid continued as incendiaries, parachute bombs and high explosives cascaded down on the hapless city.

How much more could Plymouth take? Colin wondered as he hurried through the streets towards the police station. How much more could its inhabitants endure?

The noise of the raid was deafening, explosions, crumbling masonry, the drone of the planes overhead, both bombers and fighters, with anti-aircraft guns blasting away, some from the land, some from the ships in the harbour. Searchlights scanned the sky, shafts of light occasionally pinning an aircraft on the dark breast of midnight, a target for the gunners, while on the ground beneath, new fires burst forth. Resolute firemen struggled with sand and water as they fought to extinguish the flames before they could do major harm; all enclosed within the din of battle.

As Colin was about to reach the police station, a car came up behind him. It was being driven by an elderly man who crouched behind the steering wheel, peering through the windscreen, trying to see where he was going by the faint light of the blacked-out headlamps, and the red glow from fires already burning.

Colin turned in amazement and immediately taking in the old man's peril, he flagged him down.

'You have to leave the car, sir,' he said when the driver

opened his window. 'You must park your vehicle in the event of an air raid, park it and go at once to the nearest shelter.' He reached for the door handle and pulled open the driver's door. 'Come along now, sir, and I'll take you to the nearest shelter.'

'It's not my car,' wailed the old man. 'I can't just leave it at the side of the road. It might get stolen.'

'I'm sorry, sir, but you must. Come along now. Out you get. You can lock the car for safety and then you must take shelter. When the raid is over, you can come back and fetch the car.'

'Suppose it gets bombed,' quavered the old man.

'If it gets bombed, sir, better you're not inside it.'

At last the man gave in and getting out of the car, turned and locked it before allowing Colin to lead him into the next street where there was a public shelter. Colin saw the old man into the shelter before turning again to head for the police station two streets away. He was already late on duty. He would go to the rescue centre and report finding the baby when the all-clear sounded.

# 8

Muriel went on duty that evening with such an aura of happiness about her that the other nurses in the ward noticed it at once. Patrick was in love with her and she with him and that made her in love with everyone else in the world. She couldn't stop smiling.

'Well, Nurse Shawbrook, you're looking very pleased with yourself,' remarked Sister Pearce. 'Anything we should know?'

Mu felt the colour rising in her cheeks, and she simply held out her left hand to show the ring.

'I see.' Sister Pearce's tone was less than enthusiastic. 'Well, you can't wear that on the ward. Take it off and don't wear it on duty again.' She watched as Mu removed the ring and put it in her pocket. 'I suppose that means we shall be losing you.'

'Not for the moment, Sister,' Mu answered. 'We shan't be getting married for a while yet. My fiancé,' she smiled as she said the words, 'my fiancé is in the navy. He'll be going back to sea very soon. Perhaps on his next leave.'

'I see,' came the reply. 'Well, that's enough standing about, we've a ward to put to bed.' For a moment Sister

Pearce returned to her office and shut the door. She looked back at Muriel Shawbrook, already at the bedside of an elderly man who had been brought in with a head injury after an earlier air raid. *Perhaps on his next leave.* The words, said with happy anticipation, echoed in her mind. She herself had said almost the same when Arthur Flint had returned to the front in France in 1917. 'We'll be married on my next leave,' he had promised as he'd given her that final kiss of farewell. But Arthur had not fared well. He had been picked off by a German sniper three weeks later, and like so many thousands of women, Edna Pearce had remained a spinster, robbed of marriage and a family by an unknown marksman. And now, only twenty years later, it was all happening again.

It was these thoughts and memories that were still coursing through her head when Nurse Shawbrook asked to speak to her the next morning before she went off duty.

It was with some trepidation that Mu asked to speak to her superior. She had spoken to Jean during their short break soon after midnight.

'You're a dark horse, Muriel Shawbrook,' teased her room-mate. 'You've kept him pretty quiet.'

Mu smiled. 'It's all happened rather quickly,' she admitted. 'I didn't want to talk about him because I didn't want to jinx it.' She treated Jean to a dazzling smile. 'Jeannie...' she said.

Jean looked at her suspiciously. 'Yes?'

'Are you still off this weekend, by any chance?'

'Yeees,' Jean replied cautiously. 'Why?'

'I just wondered, you see, well, I just wondered if you

could cover for me, on Saturday night. I'll give you my next Saturday, promise!'

When Jean didn't answer immediately Mu went on hurriedly.

'You see, Patrick has a forty-eight this weekend and we want to tell my family, together, about being engaged, I mean, before he goes to sea again. If I could have Saturday night off, we could go to Plymouth together on Saturday, stay the night and I'd be back in plenty of time to come on duty again on Sunday night.'

'You won't have much time in Plymouth, will you? It'll take ages to get there and then you'll spend the whole of Sunday getting back.'

'I know,' admitted Mu, 'I know, but it'll be worth it.'

'Tell you what,' Jean offered. 'You can have my whole weekend, and I'll have your next one. Deal?'

'Really? Will you?' Mu's delight shone from her eyes.

'I will, provided you clear it with Sister Pearce first. You realise she may say no, don't you?'

'Of course she won't,' declared Mu with far more confidence than she felt. Sister Pearce was known to be a bit of a tartar, and she might easily refuse to give her permission for such a switch of duty.

So it was that Mu's stomach fluttered with butterflies as she tapped on the office door.

'Come.' The tone of voice did not bode well, but Mu drew a deep breath and pushed open the door.

'Well, Nurse,' Sister Pearce said before Mu could speak. 'Isn't it time you were going off duty?'

'Yes, Sister, I'm about to go. I just wondered if I could have a word with you first.'

Sister Pearce waved her to the chair in front of her desk and said briskly, 'Sit down, Nurse, don't hover!'

Mu sat down, her knees primly together and her hands in her lap.

Sister Pearce nodded to her. 'Well?' And Muriel made her request.

Any other day Edna Pearce might have refused. She didn't hold with people rearranging their duties to suit themselves. A duty roster was a duty roster and you were expected to turn up for duty when and where you were told. She had never dreamed of altering her duties to suit her social life... until the night Arthur was leaving for the front. She had swapped duties with her best friend so that she could go to the station and kiss him goodbye, and she had done it without leave, without warning. It was the last time she had seen him, waving from the window of the train as it drew out of the station. She had lost Arthur, and all she had left of him was a faded sepia photograph on her bedside table; he forever young, she growing old. Even as she looked at the eager young face across the desk from her, the same words echoed again in her head, 'on his next leave...'

'Very well, Nurse,' she said, but without warmth in her voice. 'Provided Nurse Darwin has agreed. I shall expect you back on duty on Monday night.'

Sister Pearce picked up some papers from her desk and Muriel, her heart singing, beat a hasty retreat before she could change her mind.

When she emerged from the hospital it was to find Patrick waiting for her in the street outside. His face cracked into a grin when he saw her and she hurried over to him. He made as if to take her in his arms, but she shook her head vigorously; there were too many people about for such demonstrations in the street. Instead she took his arm and they walked sedately away to a less public place.

'Did you ask?' Patrick demanded as soon as they had found a vacant bench in the nearby park. Sitting side by side he put his arm round her and this time she did not stop him, rather she leaned into him and rested her head on his shoulder. An old woman was being pushed slowly round the park in a Bath chair and as she passed, Mu heard her say in a loud tone of disapprobation, 'Such goings-on in a public park in broad daylight!'

Her companion, probably used to such comments, simply murmured, 'But he is in uniform.'

'As if that makes any difference,' came the retort, and the couple passed on by.

Mu giggled. 'See, your uniform doesn't protect you!'

'Nor you,' Patrick agreed with a grin. 'Now tell me, have you got the night off on Saturday?'

'Yes,' cried Mu in delight. 'And Sunday too!'

'Well, I have to be back by midnight on Sunday. We can leave Saturday morning!'

'Have you looked up trains?' Mu asked.

'I've done better than that, Mu. I've scrounged some petrol and I've borrowed a car.'

Mu stared at him. 'A car,' she breathed. 'Patrick, that's fantastic. Who lent you a car?'

'Your friend Malcolm Frith,' grinned Patrick. 'He's just come back from convalescence and he drove himself down here in his father's car.'

'And the petrol?'

'Better not to ask him,' Patrick replied, tapping the side of his nose, 'but he says the tank's full and there's a jerrycan in the boot.'

'Really! But why? I mean, doesn't he need it himself?'

'Said to tell you it's part wedding present and part thank you for looking after him so well.' Patrick's arm tightened round her shoulders. 'So, we can drive to Plymouth in style and not have to hang about waiting for trains that are all full or never come at all. What time can you be ready to go on Saturday morning?'

'As soon as I come off duty, like today.'

'You'll need some sleep first, won't you?'

'I can sleep in the car,' Mu told him. 'We need to set out as early as possible so's to have the longest time when we get there.'

Patrick got to his feet. 'I've got to go, Mu,' he said reluctantly. 'I'm due back on board. But I'll see you first thing Saturday morning. I'll be waiting for you outside the hospital.'

'I'll come out as soon as I can and I'll have my bag with me so that I don't need to go back to the nurses' home. Oh, Patrick!' She turned to him her green eyes sparkling. 'Only two more nights and we'll be on our way!'

When she reached the nurses' home, Muriel went into the communal kitchen and made herself a cup of cocoa. Carrying it through to the common room she sat down in the window to enjoy the sunshine before she went upstairs to get some sleep. Someone had left the wireless on and as she drank her cocoa she could hear *Music While You Work* playing softly in the background. As she finished her hot drink, another of the night nurses, Christine Jackson, who worked on a different ward, came in and flopped down into one of the sagging armchairs.

'What a night!' she said.

'It wasn't too bad,' Muriel said. 'At least there wasn't a raid.'

'No, but Sister Drewitt made us practise for one, before settling everyone down for the night.'

'Well, it's important to keep in practice, I suppose—' began Mu, but she broke off as, with the end of the music, there came an item of news on the wireless and the mention of Plymouth caught her attention.

'...a third raid described in an earlier broadcast as "short and sharp" was in fact one of prolonged attack, leaving much of the city on fire. Firefighters from the surrounding area have been rushed to the burning city...'

Muriel leaped to her feet and turned up the volume on the wireless, but the BBC announcer had already moved on to other breaking news.

'Did you hear that?' she asked, her voice shaking.

'What?' Christine had picked up the newspaper from the table and was scanning the headlines.

'What he said about a raid on Plymouth?'

'No, not really, I wasn't listening. What did he say?'

'That Plymouth had a really bad raid last night.'

'Last night? Another one? I thought that was two nights ago.'

Two nights ago. The night she and Patrick had heard distant planes and been glad they were not directing their attention to Portsmouth this time. Had they been on the way to Plymouth, or somewhere else? How were her family? Were they all safe? There was no way of finding out immediately, they had no telephone, and unless they borrowed someone else's, or used a public call box, they would not be able to try ringing her on the one public phone in the nurses' home.

'You all right, Mu?' asked Christine, seeing the colour drain from Muriel's face.

'Yes. No. I don't know. My family live in Plymouth.' Her voice trembled. 'I hope they're all right. No news is good news, I suppose.'

Christine reached over and took her hands in hers. There was nothing she could say. The raids sounded bad, there must be hundreds of casualties.

'They'll be all right.' Mu spoke firmly, knowing as she said the words that they might not be true. 'They always go to the Parham Road shelter. They'll be safe enough, I'm sure. Except perhaps my dad, he's a warden, he won't be with them.'

Christine squeezed her friend's hands encouragingly. 'They'll have had plenty of warning,' she said. 'Can't you try ringing them?'

'They're not on the phone,' Mu sighed, before adding a little more cheerfully, 'but Patrick and I are going there on Saturday. We'll see them then.'

'Patrick?'

Even the thought of him brought a smile to Mu's lips and she held out her left hand where her ring was back in place.

Christine's eyes widened. 'Hey,' she said, 'when did that happen?'

'A couple of nights ago.'

'And you're going to Plymouth on Saturday? How did you swing that one?'

'Patrick's got a forty-eight. Jean's agreed to swap her weekend off with mine and Sister Pearce has given her permission.'

'Has she indeed! Lucky you!'

'I must have caught her in a good mood,' said Mu.

'Didn't know she had any,' grinned Christine, glad that Mu's own mood seemed to have lightened somewhat.

'It means we can stay the night in Plymouth with my family,' Mu explained. 'Patrick doesn't have to be back here until Sunday night.' She picked up her cup and turned back to the kitchen. 'We'll be off on Saturday morning.'

Mu went up to her room where Jean was already asleep in bed. She undressed and crept into her own bed, but it was some time before she went to sleep. The announcement she'd heard kept playing in her head: *...a prolonged attack, leaving much of the city on fire.* Suppose her family had been injured in that raid? But they couldn't be. They'd be safe in the Parham Road shelter. Mam had their evacuation to the shelter organised with military precision. Even the little ones knew exactly what to do. They slept in their siren suits, ready to get up and out of the house if they needed to. Mam shepherded the youngsters and Vera carried baby Freddie. It wasn't them she had to worry about, it was Dad, out on the streets. But if something had happened to him, Mam would have got a message to her somehow. Wouldn't she?

# 9

Maggie Peterson was awakened by a pounding on the door knocker. She struggled up from the cellar sofa on which she had finally fallen asleep and made her way sleepily up to the front door. Colin must have forgotten his key, she thought. Typical! Just when I'd finally dozed off!

She had had very little sleep; Roger had been hard to settle and had spent a restless night in his drawer. She had put him to bed in the cellar so that she wouldn't have to move him in the event of a raid... and what a raid it had turned out to be. What with the terrifying noise coming from the outside and Roger's perpetual grizzling, there had been little chance of a good night's sleep for either of them, but when at last everything seemed to have quietened down, Roger had finally fallen asleep, and so had Maggie.

Now, blearily awake, she threw on a dressing gown over her nightdress and stumped up the stairs to the hall. She ran a hand through her hair before opening the door, ready to scold her husband for forgetting his key, but when she opened the door, the words died on her lips, for outside was a stranger, an unknown policeman.

Inspector Gordon Droy had walked slowly up the street,

looking at the house numbers. He was looking for 34 Marden Road, the home of Sergeant Peterson, but he wasn't looking forward to meeting Colin Peterson's wife for the first time. The Petersons had only moved to Plymouth in January. He didn't know why Peterson had requested a transfer, but quite frankly Inspector Droy didn't care. He was simply grateful that he had and so had helped bring the local force a little closer to full strength. Peterson was definitely an asset to his squad, he was keen, ready to use his own initiative, but also followed orders without fuss. He was courageous, apparently unafraid in dangerous situations and always out on the street during a raid, ready to lend a hand wherever necessary. And now he was dead. He had been found by one of his colleagues, Constable Andy Sharpe, only a couple of hundred yards from the police station. He was lying at the side of the road, apparently untouched, no wounds, no blood, no apparent cause of death. But dead he was and it was almost certainly bomb blast that had done for him; the blast from the bomb which had demolished half a parade of shops a little further along the road.

Sharpe had immediately returned to the police station to report the matter, but before leaving him, he had searched Colin's pockets and brought with him his ID card, his wallet, police whistle and the truncheon still attached to his belt. Better take these with me, he thought. Can't be too careful. As a policeman he knew only too well that private possessions sometimes went missing if a body were left for too long.

'He must have been coming on duty when he copped it,' Andy said to the sergeant. 'I noticed he weren't here, but thought he'd already gone outside. Weird though, isn't it?

Not a mark on him. Laying in the street, he were, almost like he was asleep. Poor bastard.'

The station sergeant agreed. Colin Peterson had been well liked, and moreover he was the second casualty from the station in the last three days. With a sigh he reported the loss to Inspector Droy and then had made the arrangements for Peterson to be collected and carried to the mortuary.

Leaving me the unpleasant duty of breaking the sad news to Peterson's wife, thought Droy as he paused outside number 34 Marden Road. He realised that he knew nothing about the Petersons' private life. He hadn't known where they lived before today, didn't know if they had children; he didn't even know Mrs Peterson's Christian name.

Still, she had to be told, and he was the one who had to do it. It never got any easier.

Straightening his back he walked up to the front door and knocked. When there was no reply, he waited several minutes before knocking again. Surely Mrs Peterson must still be in, it was not yet nine o'clock and the last thing he wanted to do was to postpone the sad news and find someone else had told her before he had done so officially.

He was about to knock for a third time when he heard a sound from somewhere inside. Thank goodness for that, he thought, and schooled his expression to one of condolence.

'Mrs Peterson?' he said to the tired-looking woman wearing a dressing gown, who finally opened the door. 'I'm Inspector Droy. May I come in?'

Maggie stared at him for a moment and then asked, 'It's Colin, isn't it? What's happened to him? Is he hurt?'

'May I come in?' Droy suggested again and took a step forward. Maggie didn't reply, but she turned back inside, leaving the inspector to follow her. She went into the sitting room, pulling back the blackout so that the room was suddenly flooded with daylight. Only then did she turn to face him and say, 'Tell me.'

'I'm so sorry, Mrs Peterson, but I'm afraid it's sad news. Your husband was killed in the raid last night, while he was out on duty.'

Maggie's legs gave way and she sank into a chair, but when she said nothing, he went on, 'He was found this morning, lying at the side of the road. Several shops nearby were demolished by a high explosive bomb and poor Colin was killed by the blast.'

His words were greeted with a long silence before Maggie said, 'I see. Thank you for coming to tell me.'

At that moment there came a cry, the sound of a baby. Maggie looked across at the door. 'That's Roger, our son,' she said. 'He's just woken up, he's hungry.'

'Your son?'

'Yes, Roger. He's been living with my mother for the last couple of months. I only fetched him last week, once we were... settled,' her voice trembled on the words, 'here in Plymouth.'

Droy could see that she was battling with tears and he said awkwardly, 'Is there anyone who could come to you, family or friends, so that you're not alone?'

Maggie shook her head. 'No,' she answered, 'no one. It's just Roger and me now.'

'You mentioned your mother...?' Droy said tentatively.

'She's moved to Scotland,' improvised Maggie. 'That's why we had to risk bringing Roger here. She'd been looking after him while we moved.'

As the cries began escalating, Maggie got to her feet and went out of the room, leaving Inspector Droy on his own. He crossed to the window and looked out. He could see the smoke from the fires still darkening the sky. How much more is this bloody war going to take? he thought viciously. Here's this brave woman, living in a town where she knows no one, left with a child to bring up on her own, thanks to the bloody Boche. He glanced at the two framed photos that stood on the mantelpiece, a wedding picture, and a holiday snap with a pregnant Maggie smiling at the camera. Surprisingly, no pictures of the baby.

Moments later Maggie appeared at the door with a baby on her hip. 'He needs his breakfast,' she said. 'I'm sorry, but I must change and feed him.'

It was clearly his dismissal and Droy was not sorry. He didn't know what else there was to say, and perhaps it was best for the poor woman to have the child to concentrate on; the only part of her husband left to her.

'If there's anything I can do?' he began. 'Anything you need?' His voice trailed off.

'You mean apart from his father?' Maggie spoke bitterly. 'He'll never know him now, will he?' Droy didn't answer and suddenly Maggie said, 'Where is he? Where has he been taken?'

'In St Mark's church hall,' said Droy. 'That's where they've been taking those in our area to be formally identified. Will you…?' Again he broke off awkwardly.

'Come and identify him?'

'You don't have to,' the inspector said hurriedly, 'one of us can do that if you want us to.'

'No,' Maggie said, 'we'll come.' She looked down at the child on her hip. 'We'll come and say goodbye to Daddy, won't we, precious?'

'If you would like someone to go with you, please do come to the station first and I know one of his colleagues would take you there.'

Maggie shook her head. 'No, thank you,' she said. 'We shall be all right on our own.'

'Of course,' Droy replied, 'but if you change your mind, you only have to ask.' He took Colin's personal items from his pocket and the truncheon from his belt and laid them on the table. 'These are his,' he said. 'I thought you'd like them.'

Inspector Droy knew an almost physical relief when Colin Peterson's wife closed the front door behind him and he stepped out into the street. There was something distinctly odd about the way she had taken the news. Then again, he thought, he had seen quite a lot of death one way or another during his twenty years in the police force, and he knew that everyone was different; different people had different ways of handling their grief, particularly if it was unexpected. It would seem that Mrs Peterson's way of coping would be to devote herself to the baby. He and his mother really only had each other now.

When the inspector had gone, Maggie carried Roger into the kitchen where she stripped off his dirty nappy, gave him a quick bath in the sink, and then gave him his bottle.

Doing these routine things kept the knowledge of Colin's death at bay for a moment, but once they were done and she was rocking Roger gently on her knee, she allowed herself to think of him, Colin, and how they had parted the previous evening; parted in anger, she telling him not to come back. 'And now he hasn't,' she spoke into the silence, 'and he never will.'

Irrationally she felt angry with him, as if it were his fault that he'd been in the wrong place at the wrong time and had been killed by a bomb. She'd never wanted to come to Plymouth, but she'd let him persuade her, and now he was dead! Over the last months they had drifted apart, Colin throwing himself into his new job and Maggie withdrawing further. It was only since he'd brought Roger home to her that the warmth between them had been rekindled. For the briefest of time they had been as close as they used to be, until he'd threatened to report his finding Roger to the authorities, taking away with one hand what he had given her with the other. But now Colin was dead and it was her fault. She had wished Roger's family dead, so that they could be his family instead, and now Colin was dead as she had wished *them* to be.

The tears began then, slipping down her cheeks, the sobs rising in her chest and shaking her whole body. She wept until she had no more tears, and with an aching throat and an aching heart, she clutched the little body against her own. 'We're on our own, now, Roger,' she said as she held him close. 'It really is just you and me.'

Later, in the afternoon, Maggie set out for St Mark's hall. She would see Colin once more to say her goodbyes. She had no pram or pushchair, but she'd seen other women carrying babies in makeshift slings on their hips. She could do the same. No one would think it odd, everyone was having to get along as best they could, make-do and mend. Well, she'd find a scarf and make do. Better than a scarf, she found an old crocheted stole of her mother's and fashioned it into a sling, and once he was settled she walked down towards the city centre.

When she reached the police station where Colin had been based, she hesitated. Would it be easier if someone came with her to St Mark's? A hall full of dead bodies; other people who'd been killed in the raid. Could she face that alone? As she was trying to make up her mind, Inspector Droy came down the steps and seeing her standing, irresolute, on the pavement, he crossed over to her.

'Mrs Peterson?'

'I've come to identify Colin,' she said. 'Only...' She bit her lip.

'Only you don't want to do it on your own,' he suggested gently. 'I quite understand. Look, Andy Sharpe, the chap who found Colin, is in the station now. Would you like him to come with you?'

'I've heard his name,' murmured Maggie, 'but I don't know him.'

'He's a young chap, I'm sure he'd like to come and pay his respects with you.'

Maggie still wasn't sure, but she sighed and said, 'All right, thank you.'

'Will you come into the station while I find him?' suggested the inspector.

Maggie shook her head, 'No thanks,' she replied. 'I'd rather wait outside.'

Droy nodded, understanding that she could only face one person at a time, and moments later she was joined by Andy Sharpe. The inspector had said he was young, but to Maggie he seemed to be about the same age as Colin; a tall, earnest-looking man, with bright blue eyes and some strands of blond hair showing beneath his helmet.

Seeing Maggie waiting on the pavement, he crossed to join her, holding out his hand. 'I know we haven't met,' he said, 'but I just wanted to say I'm very sorry for your loss. We all thought the sarge was a splendid chap. Very well thought of.' When Maggie made no reply to his greeting he smiled at the baby in the sling on her hip and said, 'I didn't know you had children.'

'Only one,' answered Maggie. 'This is Roger. He was living with my mother until recently.' She hitched him up a little. Roger was not particularly large, but she'd carried him all the way from home, and he was getting heavier by the minute.

Andy reached out a finger to the baby. 'Hello, mate,' he said. For a moment Roger stared back at him, solemn-faced, then he clutched at the finger and smiled a toothless smile.

'Lovely little chap,' Andy said, and then silence descended as they turned for St Mark's hall.

With Andy standing at her side, Maggie identified Colin to a warden who wrote his name in a ledger. Together she and Andy looked down at his face. It was unmarked, but already it was no longer Colin. Maggie turned away, tears filling her eyes, and clutching Roger to her, she stumbled outside into the street.

Andy followed her more slowly, giving her time to collect herself before he took her elbow and they crossed the road, leaving St Mark's hall and Colin behind.

'Would you like me to walk home with you?' Andy asked. 'I could carry young Roger for a bit if you like.'

Maggie's arm tightened round the baby as she shook her head. 'No,' she said quickly. 'No, thank you. He's fine.'

'Haven't you got a pram or pushchair?' Andy asked. 'He must be heavy to carry about like that.'

'No, we were going to try and get one, but now...' Her voice trailed away and for a while, they continued walking in silence.

It was Andy who broke it and asked, 'Have you got someone who can come in and keep you company for a while? A friend? Or neighbour?'

Maggie shook her head. 'No, we haven't been here all that long and with Colin working shifts, we haven't got to know anyone round here. Well, no more than to say good morning to in the street. I suppose,' she continued, 'I'll have to get some sort of job. I mean, I'll have to provide for Roger on my own now, won't I?'

As they reached the parade of shops at the end of Marden Road, Maggie stopped outside the butcher's shop.

'I must get something to eat,' she said, glancing in through Mr Grant's window. 'Thank you for keeping me company. I'll be all right now.'

It was clearly a dismissal and Andy accepted it as such, but even so he waited as she went inside the shop. He was about to turn away when another woman came sailing out and nearly knocked him flying.

'Oh, so sorry,' she cried. 'Wasn't looking where I was going, was I?'

'Never mind,' Andy said, 'no harm done!' And then, on impulse, he added, 'If you don't mind me asking, madam, do you know the lady with the baby, who just went into the shop?'

The woman glanced back to see whom he meant. When she saw Maggie, jogging Roger in her arms as she waited to be served, she shook her head. 'No, not really,' she replied. 'That is to say, I know who she is and where she lives, but I don't know her personally. Married to a policeman like you, isn't she?'

'Yes, she is, or rather, I should say, she was.' Andy lowered his voice. 'Poor woman. She heard this morning that her husband was killed whilst on duty during the raid last night. We've just come back from identifying his body.' He glanced back through to where Maggie stood.

'Oh my goodness,' cried the woman. 'How dreadful!'

'They haven't lived here for very long, and she says she doesn't know anyone,' Andy told her. 'So she hasn't really got any friends nearby.' He looked at the woman speculatively. 'Perhaps you could pay her a call. I imagine she's going to be pretty lonely, with only the baby for company.'

Stella Todd managed to hide her surprise at the mention of the baby. 'Well, yes,' she agreed, 'I suppose she will. I live just up the road from them... her. I suppose I might pop in.'

'I think it would be a kindness,' smiled Andy. Then he touched his helmet and walked away down the street, leaving Stella Todd to stare after him.

Well, she thought as she glanced back into the butcher's where Maggie Peterson was standing at the counter, Elsie'll never believe this! And she set off to visit her friend, a little further along the road.

Elsie answered the door to her knock and found Stella on the step, red faced and excited.

'You'll never believe what I've just heard,' she said as

Elsie, realising that she was bursting with news, stepped aside and let her in.

'It's very sad really,' Stella continued, shedding her coat and following Elsie into the warmth of the kitchen. She schooled her face into an expression of sorrow. 'That poor Mrs Peterson...' She began and then paused.

'What about her? Elsie asked dutifully.

'Her husband, that nice policeman? He was killed in the raid last night.'

'Was he? So now she's a widow. That is sad, but I expect there are many more, after that awful raid. My Paul was out firefighting and in the thick of it as usual; and his friend David? He's just lost almost his entire family. Now that really is sad. Quite dreadful. Of course we've invited him to stay with us just for a few days until he finds somewhere else, it's the only neighbourly thing to do. He and Paul go back a long way.'

Somewhat irritated at being upstaged in the bad news stakes, Stella said, 'I thought I might go and call on her, tomorrow perhaps. She'll be struggling to look after that baby on her own.'

'Baby? What baby? They haven't got a baby.'

'Yes they have,' Stella said, pleased that she still knew more than Elsie. 'I saw him today. And the man I was talking to said how difficult it would be, looking after the kid on her own.'

'What man?' demanded Elsie. 'Who were you talking to?'

'Some policeman. Worked with her husband, I suppose. Anyway, he seemed to know her. He said that she hadn't any friends or family locally and asked if I would visit her.'

'What cheek!' said Elsie. 'A complete stranger!'

'Not really,' Stella replied. 'I thought it was rather kind of him.'

'I suppose so,' Elsie conceded. 'In which case, I'll come with you.'

'I thought I might go round and call in for a cup of tea, tomorrow afternoon,' Stella said.

'Good idea,' replied Elsie. 'I'll call for you after lunch, shall I, and we'll go together.'

'Yes, all right,' agreed Stella a little reluctantly. Trust Elsie! she thought. She never likes being left out.

Andy Sharpe would have been surprised that his sudden suggestion was to be acted upon so quickly. He had had another idea himself, something to help poor Colin's widow, and having mulled it over as he returned to the police station, he went straight in to find Inspector Droy.

'You realise Sergeant Peterson's wife is left alone with a young baby, and as far as I can make out, very little means of support. I wondered if we could have a whip-round for her, put a little cash together to help out just until she gets things sorted.'

Droy looked doubtful. 'Have to be careful,' he said. 'We haven't done that for anyone else.'

'No, sir, I know, but she's new to the area and hasn't any friends down here. Just a few bob to help tide her over, like. First few days. No one would have to chip in if they didn't want to.'

Droy sighed. 'Oh well, if you want to organise it yourself, but it mustn't be anything official.' He put his hand in his pocket and pulled out a ten shilling note. 'Here, this can start you off.'

# IO

Mu didn't see Patrick again until she walked out of the hospital on Saturday morning. When she had come off duty, she had hurried to the locker room to change out of her uniform into mufti. Now she wore a leaf-green blouse under a simple grey coat and skirt, and with her glorious copper hair released from its stiff starched cap tumbling about her face, she looked the picture of spring. As she emerged in the street, Patrick had a moment to watch her before she saw him and his heart contracted with love.

Late last night he had collected the car from the garage Malcolm Frith had rented for the duration. Malcolm met him there and handed over the key.

'I've filled her right up,' he said, 'and as promised there's a jerrycan in the boot. There should be enough to get you there and back. That is, if you're still going.'

'Yes, we're still going.' Patrick sounded surprised. 'Why wouldn't we be?'

'Well, Plymouth, you know?' Malcom raised an eyebrow. 'Heavy raids the last few nights? They say the whole city is ablaze. Wouldn't be my destination of choice.'

'What have you heard?' asked Patrick. 'I haven't been listening to the wireless these last few days, too busy.'

'It was on the BBC earlier today and again this evening. They've taken a real pasting again.'

'We'll be going,' Patrick assured him. 'It's where Mu's family live...'

'If they're still alive,' Malcolm said quietly.

'That bad?'

Malcolm nodded. 'Sounded like it,' he said.

'All the more reason to go, then,' returned Patrick. 'Mu will want to know that they're all right, and if the raids have been as bad as you say, it'll be the only way of discovering.'

'Fair enough,' conceded Malcolm. 'Hope you find them.'

Patrick thought of the chaos that had reigned after the last huge raid on Portsmouth just over a month ago. Finding out anything about anyone had been a complete nightmare. Plymouth would surely be much the same. He wondered if Mu had heard the news and if not whether he should warn her of what they might find. He'd have to wait and decide when he saw her in the morning.

'I'll have the car back well in time on Sunday,' he promised. 'Due back on board by midnight.'

'Just lock her up in the garage,' Malcolm said. 'And bring the keys with you.' He held out his hand and said, 'Good luck, Patrick. May not be an easy weekend. See you aboard.'

Watching her now Patrick wondered again if Mu had listened to the wireless as well. Probably not, he thought. She'd only just this minute come off night duty, so he hoped that she hadn't. He decided that if she didn't mention the news, he wouldn't either. He would keep what Malcom had told him to himself. He didn't want her to be worrying all the way to Plymouth; he was well able to worry enough for both of them. Sufficient unto the day... Plymouth could wait until they got there.

When Mu saw him waiting on his usual corner she hurried across to him, her eyes alight with happiness. Taking her overnight bag from her, he kissed her lightly on the cheek.

'Got everything you need?' he asked, glancing down at the small bag.

'Yes,' Mu assured him. 'I don't need much.'

'Right,' he said. 'Let's go. I'm parked just round the corner.'

She took his arm, and moments later he was opening the door of a smart black car and ushering her into the passenger seat.

'Nice car,' she said admiringly. 'Does it really belong to Malcom Frith?'

'Certainly does,' replied Patrick. 'Well, his father anyway. Let's hope she goes as well as she looks.' He indicated the back seat. 'I thought you might be sleepy so I've put a cushion and a blanket in the back, so's you can try and catch up on a bit of shut-eye.'

It was a long journey, despite the roads being comparatively empty, and it wasn't long before Mu moved from the front and, curling up on the back seat, fell fast asleep. When she woke again later, they stopped at the side of the road and ate the cheese sandwiches and drank the cold tea Patrick had brought. For a short while they both forgot the war as they sat on the blanket and shared their first picnic together, but there was no time to waste. Mu got back into the front seat beside Patrick and they drove on. At last they reached Exeter and Mu began to recognise some of the countryside.

It was well into the afternoon when they reached the top of Haldon Hill, where, looking down towards Plymouth they saw a smudge of grey hanging in the sky, a cloud of smoke, marking the city where fires still burned.

'Is that really smoke?' breathed Muriel. 'Are there fires still burning?'

'Almost certainly,' Patrick replied. 'Remember how long it took to put them out in Portsmouth, back in March?'

Mu certainly did. Two consecutive night raids had pounded Portsmouth and swathes of the city had been destroyed by high explosives and fire from incendiaries. Fire brigades had come from miles around to help put out the fires, and it had taken some days to extinguish them all.

She remained quiet as they drove on towards the city, but as they drew nearer, she gazed in horror at the destruction and desolation that lay spread before them. When they reached the outskirts they headed towards the city centre but the nearer they got, the more difficult it became, their way was blocked with rubble, with craters in the road and closed streets where unexploded bombs still threatened and fires still smouldered. At last they gave up trying to drive and Patrick parked the car in a relatively undamaged side road and from there they set out on foot. Mu led the way and together they threaded their way through the streets towards Suffolk Place. All the time Mu was trying to ignore the devastation about her. Some houses were still standing, apparently untouched, others had been reduced to rubble, and many were half way between the two.

At last they turned into Haversham Road and Mu said, 'We're nearly there. Suffolk Place is the next street.'

As she turned the corner she gave a cry of anguish and

came to an abrupt halt. Most of Suffolk Place no longer existed. Wreckage had turned the little street into a wasteland. Apart from a couple of defiant walls, most of the houses had completely collapsed, the debris blasted in every direction. Heaps of stones, broken bricks, charred wood and twisted metal tossed aside were all that remained of her home and those of her neighbours. Shattered glass crunched under her shoes as she took a hesitant step forward, and she froze, staring.

'It's gone!' she whispered. 'Our house has gone.' She pointed to one of the heaps of brick, with a shredded front door lying across it at an angle. 'Our house!' She turned to Patrick with tears streaming down her cheeks and he gathered her into his arms and held her close as her body was convulsed with sobs. Looking over her head he could see that the whole row had been destroyed, perhaps by one high explosive bomb. Beyond the debris he saw there were small squares of garden behind the houses and in the Shawbrooks' was the hump of a half-buried Anderson shelter. It was unlikely anyone sheltering in that would have survived the bombs. Then he remembered what she'd told him. He held her a little away from him and asked gently, 'Didn't you say that your mother always took them to the public shelter in the next street?'

Mu gulped and nodded.

'Just because the house has been demolished,' he said, 'it doesn't mean that anything has happened to your family. Like you said, they were probably safely in that street shelter. They may have nowhere to live now, but it doesn't mean that they were killed when the house was destroyed. We should go to the nearest rescue centre and see where they are now. There'll be places, however temporary, for those made homeless. All we have to do is find them.'

His words had the desired effect and taking his proffered handkerchief, Mu wiped at her cheeks and blew her nose. 'Of course, you're right,' she said as she scrubbed at her eyes again. 'They wouldn't have been in the house, they'd have been in the shelter. If we go to the rescue centre we can ask where they've been taken.'

'Which way to the nearest centre?' said Patrick, realising that practical action was needed now to keep Mu's hopes alive. They must do something practical to find her family.

'I'm not sure, but I know where Dad's wardens' post is, so we'll go there. He'll know where they are.' With a final glance over her shoulder, Mu turned her back on the pile of debris which had once been her home, and led the way back into Haversham Road.

The wardens' post was half a mile away, and they had to pick their way through the bomb-damaged streets that lay between. Everywhere there were people, workmen searching through rubble for possible survivors, others clearing the roads for the rescue services, fireman still dousing outbreaks of flame that erupted from smouldering wreckage, and people simply staring in disbelief at the destruction all around them. As if silence would invade her mind with doubts and allow her fears to take over, Mu kept on talking.

'Of course,' she was saying, 'Dad may not be there at this time of day. If he's been up all night he'll be somewhere to try and get some sleep, ready for tonight. He's probably with Mam and the children, wherever they are, but the people at the post will know. It's the obvious place to go.'

Patrick rather agreed with her, but with chaos all round them he wasn't so optimistic that it would be as simple as just asking. There must be so many homeless after four nights of raids, that it could take some time to learn where all the displaced families were being housed.

They reached the post where her father should have been, but there was no sign of him. Queues of people were waiting patiently to be registered for help, for food, for clothes, for a place to lay their heads. Most of them having given their names were being redirected to the feeding station in the next street where they could get a hot meal. Patrick and Mu waited as patiently as they could, but just as they were reaching the head of one of the queues, a voice hailed her.

'Muriel? Muriel Shawbrook?'

Mu turned round to see a familiar face, a man she knew she ought to know, but for a moment couldn't place.

'Muriel! It is you, isn't it?' And seeing the confusion on her face he said, 'Paul Jefferson, old friend of your father's.'

'Oh, yes,' said Mu, 'sorry, Mr Jefferson, I knew I recognised you, but I couldn't think.'

'Well, it's been quite a while since we saw you, but I couldn't miss your beautiful hair.' Paul hesitated, suddenly realising that Muriel wasn't alone. She and the good-looking man with her must be looking for her father, and if that were the case she probably did not yet know the fate of her mother and brothers and sisters.

He smiled at Patrick and said, 'How d'y'do? I'm a friend of Muriel's father.'

Before Patrick could reply, Mu said, 'And this is Patrick. We're looking for Dad. Do you know where he'll be?'

## II

The raid that killed Colin Peterson that Wednesday had been the fiercest yet, lasting almost until dawn. The night was filled with the clamour of the raid; ack ack, explosions, crashing masonry, and most terrifying of all, the shriek of the dive bombers, as they hurtled out of the night to drop their fearsome load on the already burning city. Buildings became infernos and Paul Jefferson and his volunteer crew were working flat out to extinguish the smaller fires with stirrup pumps and buckets of sand, while the huge blazes that consumed shops, offices and homes alike, were left to the professional fire fighters with fire engines, hoses and ladders from around the county. It was the third consecutive night of blitzkrieg and the whole city was shaken to its foundations. Paul was exhausted and when at dawn he was sent for a break, he wondered if he could ever drag himself back to his post to continue fighting fires. But no one gave in. The moment the raid was over and the all-clear sounded, people emerged from shelters and cellars, and busloads of citizens returned from the refuge they had sought on Dartmoor or the outlying countryside, ready to help those who had not only fought throughout the night risking their lives to save others, but now continued their rescue work into the day, the clearing up, the searching and the laying out of the dead.

David Shawbrook had been out on the streets with one of the rescue parties all night. As the sun rose to reveal the extent of devastation, more and more volunteers poured out to give respite to those who had given their all.

For the next few days the civil defence services toiled throughout the city, searching, clearing, dealing with outbreaks of fire smouldering under the debris, only to burst forth again to demand attention. Water mains had ruptured, and several gas pipes burned merrily in the sunshine. There was lurking danger from unexploded bombs that lay undiscovered amid the rubble, threatening to ambush the unwary before the sappers could defuse them. At the end of each day, people streamed out into the countryside, terrified that the Luftwaffe would be back, determined to finish the job, leaving no stone standing upon another.

Both Paul and David worked themselves to exhaustion, only snatching a quick meal and few hours' sleep in Paul's house before returning to their posts for their night-time shifts.

Respite from the bombing was a blessed relief, and it was on Friday night that David decided that he could wait no longer. He couldn't leave poor Mu in ignorance of the fate of her family any longer, neither could he bring himself to ring her at the nurses' home and tell her on the telephone. He had no idea how long it would take to get to Portsmouth, but he had made up his mind he must go.

As soon as the sun was fully up, David slipped away from the frantic busyness of the streets and made his way to the station. He had some money and the clothes he stood up in, albeit they were certainly the worse for wear, covered in dust and soot, his shoes scuffed and filthy. There was a cafe at the station which was serving breakfast and, having done his best to make himself presentable in the men's lavatory, David had a bacon sandwich and a cup of tea while he waited for a train... any train that might be going in the right direction. Miraculously, the railway lines had not been hit. Though much of the land on either side of the track was now a wasteland, trains were still running, so David bought a ticket and waited on the platform. The first train to arrive was on its way to Exeter and he climbed aboard. It was the first leg of his journey to Portsmouth, but it wasn't until nearly nine hours later that the fourth train on which he had travelled brought him into that city. He had managed to get some sleep, lulled by the rocking of the train, but the night's exertions had left him drained physically and mentally and when he was jerked to wakefulness as the train stopped at yet another signal, he awoke unrefreshed.

When he finally reached his destination, he stepped out onto the street, and looked about. He knew Mu lived in the nurses' home. He didn't have an address, but it must be close to the Royal Hospital. It would be the place to start and the quickest way to get there would be to lay out money for a taxi.

When the taxi deposited him outside the main entrance of the hospital, David stood for a moment before going in, dreading what he was going to have to do. Still, he'd come this far, and he went inside to ask at the reception desk. He was greeted by a woman of about fifty, who looked about as tired as David felt. She eyed him with disfavour, taking in his scruffy clothes and asked in a weary, end-of-shift voice, 'Good afternoon, sir. Can I help you?'

'I'm looking for my daughter,' David replied. 'Nurse Shawbrook. Can you tell me where to find her?'

'I'm sorry, sir, but I don't think I can help you.'

'But surely you can tell me if she's on duty right now!'

'No, sir, I haven't got that information.'

'But somebody must know,' cried David in frustration. 'I've come all the way from Plymouth! I have to find her.'

Seeing that he was not only dishevelled, but clearly exhausted, the woman relaxed a little and managed a smile. Leaning forward, she said quietly, 'The quickest way to find out would be to go to the nurses' home and ask. There's sure to be somebody who'll be able to tell you. They have all the rosters there.'

'Thank you,' David said, relief in his voice. 'Thank you very much. Can you tell me how to find the nurses' home. Is it far?'

'No, just round the corner.' She pulled a piece of paper towards her and wrote down the address. Giving him directions, she added, 'You can't miss it, it's a square box of a building backing onto the hospital wall.'

David thanked her for her help and as he turned for the door she said, 'I hope you find her all right.'

Once out in the street again, David followed her instructions and soon found himself outside the building she'd described. There was nothing to indicate that it was the nurses' home, and for a moment or two he waited, hoping someone would go in or come out so that he could ask. He stared up at the building, an unattractive square block, and wondered if Mu was inside. As he stood irresolute on the pavement, the front door opened and a girl came out and ran down the steps. She wasn't in uniform, so David didn't even know if she was a nurse, but he hailed her tentatively.

'Excuse me, miss,' he said.

The girl paused, but seemed on the point of turning away. 'Yes?'

'Sorry to trouble you, miss, but am I right in thinking this is the nurses' home?'

The girl eyed him warily. David didn't really blame her, despite his efforts to clean himself up, he knew he still looked pretty disreputable.

'It's just that I'm looking for my daughter, she's one of the nurses and I wasn't sure I was in the right place. Perhaps you know her? Muriel Shawbrook? I'm her father. Is she here?'

'Mu?' The girl relaxed a little. 'Yes, I know her, but we don't work the same ward so I don't know if she's in the house.'

'I must find her,' David said. 'It's most important.'

The girl looked at his ravaged face and saw that he was almost at the end of his endurance. 'I'll go back in and ask if anyone knows,' she said, 'but she's probably on the ward.'

The girl turned back up the steps and when David waited uncertainly on the pavement she smiled and held out her hand and said, 'Come on. Come in, it's starting to rain.'

'Thank you, miss...'

'Eltham, Alison Eltham.'

'Miss Eltham.'

Alison smiled at him and opening the front door, led him into a common room where several nurses were relaxing, drinking tea.

'Anyone know where Mu Shawbrook is?' she asked. 'This is her father.'

'Mu? Didn't someone say she'd got the weekend off, lucky devil?' Mandy, the girl who had answered turned to another and said, 'Isn't that what you said, Christine? That she'd swapped weekends with Jean? *She'll* be here in a minute, cos she's working Mu's shift tonight.'

'But Muriel?' cried David in dismay. 'If she's not working, where will she be?'

'I think she said she was going home... to Plymouth? I might have got it wrong, it's an awfully long way to go for one night, but I think that's what she said.'

David stared at her in stupefaction. 'But I've just come from there. I've just come from Plymouth.' For a moment his head swam and the room shimmered about him. The girl called Christine jumped to her feet, and catching his arm helped him into an armchair.

'Ali, get a glass of water, quickly.' Alison went to the sink in the corner of the room, as David sat back in the chair and closed his eyes.

'Mr Shawbrook? Mr Shawbrook? Are you all right?'

David could hear the anxious voice as if from a great distance. He knew he had to open his eyes, but somehow they wouldn't obey him. He was too tired... too tired to make such an effort. Someone put a glass of water to his lips and he took a tiny sip and then another, but he still didn't open his eyes.

'Let's leave him for a while,' suggested Alison. 'He's obviously exhausted and if he's come all the way from Plymouth, it must have taken him hours.'

At that moment the telephone in the hall rang and

Mandy went to answer it. She had a short conversation with whoever had called and then came back into the room. 'Let him sleep,' she said softly. 'That was Mu, or rather that was her fiancé. There was another heavy raid over Plymouth last night. Mr Shawbrook's a warden and was up all night.'

'Mu's fiancé?' The news was greeted with surprise. 'I didn't know she had one.'

'Nor did I. When did that happen?'

'But what did he want?' asked Christine. 'Was he looking for Mu?'

'No, Mu's with him, they're in Plymouth. They went to see her family and she's looking for her father.'

'But why would she ring here?'

'She thought he might come here, looking for her.'

'What her fiancé said was that they had gone to Plymouth to find her family and at the same time her father had set out to find her.' Mandy shook her head. 'He said they must have crossed on the way. Anyway, he said they're coming straight back, and if Mr Shawbrook arrived looking for Mu, to look after him here until they get back.'

'But they may not be back for hours,' protested Christine, 'and I for one have to go on duty within the hour.'

'He can't really stay here, can he?' sighed Alison. 'Imagine Sister Roderick's face if she found out we had a man asleep in the common room!'

'Better than in one of the bedrooms,' pointed out Christine with a grin. 'Look, you can see he's all-in. Let's let him sleep and we'll pass him over to the day shift until Mu and her chap get back.'

It was the best they could do; they took a cushion and tucked it under David's head and someone fetched a blanket to cover him. Christine risked taking his shoes off, and all the while nothing they did roused him or even disturbed his slumber; he was dead to the world.

It was Alison Eltham who decided that they must tell Sister Roderick, sister in charge of the nurses' home, about their unexpected guest. Far better, she said, to explain who he was and why he was asleep in the common room than let Sister find him for herself.

'Up to you,' Christine said. 'Rather you than me. Only you'll have to look sharp, or you'll be late on duty.'

Alison knocked on the door of Sister's lair and on being instructed to enter, drew a deep breath and went in to explain what had happened. To her surprise, Sister Roderick seemed to accept the situation and told her to leave Nurse Shawbrook's father where he was and she would attend to him when he woke.

'You could have knocked me down with a feather,' she said to Christine when she caught her up in the locker room. 'She went into the common room and had a look at him and then told me to hurry up, or I'd be late.'

'I wonder why he came?' mused Christine. 'It's a long way to come just for a night, isn't it?'

Alison shrugged. 'Not our business, is it?'

'No,' agreed Christine, 'but you can't help wondering, can you?'

# I2

'All of them?' Mu whispered, her face ashen. 'All of them?'

Paul Jefferson swallowed before answering; there was no easy way of telling her, but he'd had to do it. 'It was a direct hit, Muriel. There were no survivors.'

'Mam? The children?' Mu couldn't take it in. 'All of them?' Seven members of her family, wiped out at a stroke. Her legs seemed to fold beneath her and Patrick caught her as she sank to the ground. Holding her firmly in his arms, he lowered her onto a nearby bench and sat down beside her, keeping her within the circle of his arm.

'Your father and I,' Paul said, 'we went to the shelter as soon as we heard. When we got there, rescuers were already there, digging...' His voice trailed away as he recalled the obliteration of the Parham Road shelter, the crater, the few remains. There had been frantic digging, but almost nothing to find. He went on softly, 'They'd have known nothing about it, Mu.'

Muriel shivered and Patrick said, 'Let's get you somewhere warm, and get something hot inside you.'

'I know a place,' Paul said, and led them to the Black

Horse a couple of streets away. He knew it well, the pub where the men from his fire crew went for a few moments' break from the never-ending fight against the fires that threatened to devour the city. Its windows were striped with tape against blast, its frontage heavily sandbagged, but its front door was defiantly open. The bar was crowded with people looking for food and a few moments' respite from the devastation of the streets outside, and the three of them went into the warmth it offered. Paul was hailed by various men eating sandwiches and downing a pint of beer, but he simply acknowledged their calls with a wave and led the way through into the snug.

'Mu needs a hot drink, hot and sweet,' Patrick said once he'd settled her in a chair in a corner by the fire, and so saying he went to ask for some tea.

'Your dad thought they might have taken shelter in the Anderson for some reason,' Paul was telling Mu as Patrick rejoined them, 'not gone to Parham Road this time, so we went back to Suffolk Place in the hope...' He sighed and went on, 'But the shelter was empty and the house half collapsed. Even then he didn't give up hope. He insisted on going inside, you know, to be sure...'

'He went in?' Mu looked confused. 'Went in? But there was nothing left to go into! The whole house was a heap of rubble!'

'Not then it wasn't,' Paul said. 'It was quite badly damaged, but it was the second raid that finished the job, finished off Suffolk Place. Your dad went back again then and saw it as you saw it... nothing but a heap of rubble.'

'But he went inside, the first time, the time you were with him?'

'Yes, and damned dangerous it was, too! He was lucky to come out again alive. But he was sure there was no sign of anyone there, just a few footprints in the dust. Souvenir hunters, he reckoned. They've no respect for anyone's property.'

'Poor Dad.' Mu's voice broke on a sob. 'Poor dear Dad!' Patrick leaned forward and took her hand in his and she clung to it as if she were drowning.

'He came to ours for a couple of days,' Paul said. 'Stayed in our spare room. We were pleased to have him. It's difficult to find shelter anywhere if you're bombed out after a big raid like that. But he was determined to come over to Portsmouth to tell you himself, face to face, like. Said it wasn't something he could tell you over the phone.'

Mu nodded dumbly. 'Poor Dad,' she repeated. 'Now there's only him and me and Tony. Does Tony know? Has Dad told Tony yet?'

'I don't know, Mu,' answered Paul. 'He said he was going to write to let him know what had happened. But he said at least you were within reach and as soon as he wasn't needed here he was going to come and tell you himself. I haven't seen him since crack of dawn this morning, so I'm pretty sure he went today.'

'But how was he going to find me?' wondered Mu. 'It was Mam who had the address.'

'Nurses' home?' answered Paul. 'Said he was going to look for you there.'

'So, he could be there now,' said Patrick, suddenly struck with an idea. 'We can try and ring and see if he's got there. Let's see if we can get a line and put through a call.'

'What good's that?' said Mu miserably.

'The good of that, darling heart, is to leave him a message. To tell him we're coming and to wait for us; to wait for us in Portsmouth, and we'll drive back and find him.'

Mu said nothing, just stared at him. She was beyond making decisions.

'Sounds like a plan,' put in Paul. 'If you can warn him to wait, you can meet up there. You don't want to cross over again.' He looked again at Patrick. 'Did you say you've got a car?'

'Borrowed,' said Patrick.

'That's good,' Paul said. 'Don't have to rely on the damned trains.'

'We were coming to tell them all,' whispered Mu. 'That's why we came.'

Paul looked confused. 'Tell them? Tell them what?'

Mu didn't reply, just closed her eyes and shook her head, so it was Patrick that answered.

'Mu and I are going to be married,' he said. 'I asked her the other day and we came here to tell her parents.'

'And now it's too late.' Mu gave in to the sobs which were almost choking her. 'Mam'll never know!'

At that moment a waitress brought them the tea and sandwiches that Patrick had ordered, and Paul poured the tea. Mu said she didn't want any until the cup was in her hand, and then taking a sip, she found that she was very thirsty and tea was what she needed most.

In the meantime, Patrick went to find the nearest public telephone.

'I managed to get through,' he told them when he came back into the lounge. 'He's there. He's asleep on the sofa in the nurses' home. The girl I spoke to, Mandy, is it? She said he'd simply sat down and fallen asleep.'

'But he can't stay there!' cried Mu. 'He won't be allowed.'

'Darling, this girl said they'd look after him, and when we get there we can find him somewhere to stay.' He picked up his cup of tea and drank it down in one long swallow before standing up.

'Come on, Mu,' he said, wrapping a couple of sandwiches in his handkerchief and stuffing them into his pocket. 'We've got to get going. It's going to be a long old drive.'

Paul walked back to the car with them and waited while Patrick settled Mu in the passenger seat and closed the door.

'Sorry it was me had to break the news,' Paul said, 'and not her dad, as he'd intended.'

'You had to tell her,' Patrick reassured him. 'In the circumstances, you couldn't not. Don't worry, we'll find her father as quickly as we can. They need to be together at a time like this.'

*At a time like this*. The words echoed in his mind as he took the road back towards Exeter. What is 'a time like this'? How often does a young woman suddenly discover that she has lost seven members of her family all at the same time? Mu was clearly in shock, but when the truth finally made itself real, how would she cope with such a loss?

'Take it steady on the way back,' Paul had said as Patrick got into the car. 'It's a long way to drive for the second time in one day.'

Paul was right, and added to the distance were the dangers of driving at night, with only a pinprick of light from the shielded headlamps. For a long time neither of them spoke.

Patrick was concentrating on the road and Mu was staring out of the window. It was after they had navigated their way round Exeter that Mu finally broke the silence.

'We were the biggest family in our street,' she said, almost as if they were already in the middle of a conversation. 'Tony's the eldest, he's twenty-four, next is me. Us two were the war babies. Then there's a bit of a gap before Vera was born, she's...' Mu gulped before saying, 'was... eighteen. Sammy, thirteen' – this time Patrick noticed that she left out the 'is' or the 'was' – 'Joey eleven, Winnie, nine,' she continued, 'and Angela seven. "Angel" we called her, and baby Freddie, only nine months. Eight of us. And now there's only Dad, Tony and me. What a waste of life, Patrick!' Her voice was filled with bitterness. 'Why were they born at all if they were meant to die so young? What was the point of that? Is there a God, d'you think? I don't think there can be, but if there is, why's he taken them away before they've even started their lives?'

Patrick knew these were rhetorical questions and he made no effort to answer them, just listened, Mu's voice scarcely audible over the roar of the car's engine.

How noisy it is! she thought irritably as once again she retreated into silence. This car!

'Tell me about them,' suggested Patrick. 'Tell me about them so that I can picture each one of them.' And thus they passed the next part of the journey, Mu speaking of her brothers and sisters, her parents and their lives together in Suffolk Place. When she finally lapsed into silence and drifted off into a restless doze, Patrick felt even more aware of the enormous gap that had been left in Mu's life.

How on earth am I going to fill all that space? he

wondered. The emptiness left by seven people who have always been there, part of her life and now vanished, gone for ever?

When they reached the nurses' home, it was already late and the front door had been locked for the night. Mu knocked loudly, several times, before the door was opened by Sister Roderick.

'Ah, Nurse Shawbrook,' she said. 'I've been expecting you.'

'Is my father here?' demanded Muriel.

'No, he's not. You'd better come in and I'll explain.'

When Patrick stepped forward as well, she said, 'Your friend can wait outside, then he can take you to find your father.'

Mu turned to Patrick. 'Sorry,' she whispered, 'I won't be long, I've just got to find out where Dad is now.'

Patrick understood. He knew the rules of the nurses' home: no male visitors.

Sister Roderick allowed Mu into the hallway and then said, 'Your father couldn't wait here, of course. Nurse Burford took him round to the Royal Oak when she got off duty and he got a room there for the night. You'd better go there straight away and find him. He'll be waiting up for you.'

When he'd woken up, David Shawbrook had found himself faced with the sister in charge, and realising that she needed to know the situation, the reason for his visit, he had taken her into his confidence. Sister Roderick was not known as a sentimental woman, but even she was horrified at the news he was bringing and had suggested that he take two rooms at the Royal Oak so that his daughter could stay there with him for the night. Looking at Muriel now, she did not know if she already knew the fate of her family, or if her father still had to break the dreadful news, but Sister Roderick was certain that both the young nurse and her father would be in a state of shock and they should be together.

'I understand you're not on duty until Monday night,' she said. 'I suggest you spend the time with your father and then come and see me on Monday morning.'

'Thank you, Sister,' Muriel replied. 'I will.'

She let herself out into the street and heard the door being locked behind her. 'He's at the Royal Oak,' she told Patrick. 'It's a pub round the corner. We go there sometimes. Come on.'

Together they walked the short distance to the pub. It was already in darkness, no glimmer of light escaping from its curtained windows, but when Patrick pushed the door, it swung open. It was late and the bar was closed, but David Shawbrook was sitting on the end of a sofa, staring into the empty fireplace, nursing a glass of whisky. The landlady, Betty Price, who was clearing up behind the bar, looked up to see who had come in, and saw a tall man holding open the door and a young girl poised on the threshold and knew her guest's daughter had arrived. Quietly she went through the baize door to the kitchen, leaving them alone. At the sound of the door David looked up from his contemplation and seeing Mu in the doorway, got to his feet and held out his arms.

With a childlike sob of 'Daddy,' Mu rushed into them and both weeping, they held each other close, tears mingling on their cheeks as Mu repeated over and over, 'Daddy! Oh,

Daddy! I can't bear it. I can't bear it. Mam and the kiddies. All of them!'

'So you already know,' David murmured when he finally let her go.

'Paul Jefferson told me. We were looking for you and… and… and—' Mu's voice broke on another sob, 'and he said you'd gone to Portsmouth to find me… and… and told me why.'

'I came to tell you myself,' said her father, 'but you weren't here.'

'Patrick and I came to Plymouth to see you all.'

'Patrick?' For the first time David seemed to be aware of a third person in the room, a tall young man waiting patiently just inside the door, unwilling to intrude on their private grief.

'Patrick drove us to Plymouth to see you all,' Mu wept. 'We'd come to tell you, but now it's too late!'

'Too late for what?' David looked confused. 'Why were you coming?' He glanced up at Patrick and said, 'Who's he?'

'Patrick,' Mu said. 'He's Patrick. I told Mam about him. He's the man I'm going to marry. We came to surprise you all!' And with that Mu began to sob again.

David put his arms round her and held her close. He looked over her shoulder to the man still standing by the door.

'You and Muriel's going to get married?'

'Yes, sir,' replied Patrick. 'Sub Lieutenant Patrick Davenham, RNVR. With your permission, sir, we plan to get married on my next leave.'

## 13

When Muriel and her father met over the breakfast table the next morning, it was clear that neither of them had slept particularly well. Mu looked pale and drawn, with dark circles under her eyes. She had lain in the darkness, thinking through the conversation she and her father had had, when Patrick had left them alone together.

Neither of them had known what to say to the other, but eventually it was Mu who broke their uneasy silence.

'Does Tony know?' she asked.

David shook his head. 'Not yet,' he said. 'I'll have to write, but it'll be such a difficult letter, I've put it off. I wish I could tell him myself.'

'Thank you for coming to find me,' Mu said.

'I had to see you,' replied her father. 'I had to see for myself that you were still alive.' And it hung in the air between them that Tony, on active service abroad, might not be.

When Betty Price had shown them up to their rooms she had suggested a brandy nightcap might help them sleep, and Mu had carried a glass up with her, but as she lay in bed with her thoughts in turmoil, the brandy simply added to her feeling of disorientation. When she closed her eyes the world seemed to spin and she quickly opened them again and waited for it to slow down.

What was Dad going to do now, she wondered, all alone in Plymouth? Who would look after him? Where was he going to live now that their home was no more than a pile of rubble? He had told her that the Jeffersons had very kindly offered him their spare room for a while, just until he found a new place of his own, but Mu knew that wasn't going to be easy. There was so much to do, to think about, to be decided, Mu felt that she would never sleep again, but the day had taken its toll and with a little help from the brandy, she finally drifted into an exhausted sleep.

David had kissed his daughter on the landing, holding her tightly against him for a moment before saying goodnight and going into his room. His sleep in the chair in the nurses' home had not been all that long, but it had taken the edge off his tiredness and now he moved restlessly about the room, trying to see a way forward. Though he had told Muriel how kind the Jeffersons had been, Paul saying that he was welcome to stay as long as he liked, David had no intention of staying there for a night longer than he had to. It was clear that Elsie wasn't best pleased with the arrangement and he didn't want to be the cause of any marital disharmony for his old friend.

He'd already decided that he must go back to Plymouth first thing in the morning. He'd be needed there again if there was another raid, and life had to go on. The only way he could begin to deal with such a tragedy was to work, and to keep working, until he was fit to drop. That way, he thought, there'll be no time to dwell on what's happened. Work and sleep, one to fill the night on the city streets, the other to pass the empty day. He'd find himself a room somewhere and then live each day as it came, one day at a time. He would survive, but he was very worried about Muriel. How would she cope with what had happened when the reality of her loss hit home? And who was this Patrick she'd sprung on him? She said her mother had known about him. Well, perhaps Nancy had, but he certainly hadn't; didn't know him from Adam! Patrick had said they were going to get married on his next leave... with his permission. Cheeky that. What would happen if he didn't give it? But, as he'd taken his leave Patrick had reminded Mu that he was rejoining his ship tomorrow and sailing soon after.

'He'll be no support to Mu there, will he?' David demanded of his bedroom. 'She'll be on her own here in Portsmouth, with me in Plymouth, Tony in North Africa or somewhere, and this Patrick on the high seas.'

Betty served them a kipper each with toast, no butter but with a smear of raspberry jam, and a strong brew of tea. As they sat over their second cups of tea, they spoke at last of what they were going to do next.

'I'm heading straight back... to Plymouth,' David said, almost saying 'back home' but catching himself in time. 'I need to be there tonight, or at the latest tomorrow. My post will be short-handed without me and I doubt if Jerry's finished with us yet.'

'But where will you live?' asked Muriel. 'You can't stay with the Jeffersons permanently, can you?'

'No,' replied her father firmly. 'I'll find somewhere, don't worry. And when I do I'll let you have my address, so we can stay in closer touch.' He managed a brief smile. 'I did a lot of thinking last night before I fell asleep.'

'So did I,' Mu agreed. 'And I've come to some decisions, too. I don't want to stay here by myself, with you back in Plymouth by yourself. We need to be closer. I'm going to try and get myself moved to Plymouth. I'll see if I can get a transfer to the City Hospital or perhaps the Prince of Wales. I'm sure that in the light of what's happened it could be arranged on compassionate grounds. I know I'd have to live in the nurses' home there too, but at least we'd be in the same city. I'd be able to see you on my days off, wouldn't I?'

'I suppose so,' replied her father, adding with a gleam of hope in his eye, 'Do you think the hospital would let you?'

Mu shrugged. 'Don't know,' she said, 'but it's worth asking.'

'What about your boyfriend, this Patrick?'

'My fiancé, Dad,' Mu corrected him. 'Well, as he told you last night, he's about go back to sea, so I won't see him for ages wherever I live.'

'He may not be so happy about it when he gets home for his next leave. Said you were getting married then.' He looked into her pale face. 'Are you?'

'That was before…' Mu said flatly. 'Everything's different now.'

Mu walked with David to the station and saw him on to the first of the several trains he would take on his way back to Plymouth. In her pocket was the piece of paper on which David had written the Jeffersons' address.

'Even if I've moved out,' he said, 'they'll know where I am. It's a pity they aren't on the phone, but if necessary I can leave a message for you at the nurses' home.'

The train steamed up to the platform and David gathered Mu into his arms, holding her tightly for a moment.

'Look after yourself, little Mu,' he murmured. 'Stay safe and come back to Plymouth.'

Mu returned the convulsive hug and then he let her go and turning sharply, climbed into the train. The engine let off steam, the guard blew his whistle and the train started to move. Mu could see her father at the window and for a moment or two she ran along beside the train, waving, until it gathered speed and left her standing, bereft, on the platform. She stood alone watching the train disappear round a curve and fought to hold back the tears. Dad had gone, Patrick was going and there was nobody in Suffolk Place waiting for her to come home. Never had she felt so alone.

The bustle of the station went on around her, but at last she turned and went out into the street. Patrick had said he would come and find her at the Royal Oak in the morning and she turned her footsteps back towards the pub.

It was too early for the bar to be open, but when she pushed on the door, she found it unlocked and let herself in. Patrick was waiting for her in the lounge and as soon as she saw him, control of her emotions gave way, and she began to weep. Patrick stepped forward and gathered her into his arms, holding her close until her sobs began to subside. At last she accepted his handkerchief, drying her eyes and blowing her nose.

'Sorry,' she murmured as they sat down together on the sofa.

'Don't be,' Patrick said, still holding her firmly in his embrace.

'Dad's gone,' she told him. 'He's gone back to Plymouth.'

'I guessed he would,' Patrick said. 'What are you going to do?'

'I'm going to go too,' Mu answered. 'If I can get a transfer to one of the hospitals there. Nurses are needed everywhere, so I don't suppose they'll mind which one I'm working in.'

Patrick nodded. It made sense, Mu moving to be nearer her father, but even so he found he was disappointed. She wouldn't be waiting for him in Portsmouth when he came home on leave. She was still speaking, and he realised he'd missed part of what she was saying.

'What?' he broke in. 'What did you say?' He watched in dismay as she removed her engagement ring and laid it on the coffee table in front of them.

'I said, I can't marry you, Patrick. Dad needs me, now. With Tony abroad somewhere, I'm the only one he's got left.'

'No, well, if you really think that.' Patrick sounded confused. 'But you mustn't give me my ring back. We can wait as long as you like to be married, but surely there's nothing to stop us being engaged, is there? Mu, darling Mu, I just want to know that you'll be waiting for me when I get back.'

'But don't you see, I won't be, will I? I shall be away, living in Plymouth.'

'I don't care where you'll be,' Patrick said, 'as long as I know you'll be waiting for me. You never know, maybe the ship will dock in Plymouth next time.' He managed a smile. 'And there you'll be.'

'Patrick, I thought it all through last night when I couldn't sleep and I made my decision then. Now's not the time to be thinking of getting married, or even of being engaged. I've lost my whole family. I can't look forward to any sort of future without them, not now, not yet, maybe not ever. It's not fair to you... to keep you on a string—'

'Maybe I like being kept on a string,' interrupted Patrick, 'if it's you holding the other end.' She managed a brief smile at this, but she shook her head, slipping out of his encircling arm. 'Patrick, I'm so sorry,' she whispered, 'but I can't, I really can't.'

'All right, Mu, I understand, I really do.' He reached for her hand, needing some physical contact with her, afraid he might truly lose her if he let her go. 'But I love you more than I thought was possible to love anyone, and if and when you change your mind, as I'm praying you will, I'll be waiting for you.' He picked up the ring and handed it to her. 'Keep the ring to remind you that I love you, and when you feel able, please, my darling, let me put it back on your finger.'

Mu shook her head again. 'No, Patrick, that would be wrong. You might fall in love with someone else and need it for her.'

Patrick gave a rueful smile at this and said, 'No, Mu, if you want me to keep it safe for you, then I will, but this ring is yours and always will be. It will be ready when the day comes that you feel able to wear it again.'

He got to his feet. 'I'm on HMS *Cumbria*. We sail before dawn,' he said, 'though I shouldn't be telling you so. I've no idea when we shall be back into Pompey again. May I write to you, Mu?'

'Better not,' Mu replied, 'and anyway, I don't know where I'll be.'

'Wherever you are I'll find you,' Patrick promised. 'And

you can always write to me care of the navy.' He held out his hands to her and though she stood up as well, she didn't take them, holding hers tightly together so he wouldn't see them shaking.

'I'll go now,' Patrick said, 'but just remember, Mu, I love you and I'll be waiting for you.' With that he turned on his heel and strode out of the pub into the street.

Muriel watched him go, dry-eyed. For now she had cried all the tears that she had.

As he walked away from the Royal Oak, Patrick realised that he had to accept, at least for the time being, what Mu had said. The enormity of what had happened to her family was beyond her comprehension. She would never really get over it, but perhaps in time she would manage to come to terms with it and allow herself to go on living when they could not. All she could cling to now was her father, and her father to her. They needed to be together, Patrick could see and understand that, but he wasn't prepared to give up hope of a future together with Mu. She had said don't write, but that was one stricture that would not bind him. He would write to her as often as he could; it would be up to her whether she even read his letters, let alone answered them, but Patrick would not give up. He would write to her care of the nurses' home and if she did indeed manage to get transferred to Plymouth, he was sure the letters would be forwarded to her there.

For an hour Patrick walked aimlessly through streets already laid low and battered by raids earlier in the month. Despite the continued efforts of the civil defence teams, minimal clearing had been achieved since the last raid, leaving some parts of the city little more than heaps of rubble. When he and Mu had planned their weekend, they'd expected to spend Sunday together with a leisurely drive back from visiting her family in Plymouth, the last few hours before he had to return to his ship; but now the world had changed. He was alone, and without Mu it seemed pointless to stay ashore. He would be better off aboard the *Cumbria* with his shipmates, getting ready to take her to sea, and so, slowly, he turned his back on the city and made his way towards the docks.

Following her completed sea trials, HMS *Cumbria* lay at the anchorage of Spithead, between Portsmouth and the Isle of Wight, the majority of her ship's company already aboard, those with a few days' precious leave, such as he, would return by *Cumbria*'s boats before leave expiry at midnight. He knew boats would be running most of the day and reaching the quay, he had little difficulty in getting a ride out to his ship.

As the boat crossed the water, he looked back at the city; was that the hospital tower he could see? Had Mu gone back to the nurses' home? What would she be doing? With determination Patrick thrust these questions away. For the time being he must push Mu, if not out, at least to the back of his mind. For now he belonged again to the navy and he was returning to the war.

## 14

The swooping wail of sirens split the darkness, warning the people of Portsmouth of incoming enemy aircraft; and the people of Portsmouth once again dragged themselves from the warmth of their beds to take shelter from the onslaught. Searchlights swept the sky, lighting the ghostly barrage balloons, bulbous silver whales hanging above the city; ropes of steel trailing to slice, as with cheese wire, the wings of enemy aircraft should they venture too low. Out over the sea, distant at first, but with ever-increasing roar reverberating among the drifts of clouds, came the sound of approaching planes, coming low and fast across the water. Not an alert... a raid.

Mu was lying awake in the darkness. Having slept the sleep of exhaustion during the day, sleep had deserted her now and with the howl of the sirens, she threw back the blankets and got out of bed. Jean had insisted on taking the second nightshift as planned, but to the sound of sirens repeatedly wailing their warning, Mu threw on her clothes and made for the door. It was time to be up and doing, to fight back in the only way she knew. They would need every pair of hands in the hospital tonight and she joined the other off-duty nurses who were hurrying over to the wards to offer their help. Even as she ran into the locker room to change into her uniform she could hear the planes coming in overhead, screaming out of the night to deliver death and destruction from the air.

The first wave dropped incendiaries that landed, fizzed, burst into vicious flame. As she crossed the hospital grounds Mu could see sudden bursts of red and orange, blossoms of fire that leaped and danced, spreading quickly on the breeze; some close to the hospital itself, others distant flares and flickers. All too soon, she thought, her heart constricting with fear, there'll be more bombers loaded with high explosives, targeting the naval dockyards... the ships in the harbour... Patrick's ship.

When Mu reached the ward, she found Sister Pearce directing the nurses to prepare for possible evacuation. She accepted Mu's arrival without comment, simply setting her to cover those bedridden with a cage and blankets to protect them from any flying glass. The nurses moved about the ward with calm, reassuring faces, doing all they could to soothe the alarm of their patients. Beyond the hospital walls the sky was filled with the sound of the aerial battle as fighters from RAF Tangmere fought to harass the invading enemy, driving them back over the sea; with the unremitting clamour and explosions near and far, it was extremely difficult to remain cool. Mu was manoeuvring one of her favourite patients, an elderly man with a broken leg, named Harry Thomas, into a Bath chair to move him to the safety of the hospital's underground shelter, when the whole building rocked and shook about them. The sound of falling masonry made them all instinctively duck, though had it been above their heads there would have been nothing they could have done to save themselves.

'Take him on down, Nurse,' came the brisk instruction from Sister Pearce, 'we haven't got all night!'

'Right dragon she is,' remarked Harry as Mu started to push him out of the ward and along the corridor.

'She's anxious to get you all out of the ward and safely to the shelter,' answered Mu with a smile. 'You mustn't grumble at her. Right, here we are.' She stopped at the top of a staircase where two large sailors, sent from the naval barracks to assist, were waiting. 'Can't get you down the stairs in the chair, Harry, and daren't use the lift during a raid, so these strong blokes are going to carry you.'

One of the seamen reached into the chair and saying, 'Harry is it?' lifted Harry bodily from the chair and carried him over his shoulder down the stairs. The last Mu saw of them was Harry peering up at her and shouting, 'Mind my bloody leg, you great oaf!' Grabbing the handles of the chair she set off back to the wards for her next patient. Even as she hurried through the door, the building was rocked by another explosion, closer this time, shattering the windows; leaving the glass to hang like crazy paving held together by the criss-crossing tape, as a plume of flame spurted up the wall outside.

'Come along, Nurse,' cried Sister Pearce. 'Get these beds along the landing!'

The four nurses still in the ward reached for the beds of those who were unable to move, and with tremendous effort, two to a bed, pushed them out of the ward and along the corridor to the stairs where several more servicemen, soldiers from the barracks, seamen ashore, had appeared ready to help with the evacuation of patients from the wounded hospital.

'Ambulances outside,' one called out, and he and his mate plucked another elderly man from his bed and carried him between them downstairs.

'Where are you taking me?' asked a querulous voice.

'Down to an ambulance, mate, and away to another hospital. This one's on fire. You'll be all right, you will. Just hold on tight.'

The relay of servicemen and patients went on until the whole floor was evacuated. Mu, Jean, and the other two nurses, directed by Sister Pearce, made a tour of the wards on this floor to ensure no one had been left behind. It was only when part of the ceiling collapsed behind them and a lick of flame took hold of some abandoned bed linen that they made a run for the end of the corridor and the stairs. By the time they were outside in the grounds they could see that the casualty ward had been blown apart and that the sailor had been right: much of the hospital, including their ward, was now on fire. Flames leaped into the sky, the heat becoming intense, the smoke swirling. The patients who'd been taken to the underground shelter had been moved again and loaded into whatever vehicles were available and taken to other institutions, a cottage hospital, nursing homes, a convent; those able to walk, to church halls. Nurses from all the wards, their hair, hands, faces and uniforms overlaid with smuts and ash carried on the wind, were gathered outside, being directed to travel with the patients and see that they were made as comfortable as possible in their temporary places of refuge.

All the while the air raid continued. Firefighters,

professional and volunteers, plus the man in the street, were stretched to breaking as they fought the incendiaries released by the first wave, pumping water, smothering with sand, beating out the first burst of flame before it could ignite its surroundings, but despite extra hands from the naval base and army barracks, they were too few and the incendiaries were too many. A second and third wave of bombers had continued to sweep in with their payload of high explosive bombs and parachute mines, despite continual harassment from Fighter Command and the relentless pounding of the anti-aircraft guns in the city and from the ships lying in the harbour.

At the sound of the first alert, the ship's company of HMS *Cumbria* had been called to action stations. Patrick, officer in charge of one of the forward guns, scrambled with his crew to be at the ready. They scanned the darkness for the first sight of the Luftwaffe planes and then, suddenly, there they were, bursting through a bank of cloud, coming in low out of the night, the whole of Portsmouth laid out below.

'Fire at will!'

The crew needed no second telling and at once they were swinging the barrels skyward to blast the enemy planes as they roared through the ever-moving beams of the searchlights criss-crossing the sky.

Within moments the incoming planes began to deliver their load, incendiaries cascading from the sky to set light to the city, lying helpless below. Their bomb bays empty, the planes peeled away, making way for the next wave and the next, pounding their firelit target with high explosive.

Patrick and his team worked with automated precision, loading, aiming, firing, reloading and firing again.

Even as they continued their fire, there was a rumble from the depths of the ship and *Cumbria* lifted her anchor and began to move clear of the harbour. Leaving the Isle of Wight on her starboard bow, she headed out to sea. A target herself, *Cumbria* continued her anti-aircraft fire as she slipped away into the night. The departing aircraft flew low overhead, strafing the ship with machine gun fire. Ducking instinctively at the rattle of the guns, Patrick and his men continued loading and firing, aiming for the underbellies of the planes above. One burst from a Heinkel making a pass above took out two of their crew, flinging the men aside like two rag dolls. Patrick glanced across at them, one was beyond help, the other lay on his side, blood pouring from a wound in his arm.

'Keep going,' Patrick yelled, and grabbing the wounded man, he pulled him into the shelter of a bulkhead from where he could be taken below to the medics.

Glancing back towards the shore Patrick could see the angry sky glowing orange above the city, the inferno below beyond the scope of the fire brigades fighting desperately to contain it as the water from ruptured mains spouted wastefully away.

With the dawn came the all-clear. Portsmouth was still ablaze, smoke roiling up into the sky, an occasional boom as a delayed action bomb exploded, an afterthought from Hitler to instil uncertainty and fear in those who thought they had come safely through the raid.

HMS *Cumbria* had left the illusory safety of the harbour and steamed out into the channel to take up her station on the western approaches. Patrick looked back towards the city, still burning under an angry sky.

Mu. Where was Mu? Had she taken shelter? Was she safe?

Under that same angry sky, Mu looked at the remains of the hospital where she had worked for so long. It had been damaged in previous raids, but now some parts had been reduced to rubble and the rest looked uninhabitable. With help from the servicemen, they had saved all the patients. Not one had been lost, they were all in safety somewhere about the town. Safe until next time.

Looking out across the harbour towards the Isle of Wight, she saw that the *Cumbria* had disappeared. Patrick's ship was gone, and Patrick with it. She might never see him again. Safer not to love him, she thought miserably. Safer to put him out of her mind and out of her life. Safer for him… because people she loved tended to get killed.

## 15

Friday morning was extremely frustrating for Maggie. She had walked to the local food office carrying Roger, as the day before, in the sling on her hip. There were long queues to the counters as people, bombed out and homeless, waited for emergency ration books, their own having vanished into oblivion with their homes.

When at last Maggie reached the front of the queue, she was faced with a small woman seated behind her counter, a name plate in front of her proclaiming her to be Miss J. Hooper. Miss Hooper was a woman of indeterminate age, with a narrow, weary face, her iron-grey hair scraped back into a bun, who peered out at Maggie with sharp grey eyes from behind steel-rimmed spectacles.

'Name!'

'Margaret Peterson.'

'Address!'

Maggie gave her address and before the woman could ask any more questions she said, 'I need a ration book for my son Roger.' She gave Roger a hitch higher on her hip, as if to make the point that he was a real child, needing a ration book. 'His is lost.'

'Lost?' Miss Hooper's voice, already cool, dropped several degrees.

'He's been staying with my mother.' Maggie rehearsed her prepared explanation. 'We only moved here a few months ago and she looked after him during the move and while we were settling in.'

'I see.' Miss Hopper's voice lacked all expression. 'And?'

'And when my husband went and fetched him home to us, he came without Roger's ration book.' The woman across the desk made no comment, simply stared at Maggie and waited.

'My mother-in-law swears she put it into his suitcase, but it certainly wasn't there when I came to unpack.'

'Who did you say had the care of your son?' asked Miss Hooper.

'My mother… in-law.' Maggie's hesitation was minimal but Miss Hooper latched on to it and repeated, 'Who?'

'My mother-in-law.'

'Living where?'

'London, where we used to live, in Hackney.'

'Your mother-in-law.'

'Yes.'

'Not your mother?' Miss Hooper's eyes never left Maggie's face and under her stare Maggie felt the colour flood her face. She knew she'd made a mistake, but there was nothing she could do but go on. She ventured an apologetic smile. 'It's very difficult to get to the bottom of it,' she said, 'dealing with my mother-in-law and that.'

At that moment Roger, uncomfortable and bored, began to grizzle. Maggie tutted at him and jiggled him on her hip, but to no avail. The grizzling continued.

'Birth certificate!' snapped Miss Hooper.

'Birth certificate?'

'The child's birth certificate. I need to see his birth certificate. I can't just hand out *extra* rations,' she emphasised the word extra, 'just on your say-so. How do I know he's your baby?'

Inwardly Maggie began to quake, but outwardly she managed to appear calm.

'I see, I didn't know.'

'I need his birth certificate… and your identity card.'

'I've got that with me, of course,' Maggie said, beginning to back away as Roger grew more vociferous, 'but his birth certificate is at home. I'll have to come back.'

Even as she turned to go, the woman called, 'Next!'

As she moved towards the door another woman caught hold of her arm. 'She's a right cow, that one,' she hissed. 'If you're coming back to try again, come on Thursday afternoon. She don't come in that afternoon.' She gave Maggie a broad wink, but Maggie turned hurriedly away. How dare that woman think she was trying to cheat! To pretend he was her baby, simply to get extra rations! All she was doing was trying to get Roger his fair share!

Well, Maggie thought as she pushed her way out into the open air and set off back up the hill, at least I have his birth certificate, but if they ask for his identity card I'll be stuck.

Her own Roger had died so soon after his birth, the only documentation Maggie held for him were his birth and death certificates. There was no help for it, she would have to come back again with the birth certificate, her own identity card and, for good measure, her marriage certificate, to prove the reason they shared a surname. Perhaps she would take the other woman's advice and return on Thursday. Even if Miss Hooper was still at her window, Maggie would make sure she queued at a different one, perhaps with a man behind the glass.

She had made a stupid mistake when talking to Miss Hooper and so aroused her suspicions. It would better to hone her story a little more before she tried it on someone else. She must remain relaxed and easy as she trotted out the mother-in-law story, and that was the one she must stick with now, just in case. She had told Inspector Droy that it was her own mother who had been looking after Roger, but he and Miss Steel-rims Hooper were very unlikely to meet and compare stories.

When she got home again, she put Roger down on the living room floor and stretched her back in relief. One of the first things she would have to buy must be a pram or a pushchair. Roger was only going to get bigger and she wouldn't be able to carry him for long. Leaving him propped up on the floor, she kicked off her shoes and put the kettle on. She was gasping for a cup of tea.

It was at that moment that there was a loud, prolonged ring on the doorbell. It made Maggie jump out of her skin. Who could it possibly be? She wasn't expecting anyone, she didn't know anyone to expect! Leaving the kettle on the stove, she stuffed her feet back into her shoes and opening the front door, found two unknown ladies on her step.

'Yes?' Maggie spoke discouragingly; she didn't know them and she didn't want to.

'Mrs Peterson?' It was Stella Todd who spoke. 'You don't know me, at least only by sight, but yesterday, when I saw you and your baby at Mr Grant's, a friend of yours told me of the desperately sad news – about your husband? He suggested that you might welcome a visit, you know, an offer of moral support?' She held out a hand and said, 'Stella Todd. I live just down the road at number fifty-three.'

'We're both neighbours of yours,' put in the other woman. 'I'm Elsie Jefferson, back the other way at number eleven.' She did not offer to shake hands as Maggie had not taken the hand Stella had extended, but she took a step forward as if to come into the house and went on, 'We felt it would be a Christian kindness to come and offer you our condolences.'

This woman, Maggie realised, she did recognise, and wished she did not. Several times she had been plucking up courage to speak to her in the shops, but had been deterred by the supercilious stare that had rebuffed her even before she had opened her mouth. Now, however, faced with two of her neighbours offering friendship, she drew a deep breath and said, 'Thank you, that's very kind of you both.' Reluctantly she stepped aside and went on, 'Won't you come in?'

The two women followed Maggie into the flat. She led the way into the sitting room where Roger sat against the sofa, propped with a cushion. For a moment the three women paused awkwardly, before Stella, seeing the baby sitting on the floor cried, 'Oh, the little dote.' Squatting down beside him, she reached for his hand and said, 'Hello, pet! And who might you be? Eh?'

'That's my Roger,' Maggie said.

Roger looked at Stella solemnly for a moment and she peeked at him through her fingers. She was rewarded with a gurgle of laughter, and within moments they were playing peep-bo around a cushion.

'Stella and babies.' Elsie's tone was mildly scoffing. She had no interest in babies, or children in general. She had never had any, didn't want any, and as she always said if the question came up, 'What you don't have, you don't miss.'

With Roger and Stella happily entertaining each other, Maggie turned to Elsie.

'Can I get you a cup of tea?'

'That would be most welcome,' Elsie replied, 'but only if you can spare it.'

'Of course,' Maggie replied. 'I've already got the kettle on. Please do make yourself comfortable and I'll bring it in.'

Elsie had been on the point of following Maggie into the kitchen, she always liked to see how other women kept their homes, whether they were as clean and comfortable as her own, but it was clear that it was too soon for that informality, so she simply said, 'Thank you, I will,' and made do with looking at the living room shelves, inspecting the ornaments and touching a finger in search of dust. There was little to take her interest except the photos on the mantelpiece; Maggie and her husband on their wedding day and an expectant Maggie apparently on holiday. She peered at them, trying to guess how long after the wedding the baby had arrived; some time, it would seem, from the lines on his mother's face. Of him there were no pictures, which surprised Elsie. Her friend Stella only had one daughter, Harriet, but she had framed photos, charting her daughter's childhood on every available shelf. Elsie had always thought such an abundance of Harriets surrounding you while you drank your tea was far too many. Surely one nice studio portrait photo would be enough to remind you of your beloved daughter when she no longer lived with you. And now there was a grandson, too, young Johnny. Goodness knows, Elsie thought not for the first time, where Stella will find room for all the photos of him as well.

As Elsie made inventory of how Maggie Peterson decorated her shelves and Maggie hurriedly put her best china cups on a tray with milk jug and sugar bowl, Stella and Roger were becoming the best of friends. Stella always had had a way with babies, able to pacify them when necessary, prepared to deal with dirty nappies, happy to give a bottle or spoon Farex into their questing mouths. She was only sad that her daughter and grandson were now living in Liverpool, too far away for wartime travel.

Maggie paused a moment before picking up the tea tray. The last thing she had wanted was to have visitors today, but they had come and so she must make the best of it. It might be helpful, she thought, to know one or two people nearby and so she might as well start with these. Stella seemed pleasant enough, but Maggie was conscious that Elsie would be judging her in some way and she was determined not to let herself down. With resolution she put the teapot onto the tray and carried it into the living room. Setting it down on the small coffee table in the centre of the room, she forced a smile and began to pour.

'What a lovely little chap,' Stella said, as she accepted the cup and then placed it safely out of reach of Roger's small fists. 'We've been having lovely fun, haven't we, pet?'

Elsie, eager as always to know everything about people said, 'Where have you been hiding that baby? I've seen you about several times, but you've never had him with you, have you?'

Maggie knew a spike of anger at Elsie's rudeness, but even as she was about to make a retort, she realised that answering the question in front of two of her neighbours might be the perfect way to have her story of Roger staying with his grandmother for a while circulated locally without her having to say any more to anyone.

'No,' she said, 'because we didn't bring him with us. My mother-in-law...' she'd got it right this time, 'my mother-in-law offered to look after him until we were settled.' She gave a sad smile. 'Colin had only just collected him a few days ago... and now...' Her voice broke on a sob. 'And now he's been killed and Roger and I only have each other.'

'Couldn't you take him back to your mother-in-law?' suggested Elsie. 'She could help you look after him.'

'No,' wept Maggie. 'She and I have never got on, but she adored Colin, of course. She'll be in pieces when she hears about his death. Her only boy.'

'Haven't you told her yet?' Elsie couldn't keep the surprise out of her voice, and her words earned her a reproving look from Stella.

'I'll have to write to her,' Maggie said. 'She's not on the phone.'

'You could send her a telegram,' Elsie suggested, unrepentant.

'No, I couldn't.' Maggie was in tears again. 'We may not get on, but I do need to tell her exactly what happened to him.' She turned fiercely to the other two. 'I loved my husband and she loved him too. The least I can do is break it to her as gently as I can.'

Stella felt they had outstayed their welcome. She was used to Elsie's forthright manner, but a grieving widow didn't need to be subjected to it. She got to her feet and turning to Elsie she said, 'Come on, Else, it's time we were going. Thank you for the tea, Mrs Peterson. We are truly sorry for your loss and if there is anything I can do to help, please don't hesitate to ask. Number fifty-three. I'm usually at home, though I do volunteer with the WVS for a few hours a week. We all have to do our bit, don't we?' She moved towards the door, the determination in her eyes dragging Elsie along with her. Maggie came to see them out and as Stella passed outside, she turned back and said, 'By the way, I saw you carrying young Roger in a sling this morning. He must be quite heavy for that. My daughter Harriet left a pram here when she moved up to Liverpool to join her husband. It'll want a bit of a scrub because it's been in the cellar for a while, but if you'd like to borrow it, well, I know you'd be more than welcome to.'

Maggie's eyes brightened at the suggestion and she whispered, 'Really? Oh, Mrs Todd, that would be marvellous. Colin couldn't bring the pram on the train when he fetched Roger. We were going to get one when we got here.'

'Well, borrow ours until you do. I'll give it a clean and bring it round to you, shall I?' And when Maggie beamed her thanks she smiled and said, 'I'll look it out then.'

'I bet you don't see that back,' remarked Elsie spitefully, once the door had closed. 'She looks the acquisitive one, to me.'

'For goodness' sake, Elsie,' snapped Stella. 'Give it a rest, can't you? You don't know anything about her!' And stunned at the anger in her friend's voice, Elsie said no more.

# 16

Stella had been as good as her word and two days later brought Maggie her daughter's pram.

'I've given it a good scrub,' she said, 'and it doesn't look too bad. And I've brought the pram blankets with me in case you don't have anything the right size to use.'

'Oh, Mrs Todd,' Maggie cried, 'you're so kind. You don't know what a help this will be.'

'Don't mention it, my dear, that's what neighbours are for.' She paused a moment and added, 'And if you ever wanted someone to keep an eye on the little chap for an hour or so, I'd be more than happy, you know.'

Maggie thanked her with genuine gratitude. She knew that next afternoon there was to be a funeral service in Efford Cemetery for those killed in the recent raids. Colin would be buried in a mass grave with most of the other victims. She knew she must go and had thought she would have to take Roger with her. Now, when she mentioned it to Stella, the old lady jumped at the opportunity.

'It's no place for a baby,' she said. 'I'm more than happy to look after him. Shall I have him with me or would you rather I came to you?'

Aware that Stella couldn't fail to notice the lack of baby equipment in her flat, and not wanting any awkward questions asked, Maggie said she would bring him round to number fifty-three.

Next afternoon, dressed soberly in a dark coat and skirt, Maggie left Roger with Stella and set off to say her final farewell to Colin. When she reached the cemetery she joined the silent crowd of the bereaved and those who had simply come to pay their respects. The grave, where all the victims lay together, was covered with Union flags and flowers. Clergymen from every denomination took part in the short service, and as Maggie closed her eyes and tried to pray for Colin, she found he had already slipped away from her. The man she had loved no longer felt real; he was gone, leaving only shadows. The feel of his arms about her, the warmth of his lips on hers, his laugh, were insubstantial memories. What was real was the bleakness that was surrounding her now. Opening her eyes again she stared blankly at the flags which covered the ground.

Buried beneath those flags is all that's left of my Colin, she thought. There'll be no stone to name him. Grass will soon claim the ground above him and he'll lie with all the others, the known and unknown casualties of this bloody war.

As the Bishop of Plymouth gave the final blessing, Maggie turned and edged away through the silent crowd. Others were making a discreet departure, leaving their loved ones behind beneath the flags. As she reached the road, she was overtaken by a tall man who, she saw to her horror, had tears streaming down his cheeks. She looked away hurriedly, embarrassed. She had never seen a man cry like that. Men were meant to be strong, not prone to tears. Normally, the man himself would have agreed with her, but he had just been to the funeral of seven members of his family. Maggie walked quickly in the opposite direction, hurrying back to the only family *she* had left... his grandson.

When Maggie had collected Roger from Stella and been persuaded to share a pot of tea, she pushed the baby back along the road. When she reached the house she saw there was a man waiting outside. For a moment she wondered who it could be and assumed that it must be a visitor for one of their tenants in the upstairs flat, but on hearing her footsteps, he turned and she saw that it was the policeman, Andy Sharpe. Today he wasn't in uniform but dressed in jacket and flannel trousers; definitely off duty. She sighed inwardly. She had had enough of visitors, she wasn't used to them and today was not the day for them. However, he'd been kind to her before and if he hadn't spoken to Stella Todd, she wouldn't have come calling and Maggie wouldn't have a pram for Roger.

'Mrs Peterson, good afternoon.'

'Hello, Constable Sharpe. This is a surprise.'

'I don't want to disturb you, but I wondered if there was anything you needed? Anything I could do?'

'No, thank you,' murmured Maggie. 'I'm just back from the funeral at Efford. Difficult day,' she added, rather pointedly, making no move to go inside or invite him to do so.

'I know, I saw you, but afterwards, when I'd looked for you, you'd gone.'

'I didn't want to see anyone.' *And I still don't* remained unspoken, but hung in the air between them.

'Well, I won't keep you now,' said Andy, 'I just wanted to give you something.' He reached into the inside pocket of his jacket and, drawing out an envelope, handed it to her.

Surprised, she took it and saw that it had her name on it. 'What's this?'

'It's for you... and the boy.' He glanced down at Roger sitting happily in the pram playing with his toes.

'For us?' Maggie opened the envelope and pulled out a handful of bank notes, several pounds and a folded white fiver. She looked up at him and asked, 'What's this for?'

'For you and the boy,' repeated Andy. 'We had a whip-round at the station. The sarge is owed pay and that will be coming, of course, but we thought, that is, I thought, you might need a little something to tide you over.' He nodded at the pram. 'I see you've got a pram already,' he said,' that's what I thought you might get, but I'm sure there's lots of other things you could do with.' There was an awkward pause and then he went on, 'We all thought very well of him at the station, you know. He was a good copper and an honest man, hardworking and always ready to give a hand's turn. It's just a little something in his memory.'

Maggie put the notes back in the envelope and tucked it into the pram behind Roger. 'It's very kind of you all,' she said. 'Was it your idea?' When Andy did not answer at once, she continued, 'I'm sure it was. You're very thoughtful. There are several things I need for Roger. I shall spend it all on him.'

Still she did not invite him to come inside, but turned and opened the door into the hallway. He stepped forward and lifted the pram, baby and all, over the step and set them down outside her front door. Rather belatedly Maggie thanked him and said, 'Do you want to come in?'

Knowing from her tone that his answer should be 'No thank you,' it was the one he gave and he stepped back onto the pavement. 'Don't forget, if there's anything we can do, down at the station I mean, you only have to ask.'

'Thank you,' Maggie said, smiling at him at last. 'And please thank your colleagues for their generosity. It won't be wasted, I promise you.'

When he had gone, Maggie manoeuvred the pram through her own front door and closed it behind her. Last night she had put Roger into the pram to sleep. He needed a proper cot, but at present the pram was quite large enough and far better than the drawer.

Maggie had planned to return to the food office on Thursday, but when the day arrived, she found she couldn't face it, not yet. She was going to have to hand in Colin's ration book. She couldn't risk using the coupons when, thanks to Elsie Jefferson, so many people, including Mr Grant the butcher and Mrs Hodge at the dairy, knew that Colin had been killed in the Wednesday raid. She had seen Elsie again and they had passed the time of day, but it was clear that Elsie felt she had done her duty by calling on Maggie that first day.

Roger kept Maggie busy. She'd had no idea how much work a baby could be, especially as she hadn't worked up to it from birth through the first, now missing, eight months. However, as she discovered what she needed, she began to spend the money from the police station whip-round. She visited the salvage warehouses where furniture saved or retrieved from ruined houses was stored and was given or sold to those left with nothing. She even took the baby clothes from the trunk in the cellar and swapped them for clothes that would fit Roger now. However, by the second week she was desperate: she needed food and extra milk for Roger; sharing her own meagre rations with him as she had been, was not enough for either of them.

So, when the next Thursday came round, Maggie set off resolutely to the food office. She knew it wasn't going to be easy, but she needed rations for Roger, and securing a replacement ration book was the only way she was going to get them. The queues at the counters seemed as long as before and she almost turned back. She stood for a moment in the doorway and studied the faces of those behind the glass partitions. She could see no sign of Miss Steel-rims Hooper. Perhaps that woman the first day had been right and she wasn't there on a Thursday afternoon. Maggie was glad she wasn't, but she decided to follow her own plan, and manoeuvring Roger and the pram through the door, she joined the queue that ended up in front of a young man with thin blond hair and a frightened smile. When she reached him she saw that his name was Mr P. B. Court. Straight into the charm offensive she had practised in front of the mirror that morning, she treated him to her most engaging smile and said, 'Good afternoon, Mr Court. My name's Margaret Peterson.'

Peter Court wasn't used to ladies he didn't know smiling like that at him. He was a small, shy man, who had been turned down for active service because he was partially deaf. In the daytime he worked at the food office and at night he was a volunteer fireman. His deafness wasn't so apparent behind his counter. He could hear enough for his ability to lip read to enable him to do his job.

'Good afternoon, Mrs Peterson,' he replied. 'How may I help you?'

'I'm afraid I've got a problem, Mr Court,' said Maggie and she launched into the story of her mother-in-law and the lost ration book.

'I've brought my son's birth certificate,' she delved into her handbag and produced it.

Peter Court looked concerned. 'Have you got his identity card?' he asked.

'No,' Maggie replied. 'That's part of the problem. My husband...' she gulped and started again, 'my husband, Police Sergeant Colin Peterson, had it with him... and... and he was killed in those dreadful April raids.' The tears that slipped down her cheeks came unbidden. She hadn't planned to cry, but once she started she found it hard to stop. Angrily she dashed her tears away and blew her nose.

'Oh, oh, my dear lady...' Mr Court was all consternation. The supervisor wouldn't like to see a weeping woman at his window. They'd think it was his fault.

'Sorry, so sorry!' Embarrassed, Maggie gave her nose a final blow before shoving her handkerchief back into the bag.

'No, no,' said the wretched Mr Court as he saw the supervisor bearing down upon him. 'Don't worry, please. I'm certain we can sort everything out for you.'

'Mr Court!' Mr Saunders', the supervisor's, voice was brisk. 'What seems to be the matter here?' As Maggie regained her equilibrium Mr Court related Maggie's story to his boss, mentioning the lack of identity card.

'You see, the problem is, madam,' Mr Saunders said, 'we have no way of knowing that the child is yours. I don't doubt that he is,' he added hastily, 'but rules are rules.'

'I've brought my husband's ration book to return to you,' Maggie said, 'and as well as Roger's birth certificate, which names both of us as his parents, I have our marriage certificate.'

Mr Saunders gave the documents a cursory glance and then said, 'I really can't see the problem, Mr Court. The lady is clearly who she says she is and the child is clearly hers. The situation is none of her making, and you should not have brought her to tears like that. Please apologise and issue a replacement ration book for the child without delay.' Then, inclining his head to Maggie, Mr Saunders moved away, leaving the hapless Peter Court muttering repeated apologies to Maggie.

'Please don't apologise, Mr Court,' Maggie said. 'None of it was your fault, it was just explaining about Colin... you know.'

Ten minutes later Maggie was pushing the pram back down towards the door. Once again, a woman – the same woman? Maggie didn't know – grabbed her arm and grinned at her. 'Tears works a treat, don't they, love? Don't do it too often, though, spoils it for the rest of us.'

Maggie froze and then turning on the woman, she jerked her arm free and muttering through her teeth, said, 'I have lost my husband. The child has been robbed of a father. How dare you, you, who don't know me, suggest anything else!'

The woman shrugged and answered, 'No, I don't know you, but I know the likes of you. And I'll know you again if I see you.'

Angrily, Maggie walked away, pushing the pram through to the street. As she got out into the fresh air, relief flooded through her; the whole ordeal was over. She had got what she had come for. Now she could go to the shops and buy food for both of them. Roger had been officially recognised as hers, hers and Colin's, even though Colin was no longer here to claim him.

## 17

Muriel walked along the corridor in the City Hospital in Plymouth to ward five where she had been sent to work. It had been surprisingly easy to move from the Royal Hospital in Portsmouth, or what was left of it, to work in the City Hospital in Plymouth. The hospitals in both cities were struggling with the aftermath of the March and April raids, with the deaths of patients, staff, nurses and doctors; with the obliteration of buildings and the loss of bed spaces within them, with the general confusion inflicted by the bombers.

Muriel, having explained the situation, was released from the Royal in Portsmouth and within a fortnight she was working on the wards at the City in Plymouth. She was found a room in the nurses' home, after the raid its previous occupant no longer requiring it, and she settled quickly into the familiar hospital routine, little different to what she was used to.

After a day off, which she spent with her father, trying to find him somewhere permanent to live, she had been assigned to a night shift on a different ward. It was her first night duty since the terrifying raid on Portsmouth, and she was looking forward to it with some trepidation. Would she hold her nerve if there were raid tonight? She knew she must switch her mind away from the memories of that Sunday with its explosions and fires and the drone of aircraft overhead.

She had lost her way in the unfamiliar corridors, and when she presented herself apologetically to Sister Brock in ward five, she found that other night nurses were already moving about the ward, and she was greeted with a glance at the clock and a brisk, 'Nurse Shawbrook, is it? Time to settle the patients for the night.' She had been dispatched round the ward to take bedtime temperatures. Most of the patients were women injured in one of the recent raids. Broken bodies, dragged from ruins, plastered and bandaged; damaged minds suffering nightmares of being blasted, buried and burned.

As she made her way along the row of beds, she took time to stop and speak to each patient, greeting them with a smile and telling them her name.

'It's my first time on this ward,' she'd say. 'I'll do my best to look after you.'

When she came to the last bed, bed number ten, she found that the occupant, a young woman, was already asleep. The woman, scarcely more than a girl, had a broken leg, resting beneath a blanket-covered cradle, and a bandage round her head, partially masking her features. One arm rested outside the covers, and the other was tucked under her chin. It was the sleeping position Muriel immediately recognised, making her stare at the girl in stupefaction. Quietly, she picked up the notes clipped to the bottom of the bed. The box marked 'Name' had the word 'Unknown' inscribed in it. General information simply marked the patient as Female, aged approximately 16–20, gave her height and weight and listed her injuries, including 'temporary amnesia'. Mu couldn't believe her eyes, eyes that were filling with tears as she stared down at the face of her sister, Vera.

'Vera!' she breathed. 'Vera, is it really you?' She put out a hand to touch her sister's face.

'Nurse! We haven't time to stare at sleeping patients. Nor do we wake them up when they are already settled!'

Staff Nurse Drew was at her elbow. 'And I can assure you that you have no need to read her notes. In the meantime, Mrs Ford needs the bedpan, *if* you could help her on to it in time.'

'Yes, Staff. Sorry, Staff,' Mu said quickly. She moved towards the bed the staff nurse was indicating on the other side of the ward, but she said as she did so, 'Is the girl in bed ten unidentified?'

'Well, you've looked at her notes so you know that she is,' snapped the staff nurse. 'Mrs Ford's bedpan!'

Muriel moved quickly to Mrs Ford, easing her up onto the bedpan. Mrs Ford was an elderly lady who had been dug out of the ruins of her kitchen. Bruised from head to foot but miraculously with only a couple of broken ribs, she was in pain whenever she tried to move. Now, as Mu helped her settle uncomfortably onto the pan, she sighed. 'Thought I wasn't going to hold it in,' she observed, 'an' now I can't go at all. Ain't it always the way?'

Mu smiled at her. 'It often happens,' she agreed, 'but there's no hurry. I'll come back when you've finished.'

Leaving Mrs Ford to relieve herself in peace, she returned

to where Sister Brock was sitting filling in some forms at the nurses' station. She looked up impatiently.

'Have you finished your round, Nurse?'

'Yes, Sister. At least, I need to tell you something.'

'It can wait,' snapped Sister Brock. 'You can see I'm busy and so should you be!'

'She's my sister,' went on Mu as if the sister hadn't spoken. 'Over there.' She pointed to the end bed. 'The girl in that bed, the unidentified one? She's my sister.'

'Don't be ridiculous, Nurse. She couldn't be, or we'd know who she was.'

'I know who she is,' Muriel said firmly. 'We thought she was dead... with the others!'

'Others? What others? I wish you'd make yourself clear, Nurse.'

'My mother and my younger brothers and sisters were all in the Parham Road shelter...' Mu swallowed, for a long moment unable to go on. At length she whispered, 'We thought Vera was there with them. My father and I, we thought she was dead too.'

Now, she really did have Sister Brock's attention. Sister Brock had seen the chasm in the road that was all that was left of the Parham Road shelter and its occupants. She knew that the number killed had been only an estimate, that not all the bodies could be identified, and here was this nurse saying that the unknown patient in the ward was her sister and she'd been in the Parham Road shelter.

'Are you quite certain?' she said, still sounding doubtful. 'There were no survivors, I believe.'

'I'm not mistaken, Sister,' asserted Muriel. 'I know my sister when I see her.'

Sister Brock paused. It could be hope leading this young nurse to think she had found her dead sister. 'I mean,' she said, 'well, it's just that that patient is bandaged round her head. You could be mistaken.'

'I'm not,' insisted Muriel.

'I see,' sighed the sister. 'Well, she doesn't remember who she is or what happened to her. Dr Caster says that the amnesia is probably temporary, and in time things will come back to her. That something may prompt her to recall.'

'I could be that prompt,' said Mu excitedly. 'Or my father. He could come and see her, couldn't he? Where was she found? Do you know?'

'I'll have to look that up,' said the sister. 'And check when she was brought in, whether it was the night the shelter was hit.'

At that moment Staff Nurse Drew appeared and asked acidly, 'Do you intend to leave poor Mrs Ford on the bedpan all night, Nurse?'

Mu turned back to see Mrs Ford, still waiting for help, waving to attract her attention. 'Sorry, Staff,' she said, and hurried back to her patient.

'She's every which way,' Nurse Drew complained to Sister Brock. 'I found her just now, standing over bed ten reading her notes. I said to her, no cause for her to read them, all she had to do was be sure that the patient was comfortable and move on.'

'She says it's her sister.'

'She says what?'

'In bed ten, she says it's her sister!'

'Can't be,' Staff Nurse Drew said. 'Hasn't she just come from Portsmouth?'

'Transferred because her family needed her here.'

At that moment there was a cry of consternation from Mrs Ford. 'Oh my lordy, girl. What on earth's the matter?'

The two nurses spun round to find Nurse Shawbrook standing beside Mrs Ford's bed, tears streaming down her cheeks.

Staff Nurse Drew was immediately beside her, hissing, 'Pull yourself together, Nurse. Get into the ward kitchen until you have!' Then with a complete change of tone she turned to Mrs Ford. 'Now then, Mrs Ford, let's get you more comfortable, shall we?'

Mu beat a hasty retreat to the ward kitchen where she mopped her face and blew her nose.

*Vera's alive! Vera's alive! Vera's safe.*

The words repeated themselves in her head. And then another thought struck her. If Vera didn't die in the Parham Road shelter, perhaps the others didn't either. Perhaps Mam and the children are alive somewhere, waiting to be found.

Sister Brock came into the room and said, 'Are you fit to work, Nurse? You're no good to me if you're going to burst into tears all night.'

'Yes, Sister,' Mu promised. 'I'll be fine now. It was just the shock of seeing her when we thought she was dead. I can't wait to tell my father.'

Once the ward was settled for the night, Mu crossed over to the bed in the corner. The patient hadn't moved. How often had Mu seen her sister sleep in that position when they had shared a room as children? Vera sleeping with her hand tucked under her chin.

Sister Brock summoned her back into ward kitchen.

'When she wakes in the morning, you are to go to see

to her, and we can see if she recognises you. She may not, but it is possible the sight of you will jolt her memory. Whatever happens, when you go off duty you'll have to go to the almoner and tell her that our unidentified patient is your sister.' Her eyes rested on Mu's face for a long moment. 'You are quite sure, Nurse? It isn't just wishful thinking?'

'No, Sister, I'm quite sure, and my father will confirm it as well.'

'He'll have to come in to see her,' agreed Sister Brock, 'especially if she doesn't regain her memory.'

'Is her head wound bad?' asked Mu.

'No, it's a nasty gash on the side of her head that required stitches, and she was almost certainly concussed, but it's healing nicely. Her leg is broken, as you can see, but it's been set and should mend well enough. We shouldn't have to keep her in for very long once she's able to move with crutches. It would be more difficult to discharge her if she had no one to look after her, but if she's got family...'

'She's got our father and me.'

When the ward woke in the morning and the night staff prepared to hand over to the day nurses, Sister Brock sent Mu to take a cup of tea to the patient in bed ten. She was still not convinced that Mu was right. A likeness and a thread of hope could be all that linked them.

Mu walked round the bed so that Vera could see her and seeing that her sister was already awake, she pulled the curtains round the bed.

'Hello, Vera,' she said gently. 'How are you feeling this morning?'

The girl did not react to the use of her name, but she

answered easily. 'Not too bad. My head hurts and my leg hurts, but I'm all right.'

'Well, I'm Nurse Shawbrook, Muriel Shawbrook, and I've brought you a cup of tea. Shall I prop you up so that you can drink it?'

The girl thanked her, but again there was no reaction to Muriel's name.

'I'm new on this ward,' Mu said conversationally, 'so I'm getting to know everyone. How do you come to be here?'

'Don't know,' replied the girl. 'Don't remember. They found me in the street after a raid.'

'And you had no identity card on you?' wondered Mu.

'Must have been in my handbag, but they didn't find that.'

'I wonder you weren't in a shelter somewhere,' said Mu casually.

'I don't know! I can't remember! I don't even know my name!'

'I know, but try not to worry,' Mu said, hearing the note of panic in Vera's voice. She was convinced that, without a doubt, this girl was her sister Vera. Her voice confirmed it. She would know Vera's voice anywhere. 'I'm sure things will come back gradually given time. You're quite safe in here and no doubt your family will be looking for you.'

When they went off duty, Sister Brock took Mu to the almoner's office where they explained to Mrs Holt, the almoner, what they had discovered. Once again Mu was subjected to a stream of questions. Was she quite sure in her identification? Was she certain it wasn't simply a question of similarity and misplaced hope?

'It is definitely my sister,' she asserted. 'I know her face even when partially bandaged; I know her voice, I recognise her hands with their bitten nails. It is, without doubt, my sister, Vera Shawbrook. If you need further confirmation my father will come in and give it.'

'She didn't recognise you,' Mrs Holt pointed out.

'No, she didn't, but Sister Brock had warned me to expect that.'

'She didn't respond when you called her Vera.'

'She wasn't surprised either and she answered the question I put to her perfectly normally.'

'Well,' said the almoner, 'I can provisionally accept what you say, but I must speak to the doctor and see what he suggests.'

'In the meantime, I shall go and find my father and bring him here,' Mu said. 'She may recognise him, or begin to remember things as we keep addressing her by name.'

'I'll speak to Matron about bringing him in as a visitor,' said Mrs Holt. 'Normally visiting day for ward five is Tuesday early evening, but in this case I'm sure an exception can be made.'

The moment Mu was out of her uniform, she hurried to the wardens' post where her father would have been on duty all night, in the hope of catching him, but he had already gone. He was still lodging with the Jeffersons, and so Mu made her way there.

Elsie opened the door to her knock and seeing Mu on the step said, 'Oh, it's you. Your father's just got back. You'd better come in.'

David Shawbrook was in the kitchen drinking tea and eating toast with Paul.

'Hello, Mu,' he said with a smile. 'You're a nice surprise.'

'Dad,' Mu said, 'I need to speak to you.' She glanced at the Jeffersons, both waiting expectantly to hear why she had come. 'Shall we go for a walk, Dad?'

'Yes, of course, love. Just let me finish my tea.'

Mu waited, sitting awkwardly on the stool Paul had set for her, while Elsie joined the men at the table. Rather belatedly Elsie offered her tea, but Mu refused.

'No, really, thank you, I had one earlier.'

David, realising that whatever it was Mu had come for wasn't going to be discussed in front of the Jeffersons, and recognising her urgency, downed his tea and picking up his toast said, 'Right, I'll bring this with me.'

Once they were outside in the morning sunshine, he said, 'What's the matter, Mu? What's the matter? Have you heard of somewhere?'

'No, Dad, not that, but better.'

'Better? What?'

'I've found Vera.'

'Found Vera?' David stopped in his tracks and spun her to face him. 'Found Vera? What do you mean found Vera?'

'She's in the hospital, Dad. I was sent to a different ward last night and there she was. She's got a broken leg and a gash on her head, but she's all right.'

'But why didn't we know? Surely she could have got a message to me somehow!'

Mu took his hand and led him into the small park at the bottom of the hill, where they sat down on an old wooden bench. 'She's lost her memory, Dad. She doesn't remember her name, she has no recollection of the raid. She just says they've told her she was picked up in the street. The almoner says they need further confirmation that she is who I've told them she is, so you're to be allowed to come into the ward and see her.'

'Let's go!' cried David jumping to his feet. 'What are we waiting for?'

'I'm not sure when they'll let you in,' warned Mu, getting up as well. 'They're very strict about visiting times.'

'Can but try,' David said as he set off in the direction of the hospital.

When they got there, Mu took him straight to the almoner's office, where Mrs Holt greeted them with the news that Matron had given her permission for them to visit ward five so that David could confirm that the unidentified patient in bed ten was indeed his daughter. As soon as he saw her, lying in her bed, he turned to Mrs Holt who had accompanied them and nodded emphatically.

'Yes,' he said as he dashed the tears from his eyes, 'that's my daughter, Vera.'

# 18

Muriel and her father walked out of the hospital still almost unable to believe that Vera was alive. She had been asleep when they had gone into the ward and they hadn't woken her. Day Sister Chapman had said, 'I think it better to leave her asleep this time. Of course you can visit again, Mr Shawbrook, and you, Nurse, will be nursing her at night. Maybe seeing you often at her bedside will provoke her memory.'

David had longed to shake Vera awake, to grasp her in his arms and hold her close, but he realised that might frighten her, especially if she didn't recognise him, and he saw the wisdom of what Sister Chapman was saying.

'Come back in visiting time on Tuesday,' said the sister, 'and see what happens when she's properly awake.'

'Now I've definitely got to find somewhere else to live,' David said to Mu, as they walked away, 'so that when she comes out of hospital she'll have a home to go to.'

Mu agreed. 'But let's not tell anyone our news yet. I don't know about you, Dad, but I don't want to discuss it with anyone. I couldn't put up with people gushing excitedly at me. So do you mind if we wait a while before telling anyone we've found Vera?'

'Fair enough,' agreed David. 'I'd only tell the Jeffersons anyway.'

'Do you mind not telling even them?'

'Not if you feel strongly about it, love.'

'The thing is,' Mu said, 'Vera can't have been in the Parham Road shelter, can she? She was found in the street.' She paused and then, taking a deep breath, asked, 'Dad, do you think Mam and the little ones weren't in that shelter either? Could they be somewhere safe, not knowing how to find you?'

David stopped walking and taking Mu's hands in his, turned her to look at him. 'It did cross my mind for one crazy moment,' he admitted, 'but I know if your mother was still alive, she'd have made contact with me.'

'Suppose she's lost her memory too?'

'Even if she has, it would be unlikely that they all have, and the children are quite old enough to have told someone their names and where they lived.' He squeezed Mu's hands gently and said, 'I'm afraid you have to accept that despite the miracle of Vera being alive, the others are not. She won't know what's happened to them, so we have to be prepared. When and if she does get her memory back it's going to be a dreadful shock... particularly losing her own little Freddie.'

Each night after that, when Mu was on duty, she spent time talking to Vera, gently probing what she could and couldn't remember, but when the moment of recollection actually came it was in the middle of the night, when the rest of the ward was asleep.

Suddenly Vera sat bolt upright in bed with a cry of desolation. Mu was immediately at her side, taking her hands and trying to soothe her.

'Vera, dearest, whatever is the matter? Tell me.'

Vera stared wildly round the night-time ward, lit only by the lamp on the nurses' desk, completely disorientated. 'Where am I?' She shook Mu's hands up and down. 'Tell me where I am!'

'You're in hospital, Vera. You were caught out in a raid and you were brought here.'

Vera stared up at her. 'Mu?' she whispered incredulously. 'Mu? Why are you here? How long have I been here? Where's Freddie?'

'Freddie?' Mu answered carefully. 'Where should he be?'

'With me. He got left in the house and I went back to fetch him, to take him to the shelter. Where is he now?'

'And did you get him?'

Tears sprang to Vera's eyes and she shook her head. 'I don't know. I can't remember.'

'Never mind now,' soothed Mu. 'You've remembered who you are, that's a step in the right direction. The rest will all come back if you give it time.' She handed her sister a clean handkerchief. 'Here, dry your eyes and blow your nose. There's nothing to worry about at present, so you must get better quickly and come...' Her voice trailed away as she realised what she had been about to say... *come home*. She amended it to, 'And come out of hospital.' For a moment she clung to Vera's hands before she went on, 'Now, I'm going to get you something to help you sleep, and we'll find out about Freddie in the morning, all right?'

Sister Brock had been watching the interchange from

the door of her office and when Mu gently disengaged her hands from Vera's and came across to her, she said, 'She's remembered.'

'Not everything,' replied Mu, 'but she recognised me and some parts of the evening when she was injured. She was out looking for her son Freddie during the raid.'

'Her son!' exclaimed the sister.

'She doesn't know our mother and brothers and sisters have been killed. My father and I want to find the right time to tell her... if there ever could be a right time. May I give her something to help her to sleep now, Sister?'

Sister Brock went into the ward kitchen and came back with two white tablets. 'Give her these, and she'll sleep like a baby.'

Obediently Vera took the tablets Mu brought her and closing her eyes, lay back against her pillows, but it was only a moment before she opened them again and asked, 'Why are you here, Mu? I thought you were in Portsmouth, nursing.'

'I was,' agreed Muriel, 'but now I'm here in Plymouth... nursing,' adding when Vera asked why, 'They needed extra nurses to come here after the recent bad raids. I volunteered and here I am! Now get some sleep, and I'll see you when you wake up in the morning. All right? I promise I won't go without saying goodbye.'

Once the dam of her memory had burst, other deeper memories came floating to the surface, and by the time her father was able to visit her properly, she was able to tell him what she thought had happened that fateful night.

'I was late home from work, and when the raid started I went straight to the shelter. Mam was there already with the children, but she had thought I was fetching Freddie as usual, but I hadn't and we realised that he must still be at home, so I went back to find him.'

'Dad.' Vera suddenly broke off and said, 'Dad, why hasn't Mam been to see me?' Her voice trembled. 'I want to see Mam.'

And so it fell to David to tell her what had happened to the rest of the family, and everyone else in the Parham Road shelter. Vera stared at him in blank disbelief. 'But I should have been there too,' she whispered. 'I should have been with Mam and the children... and Freddie.' She sank back against her pillows and closed her eyes, fighting the tears that tried to squeeze from beneath her lashes. David waited beside her in silence. No comforting words would comfort her, no soothing voice would soothe her. Silence was the only response to her despair.

For a long while David thought she had fallen asleep, but suddenly her eyes sprang open and she said, 'Dad, if I didn't fetch Freddie, where is he?'

'I don't know, pet,' David replied gently. 'But I went to the house immediately after...' He paused, almost saying *after I'd seen what was left of the shelter*, but he caught himself in time and changed it to, 'After the raid. Paul Jefferson was with me. The house was damaged, but I went inside anyway. There were footprints in the dust, leading into the children's room, but Freddie wasn't in his cot.'

'So someone must have taken him,' cried Vera. 'Haven't you been looking for him? Why haven't you been looking for him?'

'Because I didn't know he'd been there. I assumed both you and he were in the shelter with your mam and the other children. Mu and I thought you were all killed that evening. Mu finding you in here was an absolute miracle. And even then we didn't know that Freddie might still be alive.

'If someone found him, Vera, they must have surely reported it to the authorities. There'll be a record of him somewhere, a children's home, probably, and we'll find him in no time.' David spoke with more conviction than he felt. He knew the chaos that had reigned after that particular raid. Streams of people, himself included, had found themselves suddenly homeless and finding somewhere to sleep had been a major problem. Not everyone had friends to take them in. But surely if somebody had rescued Freddie, which seemed the logical explanation for his disappearance, they would have notified someone official, the police, one of the hospitals, a warden like him.

When he saw Mu as she came on duty that evening, he told her what Vera had said.

'And there was no one at the house?'

'No, I told you. Someone had been there, but I assumed it was looters or scavengers. It never dawned on me that Freddie would have been there by himself.'

'I wonder if anyone saw anything,' Mu said. 'I mean, they might have and not realised what they were seeing.'

'Maybe,' conceded her father, 'but one thing we do know is that Freddie was not in the house when it was flattened in the next raid. He must be out there somewhere, in a home or a refuge, or even in hospital.'

'We must check the children's ward here,' Mu said excitedly. 'Make sure he wasn't handed in here for some reason. They wouldn't know who he is, any more than they knew who Vera was.'

Mu was as good as her word and when she came off duty she went straight to the children's ward and spoke to the sister in charge, Sister Newman. Once she'd explained what had happened and that she was looking for her baby nephew, Sister Newman shook her head.

'I'm sorry, Nurse, but though we have had several babies brought in, there were none unidentified. You should try the Prince of Wales.'

Mu had already decided to try the other Plymouth hospitals and she replied, 'Yes, Sister, I certainly will, but if by any chance you hear of an unknown baby, please will you let me know?'

Sister Newman promised that she would and that she would leave a message in her office for the night staff. 'Just in case.'

Before going back to the nurses' home for some well-earned sleep, Mu went back to Suffolk Place. Nothing had been done to clear the debris, and the heaps of rubble were as she had seen them last. If her father had not actually been inside their old house before it was completely flattened, they would have assumed that poor little Freddie, alone and frightened, had died in the second raid.

When she met with her father again to tell him what she had been doing, he said, 'I think I must tell the Jeffersons, Mu. You never know, Paul might hear something at the fire station which would help us, and Elsie volunteers with the WVS, she might learn something. The more people who know we're looking for a lost baby, the more likely we are to hear of him.'

Mu had to agree, but she was never comfortable with Elsie Jefferson, and didn't like the idea of her spreading their news abroad. She could just imagine her saying, 'And can you imagine, leaving a baby in a house *by mistake* during an air raid? What desertion!'

Mu had no wish to hear what Elsie thought of the situation. She was still hoping to find her father somewhere else to live, and now they needed somewhere with room for Vera as well, the matter was becoming more pressing – the hospital needed her bed.

Days passed; occasionally there were other alerts, and planes were heard overhead but headed somewhere else. On other nights they received the attention of the bombers, and though it was nothing like the ferocity of the late April raids, everyone knew that some night or other the Luftwaffe would be back with a vengeance, determined to complete their unfinished business with Plymouth.

When David told Paul and Elsie about the missing baby, it was clear that Elsie saw at once that she might be asked to have both David and Vera in the house.

'Oh, dear,' she sighed. 'I wish I could have her here, but of course there's only the one room and you'll want to be together, that's only natural.'

'Don't worry, Elsie,' answered David. 'We'll find somewhere together. She won't be out for another week or so.'

'Just imagine,' she said as she passed the news on to Stella, 'leaving a baby alone in a house during an air raid!' Her words were almost exactly as Mu had expected, but luckily she didn't hear them. Mu and David made a list of all the places they might search for a lost baby – hospitals, children's homes, rescue centres – and between them they visited them all, but they could find no unidentified babies. At David's request, Paul asked at the fire station if anyone had heard of a baby being found, but no one had. Too many families were now homeless and often children were separated from their parents and being cared for in children's homes. Other mothers, very often without the support of their husbands who were away fighting, had evacuated themselves and their children, taking them out into the countryside where the bombers seldom strayed. None of the authorities knew anything about little Freddie Shawbrook. Mu would not give up, however. She returned to Suffolk Place and knocked on doors in the surrounding streets, asking if anyone had seen or heard of someone rescuing a baby from number 21 Suffolk Place. If there was no reply to her knock, she made a note of the address and went back again and sometimes yet again, until she was able to ask her question and cross that house off her list.

Persistence finally paid off when she called at the home of Jane and Ernie Drake at the far end of Haversham Road.

# 19

That same afternoon, Maggie and Stella were sharing a pot of tea in Stella's sitting room. Despite the difference in their ages, they had become friends, their common love for baby Roger bringing them together, and Maggie often dropped in to Stella's house for a chat. She heard how Stella and her husband, John, had lived in that house ever since they were married, how her daughter, Harriet, had been born and brought up there and she wondered how anyone could live in one place for that number of years.

'Of course,' Stella told her, 'when John died five years ago, the house was far too big for me. Harriet was married and I wondered if I should sell it and buy somewhere smaller, but then I thought no, it's been my home for so long, I don't want to move to somewhere smaller. You don't, do you, if you've been happy somewhere and it's full of happy memories?'

'I suppose you don't,' conceded Maggie, 'but when I was a child, my parents moved about a lot for my dad's job. Colin and I lived in London when we were married, and I didn't really want to move, but we did because Colin got a new job and the promotion he wanted with the Plymouth police.'

'What did your father do?' asked Stella.

Maggie hesitated and then said, 'He worked for a firm that sold gardening tools. He was always being moved from place to place. Sometimes we moved with him and others he went by himself.'

There was no need to tell Stella how often she and her mother had had to do a moonlight flit when her father disappeared and the rent hadn't been paid. When the day came that her father failed to come home at all, neither she nor her mother were sorry. They never discovered what had happened to him, but they both knew they were better off without him. Maggie got a job behind the counter in a grocer's shop, her mother took in laundry and their lives settled down to some regularity.

She had met Colin when he came into the shop one day for a pound of cheese, returning twice more before finally plucking up the courage to invite her to go to the pictures with him. She accepted and his courtship began. After a couple of abortive love affairs that led nowhere, Maggie was looking for security and the security Colin could offer with a regular pay packet outweighed the fact that she found him rather boring. She'd set out to charm him, with smiles and good humour, and found that, accidentally, she'd grown fond of him. Both of them wanted children, and so happy each to find in the other what they had been looking for, they were married. It was a step up for Maggie. Her mother had always had to work to keep her family fed, but Colin did not want Maggie to work.

'Why on earth should you?' he demanded when she suggested she should stay on at the shop. 'I'm perfectly able to provide for my wife, thank you very much! I'll not have people saying any different.'

He was as good as his word, giving her housekeeping money every Friday, sometimes with an extra five shillings to spend on herself, and all was well in her world.

Two miscarriages later it seemed they weren't going to have a family after all, and gradually she became discontented. Colin was Colin and still rather boring, and she had begun wondering how much longer she could put up with him when she fell pregnant for the third time. This time she carried the baby for seven months before he was born prematurely and only survived a few hours.

She was left in the depths of depression, low in mind and spirit, refusing to do anything. When Colin had suggested the move to Plymouth, she didn't want to go, but she hadn't the energy to stand out against it for long.

It'll be a change of scene, I suppose, she thought wretchedly, and if I don't like it, well, I'll take after Dad and one day I won't come home again.

They had moved and it had been almost worse than before, until Colin had brought home little Roger. Now she had the baby, and she didn't have Colin. Despite the fact that she had been thinking of leaving him, Maggie was surprised when she realised just how much she missed him. She found herself listening for his key in the door and his cheerful call, 'Maggie, I'm home!'

Now, she and Stella were sitting in Stella's lounge drinking tea, with Roger playing on the floor between them. He was on the move, crawling everywhere and pulling himself up on the furniture. He had finally grown some hair, the soft fluff becoming a covering of auburn velvet. Gurgling with delight, he set off towards Stella at a rate of knots and pulling himself up on her knees, edged his way round her chair.

'He'll be walking in no time, the clever boy,' Stella remarked.

'Yes, it won't be long,' agreed Maggie, 'and then I'll have to put him on reins when we go out. I'd hate to lose him!'

'Yes,' agreed Stella. 'I always had Harriet on reins once she was walking. That way I could take her into shops rather than leave her outside in the pram... Do you take the *Western Morning News*?'

'No.' Maggie sounded surprised at the sudden change of subject. 'Why?'

'Oh, no reason really,' Stella said. 'There was a short piece in it the other day about a baby that is missing. I just wondered if you'd seen it.'

'No,' replied Maggie, the colour fading from her face.

'I've got it here somewhere.' Stella started rooting through a pile of papers on the table beside her chair. 'If you'd like to see it. Ah! Here we are.'

'Sounds very sad,' answered Maggie, holding out her hand for the paper that Stella had pulled out. She glanced at the piece beneath a small headline 'Missing baby' and felt her head begin to spin. She looked up from the paper and found Stella looking at her in concern. 'Are you all right, my dear? You look a bit peaky today.'

Maggie gave an awkward little laugh and said, 'No, I'm fine, just a bit tired. Roger had me up in the night a couple of times and I didn't really get back to sleep.' To cover her confusion she put down the paper as if it was of no interest and, leaning across, scooped the baby into her arms and kissed his head. 'Naughty boy, weren't you?' She mustered a smile and went on, 'Still, when he goes down for his nap, I'll try and catch up on an hour's sleep.'

'Very sensible,' agreed Stella, wishing she hadn't mentioned the missing baby. The poor girl's had enough to bear with the loss of her husband, she thought. No need to tell her of other people's troubles.

Maggie left soon after, saying it was time for Roger's nap. 'May I take the paper?' she asked casually as she gathered him up and put him into the pram.

'Of course, my dear,' replied Stella, 'but it's several days old. I've got yesterday's, if you'd rather have that.'

'Thank you,' Maggie smiled, 'may I take both? I haven't read a paper for ages.'

'Yes, do, take both. I've finished with them.'

Maggie hurried back along the street, looking about her, as if afraid she might be seen.

Don't be stupid, she told herself, the neighbours are used to seeing me with a baby these days, they have absolutely no reason to think he might not be mine.

When she was safely inside her own front door, she put Roger into the second-hand cot she had bought with some of Andy's money and sat down with the paper to read the article properly.

### Missing Baby

Baby Freddie Shadbroke (9 months) is missing. During the raid on the night of 21st April, Freddie was accidentally left at home when his family went to the Parham Road shelter. When his father, a warden who had been on duty during the raid, returned to the family home in Suffolk Place, there was no sign of him. Freddie had disappeared.

'Some kind person must have found him and taken him to safety,' says sister Muriel. 'We are desperate to find our little Freddie. If anyone has any information as to where he is now, please, please come forward and contact us through this newspaper.'

Maggie read the piece through twice. There was no doubt about it, the missing baby Freddie was the one Colin had saved, her Roger, and now his family were looking for him. How could anyone forget to take their baby to the air-raid shelter? she wondered incredulously. And yet they had. This required very careful thought.

'*We are desperate to find our little Freddie,*' his sister was quoted as saying.

'But not careful enough not to have lost him in the first place,' Maggie answered her aloud. 'If my husband hadn't rescued him, he would have died! He's only safe and well because *my Colin saved him.*'

Yes, Colin had saved him, but she knew that if Colin hadn't been killed when he was, he would have reported finding the baby and someone would have come to take him away; to give him back to a family that had left him to die in a house all by himself.

Well, not if she had anything to do with it. Colin would have reported his find, but she wouldn't. There was no way she was going to give Roger up now, so she needed to make plans, decide what she was going to do... just in case.

Suppose someone else knew of Colin's rescue? Well, she

hadn't told anyone, and as far as she knew Colin hadn't either, and since no one had come looking for the child, it seemed unlikely.

Surely that means that we're safe and there's no need to panic, she thought. Just keep our heads down and we'll be fine.

What reason could anyone have to suspect her Roger was the missing baby? The only time he'd come into contact with officialdom was when she had been to the food office. They would have the date when they had provided him with a new ration book, but that was some time after the other baby went missing and it was unlikely they would make a connection; after all, she'd shown them the birth certificate naming the baby in her arms as Roger Peterson. He was clearly hers. Still, she felt uneasy.

That night she did not sleep well. She dreamed that the fire brigade turned up on her doorstep and said that if she didn't hand Roger over immediately they would set fire to the house. She was screaming at them to go away, but they drove their fire engine right up to the house and played the powerful hose in through the door as if putting out a fire. She woke up shaking to hear Roger crying and the sirens warning of yet another raid. How she hated that sound!

Over the next couple of days Maggie tried to decide what to do. Should she simply stay where she was and carry on, or should she move away? If the father and sister were determined in their search, wouldn't it be safer to leave Plymouth? But where, and how would they live?

Gradually, the glimmerings of an idea came to her. Lots of mothers had been moving out into the country and surely she could do the same, saying it was because of the raids. She didn't need to live in Plymouth now for Colin's job and she was going to take baby Roger to the safety of the country. People would accept that. Colin's salary had died with him and though money came in from the Clays in the upstairs flat, giving her a small regular income, apart from sixty pounds left in the bank from the legacy, the house was her only asset. If she moved away, she could let the ground-floor flat as well as upstairs and that would give her enough money to live on. When Roger was old enough to be left with someone she would find a job, part time probably, and she'd simply stay away until the search for the baby had died down. All she had to do was find somewhere safe to go.

It shouldn't be difficult to let the flat, people were desperate for housing after the raids. She knew that even Stella was thinking of letting her spare bedroom if she could find a nice single lady in search of a roof.

Next afternoon she went to see Stella and mentioned the idea.

'We don't need to stay here in the city for Colin's work any more,' she said, 'and after last night's raid, I want to take Roger safely away from the bombing. I'm sure Colin would want me to move to the comparative safety of the countryside to keep his son safe. If I could rent out my flat in the meantime I'd have some money coming in, and at the end of the war I could come back and the house would be waiting for me.'

*If it survives the bombs.* Both of them had this thought, but neither of them gave voice to it. And anyway, Stella thought, if it were to be bombed, far better that Maggie and Roger were not in it.

Stella thought of Elsie's complaints that Paul's friend David seemed to have moved in for the duration, and, what was more, he'd want his daughter with him when she came out of hospital. There would be room enough for both of them at a pinch, but Elsie was determined that it should not come to that. She had spent a good deal of time looking out for somewhere suitable for the two Shawbrooks.

'Thank goodness the older girl is accommodated in the nurses' home,' she said to Stella. 'We certainly couldn't take in three of them.'

Would Maggie's flat do for them? Stella wondered, if Maggie was really going to move to the safety of the countryside? Should she suggest it to Maggie? It would have to be before mentioning it to Elsie, otherwise Elsie would blame her if it didn't work out.

'Actually,' she said casually, 'if you're really thinking of moving out into the country I might know someone who's looking for a place to live. A man and his daughter, bombed out. She was injured in the raid and is about to come out of hospital. They need somewhere to live and would probably be pleased to rent the flat from you.'

Maggie's eyes brightened. She had been wondering how to go about finding the right people to take the flat. She didn't want just any old person living there. She wanted to be sure it would be looked after, so that when she came back with a little boy rather than a baby, it would still be her home.

'If you like I can find out if they're still looking for somewhere,' Stella suggested.

'Oh, yes, please,' Maggie replied. A man and his daughter

sounded just right; she didn't want a large family trying to cram itself in.

Maggie had given careful thought to her plan, but the question still remained as to where she should go. Surely there was no real hurry. If Stella really did know someone suitable as tenants for her flat, then would be the time to make her decision.

However, her decision was made for her later that evening when she sat down to put her feet up. Opening another newspaper that Stella had passed on to her, she spent a few minutes looking for any further mention of the missing baby. There was none, but as she scanned the pages she saw an advertisement in the personal column, an advertisement which leaped out at her.

Help Required! Lady, honest and hardworking, wanted to help in country house. Remuneration by arrangement to include occupancy of estate cottage. Apply Bridger, Box Number A243 *Western Morning News*.

Maggie read it and read it again. Surely, she thought, it could be the answer to all her problems; a job in some outlying village where no one had heard of the lost baby. After a while, when the war had moved on, she and Roger would be able to return home to the house in Marden Road. It was a possibility, so she cut out the advertisement and slipped it into the kitchen drawer. She would sleep on the idea.

Next morning she took the advertisement out and read it through again. It would do no harm to answer, she thought, and pulling a pad towards her she began to write a reply.

When Stella called round to Elsie to tell her of the plan, Elsie was delighted. 'But you must be the one to organise it all,' she said. 'I don't want Paul saying I turned his best friend out into the street.'

'But you wouldn't be,' objected Stella.

'Paul would say that I am,' replied Elsie. 'I didn't mind when it was just David for a couple of days, but I really don't want to take in the whole family.'

Stella forbore to point out that 'the whole family' was just two adults, and said, 'Well, if you'd rather it didn't come from you...'

'It's just that you and that Maggie have become quite pally lately,' Elsie said, 'so she'll probably take them on your recommendation and that'll suit everyone.'

Mu was still on nights, Vera not yet out of hospital though due to leave in the next few days, so it was David alone who went to meet Maggie Peterson at her flat the following week. They had arranged a time and Maggie had asked Stella if she could leave Roger with her for the afternoon. It would be difficult if he woke up and began to cry.

Stella was quite happy to agree. She had not mentioned to Maggie that the man coming to look at the flat had recently lost most of his family in the Parham Road shelter disaster. There was no need for that, but she did think it would be far better not to confront him with a bouncing baby boy.

'Of course I'll have him,' Stella said. 'Just pop round and collect him when you've finished with Mr Shawbrook.'

David arrived promptly and Maggie showed him into the flat.

He seems a decent enough bloke, she thought as she led him through the rooms. And if it's just him and his daughter, they'll have plenty of space.

'When were you thinking of moving away?' David asked her when he'd seen the whole place and decided to take it.

'As soon as I've let this place,' she said. 'My husband was killed recently and I want to take our son out of the danger area as soon as I can.'

'I'm so sorry for your loss,' David said softly, still unable to come to terms with his own. 'It's very sensible to take the child out to the country somewhere. I doubt if we've seen the last of the Luftwaffe yet.'

They agreed a rent and arranged for David and Vera to move in after the weekend. It would be the perfect place for them. Maggie was leaving the flat fully furnished, they would bring nothing but the few clothes they had acquired since they'd lost everything.

'You won't mind if I leave a suitcase in the cellar cupboard, will you?' Maggie asked David as she showed him to the door. 'It's only got a few bits and bobs I shan't need with me.'

'No, that's no problem,' David replied. 'It'll be quite safe here till you come back.'

There was no real hurry for Maggie to leave, but she didn't want to lose these very acceptable tenants. There was always the nagging thought in the back of her mind that Roger's real father was still searching for him and might come knocking on her door without warning. Better to have disappeared.

## 20

When Mu knocked on the door of the Drakes' terraced cottage it took so long for an answer that she was already turning away, about to mark it as 'not at home' on her list.

'Can I help you?' A woman was standing in the doorway.

Mu turned back and smiled. 'Well,' she said, 'I'm not sure but I'm hoping you can. I'm looking for a baby, and—'

'No babies in this house any more, I'm sorry to say,' replied the woman. 'Just a hulking great lad of eleven.'

'No, well, I mean I'm not looking for a baby, but for information about my nephew. He's disappeared.'

The woman looked doubtful. 'Don't know why you think we'd know anything,' she said. 'I don't know who you are and I certainly don't know where your nephew is. Run away, has he?'

'No, he's only nine months. It's just that somehow he came to be left in the house when the rest of my family went to the shelter and no one has seen him since.' She smiled at the woman, feeling that she might be more sympathetic than some of the other people she'd spoken to. 'You live just round the corner, you see, and if someone came and took him to safety, well, you might have seen or heard something about it and be able to help.'

'I see.' The woman looked thoughtful. 'When did this happen, then?'

Mu turned and walked back to the front door, a glimmer of hope in her eyes. 'It was the first night of the dreadful April raids,' she said, 'the night of Monday the twenty-first.' The woman standing in the doorway looked at her consideringly. For a long moment there was silence between them and then she said, 'You'd better come in.'

Mu stepped forward and held out her hand. 'Thank you,' she said. 'My name is Muriel Shawbrook and my family live… lived at 21 Suffolk Place.'

The woman accepted her extended hand and replied, 'Jane Drake, Miss Shawbrook. How do you do?' She stood aside to let Mu precede her into the house. Once inside she opened the door immediately to her left and again stood aside to let Mu go first. The room they entered was clearly the 'front room', kept for best and only used for visitors.

'Please sit down,' Jane Drake said. 'I'll give my Ernie a call, he came in from school just now.'

Mu did as she was asked and waited while Jane Drake disappeared to the back of the house. She heard Jane calling and then the sound of footsteps on the stairs. Moments later Jane returned followed by a skinny boy of about eleven who stood awkwardly in the doorway when faced with an unknown visitor in the front room.

'This is my son, Ernie,' Jane said. 'I think he might be able to help you.' She turned back to her son and said, 'Come in, numbskull, and talk to Miss Shawbrook. She wants to ask you some questions.'

'I don't know nothing,' replied the boy sullenly.

'You don't know what she's going to ask you yet,' remarked his mother.

'Well, I don't know nothing about nothing.'

'Yes, you do. About the policeman rescuing that baby from a bombed house in Suffolk Place. Tell her about that.'

Ernie gave an exaggerated shrug. 'Weren't nothing. I heard a baby crying and this cop went into the house and fetched him out.'

'Wait a minute, Ernie,' Mu said. 'Let me explain what's happened, and then you can tell me about the policeman and the baby.' She waited until Ernie gave a nod and edged his way into the room. Despite his truculence, he was actually very interested to hear what this lady had to say. He hadn't told Mum about his escapade, not straight away, but in the end when he realised that his mother knew full well he'd been out in the early hours and was about to give him a hiding for going, he had told her about hearing a baby cry in an empty house and the daring rescue by the policeman.

'If I hadn't been out, Mum, then no one wouldn't have found that baby and it'd be dead by now. He *told* me I'd saved its life 'cos he hadn't heard it cry.' He could see his mother was intrigued and hoped that him saving the baby's life might spare him a beating. 'I asked him what would happen to it and he said it would be taken into a children's home and looked after.' He looked at his mother anxiously. 'I'd hate to be put in a home,' he said. 'I'd run away again as soon as I could, but a poor little baby can't run away, can it?' And Jane had agreed that it couldn't. She had realised that Ernie couldn't have made up such a story, so she believed him and, secretly proud of him, she scolded him for creeping out of the house in the middle of the night but let him off the beating. Neither of them mentioned the baby again. Ernie told his mates Sidney and Joe about the cop and the baby, but they were far more interested in any souvenirs he might have found and suggested they go and look in the ruins of the Lord Howard, because as Joe said, 'There's sure to be some good stuff in the pub. Stands to reason!'

Ernie and his mother might not have talked about the rescued child again, but Ernie had thought of it quite often and wondered what had happened to it. Maybe its mother had found it again and it was happily back at home. Ernie hoped so, but he knew that the house where he'd had found it had been demolished the following night because he'd back been to look, so, he supposed, it must have had to stay in a children's home and wait for its mum to find it.

Now, he listened to what the visiting lady said. 'My family have lived in Suffolk Place all my life. I don't live there any more, I've been nursing in a hospital in Portsmouth, so I wasn't there during the raid on the twenty-first of April. Nor was my father, but most of my family were and when the sirens went, they all went to the public shelter.' She did not name the shelter, even thinking about it brought a lump to her throat, but she swallowed hard and went on, 'I don't know what happened, but somehow the youngest child, a baby, got left behind. Do you know anything about him, Ernie? Don't worry, you aren't in trouble if you do, but we can't find him and we do know that he wasn't in the house the next morning when his granddad went to look at the damage.' She gave Ernie a reassuring smile. 'Anything you can tell us, anything at all about that baby, would be very helpful. We're so worried about him.'

For a long moment Ernie did not reply and then he said, 'He said he was going to take it to a rescue centre.'

'He? Who's he, Ernie?'

'I don't know,' returned Ernie. 'Some copper. Didn't tell me his name, did he?'

'A policeman? He took him?'

'It was *me* what found him,' Ernie hastened to say, anxious that the credit shouldn't go to someone else. '*Me* what heard him crying, like, and I was going to go in the 'ouse and look, but then this copper come along and said I wasn't to go inside. He thought I was looting and I told 'im that I'd heard a baby crying in the house, an' he listened an' then he heard it too, so he told me to wait across the road until he come out again. Said if the 'ouse fell down I was to go for 'elp, from the firemen what were putting out the Lord Howard.'

'So what happened?' prompted Mu.

'The copper went in the 'ouse and then a few minutes later he come out again with this baby in his arms. The baby had stopped bellowing, and he carried it across the road. He told me to scoot off 'ome cos I shouldn't be out at that time of day and without my gas mask. Said my mum would be worrying, so I went 'ome. So, I don't know what he done with the baby, 'cept he said he was going to take it to the rescue centre and they'd put it in a home to be looked after. All right?'

'Ernie, that's wonderful news,' cried Mu. 'If a policeman took him then I can go to the police station and find out where he took him. Thank you. Thank you so much for telling me what happened. If it hadn't been for you, baby Freddie wouldn't have been rescued.'

Hoping to be even more of a hero, Ernie added helpfully, 'Is that 'is name? Well, I can tell you he didn't 'alf stink.'

Both women laughed at that and Ernie looked offended. 'Well they do, don't they? Babies?'

'You certainly used to,' agreed his mother with a smile. Turning back to Mu she said, 'I hope what Ernie's told you will help you find him. The policeman will at least know where he took him and you'll be able to follow on from there.' She paused a moment and said, 'Would you like a cuppa before you go?'

Mu looked a little embarrassed. 'Do you mind if I don't?' she said. 'I've just got time to go and give my father the news before I'm on duty again at the hospital, you know...'

'Of course,' Jane Drake said. 'I quite understand, if it was Ernie, I'd be out of the door by now.'

As Mu left the house she took a ten shilling note from her bag and said, 'This is for you, Ernie, for being such a hero. It was you who found him, and by telling the policeman, you saved his life. He's safely somewhere – all I've got to do now is find that policeman and ask where.'

'Oh, Miss Shawbrook,' cried Jane. 'Ernie don't need a reward.'

'Well, I think he does,' Mu said firmly. 'Anyway, I'd like to give him one.' She held out the ten shilling note to the boy, who, eyes wide at so much money, glanced at his mother before he took it and stuffed it into his pocket.

'That's very generous of you, Miss Shawbrook,' said his mother, 'and unnecessary.'

'Not to me, Mrs Drake, not to me.'

'He had stripes on his arm,' Ernie suddenly volunteered.

'Who did? The policeman?'

Ernie nodded.

'So, he was a sergeant?' asked Mu.

'If that's what stripes means,' said Ernie, who, from choice, steered clear of all coppers.

'That's what they mean,' answered Mu. 'That's a very helpful thing to know. Thank you, Ernie.'

'When you find him, the baby, will you bring him round and show him to Mum?'

'I certainly will,' promised Mu, and with that she took her leave and headed back into the town. The only thing they had to do now was to find the right police station and the right sergeant, but first she must give Dad and Vera the good news. Freddie had been rescued by a police sergeant and it would be only a matter of time before they would have him safely back with them. All they needed was somewhere to live, and they could, perhaps, begin to face the rest of their lives.

## 21

Mu found her father at the Jeffersons' and told him the wonderful news.

'I know what's happened to Freddie,' she cried. 'He's alive and safe... somewhere. I found a boy called Ernie who heard a baby crying inside a bombed house, our house, and he told a policeman. When the policeman heard the crying too, he went into the house and carried the baby out. It was his footprints you saw in the dust, Dad. Ernie says that the policeman was very brave because the house was about to collapse.'

'It certainly was when I went inside,' agreed her father. 'So, what happened to the baby?'

'The policeman told Ernie that he was going to take him to a rescue centre and he'd probably be looked after in a children's home.'

'Did he? Then that's where we must look.'

'But we've been round the rescue centres in that area, and no one had any record of an unidentified baby,' sighed Mu. 'We've been to all the authorities and no one knows anything.'

'Well, now we know it's a police sergeant, it should make him easier to trace,' David said.

'Somewhat,' agreed Mu ruefully, 'but there must be dozens of those in the City of Plymouth police.'

'Yes, I know,' replied David, 'but think about it, he was patrolling our street, wasn't he? So he must have come from a station in our area, don't you think?'

'I suppose so,' Mu said. 'That certainly gives us a place to start, and presumably if we don't find him straight away, they can put the word out. Find out if a sergeant from another district found him. Oh, Dad, at least we know Freddie didn't vanish. We know he was rescued. I can't wait to tell Vera, she'll be so excited. And tomorrow when I come off duty I shall find our nearest police station and make enquiries.'

'Well, we have some more good news for Vera when you see her tonight,' David told her. 'I've found us a place to live, not far from the Jeffersons, actually. There's a widow with a young child who wants to get out of the city and she's letting her flat. We can move in after the weekend.'

'Oh, Dad!' cried Mu. 'That's wonderful news. Vera'll be delighted. She can't wait to get out of the hospital.'

Mu was quite right. When she went onto the ward that evening, she told Sister Brock that her father had found a place to live for himself, and Vera too.

'That's very good news, Nurse,' replied the sister. 'She's fed up in here and can easily go home now that she can manage on crutches. And,' she added ruefully, 'we need the bed.' She smiled at Mu and said, 'Go on, go and tell her.'

Mu went across to Vera's bed, and reaching for the cubicle curtains she swished them round the bed.

Vera looked up, startled. 'Mu?' she said. 'What's going on?'

'I've got some news for you,' replied her sister.

Vera's face brightened. 'Really? Are they going to let me out at last?'

'Yes, Sister Brock says you're ready to be discharged, but that isn't what I've come to tell you.'

Vera gave a shrug. 'So? What?'

Mu considered telling her about the flat, but that wasn't the important thing just now. Freddie must come first.

'Vera, just the most wonderful news,' she whispered as she sat down beside the bed and took her sister's hands. 'We've just had some news about Freddie. He's definitely alive! A policeman rescued him from the house and carried him to safety.'

Vera stared at her for a moment and then burst into violent tears, her body shaking with huge, gasping sobs. Mu held her hands tightly. 'Oh, Vera, don't cry. Don't cry! We'll find him now, you'll see. Just a couple more days and we'll have him back, I promise you!'

But Vera couldn't stop; her Freddie was safe, but she felt no joy, just an aching knowledge that her mother had died knowing that she had forgotten Freddie. She had deserted her baby so that she could have a drink with Charlie who, she suddenly realised, must be dead as well, as he had gone with her to the Parham Road shelter. Mam had trusted her to look after her own son and she had let her down, let them both down.

Mu reached across the bed and awkwardly gathered her sister into her arms.

'Sh, sh,' she soothed. 'It's all right, Vera. It's all right. Freddie is all right.'

'But Mam doesn't know,' sobbed Vera. 'She doesn't know and it's too late to tell her.'

She doesn't know about me and Patrick either, thought Mu, entirely forgetting there wasn't any 'me and Patrick'. Everything is too late. Mam isn't there to tell… anything.

'Listen,' she said in her most rallying tone, 'Dad's found a flat for you and him to live in. You can move in after the weekend, the two of you. You can look after Dad and he can look after you, and I'll be just round the corner in the nurses' home.'

'But the others are all gone. Mam and the children!'

'Yes,' said Mu, fighting her own tears as the knowledge struck her afresh, 'so we have to look after each other… and particularly Freddie.'

'Where is he?' Vera's sobs were dying away. 'Who's looking after him now?'

'He was rescued by a policeman and is being looked after in a children's home,' Mu told her again. 'He'll be fine, and all we have to do is contact the city police and ask which of them found him.'

At that moment the curtains were drawn back and Sister Brock appeared at the bedside, all starched apron, starched cap and starched face. She had heard Vera's outburst, as had the entire ward, and had given her some moments to regain control of herself. She had no idea what Mu could have said to provoke such an outburst, but the work of the ward must go on and it was time for the disturbance to stop.

'Nurse Shawbrook,' she said in a cold tone, 'Mrs Ford needs a bedpan. Please see to her at once. I will settle your sister for the night.'

'Yes, Sister,' replied Mu meekly, 'sorry, Sister.'

When Mu had disappeared to attend to Mrs Ford, Sister Brock pulled the curtains back round Vera's bed and took Mu's place on the chair at her bedside.

'Now then, Vera,' she said, her voice firm but gentle, 'what's all the fuss about? Don't you want to go home? Your sister told me that your father has found a place for you both to live. That's good news, isn't it?' Passing the girl a clean handkerchief, she said, 'Come on, blow you nose and tell me what's the matter.'

Vera responded to her tone as she would have if she were still a child, and taking a few gulping breaths she did as she was told and blew her nose.

'They've found Freddie,' she said flatly.

Sister Brock knew that Vera had a son and had been looking for him when she was caught out in the raid. 'Well, that's wonderful news, isn't it?'

'It was my fault that he got lost.'

'You went to find him.'

'I should have taken him to the shelter when the sirens went. I forgot him. I forgot him because I stayed out late, having a drink with someone.'

'And if you had been at home, you'd have carried him to the shelter.' Sister Brock knew what she was going to say next would be very difficult, but she also knew that it wouldn't help Vera to let her carry the blame for what had happened to her family. She had not been killed with them and she felt guilty. Survivors often did, but it was something she was going to have to come to terms with. 'If you had carried him into that shelter, you wouldn't be here now,' she said, matter-of-factly. 'He wouldn't be alive and your father and sister would have lost the two of you as well. Don't forget, you're not the only one who was robbed of her family by that bomb. Your father and sister are having to cope with their loss too, aren't they? Don't you think your mother would be thrilled to know that you and Freddie have both survived? That your father and sister have some of their beloved family left? She would want you to go on and live your life to the full, to bring up Freddie as the best mother you can be. You cheated the Nazis and you cheated death. Your mother would trust you to make the most of what you've been given. A second chance.'

'You don't know that,' said Vera truculently.

'Yes, I do,' said Sister Brock. 'I wasn't always a crusty old spinster trying to teach nurses their job. I was just nine when my parents died in the Spanish flu epidemic after the last war. They both died and I thought it was my fault.'

'But that's stupid!' exclaimed Vera.

'Yes, of course it is; but like me you have to learn that it isn't your fault that you survived and they didn't. You have to make the most of everything in the rest of your life, and in particular your little boy. Now then,' Sister Brock got to her feet, 'time you were settling down. In a few days you'll be back with your family, including Freddie, and he'll need all the love you can give him.' She pulled open the curtains, letting Vera see her sister helping another patient brush her teeth, holding the bowl as she spat.

'Your sister is a born nurse,' Sister Brock remarked. 'Perhaps you're a born mother. You'll never know until you try, will you?'

## 22

When David Shawbrook had left, Maggie had walked down to Stella's to collect Roger.

'It's all agreed,' she said. 'They move in next week.'

'That soon?' Stella was surprised.

'Well, his daughter is coming out of hospital then and he needs somewhere to bring her home to. I want to leave as soon as I can, because, as he said when we were discussing it all, he doesn't think the Luftwaffe have finished with us yet and if he's right, I don't want to be here when they come back.'

'Even so, it's very sudden. Where will you go?'

'Well,' said Maggie slowly, 'I was wondering…'

'If you could come here? I suppose—' Stella began doubtfully, but Maggie interrupted her.

'No, I wouldn't dream of imposing on you, Stella. I just wondered if you could have Roger for the day tomorrow so I can go and see someone about a place I've heard of that might do. I shan't be fussy, you know, a little house or cottage will do the two of us nicely.'

Finding she was relieved that Maggie had not wanted to move in with her, Stella asked no more. Maggie would tell her when she knew more herself and she was happy enough to look after Roger for the day. She doubted that Maggie could just turn up somewhere and find a place to live, but at least she was going to look. There had been a time when she would hardly leave the house, but since Colin's death she'd had to do so and she seemed to have overcome her fear of being out of doors.

If Stella had known it, Maggie had already found a possible place for her and Roger to live. She had received a reply to her letter to the box number. A Colonel Bridger had written from an address in a village called Martindell outside Exeter. An estate cottage was indeed being offered rent free in return for some inside work at the big house, Martindell Manor. It sounded ideal. She and Roger would disappear into the countryside, with a place to live, a mother sensibly evacuating herself and her son from blitz-burned Plymouth. The colonel's letter summoned her for immediate interview. It wasn't that far, and with Stella looking after Roger, Maggie could be there and back in the day; she could see the cottage and discover what she might have to do in return for living there. She was determined not to skivvy, but she wouldn't mind helping with some of the household chores. She reckoned she could strike a decent bargain with this Colonel Bridger at the big house; after all, it was almost impossible to get servants these days with the men called up and the single women about to be. As a widow with a small child she wouldn't be conscripted, but this way, she thought, she would still be doing her bit.

Maggie took the train to Exeter the next morning and from there the local, stopping train which passed through

Martindell. Asking at the station, she was given directions to the manor which stood behind a grey stone wall just beyond the village green. She found it easily enough and passed through crumbling stone gateposts bereft of their iron gates, long since gone for salvage. As she walked up the overgrown drive towards the manor, she could see that it had once been a beautiful house set in well-laid out gardens, but now those days were over; the whole place was quietly disintegrating. Clearly there was no money to look after it and the owners must be offering the cottage to tempt someone into agreeing to work for almost no wages. If the cottage was anything like habitable, Maggie decided, she would take it. Roger could be wheeled over to the manor house in his pram, and with luck she might find a girl in the village who would occasionally look after him at home for a shilling or two.

When she finally rang the front door bell, the door was opened by an elderly lady, who peered out at her through the broken spectacles balanced on the end of her rather chubby nose. She had a halo of white hair about her head and looked like nothing as much as a confused dandelion clock.

'Yes?'

'Mrs Bridger?'

'Yes?'

'I'm Margaret Peterson. I saw your advertisement in the paper and sent a reply. Colonel Bridger – your husband? – asked me to come... and meet you.' She had nearly said for an interview, but having seen the frailty and confusion of Mrs Bridger, she decided to go for equality. She might work for this woman, yes, but it would be on her own terms.

'Ah, I remember,' Mrs Bridger said. 'My husband will want to see you. He's in his study.' She turned and led the way into the house, the interior of which was in dire need of a good clean and polish. A huge chandelier hung in the hall, but it was festooned with cobwebs, as were the banisters of what had once been an elegant staircase curving up to the floor above. Maggie followed her through the hall into a well-proportioned, south-facing room where an elderly gentleman was sitting at a large desk with papers laid out in front of him. He was a man from another age with white mutton-chop whiskers and white, furry eyebrows which met each other over the bridge of an eagle nose, but he fitted perfectly with his surroundings. This room, too, was in great need of a duster, but the furniture itself looked comfortable if well-worn and it was clearly where the gentleman spent most of his day.

'Colonel,' the woman announced. 'Mrs Peterson is here.'

'Ah, capital!' cried the colonel and got to his feet. 'You can leave us, my dear,' he added, turning to his wife. 'I'll sort this out.'

And sort it out he did.

When they were alone together, Maggie explained that she had recently been widowed and that she wanted to bring the baby out of Plymouth to the comparative safety of the countryside.

'And I need a change of scene,' she said, allowing a break in her voice. 'Away from the bombs and away from painful memories.'

The colonel said he quite understood and remained unfazed when he heard that she'd be bringing a baby with her. 'That's no problem, my dear, clean country air'll be good for him,' adding as an afterthought, 'The memsahib likes babies.'

'Can you cook?' he asked hopefully. 'Not very good in the kitchen department, the memsahib. Can't work out the rationing. You know how?'

Maggie said she did and the colonel looked relieved.

'Sounds as if you're just what we're looking for,' he said. 'Will you take the job? It's all got a bit beyond the memsahib without help.'

'If I like the cottage,' Maggie replied. 'But if I'm going to cook your meals as you suggest, my son Roger and I are going to eat here too.'

With this all agreed, Maggie knew she would accept the job whatever the cottage looked like.

'When can you start?' asked the colonel. 'The last woman walked out after two weeks without giving notice. It's been a bit of a strain.'

Maggie could well see it had, and it must have been a strain on 'the last woman' as well. But the whole set-up suited her purposes very well. No one would find them living in a cottage belonging to a ramshackle old manor house, owned by a rather decrepit, elderly couple who seldom passed through the gateless stone posts at the end of their drive.

'Come along,' said the colonel, 'I'll show you the cottage, it's not far from us and it's not far from the village.' He led her out through the French windows that opened off his study and across what had once been a lawn. Now it had been dug up and was planted with neat rows of vegetables.

'Digging for victory,' he said with a wave of his hand. 'Not us doing the digging, far too old, a local farmer, Bill

Merton, lives at Hawthorn Farm. He rents our last couple of fields as grass keep for his sheep. Pays us a pittance, but he looks after our vegetable plot for us. Turns up and digs potatoes and things. Leaves vegetables on our doorstep. All helps!'

He led the way out of the garden, following a narrow track across a small field to a stand of trees. The cottage was tiny, sheltering beneath the trees and looking out across the fields towards the village.

The colonel unlocked the front door and stood aside for Maggie to enter. Passing him she stepped straight into the one room downstairs, a kitchen with an old range and a large Belfast sink with a pump handle above it. A table and two chairs stood by the window and an old dresser was stacked with an assortment of crockery. There was a rough-finished wooden door in one corner and when Maggie investigated it, she found to her surprise that it concealed an indoor lavatory. She had been afraid of an outside privy, but at least this unexpected convenience meant she wouldn't have to venture outside in the middle of the night. No hot water, but the pump over the sink meant that she did have water indoors. Certainly not all mod cons, but she knew she could cope without them; they would be safe here. That was the main thing.

'Bedrooms upstairs,' said the colonel pointing to steep narrow stairs leading to the floor above. 'I can't manage those stairs now, but I'm sure a young lady like you will have no problem.'

'I'll go and look,' Maggie said, wanting to see exactly what had been provided.

Two bedrooms squatted under the eaves, furnished

with an iron bedstead with a thin mattress on each. She'd demand bedclothes from the big house. The whole cottage was sparsely furnished, but it would be enough for her and Roger.

'All well?' asked the colonel when she came back down.

'I'll need a few things to make it habitable,' she said, 'but I'm sure there are a few spare bits and pieces in the big house?'

'Of course.' The colonel agreed readily enough, anything to ensure this woman came to help with his wife and his house. The two of them spent almost an hour together and by the end they had come to an agreement with regard to the cottage and the remuneration as advertised. He held out his hand and they shook on their deal.

'We'll be here within the week,' Maggie promised.

## 23

When Maggie got home from Martindell she went straight to Stella's house to collect Roger.

'Have you been a good boy?' she cooed as she gathered him into her arms.

'Good as gold,' Stella smiled, 'haven't you, my pet?'

'Thanks so much for having him,' Maggie said.

'No trouble at all,' replied Stella. 'You know I'm happy to look after him whenever I can.' She looked speculatively at Maggie and asked, 'How did you get on? Was the place you went to see any good?'

Maggie was ready for that question and she gave a rueful smile. 'Well,' she said, 'it would have been, but another couple got there first. It was a pity really, as it would have been perfect.'

When she didn't enlarge on this Stella said, 'Why, what was it?'

'It was a village pub. They wanted someone to live in and work in the bar. I would have had board and lodging and Roger would have been there with me, so that he was upstairs when I was working in the bar, or helping in the kitchen.'

'And someone else got there first? Didn't the publican know you were coming? I thought you'd arranged to meet.'

'We had,' agreed Maggie, 'but he didn't keep his side of the bargain, he told me he was so desperate for help that he took this other couple on.' She gave a frustrated smile. 'You know what I think? I think it was because I was going to bring a baby with me. Roger and I would have shared a room, but he didn't want a baby on the premises and decided to go with the others. He said, "First come first served"!'

'So what are you going to do now?' Stella asked.

'Go on looking, I suppose.'

'But you have to be out to let your tenants move in after the weekend.'

Maggie sighed. 'Yes, I know. I suppose I should have confirmed the pub place before I said they could have the flat so soon.'

'Yes,' Stella said firmly, 'you should.' Then her face softened. 'Well, if the worst comes to the worst, you'll have to move in with me for a few days, just until you find somewhere definite. I still think you've made the right decision, to move out of Plymouth as soon as you can. It must be our turn for some more raids soon.'

'Stella, you are a very generous woman and I promise that if we do have to beg a bedroom from you, Roger and I will do our best to find somewhere else as quickly as we can, so that we don't outstay our welcome.'

As she walked home Maggie found she was feeling very guilty at the way she had lied to Stella, the one person who had stood her friend and helped her when Colin had been killed. But she was determined she was going to leave no trail behind her when she set off to Martindell and their new life in the country at the weekend.

I can make up some story if necessary when I come back, she thought. So much time will have passed, with luck no one will remember who said what!

Reaching her house, she manoeuvred the pram into the hallway and then through her front door. Once inside she kicked off her shoes and collapsed onto the sofa for a moment. It had been a very successful day, as far as she was concerned, but she was tired, very tired, and Roger's grizzling had begun again.

Reluctantly Maggie got to her feet again to make up a bottle and to mash up some potato and cheese for Roger's supper.

'You're very demanding, you know,' she told him as she waited for the bottle to cool.

At that moment there was a ring at the doorbell. Maggie sighed and, putting Roger back into the safety of his cot, she went to answer the bell.

Standing on the doorstep was Andy Sharpe.

'Oh!' Maggie said in surprise.

He was in uniform this time, but he smiled at her and said, 'Good evening, Mrs Peterson. Constable Sharpe, we met before.'

'Yes,' answered Maggie snappily. 'I know who you are.'

'I just wondered if I might take a few minutes of your time and ask you a couple of questions. Purely routine, but Inspector Droy asked me to call.'

Maggie sighed. 'If you must, but I'm just about to feed Roger.'

'I won't keep you long, I promise you,' replied Andy, and

she stood aside to let him in. Once they were in the living room she picked up Roger.

'You don't mind me giving Roger his supper while we talk, do you? He's hungry and if he starts to bellow we shan't be able to hear ourselves think.'

'No, of course not.'

Maggie settled Roger on her knee and began to spoon the cheese and potato mixture into his mouth. 'Well?' she said. 'How can I help?'

'We've had an enquiry about a missing baby.'

Maggie looked up sharply. 'And what has that to do with me?'

'Oh, nothing,' said Andy. 'It's just that a police sergeant was seen to rescue a baby from a damaged house in Suffolk Place after the first of the bad April raids. Someone saw him carry the baby out of a house, but we can't find out who it was or where he took the baby.'

'How strange,' Maggie said, keeping her voice steady. 'But surely the man must have reported finding the baby? I mean, that would be the first thing he'd do, wouldn't it?'

'He should do, but no one has heard anything about the baby since, and he's still missing.'

Stay calm! Maggie told herself. Speak reasonably! Think what any concerned person would say, but don't say any more.

'So how do you think I can help you?'

'Inspector Droy sent me to ask you if by any chance your husband had mentioned anything about this. Whether he had heard of such a rescue. It was just before he was killed, so he might have known about it.'

'Are you suggesting it might have been him?' asked Maggie cautiously.

'No, not at all,' replied Andy hastily. 'We know if it had been Sergeant Peterson he would have reported it straight away. But the inspector did wonder if he might have heard something about it and mentioned it to you.'

Maggie spooned the last of the cheese supper into Roger's mouth and hoisted him up over her shoulder to bring up his wind. As she gently patted his back, she shook her head.

'No, I'm sorry, Constable, I don't think I can help. Colin certainly didn't tell me anything like that. How very sad for the family concerned.'

'Particularly so as several of that family were killed in the Parham Road shelter disaster. You may remember there were no survivors. However, the grandfather and two of his daughters were elsewhere when the shelter was hit, and they have only just discovered that the baby wasn't in the shelter with the rest of the family.'

Maggie tightened her grip on Roger. How close he'd come to being killed!

'Well, I'm sorry,' she repeated, 'but I'm afraid I can't help you.'

'No, I understand.' Andy looked at the baby in Maggie's arms and a thought crossed his mind.

'How is your little chap?' he asked. 'How old is he now, I wonder? He's certainly bigger than when I first saw him.'

'He's nearly ten months,' responded Maggie guardedly.

'About the same age as the baby who's missing.' He smiled across at her. 'Going to be a copper knob by the looks of him.'

'That comes from my grandmother,' said Maggie. 'She was Irish and had lovely red hair.'

'Really? Funny how things like that often skip a generation, isn't it?'

Maggie looked at the constable narrowly and decided to take the bull by the horns.

'Are you suggesting that Roger is this missing baby, Constable?'

'Good Lord, no!' replied Andy Sharpe. 'Not at all.'

'Because if you are, I can assure you he is not and I have his birth certificate to prove it.'

'Mrs Peterson, I am suggesting no such thing,' said the policeman getting to his feet. 'But you must understand that it's our duty to make sure we have followed every possible lead, and if you or your husband had heard anything that might have helped us, well, we had to come and ask.'

He moved towards the door and continued, 'I won't take up any more of your time. Don't get up, I can see myself out. I'm so glad you're managing all right.'

Maggie relaxed a little and said, 'I am, thanks to your generosity and to the help and friendship I'm getting from Mrs Todd down the road. I think it was you who asked her to call, wasn't it?'

'I did speak to a lady who came out of the shop,' he admitted. 'I'm glad she has become a friend.' He smiled across at her. 'Well, I'd better leave you to it. Good evening, Mrs Peterson.'

Andy Sharpe let himself out of the front door and into the street. When he had walked a short distance he stopped and looked back at the house. It showed no sign of life, a quiet house in a quiet suburban street, dreaming and peaceful in the evening sun, and yet he was positive that Maggie Peterson would be looking out from somewhere, watching his departure. As he walked back towards the police station he went back over their conversation. Was it possible that the idea which had suddenly struck him could actually be the truth? Had Colin Peterson been the sergeant who had rescued the baby from the Suffolk Place house, and was that baby now resting comfortably in Maggie Peterson's arms? Surely not. What had put such an idea into his head? He couldn't put his finger on it, but something in her answers, or the way she looked as she answered, made him suspicious. She had been angry when she thought he was suggesting that very thing, but she threatened to prove the child was hers by showing him the boy's birth certificate. Why would she do that? It seemed a rather extreme reaction. What if he had called her bluff and asked to see it? Would she really have been able to produce it, or would she have had to pretend she had lost it? All of a sudden he wished he had called her bluff, but it was too late now. Even so, he thought, as he neared the station to report back to Inspector Droy, methinks the lady doth protest too much!

'How did you get on?' asked the inspector.

'She said she didn't know anything about a lost baby. Said if her husband had found it he would have reported it straight away.'

'Well, I think she's right there, straight as a die, Colin Peterson.'

Andy Sharpe nodded. 'That's what I thought at first,' he said, 'but the conversation became a bit stranger as it went along. I mentioned that the missing baby would be much the same age as her son, and she was really angry. Asked if I was suggesting her baby was the missing one. I said I wasn't, but she insisted that he was hers and she had his birth certificate to prove it. I thought that was a bit over the top – all she had to do was agree the ages and I wouldn't have thought any more about it.'

'Not much to go on,' remarked the inspector. 'You didn't ask to see the certificate, I imagine.'

'No, sir, I thought it better not to ask. If she has one, well and good, but if not better let her think she's got away with it. You see, there was something else. She was feeding the baby when I got there. I'd seen him before, but he's grown quite a bit since the last time, and his hair has come through.'

'And your point is?'

'He's a copper knob. Well, the sarge didn't have red hair, his was dark, and Mrs Peterson's is dark as well. I don't know enough about genetics, but it made me wonder if the child could be theirs. I commented on his hair and Mrs Peterson said that it was a throwback to her Irish grandmother, and so it could be, but it's also the same colour as Miss Shawbrook's, the missing baby's sister. You didn't see her, sir, when she came to the station to tell us about the child being rescued by a police sergeant, but her hair is the most stunning colour, auburn, very noticeable, and I think his will be too.'

'I see. Well, where do we go from here? We can hardly arrest her for abduction on the colour of the child's hair.'

'I been thinking about that, sir, all the way back. We can check Somerset House and see if there is a birth certificate naming her and the sarge as his parents, that would be one way forward, but that would take time in the present circumstances.' He paused and then went on, 'But there is another option. We could arrange for Miss Shawbrook to see Mrs Peterson with the child, unobserved, to see if she can definitely identify him as Freddie Shawbrook. The thing is, sir, Suffolk Place isn't far off the sarge's patch, is it? He could have been the one to rescue that baby from the ruined house. It does all sort of tie up, doesn't it?'

Inspector Droy stroked his chin thoughtfully. 'I can see that it does, Sharpe, but it also seems pretty far-fetched, don't you think? Very circumstantial.'

'Knowing Sergeant Peterson, sir, I would agree with you, but the fact remains that Mrs Peterson has a baby the right age, with the right coloured hair, so it could possibly be Freddie Shawbrook.'

'Well, we can hardly blunder in and accuse her of stealing the baby on your hunch, and the colour of his hair, Sharpe. I still think it most unlikely that Peterson found him and didn't report it. We shall certainly have to do a bit more digging before we can mention the matter to Miss Shawbrook. Mrs Peterson is a person of good character and she deserves our belief unless it can be proved otherwise. Before we say anything about her and her son to the Shawbrooks, we must find out about the birth certificate. We can get someone in London to check with Somerset House for a Roger Peterson, born sometime in July last year to parents Colin and Margaret. It would be about July, wouldn't it?'

'Yes, about then,' agreed the constable.

Inspector Droy nodded. 'And in the meantime we say nothing to the Shawbrooks. Apart from anything else it might raise hope where there is none.' He got to his feet to show that the discussion was over. 'It's an interesting idea,

Sharpe, but, as I said, a bit far-fetched. I'm really hoping you're wrong. I'd hate to think that Colin Peterson rescued that child and took him home to keep. It's most unlikely, but we'll look into it tomorrow.'

# 24

Andy Sharpe had been right, Maggie had indeed been watching him from the shelter of her curtains as he walked away from the house. She saw him stop and look back, and took a step backwards herself to ensure he could not see her.

Where had she gone wrong? she wondered. She had answered his questions patiently until he seemed to be suggesting that Roger was the missing baby. Well, she couldn't let that idea take root, she'd had to nip it in the bud. So she had jumped in with the birth certificate, but somehow, despite the fact that he had not asked to see it, she had quickly realised it had been a mistake; it had made Constable Sharpe more suspicious, not less. What would he do with his suspicions? Would he go straight back to the police station and report them, or would he think about it for a while first? There was no other evidence to suggest Roger and the missing baby were one and the same, and without evidence it would be a leap in the dark to assume that they were. How would they ever know for sure? The sister who had reported him missing would recognise him, she supposed, but it would be her word against

Maggie's, and Maggie still had the birth certificate to back her up.

For a while Maggie found this reasoning reassuring and she set about putting Roger to bed in the usual way, but once he had gone down and the silence of the flat enveloped her, she found anxiety setting in. Was that someone outside the door? Had Constable Sharpe already come back to make more enquiries? Suppose they came back again before she left for the country? If she were under suspicion, would they be watching her? If so, she might not be able to get away to the safe anonymity of Martindell Manor.

Better, she decided, to leave almost at once, to be gone before anyone came asking her more awkward questions. If she packed up their things during the night, she and Roger could slip away first thing tomorrow morning and vanish into the countryside. She would have to think up an acceptable reason for the sudden change of plans, especially for Stella, but surely she could come up with something. She still needed the Shawbrooks to rent the flat, she needed the money, but that had all been arranged when David Shawbrook agreed to take the place. He would take the rent to the bank and lodge it in her account every week.

She had also arranged for the Clays to do the same, explaining to them that she was taking baby Roger out of the war zone that Plymouth had become, and would need to draw on her money from where she was going.

'Oh,' Mrs Clay had enquired politely, 'and where are you going?'

'I've got a job working in a village inn, the other side of Exeter,' she replied with her prepared answer.

'A job?' Mrs Clay, who had never had to earn her own living, repeated the word with a sniff. 'How interesting.'

'It provides me and my son with board and lodging,' Maggie said tightly. 'And in the meantime, I've let my flat to some people called Shawbrook, a man and his daughter, so you'll still have company in the house. He is paying the rent into the bank each week, and I would be grateful if you could do the same.'

'That's not really very convenient,' grumbled Mrs Clay.

'More convenient than looking for somewhere new to live, I imagine,' suggested Maggie coldly, 'but of course, if you'd rather find somewhere else I'd under—'

'No, no, not at all,' Mrs Clay said hastily. 'My husband can walk down to the bank every week. It will be no problem.'

They had parted on a mutually cool note, but the arrangement had been set in place.

That conversation had taken place some days earlier, once she and David Shawbrook had shaken hands on their deal. She could leave in the morning without the need to speak to the Clays again.

Stella Todd was another matter. She would think it very strange that Maggie had disappeared without saying goodbye. Maggie would have to think of a way round that, but she would give that thought as she packed up all the things she would need, ready to leave first thing in the morning. She knew the train times to Exeter and Martindell, she'd looked those up for her first visit. Any train to Exeter would do, and once she'd got there she could travel onward on the stopping train, with all the other locals.

She worked her way carefully around the flat, sorting out

what they would need. All their clothes, of course, and the pram, bottles, nappies, lotion and powder, the necessities of babyhood; gas masks, ration books, identity documents.

She went through her own private possessions. Of course she must take the precious birth certificate with her, but apart from that and her bank book, she didn't need the few mementos she had collected during her life. She looked at their few important documents – Colin's will and the deeds to the house – and considered taking them with her, but she couldn't risk losing them on her travels; they'd be safer locked away here until she came back. She took down the photographs from the mantelpiece. It would look odd, she thought, if they were left behind, and she put them with the other documents into the trunk they'd brought from London. She clicked its padlock closed and pushed it back into the bottom of the large cupboard in the cellar.

It was midnight before she sat down to write a note to Stella. It wasn't an easy one to write, a lie from start to finish to someone who had been kind to her, but she knew if she simply disappeared, Stella would worry about her and if she heard nothing from her, might even report her missing to the police. This way she could simply say she'd had the chance to bring her plans forward. She drew the paper towards her, hoping the words of explanation would flow, but it was only after several false starts that she remembered with sudden inspiration that tomorrow was Friday, one of the days Stella volunteered with the WVS. She would be out from half past eight until at least lunchtime and maybe all day. Maggie could push the note explaining her hurried departure through Stella's letter box while Stella was out, and by the time she got home again, she, Maggie, would be long gone, so there could be no awkward explanations. Now the words came easily, sliding off her pen onto the paper.

*Dear Stella,*

*I'm so sorry to have missed you, but I thought I'd let you know that there has been a change of plan. I had a note this morning from the landlord of the pub where I'd hoped to work, saying that the couple who he'd taken on had proved unsatisfactory, and that the job was mine if I could get there by this evening. I didn't want to miss the chance and so I've hurriedly packed up our things and Roger and I are off to spend the rest of the war in the country. I'd like to come back sooner but only if the air raids have stopped.*

*Thank you for everything you've done for me, you have been most generous. I have taken the pram with me, but will return it when I come back.*

*One last favour, if you don't mind. I enclose the keys to the house and the flat. Please could you meet with the Shawbrooks at II on Monday morning when they come to move into the flat, and explain why I am not there to hand over the keys myself?*

*Thank you. Roger sends his love and so do I.*

*Maggie*

She read it through and stuffed it into an envelope which she addressed to Stella.

'It'll have to do,' she told the silent flat.

After a few hours' sleep, she was up and about again. She fed and changed Roger, made some sandwiches for her lunch, a bottle and some mashed pear and a packet of rusks for Roger's, and got herself ready to go. She had crammed their few belongings into one holdall which she pushed under the body of the pram and a knapsack which she wore on her back. Her handbag she put in the bottom of the pram with Roger on top of it and her purse was buttoned into the pocket of her coat.

Maggie took one final look around the flat. It was relatively clean and tidy, and she had no more time to make it more so. With a shrug she decided it would have to do. The church clock was striking nine as she manoeuvred the pram out into the street. It was a bright morning, the sun bringing welcome warmth, promising heat later on in the day. There were few people about as she set off along the road towards Stella's house, but no one she recognised to wonder where she was going. When she reached number fifty-three she walked past and looked back at the house. There was no sign of life inside and so, parking the pram behind the wall, she pushed open the gate and hurriedly thrust her envelope through the letter box and then, without a backward glance, she scurried out again and grabbing the handles of the pram, set off quickly towards the station.

If Maggie had looked back she would have seen a pale face at the window. Stella had woken early with a headache pounding behind her eyes and had decided she would not be going to join the other WVS ladies that morning. She had taken an aspirin and crawled back into her bed. When she heard the snap of the letter box she thought it was a knock on the door, and had looked out to see who was there.

Maggie? Was that Maggie? Yes, of course it was, with Roger in the pram. Had she knocked on the door and then hurried away like a naughty child? Perhaps she had suddenly remembered that it was Friday and realised that Stella would have already left to go to the WVS table at the rescue centre. Whatever, there was no point in going downstairs now, and so Stella returned to her bed and drifted off to sleep.

She didn't wake until nearly midday, and when she did, she found her headache had left her. Tea, she thought, that's what I need, and she went down to the kitchen to put the kettle on. As she reached the bottom of the stairs she saw the envelope lying on the mat and stooping to pick it up, she glanced at the inscription before putting it on the table while she filled the kettle.

With her tea made and a piece of toast and marge beside her on a plate, she reached for the envelope. She had recognised Maggie's handwriting and slit it open.

*Dear Stella...*

Stella read it through twice before laying it aside to drink her tea. What was Maggie doing? Why hadn't she come in to say goodbye? Why this odd letter?

When she'd had her toast and tea, Stella went upstairs to dress. She'd take the letter over to Elsie and see what she thought of it.

Elsie was her usual cynical self. 'What did I tell you?' she cried when Stella told her. 'I told you you wouldn't see that pram back. What happens if Harriet has another baby and comes to stay? She'll want her pram, won't she?'

'As far as I know she isn't having another baby!' retaliated Stella. Why did Elsie always try and score points? 'Anyway, she said in her note that she'll be bringing it back when she comes.'

'If she comes.'

'Of course she'll come back,' snapped Stella. 'She owns that house, for goodness' sake!'

'So, what else does she say in her letter? Where has she gone to?'

'She was offered a live-in job in a pub, so she'd be working in the pub and Roger could be upstairs asleep and she need not worry about him. Seems ideal.'

'Where is this pub, then?'

'I don't know,' admitted Stella reluctantly. 'The other side of Exeter, I think, she never actually said.'

'But why did she leave so suddenly?' wondered Elsie.

'She got a message from this place saying they were holding the job open for her provided she could be there by this evening. So she packed up and went.'

'Without saying goodbye? To you who's been her lifeline since her husband died?'

'Well, I expect she thought I'd be at the WVS today and wouldn't be at home, hence the note through the door.'

'She must have had that message from the pub extremely early,' mused Elsie. 'To get it this morning and be packed up and ready to leave by nine o'clock.'

'Well, whatever happened, she's gone,' said Stella. 'I went to the house on my way here.'

'So the Shawbrooks could move in today?' suggested Elsie with a gleam in her eye.

'I suppose so,' agreed Stella uncertainly.

'Well she isn't coming back now, is she? Young Vera's due to be discharged from the hospital soon. David could be already moved in with everything ready for her, couldn't he? The poor man's had nowhere to call his own for over a month now. He's asleep now after last night's duty, but I could tell him when he wakes up. She's left the keys with you, so there'd be no problem getting in early, would there?' A sudden thought struck her. 'Did you go in when you were passing today?'

'No, of course not,' retorted Stella. But if she were honest, she had been sorely tempted to do so, just to check if Maggie really had gone.

'Then I'll tell David the minute he wakes up,' Elsie said. 'He may even want to move in this evening before he goes out to the wardens' post.'

'You can tell him when he wakes, and you can also tell him I'm prepared to give him the keys tomorrow rather than Monday. It's only two extra days, after all. It can't hurt.'

Unless of course Maggie Peterson comes back! thought Elsie, but she certainly didn't share that thought with her friend, Stella. She wanted her lodger gone.

# 25

The next morning Stella went along to Maggie's house. She wanted to have had a look inside to make sure everything was shipshape before she handed over the keys to David Shawbrook. In the hall she met Mrs Clay coming out and instinctively said, 'Good morning.'

Mrs Clay looked at her suspiciously. Surely Mrs Peterson had said it was a man and his daughter. 'Are you the new tenant?' she asked.

'No, Mrs Clay. We've met before. I'm a friend of Mrs Peterson's. Stella Todd. I live at number fifty-three. I've come to open up the flat for the new tenants.' She shook the keys between her forefinger and thumb.

'She's gone then?'

'Yes, she's taken the boy into the country, away from the bombs.'

'Yes, she said,' replied Mrs Clay. 'Well, I can't stand here gossiping all day, I've the marketing to do.' And with that she simply turned and walked out of the hallway into the street, leaving Stella standing at Maggie's front door, key in hand.

When she had unlocked the door of the flat, Stella paused

a moment, feeling awkward. Maggie had given her the keys, but she wasn't supposed to use them until Monday.

'Don't be stupid!' She could hear Elsie's voice in her ear. 'What difference can it make?' Well, it was too late to have second thoughts. By now Elsie would have told David Shawbrook that he could move in today, and he would come knocking on the door in an hour's time. She drew a deep breath and stepped inside.

As she made her way through the silent flat she was suddenly glad that she had come. The flat, though fairly tidy, could have been made much cleaner for the incoming tenant. Maggie said she'd packed in a hurry and there was plenty of evidence of that. In the kitchen the washing up had been done, but though the crockery was clean it was stacked up in a rack on the draining board to dry. In the main bedroom the bed had been stripped, but no clean sheets had been put on the bed. Everywhere else was comparatively tidy, but the furniture needed dusting.

Oh well, thought Stella, I'd better see what I can do to smarten the place up.

By the time Mu arrived, Stella had run the carpet sweeper over the floors, cleaned the kitchen surfaces and put away the china. A bunch of marguerite daisies gathered from the back garden stood in a vase on the kitchen table, and the beds had been made up with fresh sheets from the cupboard.

Mu had arranged to meet her father at the flat, but she'd made a point of arriving some time before he did. She hadn't seen the flat before, and she wanted to be sure that it was a suitable place and not just a stopgap. However, as she walked through the rooms and saw the kitchen, the living room, the main bedroom and the small box room set up with a single bed, she saw there was plenty of room for her father and Vera without them falling over each other. Having the bedrooms on the ground floor would be a great help to Vera until she had finally thrown away her crutches. When Mu saw the cellar and took in the sofa, the tilley lamp and the primus stove she said, 'It looks as if they've been using this as an air-raid shelter.'

'I think they have,' Stella said. 'There was a time when Mrs Peterson hardly left the flat, and she refused to go to one of the public shelters.' Suddenly realising she was on delicate ground she added quickly, 'There is an Anderson out the back, I think.'

'Don't worry Mrs…? I'm sorry, I don't know your name.'

'Todd, Stella Todd.'

'Mrs Todd. I think it will be perfect for my father and sister. They need somewhere they can be together.'

'You aren't going to be living with them, are you?' Stella wondered, thinking that it would be a tight squeeze if she were.

'No, no,' Mu replied with a smile. 'I'm a nurse at the City Hospital and I live in the nurses' home. But I won't be far away if they need me. My sister is being discharged from the hospital today. She's had a broken leg and she's still on crutches, so a flat on the ground floor is perfect for her.'

At that moment there was a ring on the doorbell and opening it Mu found Vera on the doorstep balancing on her crutches while her father paid off the taxi that had brought them to their new home.

'Oh, Vera,' she cried. 'It's wonderful to see you out of the hospital. Come in and see where you're going to live!'

Stella stayed a few moments longer to explain to David why it was she and not Maggie who was giving him the key.

'It was all rather sudden,' she admitted, 'but Mrs Peterson was offered a job outside Exeter and it meant leaving at once.'

'I quite understand,' David said. 'I know she was anxious to take her son to safety in the country. Thank you for standing in for her.'

'Oh, that was no trouble,' Stella said. 'I only live just up the road at number fifty-three.' She turned to Vera who was sitting in an armchair in the living room. 'If you ever need anything, shopping or even just a bit of company, just let me know – I can always pop in.'

'You're very kind,' David said. 'We'll certainly bear that in mind.'

'I don't want that old biddy "popping in"!' complained Vera when they had shut the front door behind their new neighbour. 'I bet she's a nosy parker.'

'Perhaps,' said her father repressively, 'but it was kind of her to offer to help with shopping and such. You're not going to be able to get out and about very easily until you're off your crutches, are you?'

'Don't worry, Vera,' soothed Mu. 'I'll come shopping with you. We need to get you some more clothes for which you'll need some emergency coupons. And a new ration book.'

They had almost no luggage to bring to the flat, David carried all he now owned in one small suitcase and Vera had the few clothes that the hospital had provided from its own supply. Getting their lives back together with all the basics wasn't going to be as easy as it sounded and both

Vera and her father were glad that Mu would be about to help them.

'What was she like? This Mrs Peterson,' Vera asked her father as the three of them shared a pot of tea. 'Doesn't it seem strange to you how suddenly she left?'

'Not really,' he replied. 'As I said, she was keen to take her boy out of the danger area. Her husband had been killed recently in a raid and obviously she was desperate to protect the boy.'

Once she had seen them settled Mu returned to the nurses' home to catch a few hours' sleep before her last night on the wards. Then she had three days off before she would be back on the day shift. When she reached the home she found there was yet another letter waiting for her in her pigeonhole; a large envelope, sent to her by Jean, still in Portsmouth. It was not the first and Mu knew what it contained. She picked it up and hurried up to her room. She slit it open carefully and pulled out the contents, four letters, all with forces' postmarks, all addressed to her care of the Portsmouth nurses' home. Wrapped round them was a scribbled note from Jean.

*Dear Mu*

*I think it's about time you told your chap where you live now, or to stop writing to you. Of course I don't mind sending on his letters from time to time, but surely you must be answering them and should tell him your new address. If you aren't answering them, you should write back at least once and tell him to stop writing, that you don't want to hear from him again. That's only fair. Of course if you don't want to hear from him you only have to tell me and I won't send them on to you any more. I'll just return the next one to him marked 'Gone away!' It's not fair to keep him dangling!*

*Let me know which you want me to do.*

*Love, Jean.*

Mu read the note through again and sighed. She knew that Jean was right. If she didn't want any more letters from Patrick, she should send them back unopened. That would surely stop him writing again. She had told him the day he left that she didn't want him to write to her, and when the first letter came, even before she had moved back to Plymouth, she almost tore it across still in its envelope, but somehow, at the last minute, she just couldn't do it. She buried it in her bedside drawer and tried to put it out of her mind. As others arrived, most of them following her to Plymouth sent on by the kindly Jean, she had added them, unopened and unread to the growing pile in her bedside table.

Despite her determination to forget him and all thoughts of marriage, Patrick was never far from her mind.

He must realise by now that I'm not going to answer them, she thought, as she looked at this latest offering of four more letters. So why does he keep on writing? It's nearly two months since HMS *Cumbria* sailed out of Portsmouth, surely he knows that I haven't changed my mind; that my father and sister need me more than he does. That my place is with them. With Tony, we're the only family we each have now, and we don't even know if he's still alive. As far as we know he's in North Africa and sounds as if the fighting is pretty desperate over there.

'Oh, Patrick,' she cried in anguish, 'what am I going to do?' She picked up the letters that Jean had sent and looked at them. If she opened one she knew she would open them all. Her resolution would dissolve. Carefully she put them back into her drawer, adding the latest batch and Jean's very sensible letter to the pile. As before, she would try and put Patrick out of her mind. She would help Dad look after Vera until she was able to get about easily by herself. She would keep working at the hospital, of course, and she would try and help them rebuild some sort of life out of the ruins of Parham Road shelter. The future was far too uncertain to make any plans. The war had to be won first, and that was looking increasingly unlikely in the near future. The Battle of Britain had been won, the RAF had survived, but the Blitz had destroyed and was still destroying cities all over the country. The worst was perhaps over, but there was still the battle for the seas to be won. German U-boats were decimating shipping in the convoys from North America. Unless they, bringing in precious food and other resources, could sail in safety across the Atlantic, the country, so brave in the air and under the bombers, might still be starved into submission and all that death and destruction would have been for nothing.

Patrick was still at sea as far as she knew, but where? And what danger was he in?

With a sigh she undressed and climbed into bed. She must get some rest before going onto the ward tonight, and resolutely she closed her eyes. At last she slept, but there in her dreams was Patrick.

# 26

Patrick Davenham was looking out across the grey swell, scanning the horizon where the sea merged into the gunmetal of the sky. Despite being early June, the evening was cold. He was cold, but it was almost the end of the watch. Able Seaman Rafferty came up from below carrying a steaming mug in his hand.

'Cocoa, sir?'

Patrick took the drink gratefully, warming his hands about the mug. 'Thank you, Rafferty. It's brass monkeys out here.'

For a long moment both men stared out across the sea; a seemingly endless ocean of shifting water.

When she had sailed from Portsmouth, HMS *Cumbria* had headed out into the south-western approaches to join other naval vessels that were escorting convoys of merchant ships crossing from North America. In the weeks that followed they had patrolled the waters off the west coast of Britain, searching for the U-boats that were intent on destroying the incoming ships before they could reach safe haven and discharge their valuable cargos. Every man aboard *Cumbria* was well aware that they were a vital part of the war at sea. Such convoys were the lifeline that was keeping Britain supplied both with food and armaments and no one, British or German, underestimated the importance of their safe arrival. Hunting singly or in wolf packs, the German submarines sought the convoys, circling to attack and even on occasion sneaking undetected amongst the ships where they could attack both the merchantmen, their true targets, and their escorts.

In the few weeks they had been at sea, Patrick had seen more action than ever before. *Cumbria* had had several near misses with torpedoes snaking harmlessly past her bows, to disappear into the sea, but on several occasions, though *Cumbria* escaped, some of the ships being shepherded into safer waters had not been so lucky. Some were able to limp onward, but two had been sunk and *Cumbria* had had to pause to pick up survivors who had jumped for their lives into the icy water. Some of these men were rescued as they clung to anything which would float; covered in oil and filthy from smoke they were dragged from the surging waves which threatened to overwhelm them. Others simply drifted away, never to be seen again, their struggle to survive the continual buffeting of the sea to no avail.

Patrick envied the stoical courage of the men they managed to save as they clung to and clambered up the scrambling net let down over *Cumbria*'s side. Exhausted, frightened, cold and filthy, it was their dogged determination combined with a huge dose of luck which had kept them alive. Occasionally Patrick wondered how he would fare should *Cumbria* herself take a fatal hit. Unproductive thinking, he told himself firmly; either he would survive or he wouldn't, no point in meeting trouble head on... sufficient unto the day...

Now, as the twilight was deepening to darkness, the two men stood together for a moment, staring out across the swelling sea. In the far distance the convoy they were meeting was starting to emerge, little more than smudges against the last of the evening sky.

'Don't like it, sir,' Rafferty remarked. 'It's all too quiet.'

'That's the way I do like it!' Patrick replied, as he downed the last of his cocoa and swept his binoculars yet again across the sea. Nothing. As the darkness deepened, faint starlight provided feeble luminescence, but there was nothing to see.

Rafferty, picking up the empty cocoa mug, turned towards the companion way. Suddenly he heard an all too familiar sound, and spun back to stare out over the sea. Seconds later Patrick heard it too, the unmistakable hiss of an incoming torpedo, speeding through the waves. At that moment the alarm was given with the call to action stations. The ship came suddenly alive. Men came tumbling out of their bunks, their cabins, leaving their other duties, each sprinting to his individual action station at gun or lookout or, as with Patrick, aft with the depth charge crew. Here, over the stern, they would be dropping their depth charges, hoping to blow the stealthy submarine out of the water. The hissing torpedo passed harmlessly by, but another, unseen, was already on the way, coming from a different direction.

Patrick and his crew loaded their depth charges on the rack ready to roll into the sea behind the ship once a target had been identified. Above and forward on the bridge, Commander Rees was giving orders as the ship began to zigzag through the waves. The lookouts could see nothing, but the ping of the Asdic warned of an underwater target; the presence of danger below.

Signals were sent to the approaching convoy, warning of the enemy U-boats lying in wait. It was the last signal the convoy commander received from HMS *Cumbria* as she took the inbound torpedo amidships, a direct hit on an ammunition magazine. The resultant explosion shook the whole ship, ripping through her, breaking her back and tossing debris into the air and into the water. Fire burst from the depths of her hull, and men, with burning clothes, hair, arms and legs, flung themselves into the water in desperate attempts to quench the flames consuming their bodies. Thick black smoke belched across the sea obscuring *Cumbria*'s death throes, leaving the rest of the convoy, still steaming forward shepherded by their escorts, to guess at her destruction and the fate of her men.

The klaxon blared the order to abandon ship. Every man for himself. And so they jumped into the oily water still roiling from the explosion, trying desperately to swim away from the sinking ship, terrified of being drawn under with her as she finally shuddered and slid beneath the sea; her watery grave a resting place for more than half her ship's company, leaving the rest floundering in the sudden darkness of the sea as the blaze from her fires was extinguished.

Patrick had echoed the order to abandon ship to his depth charge crew and as they leaped out over the stern, he glanced back to see Able Seaman Rafferty, standing frozen beside the rack of unlaunched depth charges, his face white, the light of the approaching flames flickering across his face.

'Rafferty!' Patrick bellowed. 'Jump, man!'

'Can't swim, sir.'

'Time to learn,' shouted Patrick and grabbed the man bodily into his arms, hauling them both over the stern into the slickness of the water. For a moment they sank, their heads well below the waves. Rafferty clung to Patrick, almost drowning him in the process, but Patrick was a strong swimmer and kicking hard he managed to drag them both to the surface, their faces breaking out into the air for the few moments needed to gulp more air into their lungs before they found themselves dragged down into water that sucked and boiled about the sinking ship. It was enough. Patrick had seen a light bobbing on the water, and realised it must be a Carley life raft from the ship, floating free; an oval of buoyant hope with several men already clinging to it for dear life. Forcing them both back to the surface, Patrick struck out towards the raft. Rafferty was now inert and so Patrick turned onto his back and with an arm under the man's arms supported his head and towed him over to the floating raft. Even as he reached it, one of the sailors clinging to an outside rope let go and drifted away, face down in the water. His place was immediately grabbed by another. There were at least twelve men already crammed into the raft, and Patrick realised they were going to have to take turns both inside the raft and outside in the water. It was summer, but the June sun had done little to warm the ocean. The light Patrick had seen was a torch pulled from the raft's survival kit, and by its light he could see Petty Officer Pitt already installed in the raft and called to him.

'Get this man on board, Pitt. He's unconscious.'

'Have to take his turn, sir,' replied the PO. 'Probably

won't make it anyway, by the look of him. Better to give a fit man a chance.'

'Pull him inboard,' Patrick ordered. 'If he doesn't regain consciousness before it's his turn for the water again, well, so be it!'

Arms reached out for the unconscious Rafferty and he was hauled into the life raft, Patrick pushing him up from the water. There was no room for Patrick himself, either inside the raft or in the water clinging to the ropes that hung over its sides, and having made sure Rafferty was aboard, he found himself drifting away. There were voices all round him, men calling for help, clutching any debris that floated as they struggled to remain afloat in the darkness. As the darkness claimed them all Patrick began to see other pinpricks of light and realised that some of the other life rafts must have been swept from *Cumbria*'s upper deck as she went down; other floats were out there on the water offering tenuous hope to those who'd escaped the ship. But even as his eyes adjusted to the faint luminescence, all he could see were indistinct shapes, impossible to tell how near or far they might be.

Patrick could feel his clothes weighing him down, and his instinct was to try and discard them, but his head told him that even wet clothes were giving him some protection from the cold and he overcame the temptation. The sea was still turbulent from the explosion and as he rose on the waves and fell back into the troughs, Patrick saw other bodies floating, lifeless, simply drifting with the motion of the ocean.

What a way to die, he thought. He knew the convoy would still steam on towards them, but he also knew it would be too late to pick up more than a few survivors, if any. The U-boats were still lying in wait, and though with the sinking of *Cumbria* they had signalled their intention and lost the element of surprise, the incoming fleet would still have to run the gauntlet of the submarines.

He swam towards one of the bobbing lights, hoping for space in a float or a rope to cling to. The exercise helped him generate a little warmth, but the raft was drifting too fast for him to catch up. He trod water for a while, but that was exhausting and he turned on his back and allowed himself to float. He could still hear voices calling out across the water, but they seemed incredibly far away.

He thought about his beloved Mu, the love of his life. Would she ever know what had become of him? She'd hear that *Cumbria* had been sunk and most of the ship's company with her. She'd know he was one of those who had perished, either caught on board or in the water afterwards. She would never know for sure. Would she wonder? Would she think of him fondly and then move on with her life?

Before he had embarked that last day in Portsmouth, he had written to his parents in Glasgow and told them he had met the girl he was going to marry.

*You'll love her too*, he'd written. *She's agreed to marry me, but it won't be for some time, probably the end of the war*, and from there he had gone on to explain the dreadful loss of her family. *I shall write to her all the time while I'm away, but, please, if the worst should happen and I don't come home again, please will you tell her how much I loved her. Tell her that she must find someone else and live her life to the full for my sake. It is you, of course, who are named as my next of kin, so it'll be you who learn what has happened to me, so if necessary please tell her and give her my message.* He went on to give them her address at the nurses' home where he had been writing himself.

As he drifted further and further away, something bumped against his head, and turning he found himself being nudged by a corpse, floating face down in the water. Instinctively he pushed the man away, but thought, even as he did so, That'll be me very soon, drifting dead in the sea. Oh, my darling Mu, my last thoughts will be of you.

## 27

Maggie settled into the cottage at Martindell very quickly. Nothing had been ready for them when they arrived, but as the colonel explained, 'The memsahib wasn't expecting you until after the weekend.'

Maggie assured him that it didn't matter and leaving Roger in the care of Mrs Bridger, she and the colonel made several journeys to the cottage with the bare necessities she would need for the first night.

'Merton should be here tomorrow,' said the colonel. 'He'll be coming up to water the vegetables, so we can ask him to help with the extra furniture.'

When they finally got back to the house, they found Mrs Bridger sitting in an armchair, fast asleep, with Roger curled up in the dog basket with the colonel's spaniel, also fast asleep.

With a cry of alarm, Maggie swooped on the child, making him cry as she grabbed him from the dog's bed. The spaniel didn't move, simply offered the faint wag of her tail.

'Oh, you don't have to worry about her,' the colonel tried to reassure Maggie. 'Flopsie wouldn't hurt a fly.' He reached down and stroked her head. 'Would you, my pet?'

'She was supposed to be looking after him!' Maggie exclaimed, glaring at the sleeping Mrs Bridger.

'Well, he's quite all right,' returned the colonel, 'so no harm done, eh?' He crossed to where his wife was snoring softly and with great gentleness shook her awake.

She sat up with a jolt and looked about her, confused.

'Who's here?' she said. She peered at Maggie. 'Who are you?'

'This is Mrs Peterson,' the colonel told her. He turned to Maggie and asked, 'Would it be all right if she addressed you as Margaret? I think she'd remember that better.'

Maggie shrugged. 'Maggie, if she wants to.'

'Her name is Maggie, my dear. She's come to help us in the house. I think she's going to cook us some supper,' he added hopefully.

Maggie hitched Roger onto her hip and said, 'Well, I'd better look in the larder then, hadn't I? Where's the kitchen?'

Half an hour later they all sat down to a meal of thick vegetable soup, made from potatoes, carrots and some cabbage that Maggie had found in the cold safe in the pantry. There was some stale-looking bread in a crockery pot and a whole pound of butter which she found hidden in another crock with a lid.

'Where did you get this?' she demanded.

'Farm down the road,' said the colonel cheerfully. 'Swapped it for some vegetables. We all swap round here. Can't live on what the government give us, can we?'

So Maggie became part of the household and they had soon established a routine. She and Roger would come over from the cottage first thing in the morning and Maggie would prepare some sort of breakfast. When Bill Merton came up to do the garden, he brought his fourteen-year-old daughter, Josie, with him and she took over the care of Roger, while Maggie set to work to bring some sort of order to the house.

'Mad as a basket of ferrets,' Merton said that first morning with a nod at the house. 'He still got most of his marbles, but her, the memsahib, she's away with the fairies. Sometimes she thinks she's back in India and starts ordering the servants about.'

'Servants? What servants?' demanded Maggie.

'Exactly!' cried Bill. 'S'what I mean, see? She don't know if she's coming or going. Some days she'll be wandering round the place, looking for her daughter, what's been dead these ten years. If she asks you where Edwina is, it's best to answer, "She gone down to the village, madam. She won't be long." That usually soothes her. I used to think that neither of 'em was long for this world and here they are, her and the colonel. She's spry enough in the body and feeble in the head and with him 'tis t'other way about.'

Maggie got to like Bill Merton and as the days passed she gradually learned his life history. In his late forties, he had survived the last year of the Great War and come home with shrapnel in his leg, to marry his childhood sweetheart Doris. When at last she was expecting a long-awaited child, Doris had died giving birth to their daughter, Josie, leaving him to bring her up on his own.

'Wouldn't have minded getting married again,' he confided to Maggie one morning as they sat over their elevenses. 'But you got to find the right person, haven't you? Can't just live with anyone, can you? Specially not if you're set in your ways.'

With Josie to look after Roger, the two of them set about keeping Martindell Manor running. Maggie soon learned the ways of the local 'swapping' scheme, though had she been asked she might have described it as the black market. Very little money ever changed hands, but a fair amount of food substitution took place.

Maggie had registered their ration books with the shops in the village, and using the Bridgers' coupons as well, she managed to keep them all fed.

Mrs Bridger got used to having her about the house, and though she seldom called her by the right name, she ceased asking her who she was or what she was doing.

The colonel knew the answers to both those questions and he couldn't believe his luck that they had at last found someone who was prepared to stay and look after them. Maggie was worth her weight in gold. What did it matter if occasional things went missing? There was food on the table, the house was clean – at least the parts that they actually lived in were – and the memsahib was calmer and more rational than she had been for some time.

When Maggie retired to the tiny bedroom she and Roger shared in the cottage each night, she was relaxed and slept well. Here in Martindell she felt safe. If anyone was looking for her or Roger, they weren't going to find either of them here. She had taken him to the safety of the country as a wise mother would, and by the time they returned to Plymouth, the war would be over and no one would remember anything about a missing baby. It would simply be one of the many wartime casualties; sad, but in the main forgotten. Then she would sell the house and move away and her escape would be complete. In the meantime, her existence here at the manor was comfortable, the work not too onerous and there were no air raids. She had learned to handle the colonel and the memsahib easily enough; a threat to leave would ensure she got her own way and as long as they were fed, they made few demands on her.

Bill Merton watched her taking over the household and for the first time for years he wondered if he were too old to think of marrying again. Josie would soon be grown up and getting married herself and he had no wish to condemn himself to a lonely old age. Maggie might do very nicely, and the little lad was fond of Josie. A nice little family they could be if she was willing. All he knew was that her husband had been killed in an air raid a few months ago, so it was far too soon to suggest anything like that yet, but the more Bill thought of it, the more he liked the idea. It was, he told himself, just a question of biding his time.

# 28

The letter from Glasgow that was waiting for Mu when she got in from the hospital was completely unexpected. It had been forwarded from Portsmouth as had her other letters, Jean's familiar scrawl across the envelope redirecting it, but she didn't know the original handwriting. Indeed, she didn't know anyone in Glasgow, but it was addressed to her, with the right spelling of her name, and she took it up to her room to open.

One look at the contents and her heart seemed to come to a stop. It was signed Michael Davenham and, in brackets, *(Patrick's father)*. The letter was brief and very much to the point.

*My dear Miss Shawbrook,*

*It is with much regret that I write to tell you that HMS Cumbria, the ship on which my son Patrick was serving was torpedoed and sunk off the coast of Cornwall last week. Most of the ship's company perished and I am sorry to tell you that Patrick was one of them. Before he sailed last time, he wrote and told us that he had met you and he hoped you would be married at the end of the war. He asked us to contact you should there ever be news like this.*

*He asked us to say how much he loved you and that should he not return, he hoped you would be able to find someone else and live your life to the full. I did not write sooner in the hope that we might hear that somehow he survived the sinking, but a fellow officer and friend who was rescued has written to say that he saw him in the water, supporting one of his comrades, but he was not among those who were later picked up.*

*In our own grief we sympathise with yours.*

*Yours faithfully,*

*Michael Davenham (Patrick's father)*

Mu stared down at the letter, its handwriting now obscured by her tears. She could hardly breathe, and she collapsed onto her bed.

Patrick! Her beloved Patrick. He was dead and he was never coming back to her. He had died helping another man and now he was at the bottom of the sea with the ship he had loved so much. Now she would never see his face again and she hadn't even got a photo of him. She lay on the bed, the tears coursing down her cheeks, unable to stop the flow, her heaving sobs wracking her whole body. She had sent Patrick away, and now he was gone for ever. Never coming back. Never. Never. She would never see him again, or feel his arms around her, or feel his lips on hers. Never. Never. The despairing word rebounded in her brain. She had received his letters, but she had stubbornly refused to open them. He had continued to write to her despite her lack of replies; because he loved her he had written to his parents and told them about her and had asked them to contact her if the worst occurred. And now it had, what she had always dreaded: that yet another person she'd dared to love had been taken from her by this vicious war.

Mu stayed in her room and cried until she had no more tears, until her throat ached and her head thumped and her face and her eyes were swollen and red.

She had decided that very afternoon that she would, after all, open Patrick's letters. If he were asking her to reconsider, to see him again when he next had leave, she would say yes. Her father and Vera had each other now, she would be there for them as well, but they no longer needed her undivided attention. The pain from the loss of her family had not diminished, but working in the hospital and helping her father and sister had helped her to manage it. But now another blow had come to sideswipe her.

The day on the ward had been long and arduous and she needed to sleep, but though exhaustion hit her, she felt that she would never sleep again.

Finding a handkerchief, she sat up, blew her nose hard and scrubbed her eyes. She turned her tear-soaked pillow over and got up from the bed. Patrick was not coming back, there would be no 'next leave' but she, Mu, had to go on with life tomorrow and the next day and the next day and for ever without him. She would have to write back to his father, but that could wait for a while. Somehow she would have to find the words for her reply, for the sympathy owed to Patrick's parents, but not now, not yet.

Mu stayed in her room, not joining the others for their evening meal. When Betsy Harper, a colleague on the same ward, tapped on the door, she simply called through that she was going straight to bed as she had a headache.

For the next couple of days Mu worked like an automaton. She arrived at the ward spruce and ready to work, on time, but then went home to bed. She did not go to Marden Road to visit her father and sister. She couldn't burden them with yet more misery and she knew that if she told them what had happened and they showered her with sympathy, it would be her undoing. After a couple of days, she managed to write back to Patrick's parents, somehow expressing her sympathy for their loss, without intruding her own grief.

When she got home from her shift each evening, she retired to her room and gradually read all Patrick's letters. She set them out in date order, from the first, the very day he had left her in the Royal Oak, and worked her way slowly through them. There were a dozen all together, each of them telling her how much he loved her and missed her; how he was longing for the day when he could return her engagement ring and they could plan their future together. Never once did he mention the decision she had made that morning in the Royal Oak. He always wrote as if they were still engaged and only separated by the war. In each letter he wrote a little of his daily life on board, but with no mention of any action in which the ship had been involved. He made no suggestion of any engagement with the enemy, no hint that they had even been in any particular danger since they had sailed out of Portsmouth that night. She could hear his voice in the words he had written, see his smile through the endearments, and each letter ended with the same words: *Remember how much I love you, darling Mu. Remember you are mine and that I am counting the days until we can be together again.*

*Yours for ever, Patrick.*

Yours for ever, Patrick. Only now he wasn't, and never would be, *hers for ever.*

Tucked into one of the early letters was a small photograph, just a snap of him leaning on a ship's rail and smiling back over his shoulder, smiling at her. Mu would have carried it with her, but unable to do so when on duty, she bought a small frame and placed it by her bed where she could see it last thing before she turned out the light and first thing in the morning.

A few days later there was another raid on Plymouth, not much more than a quick sortie from over the sea, a flurry of bombs and an equally quick departure. David Shawbrook was on duty at the wardens' post and Vera was alone in the Marden Road flat. She still used her crutches if she was going any distance, but she had already decided that she wasn't going to leave the building if there was a raid, not even to go out to the Anderson shelter in the back garden. No, she would stay in the flat, simply decamping to the basement which was already fitted out as a shelter.

'If there's another raid,' she said to her father, 'I promise I'll go down into the cellar. After all, it's been used as a shelter before. Nothing will make me go anywhere else.'

David had accepted this. He knew Vera couldn't venture out into the streets alone yet, and that nothing would induce her to take cover in a public shelter like the one in Parham

Road. She would have to take her chances in the Marden Road cellar.

So that night, when the sirens started wailing, she made her way carefully down the stairs. Once she had closed the door she was able to switch on the lights and she settled down with her book. She knew she wouldn't sleep until the raid was over and, unable to get comfortable on the sofa, she got up and practised her walking using only a stick. She was determined to get rid of her crutches as quickly as she could. Slowly she walked across the room to the window, set high in the wall and covered with a blackout curtain, then she turned back and walked to the bookcase against the far wall. Her leg was aching, but she was determined to do five laps of this course. It was as she was completing the fourth that she noticed something poking out from behind the bookcase; a piece of black cloth, just a corner showing, caught between the wall and the wooden base of the bookcase. Vera finished her five laps and as she returned to the sofa, she paused and bent down to retrieve whatever it was trapped against the skirting. It felt soft and fluffy and as she pulled at it she realised that it was a soft toy.

She remembered that the woman who had let them the flat had a little boy, and guessed that it must be one of his, lost behind the furniture. One final pull and it came free, Vera almost falling backwards with the sudden release. She stared at what she was holding in her hand and gave a cry. It was a panda bear, sporting a purple ribbon around his neck.

Vera stared at it for a long moment and then raised it to her cheek, breathing in the familiar dusty smell. Pandy, it was Pandy, the toy from which Freddie would not be parted. At least, she reasoned, it couldn't be Freddie's Pandy; after all, there must be hundreds like him all over the country. But how strange that the baby who lived here had had one identical to Freddie's. The thought of Freddie, still missing, brought tears to her eyes. Mu had said he must be out there somewhere, that he'd definitely been rescued from the house, but so far they had no clue as to where.

'Are you a clue?' she asked the bear. 'I'll show you to Mu next time she comes round, and see what she thinks.'

She could show him to Dad, of course, when he got home, but he probably wouldn't recognise Pandy anyway. But to her surprise David did.

'That looks like the panda bear Freddie had, doesn't it. Where did that come from? Did you bring it with you?'

'No, Dad, I had nothing to bring, did I? I found it here, in the flat. It was behind the bookcase in the cellar, but,' she went on with a sigh, 'there must hundreds like him, don't you think?'

David nodded. 'Probably,' he said. 'Well, we'll see what Mu says, but I doubt if it has anything to do with our Freddie, you know, so don't get your hopes up.'

Next day was Mu's rest day and she couldn't put off going to Marden Road any longer. When she got there she was greeted by an excited Vera. Having lain awake much of the previous night she had now convinced herself that the panda was indeed Pandy.

Mu looked at the grubby bear with his purple ribbon. 'It's just like him,' she conceded, 'but Freddie wouldn't be the only baby who had one, you know.'

'I do know,' said Vera. 'But if you look, Mu, you can see where his ear got torn and Mam sewed it back on. Remember when the dog next door got him? Poor Pandy was minus an ear for a couple of days and then Angel found it in the street? Mam sewed it on. See!' She thrust the toy back into Mu's hands. 'Look, she used white cotton even for the black bits.'

Mu did remember the story although she had not been living at home when Pandy had fallen prey to the dog.

'But the woman who lives here, she's got a baby, hasn't she?' asked Mu. 'So this panda is probably his.'

'With a sewn-on ear?' demanded Vera. 'Did a dog eat his panda, too? We need to go back to the police and tell them what we've found.'

'I think they'll think we're wasting their time,' Mu said. 'They'll say what you said, that there must be hundreds of these toys about.'

'But not with a mended ear, Mu. Won't you go back to the police and at least tell them about it?'

'No,' replied Mu firmly, but she could see how wound up Vera was and relented slightly. 'But I'll tell you what I will do. I will go back to the boy who was with the policeman who rescued him and I'll ask him if Pandy was rescued with Freddie, all right? If he wasn't, well that's an end to it, but if he was…'

'You'll go back to the police?'

'If he says the bear came out of the house with Freddie, I'll go and see them again.'

'Promise?'

'Promise.'

'Today?'

'All right, today.' After all, Mu thought, what else have I got to do but think about Patrick? This will at least give me something to pass the time.

'What does Dad think?'

'He said it's very like Pandy,' Vera replied, not prepared to express her father's doubts in case Mu changed her mind. He was asleep, so he couldn't be asked for his opinion before Mu went to find young Ernie.

'So, will you go and find him, the boy? What was his name?'

'Ernie Drake.'

'Ernie.'

'He'll be at school until this afternoon,' Mu pointed out.

'I expect he'll go home for his dinner,' Vera said. 'You might catch him then.'

'So I might,' agreed Mu. 'All right, I'll go and I'll come back and tell you what he says.'

Vera was right, Ernie did come home from school to have his midday meal. When she knocked on the Drakes' front door it was Ernie himself who came and opened it.

'Hello, Ernie, is your mum at home?'

Ernie recognised her at once as the lady who was looking for the missing baby, the lady who'd given him a whole ten shillings, that Mum had let him keep.

'Hello, miss.' He beamed at her. 'Yes, she's at home. D'you want to come in?'

'If she doesn't mind.'

Ernie looked over his shoulder and called, 'It's the lady what's lost the baby, Mum, can she come in?'

Jane Drake appeared immediately, wiping her hands on a cloth.

'Miss Shawbrook, of course you can come in. You'll have to excuse the place, I'm just clearing the dinner off the table.'

'I'm sorry if I've interrupted your meal,' Mu said.

'You haven't. We've finished. Come into the front room.'

The niceties must be preserved, so once again Mu followed Jane into the front room and accepted a seat on the sofa. 'I just wanted to ask Ernie a couple more questions if I may. I won't keep you long.'

'Of course.' Jane turned to Ernie who was standing in the doorway, not sure if he should come in. Remembering the ten shilling note, he was happy to answer anything she wanted to ask him.

'Ernie,' Mu began. 'Ernie, when the policeman carried the baby out of the house, did he bring anything else with him?'

'No, miss, he didn't.'

'You're quite sure? No clothes or anything for the child?' Ernie shook his head. 'No, nothink, miss.'

'Thank you, Ernie, that's all I needed to know.'

'Nothink,' Ernie repeated, thinking it was the answer she was looking for, and then added, ''Cept for the panda. He dropped that in the gutter an' I picked it up to give back to the baby, but 'e'd cried 'imself to sleep, so the cop stuffed it in 'is pocket. But 'e didn't bring nothink else. No clothes nor nothink.'

'But he did bring the bear?'

'Yeah. Black and white with a purple ribbon round its neck. It was grubby, mind, but I 'spect the kid was fond of it, like, so he took it just in case.'

'You quite sure, Ern?' asked his mother. 'Not making up stories?' She, too, remembered the ten shilling note.

'No, honest, Mum, the cop put it in his pocket.'

Mu beamed at him. 'Thank you, Ernie. Again, you've been a great help.' She put her hand in her pocket and retrieved the two half-crowns she put ready. As they clinked in her hand Ernie held out his.

'Ernie!' reproved his mother, 'what do you think you're doing?'

Ernie hurriedly dropped his hand, but Mu took it in hers and opening his palm placed the two half-crowns into it.

'You've earned these, Ernie,' she said, and turning to Jane said, 'Please let him accept them, Mrs Drake. What he's told me today is of great importance.'

Ernie spun round to face his mother and with reluctance she nodded, and immediately he pocketed the coins. It wasn't ten shillings this time, but five was still worth having.

Mu's next stop was the police station. Inspector Droy wasn't there, but Constable Sharpe came as soon as he was told who was at the desk.

'Miss Shawbrook,' he said. 'What can I do for you?'

'It's a bit complicated,' Mu said awkwardly.

'Well, why don't you come through here and you can tell me what's so complicated.' He led the way down a corridor to a small room at the end, furnished simply with a table and two chairs. He set one of these for Mu and took the other.

'Now then, how can I help you?'

'It's a bit complicated...' repeated Mu.

'Yes, you said. Can you uncomplicate it and explain?'

'Yes, of course.' Mu pulled herself together. She had been so surprised when Ernie had volunteered the panda, entirely unprompted, that she had immediately kept her promise to Vera and gone to the police station without thinking everything through.

'My father and sister have just moved into a flat in Marden Road. The lady who owns it has taken her son out into the country to escape the bombs. Which is sensible really. The thing is, the other night my sister Vera was alone in the flat and during that raid went down to shelter in the cellar.'

'I see,' said Andy Sharpe, 'and...?'

'And she found this panda teddy. It was just like the one that baby Freddie used to take everywhere with him.'

'And she thinks it might be his.' It was a statement, not a question.

'She does. She's convinced herself that it is. We've pointed out that there must be hundreds of them about and they probably all have purple ribbons.'

'Purple ribbons?'

'It's a black and white panda bear with a purple ribbon... And I heard today from the little boy who was with the policeman who found our Freddie, that he brought out a panda like that when he rescued the child. Ernie, the boy, saw it.'

'Miss Shawbrook, may I ask you one question before you go any further?'

'Yes, of course. What is it?'

'Can you tell me the address of the flat where your sister found this toy?'

'Thirty-four Marden Road,' said Mu promptly.

'And the name of the lady who used to live there?'

'A Mrs Peterson, I think.' Mu sounded unsure.

'Then I'm afraid it isn't your little brother's panda.'

'But how can you be so sure?' cried Mu. 'It's identical, and even has a mended ear like Freddie's did.'

'Maybe it has,' replied the constable, 'but you see we did question Mrs Peterson about her son, because we think it was her husband who brought the boy out of the house. Within days he was killed in an air raid, so we don't know where he took the baby.'

'But don't you see, he could have taken it home with him, and the panda too, and when he was killed his wife just kept the baby.'

'That might have been a possibility,' agreed Andy Sharpe, 'and I have to tell you, in confidence, that it was one we have been looking into, but we have irrefutable evidence that the baby she has is her own son. I'm sorry to dash—'

'Evidence?' interrupted Mu. 'What evidence?'

'When I spoke to her about her husband and asked if he had mentioned anything to her about rescuing a baby, she said no, he had not. I wasn't quite convinced, and she saw that I wasn't, she challenged me and maintained that she had the child, Roger's, birth certificate.'

'Did you ask to see it?'

'No, I had no right to do any such thing.'

'Why not?' demanded Mu. 'If you had asked you'd have called her bluff!'

Andy Sharpe shook his head. 'No,' he said. 'I wouldn't, because she has one. We've had it checked at Somerset House in London. Roger Colin Peterson was born to parents, Colin and Margaret, née Wilson, on the twenty-ninth of July 1940. Mrs Peterson's baby is hers... not your missing Freddie.'

'I see,' Mu said flatly. 'Well, that's that!'

'I'm sorry to dash your hopes, Miss Shawbrook,' he said.

Mu got to her feet. 'Well, I did feel it was too much of a

coincidence, but my sister, Vera, she's going to be desperately disappointed. She's so sure the toy was Freddie's.'

'Perhaps it was,' said the constable. 'If it was Sergeant Peterson who rescued your baby, he might have taken the bear home with him in his pocket and finding it there later, given it to his own son.'

Mu sighed. 'It's going to be a difficult job convincing my sister Vera of that,' she said. 'It's her son we're looking for.'

'Her son?' echoed Andy Sharpe. 'I thought it was her brother... and yours!'

'Vera was very young when she had him,' Mu explained. 'At the time our parents decided to bring him up as their own, to save her reputation, but that doesn't matter any more. All she wants is to find him and bring him up herself.'

'And now her reputation doesn't matter?'

'The war has changed everything,' replied Mu. 'It's turned everything topsy-turvy, and you find out what's really important in life.' She looked across at the young constable opposite her and added, 'Poor Vera is going to be very disappointed when I tell her what you've told me. I suppose... No, it's not fair to ask.'

'Ask what?'

'Ask you to come with me and tell her? She made me promise to come into the police station, and I have, but the news that the baby who owns the panda really is Mrs Peterson's son is going to hit her hard.'

Andy Sharpe smiled at her. 'I'm off duty in half an hour,' he said. 'I'll come with you then if you like.'

## 29

Half an hour later, Mu and Constable Andy Sharpe walked back to Marden Road together. Andy knew that Mu was a nurse at the City Hospital, and he thought that her patients were lucky to have such an attractive woman to look after them.

'You haven't moved in with your father and sister?' he asked.

Mu shook her head. 'No,' she replied, 'I live in the nurses' home. Much more convenient all round. Anyway, there wouldn't be room for me in that flat, there are only two bedrooms,' adding as an afterthought, 'I thought you'd been there.'

'I have, on a couple of occasions; soon after Colin, Mrs Peterson's husband, was killed,' he replied. 'But I hadn't met her until then. They were comparatively new to the city. I don't think they'd made many friends. Colin was well-liked at the station, but we never saw anything of his wife.'

Mu led the way up the steps to the front door and Vera opened it to her knock. Her eyes widened when she saw the tall constable, still in uniform, standing on the doorstep with her sister.

'Have you found him?' she cried. 'Have you got news?'

'Vera, at least let us get in the door,' exclaimed Mu. 'This is Constable Sharpe, who's come to talk to you. He'll be able to tell you everything.'

'Andy,' put in the constable, holding out his hand. 'Andy Sharpe.'

'Well, come in then and tell me. Did you see the boy, Ernie, Mu? Is it Pandy?'

'It looks as if it might be,' Mu answered. 'Ernie said they did rescue Pandy at the same time as Freddie and—'

'I knew it,' shrieked Vera. 'I knew it was Freddie's.'

'But it doesn't prove Freddie was here,' Mu said firmly. 'Look, let's all sit down and let Constable Sharpe—'

'Andy.'

'Let Andy explain what he thinks has happened.'

'All right!' Vera turned her attention to Andy. 'Tell me,' she said.

Andy Sharpe explained as gently as he could about the birth certificate, the reason why they knew that Roger Peterson wasn't Freddie.

'We had it checked,' he said. 'Just in case.'

'What made you check?' Vera demanded fiercely. 'Why didn't you just believe her?'

The question seemed to give Andy pause, and he hesitated.

'Well?' prompted Vera. 'What made you check? Why didn't you take her word?'

'I'm not sure,' Andy replied. 'It was a combination of things, really. I'd seen her with the boy, and she was struggling. She had none of the things you'd expect a mother with a baby to have. No pram or pushchair, not even a cot.

At the station we had a whip-round for her and she bought a cot, and a lady down the road lent her a pram. After that things were easier for her, but I wondered how she had been managing until then.'

'So, what else?' Vera asked.

'Well, the boy was about the right age, and when your sister first came into the station to explain that Freddie was missing, she mentioned that he had red hair,' he glanced across at Mu, 'the same sort of colour as hers, and I remembered that Mrs Peterson's son had red hair as well. When we heard it was a police sergeant that had rescued the boy from your house in Suffolk Place, we wondered if it had been Colin Peterson. It was the kind of thing he would do, go into a ruined house to save a life, but of course by then he'd been killed himself, so we couldn't ask him. I'd met Mrs Peterson more than once by then, so Inspector Droy asked me to come and speak to her and ask if her husband had mentioned anything about rescuing a baby, or hearing of someone else doing so. She said no, he'd told her nothing like that.

'She was feeding her son at the time and it struck me that he was about the same age as your Freddie and I asked how old he was. She said he was nine months, and I said that he was about the same age as the missing baby and a copper knob too. I hadn't told her the missing baby also had red hair, but she was immediately defensive and said it was a throwback to her Irish grandmother. I made some comment about things skipping a generation and at that she challenged me directly; asked if I was suggesting that her son was the missing baby. I said no, not at all, but that was when she mentioned the birth certificate.' Andy looked from one sister to the other. 'To be honest,' he went on, 'I thought that was a bit of overkill.'

'But why didn't you ask to see the certificate there and then,' demanded Vera again, 'if you were suspicious?'

'Because I had no grounds for doing so,' Andy replied. 'But it did seem a strange reaction, and so I reported it to Inspector Droy and he organised for a check to be made at Somerset House. The report came back yesterday and so I'm sorry from your point of view, but there is no doubt that Roger Peterson is the child of Sergeant Colin and Mrs Margaret Peterson... not your Freddie.'

'I don't believe you!' Vera's face was mutinous. 'It's obvious to anyone with a brain. *He* found my Freddie and when he died, *she* kept him as her own.'

'Oh Vera, dearest, calm down,' said Mu. 'It's not Andy's fault. It's just a dreadful coincidence.'

'I don't believe in coincidence,' snapped Vera.

'I'm afraid in this case it is one,' Andy said regretfully. 'But I do promise you that I shan't give up looking for your son, Vera. We know he was brought out of your house, so someone must know where he is. Whoever rescued him, they must have taken him to a place of safety and reported where he was found. I promise you, I will keep looking until I find him.' His eyes rested for a moment on Vera's distraught face before, reluctantly, he got to his feet and said, 'I'd better go.'

'Why don't you stay and have a cup of tea first,' suggested Mu, 'if you've nowhere else you ought to be, that is.'

'No, I haven't,' answered Andy. 'Just a bedsit in Mutley, and that can wait. A cup of tea would be very nice, thank you.'

Mu went to the kitchen and put the kettle on, leaving Vera to him. She understood her sister's despair. It was a coincidence that their landlady had a son who so resembled Freddie, but it had come as a bitter disappointment to Vera. She had been building up her hopes ever since they had found Pandy. But, it seemed, Constable Andy Sharpe was still on the case and he took it very seriously, even more so since now he'd actually met Vera and seen her distress. Mu liked him. He seemed dependable, somehow, and she was sure he would keep his promise and continue the search until the boy was found.

As she returned with the tea, her father reappeared. He had been asleep most of the day, ready for his night on duty at the warden's post. Andy Sharpe introduced himself and the question of Roger's birth certificate was considered yet again, but the outcome was still the same.

When at last Mu got to her feet to leave, Andy Sharpe also got up, unfolding his long body from the chair. Vera, looking at him properly for the first time, realised that he must be well over six foot tall.

'I'll walk with you,' he said to Mu, 'if you don't mind.'

'Yes, thank you.' Mu was happy enough to have his company. She realised with some surprise that with all the excitement of the day she'd hardly had time to think of Patrick. She had not been tempted to mention him to Dad or Vera, because of the presence of Andy Sharpe, and for an hour or more Patrick had not trespassed on her mind. She had another day off tomorrow and then she would be back on nights. Work was the answer. She knew it and her father knew it, and that was part of the problem for poor Vera. Stuck in the flat all day, she had nothing to keep her mind occupied; to give her respite from thoughts of both Freddie and her lost family. It wouldn't be all that long before she could get out and about, she was becoming more mobile, but it had been clear to Mu that at present her sister's leg still pained her if she tried to do too much.

If Mu had seen Vera an hour or so later when her father had set off for his evening duties, she would have been amazed at her sister's activity. She still believed that the panda was Freddie's Pandy and when she had the flat to herself and no one was there to stop her, she decided she was going to search the place from top to bottom to see if she could find any further evidence of Freddie being there. She started in her father's bedroom, though she considered that the most unlikely place to reveal anything. She knew that the baby had been sleeping in the room that was now hers. The cot had still been standing in the corner, a cot, she'd been told, that had been bought through the generosity of Sergeant Peterson's colleagues. That was a clue in itself, Vera decided. How could the baby have lived here for nearly nine months without having a cot to sleep in? And no pram or pushchair either? Andy had told them that the lady down the road had lent Mrs Peterson a pram and that the two of them had become good friends. Vera realised that it must be the lady who had given them the keys on the day that they had arrived. She, Vera, had dismissed the idea of getting to know her, but perhaps she should think again. What was her name? Mrs Todd? Perhaps she should go and visit her and find out more about Mrs Peterson and her baby. Surely a woman would notice more about a baby than a policeman who'd only seen him a couple of times. Yes, Vera decided, she would pay a call on Mrs Todd in the morning. She lived just down the road at number fifty-three, surely she could get there on her crutches. She wouldn't tell anyone, just slip out once Dad had gone to bed in the morning.

That decided, she made a careful search of everything in her room before turning her attention to the living room. It was more tiring than she had anticipated, and by the time she had finished going through drawers and shelves, she was too tired to face the kitchen and the cellar. They could wait until tomorrow. She made herself a piece of toast and another cup of tea and went to bed. She lay awake for a while, but at least she had a plan now and for the first time since she had woken up in the hospital bed, she looked forward to tomorrow. Tomorrow was another day.

The following morning she waited impatiently for her father to come home and then go to bed, so that she could put her plan into action. Surprisingly, he seemed ready to sit with her, chatting. He, too, had realised that Vera had nothing to occupy her time or her mind and he had decided that they should make an effort to look forward and think about what she might do, once she was up and about again properly.

'You should think of getting a proper job,' he said. 'Not just barmaiding, but something more productive.'

'That was a proper job,' Vera responded fiercely. 'It was hard work.'

'Well, it's a job that anyone could do,' he remarked. 'You have more to offer than standing behind a bar pulling pints. You're an intelligent girl, what about training to be a teacher, or maybe a nurse, like Mu?' he suggested.

Vera couldn't think of anything worse than being a nurse. She had seen enough of hospital in the last few weeks to know that it wasn't all Florence Nightingale and smoothing fevered brows, more about bedpans and vomit, but she wasn't going to get into that argument now.

'I'll think about it,' she promised. Anything to get him to go to bed so that she could visit Mrs Todd.

Eventually he went to his room and Vera forced herself to wait until she heard him finish in the bathroom and close his bedroom door before she put on her hat and coat and, grasping her crutches, let herself out of the flat, out of the house and into the street. Slowly she made her way along the pavement, counting off the houses until she came to number fifty-three. She stared up at it for a moment before pushing open the gate and making her way to the front door.

From the outside it looks very similar to ours, she thought as she rang the bell and waited.

It took a while before she heard movement from inside and then the door opened a fraction and Mrs Todd peered out through the gap.

'Mrs Todd? It's Vera Shawbrook. You said I could come and call.'

'Of course!' The door was flung open and Stella Todd greeted her with a smile. 'Come in, my dear, you're most welcome. Careful over the step with your crutches. Did you really walk here on those? You should have sent a message and I'd have come to visit you.'

'Oh, it isn't very far,' Vera replied, 'and I wanted get out of the flat. I've been shut in for too long.'

'Well, my dear, it's lovely to see you. Come on through and we'll have a cup of tea.' She led the way through the house to a living room with glass doors opening onto a loggia hung with pale mauve wisteria, overlooking a small garden beyond. There was a table with garden chairs set beneath its shade.

'You sit down here for a minute and have a rest after your walk,' Stella said, 'and I'll bring out the tea.'

Stella bustled back inside, and Vera sat down in one of the chairs and looked out over the garden. Where there had once been a lawn and probably flower borders bright with colour, there were now vegetables: lettuces, peas with pods ready for picking, and what looked like earthed up potatoes and, at the far end, two tepees of sticks supported climbing plants with red flowers.

Runner beans, thought Vera. Mam had grown those in their patch of garden.

It was very peaceful here in Stella Todd's garden. There was no sound of traffic, no voices, simply the hum of bees, busy with their day's work amongst the blossom of the peach tree espaliered on the south-facing grey stone wall. Vera closed her eyes and remembered Mam's garden. She had been digging for victory too and had sacrificed her herbaceous borders to the planting of potatoes, cabbages, broad and runner beans.

'Fresh veg are good for you,' she'd said. 'Need the vitamins to keep us healthy.'

Now, sitting in the quiet of Stella's garden, Vera could hear Mam's voice quite clearly and she found she was weeping, silent tears running down her cheeks.

Stella returning from the kitchen with a tray, saw the tears. She placed the tray on the table and, saying, 'Oh bother, I've forgotten the milk,' she went back indoors for several minutes to allow Vera time to regain her equilibrium. When she returned with the milk jug, she found Vera with dried cheeks and a brave smile on her face.

'You've got lots growing in your garden,' Vera said, waving a hand in the direction of the vegetables.

'Yes,' Stella said as she poured the tea into delicate china cups. 'My husband John was a keen gardener. I'm not so keen but I couldn't let his precious garden run wild. I've a man who comes in to do the heavy work, but I can keep the weeds down and do the watering, and working in the garden keeps me close to John. I feel he's never far away.'

'Mam did our garden,' Vera said, her voice steady and firmly under control. 'Digging for victory.'

'There's a garden at the house where you're living now,' Stella said, 'but that has become a wilderness these last few months. Maggie Peterson was no gardener.'

It was the opening that Vera had been hoping for. 'Well,' she said, 'she had a baby to look after, didn't she? That's a full-time job.'

'She did,' agreed Stella, 'but Roger was never any trouble. He's a very good boy. Intelligent, too. Into everything, as babies are.' She gave a little laugh. 'He was always exploring and picking things up; always putting things in his mouth. You had to watch him like a hawk once he was on the move.'

'Did you look after him sometimes?' Vera kept her voice casual.

'Oh yes, on occasion. When they first moved here, no one saw much of Maggie. I think she wasn't very well, but once they'd got Roger back, she had to make more effort and I think it did her good.'

'When they got Roger back?' queried Vera.

'He was with his grandmother when they moved down here from London. I think they moved for Colin's job, but they didn't fetch Roger down until they were settled, you know.'

'Oh, I see.' Vera stored this nugget of information away for further examination later on.

'And then of course when poor Colin was killed, well Maggie *had* to manage on her own, so I used to help out. It's always difficult for a woman on her own, especially with a child to bring up, so I was glad to help. I think she's made the right decision to move away into the country for now, away from the bombs. She'd already lost her husband to the war, she wasn't prepared to risk her son as well. More tea, dear?'

Vera stayed another half hour or so and then, pleading things to do at home, she hobbled back down the road to their flat. The news that Roger had only made his appearance comparatively recently interested her very much. It was another tiny piece of information that suggested, to her at least, he wasn't Maggie Peterson's son.

She was tired after her morning's excursion and she lay on her bed in the afternoon for a rest. As she dozed off she was holding the panda against her cheek.

'We'll get him back, Pandy,' she murmured, 'you'll see.'

# 30

The cold was creeping through him. Patrick had kicked off his boots as they were dragging him down, but he could hardly feel his legs. He no longer had energy to swim, and he simply drifted through the dark water, barely keeping his head above the surface, waiting for the cold and the sea to claim him. He knew death was only a matter of time, and not much of that, but somehow it didn't seem to matter any more. He thought he saw a flash of light, but it was gone before it was there and Patrick knew it had been his imagination. A swelling wave lifted him and as it did so, something bumped his head, pushing against him. He raised an arm to push it away, but he wasn't strong enough, and his hand simply ran across the rough surface of whatever it was. And whatever it was continued to nudge him as if trying to push him out of the way. And then suddenly something grabbed him, a hand, grasping at his sodden clothes and holding him higher in the water.

Then a voice. 'For God's sake, man, catch onto the raft! I can't pull you out on my own! Catch hold of the bloody raft, man. Grab the rope.'

The voice sounded a long way away, but gradually

Patrick realised it was talking to him. He put out his hand again and found a loop of rope drifting past him. He caught hold of it and the raft, for that was what it was that had nudged him, did so again. There came another flash of light dazzling him for a moment, but as his eyes cleared he saw a pale face peering down from within the raft, buoyant on the waves beside him. Patrick pulled harder on the loop of rope, but it seemed to slither through his frozen fingers and he lost hold of it. Panic surged through him and he struck out again with more energy than he had mustered for some time. He managed to grab the rope again, and held on for dear life as the raft began to drift away from him.

'Hang on!' shouted the voice. 'Hang on and I'll pull you in. Don't let go or you're a goner!'

Patrick was now clinging to the lifeline with both hands and very slowly he was being hauled towards the raft, the water dragging him down, the rope holding him up. He kicked hard with his feet, trying to propel himself towards the raft and the helping hands inside it.

'Hang on!' instructed the voice again. 'You're nearly here. For Christ's sake don't let go!'

The light flashed yet again and Patrick saw that he was only yards from the drifting raft. Its canvas sides, slick with water, towered above him and he knew he could never haul himself up out of the water. They were too high, too rounded to get any purchase. The pull on the rope continued. Patrick managed to slide his forearms through the loop, so that it wasn't his hands alone taking the strain.

'Loop the rope under your arms,' ordered the voice. 'But don't let go!'

Patrick struggled to obey, but the waves were pushing him away again. It was impossible. He couldn't do it. Then he heard another voice, not from across the water, but echoing in his head. 'Patrick! I love you! Don't leave me, Patrick!' Mu's voice.

It was his last chance at life. If he didn't make it into the life raft, he was dead. He couldn't last for any longer in the biting cold of the Atlantic. With one final effort he managed to get the loop of rope under his armpits so that it strained across his back, dragging him once more towards the raft. As he reached the side a wave lifted him high and he found himself being grasped and hauled higher, until his head and his upper body were over the side, and with one final pull, he slithered into the life raft and collapsed into a heap on its rubbery floor. Someone near him let out a groan and he forced his eyes open to see who had heaved him out of the sea and given him another chance at life. A man collapsed, exhausted, beside him on the undulating base of the raft as it continued its drift through the darkness.

For a long moment neither of them had breath to say anything and then the man spoke.

'Welcome aboard HMS Rubber Duck, sir,' said the voice. 'Thought you was a goner then. 'Snot easy gettin' aboard one of these.'

The flashlight was flicked on again and Patrick saw that his saviour was one of the leading hands from a forward gun crew.

'Dixon!' He managed to speak the name.

'As ever is, sir.'

'Thank you.'

The flashlight went off and once more they were plunged into darkness. 'Got to save the battery, sir, in case we need to signal.'

'Good thinking,' Patrick said, but his teeth were chattering and the words were hard to say. He rubbed his hands against his chest, trying to instil some warmth back in his body.

'It'll be better in the morning, sir,' said Dixon. 'Once it's daylight the sun should get us dry. Maybe we'll be picked up. The convoy must be coming through any time.'

'The convoy won't stop with U-boats known to be in the area,' said Patrick wearily. 'It'll be long gone by sunrise. Any sound or sign of anyone else?'

'No, sir. There was lights earlier, but I ain't seen none for a while now. Tried calling out, but though I could hear voices they was all echoing, difficult to follow. Maybe some of 'em was picked up.'

'Maybe,' agreed Patrick, but he thought it most unlikely.

'I only saw you, sir, because I risked a moment's light in the hope of seeing another raft.'

'Thank God you did,' Patrick managed. 'I was about to let myself go.'

Despite the cold and his wet clothes, Patrick was overtaken by exhaustion and he knew he was falling asleep and that if he did he might never wake up again.

'We'd better take turns to keep watch,' he said, shaking himself awake. 'We can't risk both of us sleeping at once. I'll take the first hour and then I'll wake you up.'

There was little room to lie down, but both men were propped against the curved sides of the raft, their heads resting on the heavy duty canvas for a pillow. Both were soaking wet, both were very cold and Dixon moved closer to Patrick, hoping that their two bodies would generate enough heat to keep them alive until daylight.

Patrick managed to stave off the need for sleep by forcing himself to recite lists of things that he'd had to learn by heart as a child; the books of the Old Testament... Genesis, Exodus, Leviticus, Numbers... the kings and queens of England... Willie, Willie, Harry, Steve... Shakespeare's plays, tragedies, comedies, histories... the nightmare song from *Iolanthe*... which seemed appropriate for the nightmare he was living through now. When he'd run out of ideas, he shook Dixon to wake him, and ensured he was properly awake before he allowed himself to close his eyes.

When the sun came up they found themselves bobbing on an empty expanse of steely grey water with not another boat in sight. It was as Patrick had imagined, the convoy of merchant men and their Royal Navy guardians had passed in the night and were long gone.

The day was a hot one and once the sun had dried their clothes, it beat down unrelentingly from a clear blue sky. They again took turns to keep watch, eyes peeled for any sign of a ship, but there was none. Once they heard the drone of an aircraft and saw it high above them, drawing lazy white circles in the sky. Immediately they were on their feet, in danger of falling out of the raft as they waved and shouted in a fruitless attempt to catch the eye of the pilot, but apart from that one sighting, they could have been alone in the world.

The survival kit that had provided the torch also provided a bottle of water, some hard tack and a compass.

Carefully they rationed out the food and water, but they both knew that they would not survive more than a day or so, if that, on what they had to share. Patrick was also very aware that had Dixon not hauled him out of the water, the leading seaman would have had twice the biscuit and water. Another man might have left him to his fate in the sea, but Dixon was not another man and Patrick was filled with gratitude for his generosity.

They could see a smudge of land in the distance, lying low on the horizon, but at the mercy of the wind and the tide, they had no way of steering the raft towards the safety it offered and they resigned themselves to another chilly night on the water.

It was as the sun was beginning to set that they heard the plane again. It was much lower this time and the two men again waved frantically, in the small hope of attracting the pilot's attention.

'Where's he out of?' wondered Dixon.

'Cornwall, maybe, or perhaps the Scillies,' suggested Patrick. 'Whatever that land is over there.'

The plane continued to circle above them and then they saw the boat. A fast inshore craft heading out from the shore, bouncing over the waves and heading straight for them. Both men stood up in the unstable canvas boat, waving their arms in the air and shouting at the top of their lungs. 'Over here! We're over here!' Minutes later the boat was alongside the raft and one of its crew had tossed them a line. They were hauled close against the hull of the rescue ship, and were able to scramble up the ladder and on to the deck.

The moment they were both safely aboard, the skipper

spun the boat round and headed back towards the shore, leaving the small Carley life raft to drift on its way, driven by the tide.

'Not hanging about here,' he called. 'Never know what's lurking down below. Could get a nasty surprise.'

Luckily there were no nasty surprises that evening and the two rescued men were taken below, wrapped in blankets and given a hot drink. They were both exhausted and could hardly believe that they were safe.

'What ship are you from?' asked the skipper when he came down to see them.

'HMS *Cumbria*,' replied Patrick. 'Destroyer heading out to meet a convoy.'

'U-boat, I assume.'

'Yes, sir, torpedo amidships, hit a magazine. Explosion ripped her in two. The order came to abandon ship and she sank in less than fifteen minutes.'

'Many other survivors, d'you think?'

'Don't know, sir, there were certainly other rafts, but how many men managed to get aboard one... well, who knows. They may have sent one of the naval escorts to pick them up. We've seen no sign of any more today.'

'Well, let's get you ashore and you can make a full report.'

'How did you find us?' Dixon asked one of the crew.

'Spotted by the flying boat, out of St Mary's,' the man replied. 'Raised the alarm, so we thought we'd better come and have a look-see.'

From there on things moved fairly quickly. As soon as they were landed at St Mary's Pool they were taken ashore to the base where a doctor looked them over and pronounced them in a reasonable condition.

'Sunstroke and exhaustion,' he said. 'But really nothing that rest, plenty of fluids, some decent food and a hot bath won't put right.' He smiled reassuringly. 'Good thing you weren't out there much longer, though.'

The next few days the two men rested as ordered. They had met the pilot who had spotted them from the reconnaissance plane, an Australian, Simon Taverner, flying with the RAF.

'No worries,' he assured them when they tried to thank him. 'Saw you in a spot of bother and radioed in.'

'You saved our lives,' Patrick told him.

'No, mate. You saved them yourselves.'

'Were any others from *Cumbria* picked up?' asked Dixon.

'We've just heard the incoming convoy picked up a few,' replied Taverner. 'Came through without a U-boat attack. Probably too many escorts for them to risk their subs on this one.'

The two men were promised a lift back into Falmouth in the next couple of days. Patrick had tried to get through to his parents to tell them that he was safe, but there was little chance of getting a connection from St Mary's and he had to accept that he couldn't relieve their minds until he was back on the mainland.

And Mu. Beloved Mu. Would his parents have written to her yet, telling her that he had been lost at sea? When he managed to contact them he would ask if they had told her he was missing. Perhaps they hadn't and she didn't know he'd been presumed lost. He was hoping that he and Dixon would have some time ashore before they were assigned to another ship. Perhaps he could see her. Turn up unannounced. She'd been going to move to Plymouth and though he had no address for her there, he would go to every hospital until he found her.

'Anyone you need to tell?' he asked Dixon.

'My parents, sir,' he replied. 'I'll send them a telegram as soon as possible. They ain't on the phone.'

'They've probably had one telegram already,' Patrick pointed out.

'Well, the second one'll please them more than the first,' Dixon replied with a grin. 'Leastways, I hope so!'

In the end it wasn't until four days later that there was a boat crossing from the Scillies to Falmouth and they were able to hitch a ride. As the MTB sped across the sea, the two men looked back at the fast fading island of St Mary's, with its air-sea rescue base that had saved their lives. The sea around them was smooth and a bright silver in the sunshine, deceptively calm, apparently safe, but with the possibility of danger skulking beneath the surface.

Once ashore in Falmouth the two men split up. Dixon sent his telegram to his parents in Barnet and then, with a warrant supplied by the navy, caught a train and headed for London.

They shook hands before he left for the station. 'I owe you my life,' said Patrick simply. 'If there's ever anything I can do for you, come and ask.'

The leading seaman looked embarrassed. 'Anyone would have done the same, sir,' he said.

'I'm not so sure they would,' replied Patrick. 'But remember what I've said. I wish you good luck, Dixon. It has been a privilege to serve on the same ship as a man like you.'

Patrick took a room in a hotel and booked a call to Glasgow. He would tell his parents first and find out if they had indeed contacted Mu as he'd asked. It took some time to be connected and when trunks finally put him through, the line was crackly and he had to shout to make his mother hear when she answered.

'Mother!' he shouted. 'It's me, Patrick. I'm safe ashore in Falmouth!'

'Who?'

'It's me, Mother, Patrick!'

There was a shriek at the other end of the line and a clatter as if she'd dropped the receiver. Then his father's voice.

'Patrick, is that really you, son?'

'Yes, it's me, Dad. I'm safe. Look, I've only got three minutes. Tell me, did you write to Muriel?'

'Yes, of course. She wasn't in Portsmouth like you said. She wrote back from Plymouth.'

'That's where I thought she'd be,' said Patrick. 'I'm heading there to find her.'

'Aren't you coming home?'

'Depends how much leave they give me before I'm assigned to a new ship. Sorry, Dad, Mother, but I have to find Mu first, especially if she thinks I'm dead.'

'I see,' replied his father, trying to hide his disappointment.

'Will you tell Neil that I'm safe?'

'His unit's been sent abroad,' answered his father, 'don't know exactly where, but we'll let him know. Come and see us if you can, son, your mother would love to see you even if it's only for a couple of days.'

'I will if I can, Dad,' Patrick promised. 'Give her my love...' And at that minute the pips went, his three precious minutes were up, and the line went dead.

Patrick knew that his parents were disappointed that he was not jumping on a train to Glasgow, but his priority was Mu, and now he knew where she was, tomorrow he would be on his way to find her.

## 31

Vera spent the next evening, while her father was out, searching the rest of the flat. She found nothing more to indicate either that a baby had lived there for nearly nine months, nor that, if he had, it was Freddie. She left the cellar until last. It was the largest room in the flat, spreading out below the main rooms above. She had left it until last on purpose. It was the room where she had found Pandy, and she felt that if there was anything to find it must be down there. She didn't want her father or Mu to know what she was doing. They would probably both dismiss all her searching as a waste of time. She could almost hear her sister sighing and saying, 'If you do find any evidence that a baby lived here, it will be evidence of Mrs Peterson's boy, won't it?'

'No,' Vera answered aloud, as if Mu had actually spoken those words. 'Not necessarily. Anyway, I've got nothing else to do, have I? So I'm going to look.'

Methodically she worked her way from the bottom of the stairs which led down from the kitchen. There was a small triangular cupboard tucked in beneath the flight. Its door was so stiff that Vera thought it was locked at first, but a strong jerk finally made it give way and the door opened to reveal a dark area smelling of dust and dirt, but containing nothing but mouse droppings. The door had probably not been opened for months, which might account for its reluctance to do so now. Vera pushed it closed again and began to make her way towards the other end of the room. She pulled the cushions off the old sofa and out of the two armchairs, shaking them hard to ensure there was nothing hidden in the lining, sliding her hand down the sides of the chairs themselves, in case anything might have been caught in the cracks, but there was nothing but fluff, some shreds of tobacco and a couple of spent matches.

She gave special attention to the bookcase behind which she had discovered the panda. Removing the few books that were set out on the shelves she shook each one in case there was anything concealed in the pages. Several of them had the name Colin Peterson written inside, but none were inscribed with Maggie Peterson's name. Clearly she was not a woman who collected or even read books. In one of the drawers under the shelves Vera found a truncheon with a loop of leather through its handle, a police whistle and a warrant card, naming Colin Peterson as a sergeant in the City of Plymouth police, warranting his authority to act as such and signed and stamped by the chief constable's office and dated 13 January 1941.

Vera looked at it with interest. In his photograph, the sergeant looked steadfastly at the camera. He was not particularly good-looking, but he had a kind face and somehow looked reliable. Vera thought she would have liked him if she'd met him, but now she was more interested in the date stamped upon it.

So, she thought, the Petersons moved down to Plymouth in the middle of January this year, and yet they didn't bring their son with them. Mrs Todd had said they didn't fetch him from Mrs Peterson's mother-in-law's until they were quite settled in and he didn't appear on the scene until April. Just when Freddie disappeared!

'No one will believe me,' she said to the air, 'but I *know* her baby is my Freddie.' And, she thought, that policeman thinks so too.

Vera had liked the look of Constable Andy Sharpe. He was very tall, something she always admired in a man; Freddie's father had been more than... but better not think about him. Andy Sharpe's smile made his speedwell-blue eyes crinkle at the corners, and, she realised, while he had been here the other day, he had smiled at her quite a lot. He had looked at her and spoken to her as a real, adult person, not just a stupid girl who'd got herself into trouble with some sweet-talking sailor. He'd been kind, too, taking on board her distress, realising just how desperate she felt. She hoped he would keep his promise to go on looking for Freddie, she hoped he would call again soon to report on his progress. Well, if she were honest, she hoped he would call again to see her.

Pull yourself together, she admonished herself. This is no time to be looking at men, specially good-looking ones like Andy Sharpe. There'll be no men in my foreseeable future. Finding Freddie is the priority, the most important thing in the world now, so get on with it.

Vera returned her attention to the bookcase, and when she had finished with it there were only two places left to search: a small bureau that stood almost obscured by the old sofa, and the built-in cupboard in the corner. The bureau took very little time. There were some sheets of paper, a pencil and a steel-nibbed pen. An old inkwell, with dried up ink, and a piece of blotting paper. A small interior drawer offered more steel nibs, some paper clips and a box of drawing pins. Nothing of any interest at all. There was only the cupboard left.

Vera hobbled across to it and pulled open the door. She had not opened it before and had no idea what might be in there. There were shelves, but nothing on them, and in the bottom was an old brown trunk with a padlock closed through the hasp. Tied to the handle on one end was a handwritten label with the words: *Peterson. Passenger Luggage in Advance.*

For a long moment Vera looked at it. Clearly the trunk belonged to Maggie Peterson. She had locked it with a padlock and left it behind in the house. She must be intending to come back for it after the war and had assumed that even if her tenants found it in the bottom of the cupboard they would respect the fact that it was hers and leave it where it was, unopened.

Well, Vera thought, she'd been too trusting. She, Vera, had decided to search every inch of the flat for evidence of Freddie, and that included a hidden trunk. Thus it was when her father got home in the early evening – rather than the early morning as she'd expected – he found his daughter in the cellar with a poker, endeavouring to lever the padlock off an old trunk.

'Vera!' he cried. 'What on earth are you doing?'

'What does it look like?' puffed Vera, very red in the face from her exertions.

'But that trunk belongs to Mrs Peterson,' he said. 'She mentioned she wanted to leave it here and I told her that it wouldn't inconvenience us at all. What do you think you're doing?'

'Trying to get the damned thing open,' stated Vera.

'Watch your language, miss!' he snapped. 'No young lady should swear!'

'Dad,' Vera tried to sound calm and patient, 'I'm looking for evidence that Freddie was here, and there might be some in here. Don't you *want* to find him, Dad?'

David took a deep breath. 'Of course I want to find him, my dear, just as much as you. But we can't go snooping into other people's private property. The trunk was left here for Mrs Peterson to collect later. It's a matter of trust.'

'Well, I don't trust *her*,' declared Vera. 'Everything points to the fact that she didn't have a baby until April and now she has, just from the time Freddie went missing.'

'What points to that fact?' asked her father, sitting down on the sofa. 'What evidence do you have?'

'Well, what Mrs Todd said for a start,' answered Vera. And she told her father all that Stella Todd had told her. 'Mrs Peterson had nothing she needed for looking after a baby. Nobody knew she had a child until just after her husband was killed. Don't you think that's suspicious, Dad? No cot, no pram, no pushchair, nothing!'

'But she does have his birth certificate,' David reminded her gently. 'And it has been verified by the police.'

'I don't care,' flared Vera. 'And I'm going to open this trunk and see what's inside.'

David realised that there was no way he could dissuade

Vera from trying to open the trunk and so he sighed and sat down in the armchair and watched.

She had managed to get the end of the poker into the hasp and was levering it against the old leather of the trunk with all her might. As he watched her exertions, David had to admit to himself that he would be interested in the contents of that trunk, too. He didn't expect there to be anything to connect his grandson Freddie with Mrs Peterson's boy, Roger, it was, he had to acknowledge, simply nosiness, and he made no further protest as Vera struggled with the poker and the hasp.

At last it gave, the whole hasp pulling free from its leather surround. With a cry of triumph, Vera discarded the poker and flung open the lid. Inside there were some papers, some tiny baby clothes, a few photographs and a diary from 1937. Disappointed, Vera sat back on her heels, to be reminded by a stab of pain that she should not be placing such pressure on her newly mended leg. She gave a squeak and hauled herself up onto the sofa, dragging the trunk towards her and peering into it again.

'Just some old photos and some papers,' she said flatly.

'Well, what did you expect, Vera?' asked her father. 'A written confession of kidnapping a baby?'

'No, of course not,' Vera snapped, but then her voice softened, 'I just thought that there might... well, that there might be something, you know.'

'Yes, I do know,' responded her father gently. 'But we'll all keep looking, I promise you. That young policeman who was here, what's he called, Constable Sharpe, he's determined to find him for us.'

'I know, but I was trying to find evidence to help him.'

She reached down into the trunk and picking up the diary flicked through it. There was nothing of interest there, only the odd appointment, and the note of an address or two. Disappointed, Vera tossed it back into the trunk. She didn't spend any time on the photos, a quick glance told her that none of them showed a baby. None of them had ever seen Roger Peterson, so they had no idea whether he looked like Freddie or not. When she had first seen the snaps lying in the trunk, she had hoped they might solve the matter, but they were only Colin and Maggie. With a sigh, she turned her attention to the papers and lifted out a long brown envelope. She retrieved the document from inside and found herself looking at Maggie and Colin's marriage certificate. Married in St John's Church, Waterloo, 29 February 1936.

'They were married on the twenty-ninth of February in a leap year!' she said. Suddenly wondering if Roger's birth certificate was in the trunk in another brown envelope, she reached in again.

If I could actually see the birth certificate myself, she thought, then I suppose I'd have to believe it.

The second envelope held a will, Colin Peterson's will, in which he left everything he owned to his beloved wife Margaret. There was no mention of a beloved son, Roger. Then she looked at the date of the will and realised that it predated Roger's birth by more than a year. He obviously had not updated it after Roger had been born.

'I suppose he thought he had plenty of time,' she murmured.

'Who did? To do what?' asked David.

'It's Colin Peterson's will,' Vera said, holding up the

document. 'He made it before Roger was even thought of, but he didn't make a new one when he was born.'

'I don't expect he saw the need,' said David. 'Even if the worst happened, as it has, his wife inherits everything and she will use it to bring up their child.' He smiled ruefully at Vera. 'I don't think you can read anything into that, my dear.'

'No, I suppose not,' she sighed. But in her head she was thinking, It still seems odd to me!

She replaced the will in the envelope and set it aside with the marriage certificate. There were two more envelopes and she picked out the first, a larger one. On the outside, written in pencil, was the word 'DEEDS'. She took out the papers and saw they were the deeds to this very house. It was owned outright by Colin Peterson, and now, she supposed, by his widow. Still no birth certificate. She must have taken it with her, Vera decided gloomily. She really had wanted to see it with her own eyes.

'I could do with a cuppa,' said David, getting up from his chair and heading for the stairs up to the kitchen. 'D'you want one, Vera, before we go to bed?'

'Yes, please,' she said and as he went up the stairs to put the kettle on, she turned her attention to the last brown envelope. When she pulled out the sheet of paper and looked at it she found that she was indeed looking at a certificate, but not the one she had been hoping for. She read it and then, as the importance of what it certified hit her, she gave a shriek that brought her father thundering back down the stairs.

'Vera!' he cried. 'Are you all right? What on earth's the matter?'

Vera was still sitting in the armchair but she held a document in her hand and this she silently held out to him. He took it and a quick glance at it made him widen his eyes in disbelief. It certified the death of Roger Colin Peterson, son of Colin and Margaret Peterson, on 30th July 1940, aged one day.

'Her baby died,' Vera whispered vehemently. 'Daddy, her baby died, and she's taken mine.'

## 32

David and Vera agreed that there was nothing they could do that night, and when they had drunk the tea and eaten the sandwiches David had made, they went to bed. But though David soon fell asleep, his whole being exhausted, Vera could not. She lay in her bed and thought of Freddie. Last time she had seen him, had held him in her arms, had been two months ago. Would he remember her, or would he have transferred his love to Maggie Peterson? Babies make bonds with whoever looks after them, she thought in anguish. Suppose he doesn't remember me! Suppose he holds out his arms to that Maggie Peterson instead! She can hardly say he is her Roger now, not with me holding his death certificate in my hand.

She played out the scene in her mind, she, Vera, facing down the woman who had stolen her baby, taking Freddie from her arms and hugging him to her and he responding with his gurgling laugh. Before the air raid that had destroyed her family, Freddie had started to make recognisable sounds – 'Mm, mm, mm,' when he saw Mam; 'Da, da, da,' when David came into the house. Supposing he'd started to call Maggie Peterson 'Mm, mm'. It didn't bear thinking about!

He hadn't known Vera was his mother, but having so nearly lost him she would make sure he did from now on. Never mind who his father was. He wouldn't be the only child who grew up after the war with an absent father. He would have Dad, as he always did, but in the role of Granddad. Mu would be there as a loving aunt. She thought of Tony, somewhere, they thought, in North Africa. An uncle for Freddie when he came home from the war. They would all live as a family again, well, until Mu got married, as she surely would one day, and then he would have another new uncle. They could be a family again.

First, however, they had to find Maggie Peterson, wherever she'd disappeared to. In the morning, she decided, she would go to find Constable Sharpe with the evidence of Maggie Peterson's duplicity in her hand and show him what she'd discovered. The police would have to help her find Freddie now. It might be difficult to prove that Freddie was her baby, but they could prove he wasn't Roger Peterson.

It was the small hours before she drifted off to sleep, but her decision had been made.

She awoke to a warm day, the sun shining and softening the battered ruins of the city laid out before her. Today was the first day of the rest of her life. She felt quite different from the past month or so. She was an adult. She had taken control of her life and she was making her own decisions. They would find Freddie and she would take her rightful place as his mother.

Over the breakfast table she told her father what she had decided in the night. He listened without comment, but when she had finished he said, 'I think it's the right decision you've made, but you do realise it won't be easy, don't you?

There will always be people who point the finger at a single mother and call her child a bastard.'

'Let them,' said Vera. 'I shall ignore them and make sure Freddie knows that he's loved and wanted and not just an awkward mistake, someone to be ashamed of.'

David smiled at her across the table. 'Good for you,' he said. 'Your mam would be proud of you. But,' he continued, 'we have to find the little chap first.'

'I know,' Vera replied, 'that's why I'm going to see Constable Sharpe this morning. I shall show him what I've found and they can put it on record that the baby Maggie Peterson maintains is hers can't be, because her son is dead.'

'Perhaps we should find Mu and tell her what you've discovered. I'm sure she'd want to come to the police station with us.'

'I think she's back on nights,' Vera said. 'We might find her at the nurses' home before she goes to bed.'

'Well, I think we should try,' said her father. 'She's done a lot towards finding Freddie, and let's face it, there's still a lot more to do. We haven't found Maggie Peterson yet.'

They set off to town. Vera had dispensed with her crutches and walked slowly down the hill with only her stick as an aid. They caught a bus to the hospital and though she would not have admitted it to her father, she was very relieved to sit down and let it carry her into the middle of the city. When they reached the nurses' home David knocked on the door, but having asked for Mu, he found she wasn't there.

'She came off duty at the usual time,' said the nurse who had answered the door, 'but I haven't seen her since. She's not in her room because I went up there just now.'

'We'll just have to go without her,' Vera said firmly.

'I'm not going to wait any longer to pass on this piece of evidence.'

Reluctantly David agreed. He would have preferred to wait for Mu, but he also knew that it meant so much to Vera to show the death certificate and keep things moving that he simply said, 'All right, come on then.'

They made slow progress. Vera was determined to keep going even though her leg was becoming increasingly painful, and when at last they entered the police station she flopped down gratefully onto the hard bench that ran along one wall of the reception area.

David went to the desk and spoke to the sergeant on duty. 'We need to see Inspector Droy,' he said and then heard himself corrected from behind.

'Constable Sharpe, Dad. He's the one I want to talk to.'

'Inspector Droy isn't here just now,' said the sergeant, adding this as if he hadn't heard Vera's interjection. 'D'you want to wait until he comes in?'

'No,' called Vera from her bench, 'we want to see Constable Sharpe.'

'And what would that be about, miss?' He lifted an interrogatory eyebrow. 'Something I could help you with?'

Seeing that Vera was about to lose any cooperation from the man on the desk, David said, 'It's an ongoing matter, Sergeant. It would be helpful to see the officer that we've dealt with before.' His voice was placatory, meant to soothe the feathers ruffled by Vera's truculent attitude. 'Is he available to speak to us?'

The sergeant grunted and then opening a door behind him called through, 'Sharpe! Wanted at the front desk.'

Andy Sharpe had just been about to set out on his beat,

and he came through to the desk wondering who wanted him. When he saw Vera sitting on the bench, his face cracked into a smile and David saw that he received an answering smile and a lift of the chin from Vera.

Oh, dear, he thought. That's all we need, Vera to fall for yet another chap.

Sharpe, however, remembered that the sergeant behind the desk was watching and said, 'Mr Shawbrook, Miss Shawbrook, good morning. How can I help you?'

'He isn't hers!' Vera was on her feet, tiredness and pain forgotten in her eagerness to tell him. 'Roger Peterson isn't her son and I can prove it!'

Andy Sharpe, maintaining the formality between them said, 'I see. Well, if you'd both like to come through, perhaps we can discuss the matter.' He lifted one end of the counter and let them through. 'Inspector Droy will be back very soon, I'm sure,' he said. 'Please come this way.'

They passed the scowling desk sergeant and followed Sharpe into an interview room, where they all sat down.

'Now then,' Sharpe said. 'What's happened?'

'I found this,' Vera said, reaching into her bag and pulling out the death certificate. 'It explains how Mrs Peterson has a valid birth certificate for a Roger Peterson, but not how she has a baby which she claims to be that same Roger Peterson, when her baby died within hours of being born.' She passed Sharpe the death certificate and he studied it carefully.

'You see!' she cried triumphantly. 'Her baby died. The child she's saying is hers, can't be. He's my Freddie and I want him back.' Her voice cracked on the last words and they ended in a sob.

'It does look as if the child isn't hers,' agreed Sharpe, 'but I have to warn you that he might not be yours, either.'

'Of course he's mine,' cried Vera. 'And when I see him, I shall recognise him, as will my father and my sister. I thought you were on my side!'

'Vera, I am,' he assured her, his voice softening. 'But you must realise, we still have to find them before we can face her with this and you can identify the baby as yours.'

'Well, at least this death certificate would seem to prove that she has been lying to everyone about the child,' David pointed out. 'Clearly she can't be trusted. So, from now on we have to rely on you to up the search for Vera's son. I imagine that technically Mrs Peterson has kidnapped him and surely that is a serious enough crime for a little more time and effort to be put into looking for him.'

'Oh, with this new information, I assure you we shall be doing our utmost to find her and the child. Even if the boy turns out not to be Vera's son—'

'He *is* mine,' interrupted Vera furiously.

'Even if it turns out he's not your Freddie,' said the constable ignoring Vera's interruption, 'he is somebody's else's child and she can't be allowed to keep pretending he's hers.'

Sharpe got to his feet. 'I need you to make a statement, explaining how you came across this information,' he said. 'And then we can go from there.'

Half an hour later David and Vera left the police station, Vera having signed a statement saying where and when she had found Roger's death certificate.

'I'll keep it for now with your statement,' he said as he took them back past the front desk, 'and I'll show it to

Inspector Droy as soon as he comes in. Perhaps I should call round later and let you know what our next move will be.'

'Yes,' said Vera with enthusiasm. 'Yes, do come and tell us. We'll be waiting to hear what you're going to do next.'

As they waited for the bus, Vera said to her father, 'I'm not going to sit and wait for them. I'm going to go and see that Mrs Todd again. I bet she knows where Maggie Peterson has gone. She pretended not to know when I was there the other day, but I think she did really. They had become good friends, by what she said, and I think she just decided not to tell me. She certainly loved...' she hesitated and then said firmly, 'Freddie.'

'My dearest girl,' David said gently, 'Constable Sharpe is right. All you've done is prove that Mrs Peterson's baby is not her own son. You haven't proved that he is yours.'

'Whose else could he be?' demanded Vera fiercely.

'Anybody's,' replied her father. 'In the turmoil of those raids in April, he could be anybody's.'

'But he isn't,' asserted Vera. 'He's mine!'

Neither of them spoke again until they reached the flat, both busy with their own thoughts, but after they'd shared a scratch lunch David said, 'This afternoon I'm going to have a snooze for a while. I'm on duty again tonight, and it won't be my turn to be sent home early. Will you cook something for supper before I go?'

Vera had a quick think as to what there was to eat and remembered Mu had brought some sausages and put them in the cold safe. 'Bangers and mash all right?' she suggested.

'Just the ticket,' said her father with a smile, and

disappeared into his bedroom. He didn't get into bed at once, he sat in the chair by the window and looked across at the houses opposite. He wasn't sure which belonged to Mrs Todd, but he was sure that Vera would visit her again and he wasn't surprised when he heard the front door close and saw her walking up the street.

She really is walking much better now, he thought inconsequentially as he watched her. She's hardly even using her stick. She's a survivor, that girl!

Vera was determined to have talked to Mrs Todd again before Andy Sharpe came round later, and though she was tired from her excursion into town that morning, she set off along the road to number fifty-three.

Stella was having her afternoon rest and wasn't particularly pleased when she heard the doorbell. She got to her feet and peered out of the window to see who her visitor was, and when she saw it was Vera Shawbrook from across the road, she sighed and went to open the door. After all, she had told the girl that she was welcome to call at any time.

'Vera,' she cried, managing a welcoming smile, 'how lovely to see you. Do come in, my dear. No crutches today? Well done you.' She stood aside and Vera entered the hall. 'Let's go through to the garden, shall we? It's such a lovely afternoon. Would you like tea?'

'No thank you, Mrs Todd,' said Vera. 'I just wanted to ask you something.'

Stella sat down on one of the garden chairs and waved Vera to another. 'Ask away,' she said. 'What can I help you with?'

'Did you know that Mrs Peterson's son isn't hers?' Vera

had decided on the direct approach, hoping to surprise a truthful answer from Stella Todd.

Stella was certainly surprised, and looking confused she said, 'Not hers? What do you mean, not hers?'

'I have proof that Mrs Peterson's son Roger died the day after he was born,' said Vera.

Stella looked at her for a long moment and then asked coldly, 'What proof?'

'His death certificate.' Vera was not going to pull any punches.

'His death certificate!' Stella stared at her in horror. 'And just where did you find that?'

'In a locked trunk she left behind in the flat!'

'A locked trunk! You mean you opened it knowing it contained with Maggie's private things? That's despicable!'

'Maybe, but I need to know where she's gone.'

'And what exactly has that to do with you, miss?' Stella's voice was icy now. 'How dare you pry into her private things! You've no right.'

'I've every right!' snapped Vera. 'She's stolen something from me more precious than life itself.'

'Stolen? From you? But she doesn't even know you. You haven't even met her.'

'No, I haven't,' admitted Vera, 'but a baby was taken from our old house after it was damaged in an air raid. We know he was rescued by a police sergeant who risked his life to do it, but the child has never been seen since.'

'And you're suggesting...?' Stella's voice was still chilly.

'I'm suggesting it was Sergeant Peterson who found him and that Mrs Peterson has kept him for her own.'

'Oh, I'm sure that can't be true,' said Stella, uncertain

now. 'I mean, surely if her husband had rescued a baby from a house, he'd have reported it straight away, saying which house.'

'He certainly should have,' agreed Vera. 'But suppose he didn't?'

'But he would have,' maintained Stella. 'He was such an upright man. He wouldn't have left some family in doubt as to where their baby was.'

'But he was killed himself soon after, wasn't he?'

'Well, yes, he was, but even so I can't believe he wouldn't have reported such a rescue like that straight away.'

'It would appear that he didn't,' said Vera, 'and now Mrs Peterson has disappeared with my son, Freddie.'

'Your son!'

'My son Freddie.'

'How do you know?' began Stella. 'I mean, how do you know that he's yours?'

'Everything points to it,' Vera said. 'You said yourself that you didn't see a baby until after Sergeant Peterson was killed.'

'He'd been with his grandmother. She looked after him while they were moving.'

'They moved down here in the middle of January,' said Vera. 'I've seen his warrant card and it's dated the thirteenth of January. You didn't see her with a baby until April. She had no baby equipment; you lent her a pram. Surely if she's had that baby for nearly ten months, she'd at least have had a pram or a pushchair... don't you think? As far as I can make out, she appeared with her baby, just at the time mine went missing.'

Stella looked at her in confusion. She had heard from

Elsie that many of the Shawbrook family had been killed in the Parham Road shelter, and she'd read about the family who had lost their baby, but she had never equated the one with the other. Surely she'd have noticed the surname. It wasn't as if it were a common one. She tried to remember when she had read about the baby. She was certain that the family name wasn't Shawbrook, and yet here was this girl, a young girl at that, claiming to be the mother of the missing baby, and actually living in the flat that belonged to Maggie Peterson.

'To clear this up, we need to know where Maggie has gone to now,' Vera was saying. 'You said she was going to work in a pub in a village outside Exeter. Can't you be more precise? What's the name of the pub, or the village? I must tell you the police are looking for her.'

'The police! Is that really necessary? I mean, I'm sure there must be some mistake.'

'Well, if there is,' returned Vera, 'the sooner we clear it up the better, don't you think?'

'Well, I suppose so,' said Stella unhappily. 'But I simply can't believe that she'd take a baby that wasn't hers.'

'And you truly don't know where she's gone?'

'No.' Stella was affronted. 'I've told you I don't, and I'm not in the habit of lying!'

'I'm sorry,' Vera apologised, 'really. It's just that I'm desperate to find him, and we don't know where to look.'

'Well, I'm sorry too,' said Stella stiffly, 'but I don't think I can be of any more help to you.'

'I think the police may come to see you and ask you some questions,' Vera warned.

'That's up to them,' retorted Stella, 'but I shan't be able

to tell them any more than I've told you. Now, young lady, I'd like you to go. Please shut the front door behind you.'

Vera got unsteadily to her feet and went back through the house. She was disappointed. She had upset Mrs Todd, who had been kind to her, but had learned nothing in the process.

As she walked back down the street she saw a tall figure coming up the hill towards her and her heart lifted a little, and not simply because he might be bringing her good news. The sight of Constable Andy Sharpe raised her spirits more than she could have imagined possible, and she found she was smiling.

## 33

Mu was exhausted. Ever since she had heard the news about Patrick she had not been sleeping well. She no longer turned out her lamp, but drifted fitfully in and out of restless slumber. She hardly dare close her eyes, for when she did exhaustion would overtake her and as she sank into deeper sleep the nightmare would claim her, the same one every night. She was in the sea, cold and being dragged down, as if someone under the water was tugging at her legs, and the more she struggled the harder it was to keep her head above water. She was shouting for Patrick, but he wasn't there. More than once she woke up streaming with sweat, her bedclothes twisted round her, holding her fast.

Mu continued to go onto her ward, but Sister Brock had seen her pale face and the dark circles under her eyes and was worried about her. She knew nothing about Patrick, and assumed it was cumulative stress caused by the loss of her family in the Parham Road shelter, but she decided Nurse Shawbrook was in need of rest and recuperation and was keeping an eye on her.

Now Mu was back on night duty and it always took a couple of days for her body clock to adjust to the changeover.

She had been with her father and Vera when Constable Andy Sharpe had explained to a disappointed Vera how they knew that Roger was indeed Maggie's son, and she'd seen her sister's despair. On top of her own misery she found she could hardly cope with Vera's, but today, as she came off duty, she knew she ought to go round to Marden Road and see how they were getting on. As she reached the hospital gate she felt that even the hundred or so yards to the nurses' home was too far to walk. Perhaps she'd go round and see them later, after she'd had some sleep. She emerged into the street and was just turning towards the nurses' home when she saw a man leaning against the wall on the opposite side of the road. A man just like Patrick.

I keep thinking I'll see him waiting for me as he used to do, she said to herself as she walked away. And then all men end up looking like Patrick!

She glanced across again as the man detached himself from the wall and crossed the road to meet her.

'Hello, Mu, my darling. How I've missed you!'

For one strange moment, Mu thought she must be seeing a ghost, and then she was in his arms, clinging to him, being held so tightly that she could hardly breathe. For a long, long moment they stood in each other's embrace, neither of them speaking, neither of them daring to speak in case it shattered the dream.

An elderly lady passing by said, 'Not in the street please… you'll frighten the horses!'

That made them laugh and for a split second they broke apart, only to clasp each other again, and for Mu to murmur, 'Oh, Patrick, is it really, really you? They said you had drowned. Your parents think you're dead.'

'No they don't,' Patrick assured her. 'I spoke to them on the phone yesterday.'

'You didn't phone me!' Mu said, pulling away from him and looking up into his face.

'Because I didn't know where you were, silly girl. My parents told me you were in Plymouth, but they didn't have an address for you. I'd been planning to go to all the hospitals in the city asking for you until I found you, but I was lucky first go.' He turned her and slipped her arm through his. 'Come on,' he said. 'Are you hungry? Let's find some breakfast.'

Quite suddenly, for the first time for days, Mu realised that she was hungry, hungry and no longer tired.

Together they walked through the streets in quiet companionship until they found a café open to serve breakfast to those who worked the night shift in the docks. They took a table at the back, where they would not be interrupted by the comings and goings of the other customers. Kippers, toast and tea made a filling breakfast, but neither of them noticed what they were eating, they simply ate what appeared before them, constantly glancing across the table to be sure that the other was really there.

'I can't believe you're really here,' Mu said. 'Are you truly all right?'

'Yes, truly,' Patrick insisted. 'I'm fine and far luckier than most of those on board.'

'You helped other people,' Mu reminded him. 'You were seen heaving a man into one of the life rafts. Your father told me that in his letter. But then you just drifted away and no one saw you after that.'

'I was lucky that despite the darkness, someone *did* see

me drifting and hauled me into a life raft,' Patrick said. 'It was extremely cold in the water and I wouldn't have lasted very much longer.' He reached over and took Mu's hand. 'But that's all behind us now. I'm home again and have two weeks' leave before I have to report to my new ship, wherever she is. Enough of me, I want to talk about you, about us.'

Mu wasn't quite ready to talk about 'us' yet, so she told Patrick all that had happened since she had come to Plymouth, about finding Vera and looking for Freddie.

When she had finished he said gently, 'What an amazing story. And you think you may have found him with this Maggie Peterson?'

'We thought so, but she has the baby's birth certificate which names her and her husband as his parents, so we're back to square one. I could have told you all this if I'd answered your letters,' she said, her hand tightening in his grasp. 'Patrick. I'm so sorry I didn't. I've got them all but I didn't even open them. It was stupid of me but I thought somehow that a clean break was better, easier for both of us.' She looked up him shyly. 'I was wrong. It wasn't easy at all; it was impossible. I didn't destroy them, I kept them in my bedside drawer and I was missing you so much. I had just decided to read them after all, when I got your father's letter... saying...' Mu stopped, tears beginning to slip down her cheeks, the sudden lump in her throat forbidding speech.

'Darling!' Patrick reached across and gently wiped her cheeks with his thumbs. 'Don't. Don't cry. There's no need. I was rescued and I'm here. I owe my life to a leading seaman called Alfred Dixon. He risked his own life saving mine, and

I shall be eternally grateful to him. But there's no need for tears, not now.'

The clatter round them increased as the café filled up and Patrick said, 'Let's get out of here and go somewhere we can talk properly.' He called for the bill and they went back out into the fresh air.

They turned away from the busyness of the city centre and made their way into the peace of a green space that the bombers had missed. Melody Gardens was small, scarcely more than a couple of acres, boasting a small pond, a bandstand, and a little higher up, some benches looking out to sea.

They appropriated a bench and for a long time simply sat in the sunshine, holding hands, each aware of the proximity of the other and the comfort, the happiness it brought.

It was Patrick who finally broke the silence. Still staring out over the harbour and without turning his head, he said, 'You know I love you, Mu.' It wasn't a question, but Mu, also suddenly very interested in the view, took it as one and nodding, murmured, 'Yes.'

'And you love me?' This time it was a question, but there was no hesitation in her reply.

'Yes.'

'I've two weeks' leave,' he said. 'Will you marry me?'

'Yes.'

Her quiet answer made him turn his head at last. 'Before I go back to sea?'

'Yes.'

'Mu, sweetheart, can't you say anything more than "yes"?'

'What else is there to say?' She grinned at him impishly

and said, 'Yes, Patrick, I love you. Yes, Patrick, I'll marry you. Yes, Patrick, before you go back to sea.'

'Good,' he said smugly. 'Then I haven't wasted my money getting us a special licence. We can get married as soon as we like.'

'You've got one already?' Mu was incredulous.

'Seemed like a good idea,' he grinned, 'just in case I could persuade you if I got a forty-eight ashore, and now we've got a whole two weeks!'

He pulled her into his arms then and kissed her long and deep, but when they finally broke apart, she remained within the circle of his arm, resting her head comfortably against his shoulder. 'You really mean it?' he asked.

'Oh Patrick! You have no idea how miserable I was when I thought you were drowned. I was in despair. I couldn't bear the thought of living without you for the rest of my life; at the thought of you dying without me telling you how much I loved you and missed you. How much I wanted you home.'

'And now?'

'And now we have two weeks, and we mustn't waste a minute of them. The war is still with us. It could snatch either of us away, and leave the other alone, but if it does, if they are the only two weeks we spend together, they'll be the most wonderful two weeks of my life.'

Patrick tightened his embrace, saying 'Mu. *My* Mu.'

He was treated to a small gurgle of laughter. 'Yes, please, Patrick if you'll have me. *My* Patrick.'

'Until my dying day.'

'No more talk of dying,' Mu said, suddenly all briskness. 'The clock's running now!'

'Just one more thing,' Patrick said. Releasing her and putting his hand in his pocket, he pulled out the ring box he'd carried with him ever since he had left her in the Royal Oak that fateful morning. The box had clearly seen better days, and he said, 'The box is a mess after its swim in the sea, but the ring has survived. Will you wear it again for me, Muriel?'

'I always know you're being serious when you call me Muriel,' Mu said with a smile.

'Never more than now,' he replied, and taking her left hand he slipped the ring back onto her finger and then kissed her hand. 'I think we should go and find your father, don't you?' He got to his feet and pulled her to hers. He kissed her once more and then they set off, Mu walking on air, for Marden Road.

Due to her reluctance to visit them, Mu had not heard of the latest developments in the search for Freddie, so, when they appeared at the door, they were greeted with a shriek from Vera. Taking absolutely no notice of the naval officer who came into the room with her sister, Vera poured out her news.

'The birth certificate doesn't matter, Mu,' she cried. 'It's the death certificate that's important. Andy says they are going to follow it up and try and find out what happened. He says that they will contact the grandparents. That Maggie,' this was now Vera's way of naming Maggie Peterson, 'that Maggie told Inspector Droy that her mother had been looking after Roger, but she told Mrs Todd down the road that it was her mother-in-law who'd had him. She didn't get her story straight; it shows she's been lying about him!'

'Slow down, slow down,' cried Mu. 'What's this about a death certificate?'

'I found it in the trunk,' explained Vera. 'That Maggie's trunk in the cellar. She did have a birth certificate for Roger, but he died. I found his death certificate in that Maggie's trunk. The baby she has with her now isn't him. Her baby's dead.'

'I see,' said Mu, trying to take it all in and make sense of what Vera was saying. However, for once she had more important things on her mind. 'Where's Dad?'

'Dad?' For a moment Vera looked as if she didn't know who Dad was.

'Yes, Vera. Where's Dad?'

'He's been out all night at the post.'

'And is he home again?'

'No, not yet. Listen, Mu, Andy Sharpe is going to do some background checking to see if we can find out where that Maggie's gone and—'

'Vera!' Mu's voice was sharp enough to cut her sister off. 'Stop for a moment, will you?'

'All right,' said Vera sulkily. 'I thought you'd be pleased, that's all. You haven't bothered to come round for three days. I just wanted to tell you what's happened!'

'Yes, well, now you have, perhaps I can get a word in edgeways.'

'Go on then,' Vera said rudely. 'What have you got to say that's more important than finding Freddie?'

Mu had wanted to tell her father first, or at least tell them together, but she was about to introduce Patrick who had stood watching silently through their previous exchange, when the front door opened again and David came in.

'Hello, Mu,' he greeted her. 'Glad you've come round. I was worried about you.'

'No need, Dad,' she beamed, 'I'm fine.' She held out her hand to Patrick who took it and stepped up beside her. 'You remember Patrick, Dad, don't you?'

'Good morning, sir,' said Patrick, extending his hand. David took it and said, 'Good morning, Sub Lieutenant.'

'Who's he?' demanded Vera. 'What does he want?'

'I'm your sister's fiancé,' Patrick replied calmly, 'and I've come to ask your father's permission to marry her.'

'Marry Mu?' exclaimed Vera, stunned.

'Well she is rather beautiful, don't you think? And if I don't marry her very soon, somebody else might get there first.' He turned his attention back to David and said, 'Mu and I want to get married, straight away, sir. I have a fortnight's leave, and a special licence, so we're hoping to be married in three days' time.'

'You seem to have it all planned without my say-so,' remarked David mildly.

'Please, Daddy,' Mu said. 'His ship was sunk last week and so I've nearly lost him once. We want to have at least this time together.'

'You're of age, Muriel, you don't need my permission.'

'No, Dad, not your permission, but your blessing.'

David looked at his daughter and saw the bloom of happiness on her cheeks for the first time since their family had been destroyed. 'My dearest girl, that you have, and I wish you both every happiness.'

Mu ran to him and putting her arms round him, hugged him tight, murmuring into his ear, 'Oh, Daddy, I'm so happy.'

Vera watched from her chair, and then turning to Patrick said, 'I didn't know anything about you.'

'No,' agreed Patrick with a smile, 'but you will from now on.'

# 34

From that moment things moved so quickly Mu could hardly believe it. That evening she went to see Sister Brock and poured out the whole story of her engagement to Patrick and how he had been rescued from the sea off the Scilly Isles.

'And you didn't tell anyone that you thought your fiancé was lost at sea?'

'I couldn't,' replied Mu. 'It was all too painful and any sympathy would have finished me off.'

'Well, you're in luck, young lady. I only spoke about you to Matron yesterday. I told her what had happened to your family and said I was very worried about you. Of course I didn't know of this extra worry, but she and I both agreed that you should be given a fortnight for rest and recuperation.' Actually, Matron had agreed to a week, but Sister Brock would sort that out without Muriel Shawbrook ever knowing. 'You're no use on the ward if you're permanently exhausted. You need to get away somewhere and have a complete break. So, make your plans and come back to me in two weeks' time renewed and refreshed and ready to work.'

'Yes, Sister,' promised Mu, her eyes sparkling. 'I will.'

'Off you go then.'

'What, now? Straight away?'

'The sooner you start "resting", Nurse, the better.'

For the next two days, the search for Freddie took second place. Andy Sharpe had warned Vera that there were background checks to make before they could go any further.

'Don't worry,' he said. 'I'm on the case. Inspector Droy has told me to find the grandparents and see if they will confirm any part of her story.'

Vera was waiting to hear what he had discovered, but in the meantime Patrick and Mu were making the arrangements for their wedding. Everything had to be done in a hurry, but it didn't matter, because they didn't want a big wedding. Mu simply wanted to get married to Patrick and neither of them thought it was appropriate in the circumstances for anything but a very quiet affair. David would give her away with Vera in attendance, and though Mr and Mrs Davenham couldn't make the journey from Glasgow, Patrick's brother Neil had managed to wangle a forty-eight hour leave to come home and stand as his brother's best man. Patrick knew that there would be an element of sadness on the day, with Mu feeling the loss of her mother and her other siblings, but both had agreed they didn't want to postpone the ceremony; for who knew when there might be another opportunity for them all to be together. They were to be married in the city register office, and though it would be a very low-key ceremony it would still be a very special day.

It was a beautiful summer's day when Mu arrived with her father and Vera in a taxi to find Patrick and Neil waiting for them at the register office door. Mu was wearing a simple summer frock of chocolate and cream linen. A small hat of cream feathers was perched on her glorious auburn hair, worn swept back and folded into a smart chignon, with just a few tendrils escaping over her ears to frame her face. She wore no veil, but she carried a posy of yellow roses, which had been Mam's favourites, and seeing her in this becoming simplicity, the sunlight gleaming on her hair, her eyes alight with happiness, for a moment Patrick's eyes misted over and he knew he was the luckiest man alive.

Mu saw him waiting for her, tall and handsome, dressed in his number one uniform, a hasty replacement for the one now resting at the bottom of the sea, and her face creased into a radiant smile.

When they reached the door, David took Mu's hand that had been resting on his arm, and placed it in Patrick's hand and together the five of them walked into the building, a wedding party made more precious with the memory of those for ever absent.

A quarter of an hour later the five of them reappeared, Sub Lieutenant and Mrs Patrick Davenham pausing in the sunshine before they walked to share a celebration meal in the Anchor, a local pub where David was a regular. If David felt there were ghosts at the feast he let no sign of it show. It was Muriel's day, and he knew that if Nancy had been there to share in her joy, she would have been bursting with pride, but David certainly wasn't going to let the ache in his own heart spoil the day for her. He looked across the table at them, Mu and Patrick both exuding happiness, and felt a certain satisfaction in Mu's choice of husband. Patrick was good-looking and charming, but that wasn't nearly as important as the fact that he clearly adored Mu, and David felt she would be safe under his care and protection.

When the meal was over and their health and happiness had been toasted, Neil wished them well and set out to spend his night of freedom on the town. David and Vera took the bus back home and Patrick and Mu picked up their meagre luggage, left earlier in a back room at the Anchor, and splashed out on a taxi to the station. They caught a train to Exeter and taking another taxi arrived at the modest Queen Adelaide hotel where they were booked in for their wedding night.

Mu watched with pleasure as Patrick signed the register as Sub Lieutenant and Mrs Patrick Davenham before they were shown to their room, with the quiet mention that it was the bridal suite. Mu blushed as she overheard the remark, but Patrick simply asked the porter to send up a bottle of Champagne and two glasses.

When Patrick had opened the bottle and poured the wine, he handed his wife a glass and raising his own he said, 'To you my darling.' They touched glasses and drank his toast, and then he set his glass down and said, 'Don't you think it's about time to take off that ridiculous hat, sweetheart, and take your hair down?'

Shyly, Mu smiled up at him and answered softly. 'You do it.' And so he did.

While Patrick and Mu were away for their two-day honeymoon, Vera was aching to know what progress Andy Sharpe had made tracing Maggie's and Colin's parents. He had no idea where they might live and Inspector Droy sent

Andy up to Somerset House himself this time. He searched the records there for birth certificates, marriage certificates, and this time death certificates, so that nothing should be overlooked. He discovered Maggie's maiden name was Wilson, so much harder to trace than Colin's Peterson, not so common. But after two days of patient research, he had finally established that both Colin's parents were dead and so, only last year, was Maggie's mother. There was no trace of her father, he had not been named on her marriage certificate, and eventually Andy gave up on him. He was unlikely to have been involved in looking after a baby for six months. His research was useful in that it proved that Maggie had been lying, that neither her mother nor her mother-in-law had been alive to look after the baby while she moved house, but it did nothing to tell them where she might have gone when she left Plymouth.

'We shall have to wait until she comes back,' Andy said when he returned from London.

'But she might never come back!' cried Vera.

'Oh, I think she will.'

Andy had taken to calling in to see Vera at the end of his day and she found herself eagerly anticipating his ring on the bell, but the news he brought back from his trip to London had been very disappointing.

'She will almost certainly come back,' he said. 'Because she owns this house and if she doesn't return, well, she won't be able to realise the capital invested in it. She can't afford not to come back.'

'I think you should talk to Mrs Todd, up the road,' Vera said. 'She's the one that spent most time with that Maggie. I know she says she doesn't know where she's gone, but she might know something without realising. Once she hears that it's now a police matter and that you're looking for her for kidnapping, she might think of something, mightn't she?'

Andy didn't think it very likely, but to please Vera and to ensure no stone was left unturned, he went to see Stella Todd and explained the situation.

Stella recognised him as the policeman who had suggested that she befriend Maggie in the first place.

'Has she really stolen that girl's baby?' she asked. 'I can hardly believe it.'

'Everything points to it,' Andy Sharpe said. 'And whether it proves to be Vera Shawbrook's baby or not, it certainly isn't Maggie Peterson's, so we need to find her. We need your help, Mrs Todd.'

'But I don't know any more than I've told you already,' Stella said fretfully. 'She told me she was taking up a live-in job at a pub in a village outside Exeter.'

'And she never mentioned the name of the pub or the village?'

'No, I told you before.'

'And that didn't strike you as odd?'

'Well, it didn't at the time,' she replied, 'but I suppose it does now. It looks as if she deliberately didn't say, so that she could disappear completely for a while.'

'Well, how might she have heard about this job, do you think?'

Stella shrugged. 'How should I know? From an advertisement somewhere, I imagine. Or by word of mouth, I suppose. But I can't think who would have told her, she didn't really know anyone.'

'Did she take a newspaper, do you know? Perhaps a local one?'

'No,' answered Stella. 'No, she didn't. Sometimes I gave her my *Western Morning News* when I'd finished with it. She liked to do the crossword.'

'When was the last time you passed a copy of that on to her?'

'I don't know,' responded Stella, 'a couple of weeks, I suppose, could be three. I really don't know.'

'Perhaps she found the job advertised in that,' suggested Andy.

'Perhaps she did, I really wouldn't know. She never told me.'

It was pointless asking Stella Todd any more questions, she truly knew nothing more, but the information about the newspaper opened another line of enquiry. It might be worth trawling through the small ads to see if he could find one offering live-in work in a pub.

He wasn't going to report these findings to Vera. He thought he would simply tell her that Mrs Todd had no idea as to where she had gone. He was prepared to look through the small ads pages himself, but wasn't sure that Inspector Droy would consider it worthwhile, and if he didn't Andy might well be assigned to other work, leaving him no time for such a long shot search. However, when he was keeping her company the following evening, it suddenly struck him that it was something Vera could do for herself if she had the patience.

'You could go to the library and look through the small ads in the *Western Daily News* and see if you can see anything that looks likely.'

Vera pulled a face. 'I could, I suppose,' she agreed grudgingly. 'Can't the police do it?'

'No, they can't,' retorted Andy. 'Yours isn't the only case we're investigating, and this is something you could do to help yourself.'

'Oh, don't be cross with me,' Vera moaned.

Andy gave a rueful sigh. 'I'm not cross with you, Vera, but you have to realise that it is only with hard work and incredible luck we're going to find Maggie Peterson if she doesn't want to be found.'

Next day Vera ventured out on her own and took herself to the library. She asked for back copies of the *Morning News* and carefully worked her way through them. There were advertisements for all sorts of things, many offering small items for sale, but the situations vacant varied from day to day. She'd brought a notebook to record any that looked hopeful, but after an hour or so, she'd found nothing about a live-in job at a pub. She felt she was going cross-eyed and stretching her aching back she got to her feet and went out into the fresh air.

'I'll go again tomorrow,' she promised Andy when he came round that evening. 'But it was ever so boring.'

'I'm sure it was,' Andy agreed, 'but it still might turn up something.'

## 35

Patrick and Mu enjoyed their two-day honeymoon at the Queen Adelaide hotel, but it was beyond their means to stay there for more than two nights. The weather had remained fine and warm, and they had explored Exeter on foot on the first morning, before taking a bus out into the country where they had a picnic and walked on the moor, completely happy in their own company.

'I shall never forget these days as long as I live,' Mu said as they lay in each other's arms in bed the second morning. 'Whatever happens now, we shall have these days to treasure.'

'And nights?' suggested Patrick.

'And nights,' agreed Mu with a gurgle of happiness.

Patrick tightened his hold on her and buried his face in her hair. 'I do think it might be a good idea to have another moment to treasure before we go down to breakfast, don't you?' he murmured. And the kiss she gave him was all the answer he needed.

Later they took the train back to Plymouth and returned to the lodgings Patrick had found for himself when he had first arrived from Falmouth. Mrs Dunbar, the landlady, was a romantic and when she'd heard the good-looking naval officer was getting married and would soon be bringing his bride back to her house, she was delighted and put flowers in their room to welcome them.

Mu was touched by her thoughtfulness and made a point of thanking her.

'Well, dearie,' she smiled, 'there ain't been a bride in this house since Mr Dunbar carried me through that door in 1913 and I've lived here ever since. I hope you'll be as happy in your marriage as I were in mine.'

They went round to see Vera in Marden Road and found David there as well.

'I thought you were back today,' he said. 'I swapped shifts at the post with Hughes, so we can spend the evening together if you want to.'

'Shall I cook, Dad?' Mu suggested, wondering even as she said it what supplies there were.

'No,' he said, 'you're on your honeymoon. Vera can rustle up something.'

Seeing the stricken look on Vera's face Mu said, 'We'll do it together, shall we?'

There was very little on offer in the flat and so Mu went along to the parade of shops to see what Mr Grant could come up with. Half an hour later she came home triumphantly, with some liver wrapped in brown paper, two onions and some potatoes and a carrot.

'Here we are,' she said. 'We'll cook them all in one pot, it'll be delicious, you'll see. Come on, Vera, you peel the spuds while I chop the onions and the carrot!'

'All right,' Vera said reluctantly, and making her way to the sink she picked up a sharp knife and set to work.

'I need another knife,' Mu said. 'Is there one?'

'Don't know,' Vera said with a shrug. 'Might be one in the drawer.'

Mu opened the drawer, which seemed to be full of everything, and rummaged round for another knife. There was a small one at the back, and as she pulled it out a piece of paper came too. She was about to stuff it back into the drawer when she realised it was a cutting from a newspaper. It was from the small ads column and one of the advertisements had a ring pencilled round it. She stared at it for a moment and then said, 'Vera, come and look at this?'

'What is it?' Cheerfully, Vera set aside the potato she was peeling and came to her side.

'It's an advertisement in the personal column,' Mu said, handing it to her.

Vera read it and gave a cry.

'What is it?' asked David as he and Patrick broke off their conversation at her cry.

'"Help Required!"' Vera read out. '"Lady, honest and hardworking, wanted to help in country house. Remuneration by arrangement to include occupancy of estate cottage.

'"Apply Bridger, Box Number A243 *Western Morning News.*"'

'That's where she is!' Vera said. 'That's where that Maggie has gone. It wasn't to a pub, but to a country house. Now we can find her! Now we've got her!'

'It could be where she's gone,' David said cautiously.

'It must be, Dad,' insisted Vera. 'Why else would she cut it out and keep it?'

'Maybe she didn't...'

'Well, who else? This is her kitchen and it was in her kitchen drawer. Now we can find her.'

'It doesn't say where this country house is,' Patrick pointed out gently.

'No,' Vera was triumphant, 'but the newspaper will know. They'll know who took that box number, won't they?'

'Very likely,' said David, 'but I doubt if they'll tell us.'

'What d'you mean, they won't tell us?' demanded Vera. 'They'll have to.'

'I don't think they will,' Patrick said. 'Advertisements like that would be treated in confidence.'

'What do you know about it?' snapped Vera rudely. 'It isn't your baby that's been stolen.'

'No,' agreed Patrick, apparently unruffled by her rudeness. 'But I don't think they will simply hand over the name and address of the advertiser.'

'Well, when Andy comes, I'll tell him and he'll *make* them tell, you'll see.'

Mu turned to her sister and said softly, 'If you speak to Patrick like that again, Vera, we shall leave and you can cook your own dinner.'

'Sorry,' Vera said, though her tone didn't sound as if she were. 'It's just that this is the best lead we've had for ages. You don't know what it's like.'

'No, I don't,' agreed Patrick equably. 'But I do know it must be very frustrating.'

They returned to preparing the supper and Vera continued to chew over what they had found. 'It must be where she's gone. I've been searching the papers looking for a pub, and all the time the ad was here in the flat.'

By the time Andy Sharpe put in an appearance, they had eaten their liver casserole and Patrick and Mu were preparing to go back to Mrs Dunbar's. The minute he came through the door Vera was on her feet, almost shouting, 'We've found her, Andy. That Maggie's working in a country house. We know where she is. We can go and get Freddie back.'

'Calm down, Vera,' Andy said, almost fending her off like an excited puppy. 'Calm down and tell me what you've found.'

So they all sat down again and Vera told him how Mu had found the cutting.

'It was at the very back of the cutlery drawer,' Vera told him. 'Then we realised what it was, so now all we have to do is find out from the paper who put the advertisement in. We can get their name and address, and go and find her.'

'It's not quite as easy as that,' Andy said, 'we can't—'

'Why not?' interrupted Vera fiercely.

'If you'll just let me finish, Vera?'

Vera glowered at him but subsided reluctantly and Andy went on. 'We can't simply go to the paper and demand to know who advertised. They won't tell us. They don't hand out information like that to all and sundry.'

'But we aren't all and sundry!' protested Vera. 'It's my baby she's stolen, I've a right to know where she is.'

'Listen, love,' Andy said patiently. 'I didn't say we couldn't find out, I just said it wouldn't be easy. There are ways and ways of going about these things.'

'But surely they have to tell the police, don't they?'

'We can ask the paper, but if they refuse to tell us, we'll probably have to get a court order,' Andy said. 'I'll have to speak to my superiors, but I promise I'll do all I can to get the information as quickly as I can, all right?'

'All right,' Vera said sullenly.

Andy looked at her miserable expression and wished he could promise more. He wanted to give her a hug, but that wasn't possible in front of her family. What he had said would be the official way forward, but it would take time, and he knew that Vera wanted everything dealt with yesterday. He did have another idea, but he wasn't prepared to mention it to anyone in the room, it was definitely too unofficial. As he looked round the room, he realised that there was someone there whom he didn't recognise and was extra glad he'd given nothing more than the official response.

He smiled across at Mu and said, rather belatedly, 'Nice to see you again, Miss Shawbrook.'

Mu smiled at him. 'Mrs Davenham, now, Constable,' she said. 'Let me introduce my husband, Sub Lieutenant Davenham. Patrick, this is Constable Sharpe who has been helping us in our search for Freddie.' The two men got to their feet and shook hands.

'If there's anything we can do to help you,' Patrick said. 'I'm on leave for another week.'

Andy Sharpe eyed him thoughtfully. If his own plan came to fruition, there could well be a way in which Patrick and Mu might help.

'Thanks,' he said, 'I'll bear that in mind. Where will I find you?'

'We're in digs at 43 Elm Street,' said Patrick. 'Mrs Dunbar's.'

Andy Sharpe nodded. 'I'll remember,' he said.

'Did you notice that he addressed Vera as 'love'?' Mu asked Patrick as they walked, arm in arm, back to Mrs Dunbar's.

'Well, I did, but is that unusual? I mean I thought maybe he and Vera had an understanding.'

'I'd like them to have,' Mu told him. 'Vera needs someone to take her in hand and he seems to be able to make her behave.'

'You said she's only eighteen,' remarked Patrick. 'Isn't she a bit young to be thinking of one man?'

'She may be only eighteen, well, nearly nineteen, but she's already got herself into trouble once. She needs someone to take care of her and see that she doesn't do so again.'

'Does he love her, do you think?' wondered Patrick. 'She seems a bit prickly to me.'

'She always has been,' said Mu, 'but I hope she'll grow out of that. Especially if she's got someone to love.'

Patrick wasn't so sure, but he didn't say so, he simply took Mu's hand and led her in through Mrs Dunbar's front door and up the stairs. Once in the bedroom neither of them gave a further thought to Vera or her possible future with Andy Sharpe.

To Vera's disappointment Andy Sharpe left soon after her sister. He took the cutting with him and promised to do what was needed to find out who had posted the ad. Vera had certainly noticed his use of the endearment, and she'd hoped Dad would go to bed and leave them together for a while, but she should have known that Dad would do no such thing. He had heard the word 'love' too and he didn't want Vera getting any fancy ideas about the young police officer.

When Andy Sharpe left Marden Road he did not go home to his dreary bedsit, but set off to find someone. He looked in several pubs and eventually ran Keith Lane to earth in the Golden Lion. Keith, a reporter on the *Western Daily News*, was sitting at the bar, a half-finished glass of whisky at his elbow.

'Get you another, Keith?' Andy asked.

'Yes, why not?' Keith knocked back his drink and pushed his glass across to the barman.

Andy ordered a pint of beer for himself and said, 'Shall we go over to a table?'

Realising the cop had something particular to talk to him about, the reporter picked up his glass and followed him to a table in the corner where they would not be overheard.

'What's up?' he asked when he'd taken a sip of his whisky.

Andy decided to come straight to the point. 'You remember that story you ran a few weeks ago about a missing baby? Left in a house during a raid, known to have been rescued but never seen again?'

'Yeah, I remember. What about it? Can't see how they forgot to take it to the shelter with them, can you? You'd think they'd notice they hadn't got the baby with them.'

'Yes, you would, but that's not the point now. I'm on the trail of the person who's taken that baby and made off with him, not intending to give him back.'

'Abducted him, you mean?' Keith Lane's expression brightened. A lost baby was very sad, but so many people were missing thanks to the damn war, it was hardly front page news. But an abduction? That was altogether different. 'So, what have you got for me?'

'It's what you've got for me,' Andy corrected him with a grin, 'leading to what I might have for you.'

'I see,' Keith replied cautiously. 'What are you after?'

Andy told him about the advertisement in the paper. 'I need to know who placed that ad,' he said. 'I need a name and address for that box number.'

'I see,' said Keith again. 'And what do I get out of it?'

'A scoop?' suggested Andy. 'I'll tip you off when we're about to make an arrest and you can have the headline. After that it'll be up to you, but I'm sure the relieved mother will give you an interview if you ask her nicely!'

'You don't want much, do you!' said Keith sarcastically.

'I want to find the child,' said Andy. 'Of course we can go to a magistrate and make your paper reveal the information we need, but that's going to take a while and if the kidnapper gets wind of that and decides to move on we'll lose track of her again.'

'It's a "her," then, is it?'

'As far as we know,' conceded Andy. 'Look, the sooner we find this baby the sooner he can be reunited with his mother. All right?'

Keith sighed. 'All right,' he said, 'but I want to be the first to run the story.'

'You will be,' promised Andy.

'And no mention of how you managed to trace the mother, or my head'll be on the block.'

'Your head's safe,' grinned Andy. 'Now, how about another before he calls time?'

# 36

The following evening when he came off duty, Andy Sharpe met up with Keith Lane in the Golden Lion again, and as before Andy found the reporter propping up the bar with a whisky beside him.

'Pint of bitter for me,' Andy told the barman, 'and another whisky for my friend.'

They carried their drinks across to the same table and once they were settled and had taken the top off their drinks, Andy said, 'Well, Keith? What have you got for me?'

Keith pulled a piece of paper from his pocket, but held it firmly in his hand. 'Just reminding you,' he said, 'I get the headline when it all comes out into the open.'

'Yeah, we made a deal on that.' Andy gave Keith a long hard stare and added, 'And no going off on your own with it, Keith. If you do some sleuthing on your own, you could blow the whole thing out of the water and we could lose her and the baby completely.'

Keith Lane gave him an injured look at the suggestion, but smiled inwardly. He had been considering doing just that, using the information to find the kidnapper himself, but reluctantly had decided against it. For a start, a deal was a deal, though he'd reneged on some before now, but never with Andy Sharpe, and on more than one occasion they had been of use to each other and it would be a pity to spoil such an advantageous relationship. No, he could settle for the headline, and still be well ahead of the competition. He handed the paper with the address on it across and said, 'Don't worry, I'll leave it to you.'

When they parted it was with a handshake, each having to trust the word of the other. Andy Sharpe had decided not to go round to Marden Road that evening. He needed to find Vera's sister and her husband, for having got hold of the information he needed, they now had a part to play in his plan. When he reached Elm Street he was in luck. Mu and Patrick had been to the cinema and were just coming home again, walking up the road, arm in arm.

'Evening,' Andy said.

'Constable Sharpe!' said Mu in surprise.

'Could I have a word with you both?' he asked.

'Well, I'm not sure we can bring a guest inside,' Mu said doubtfully.

'Never mind,' said Patrick cheerfully, 'how about the Anchor?'

They retraced their steps down the hill and were soon ensconced at a table in a corner of the Anchor's lounge bar. Patrick fetched the drinks and Mu waited on tenterhooks to hear what Andy had to tell them.

As soon as Patrick was back, Andy brought out the paper Keith Lane had given him.

'I've called in a favour,' he said, 'and I now have the name and address of the person who put that advertisement in the paper.'

'How did you get that?' asked Mu in surprise.

'I expect he'd rather you didn't ask him that question, darling,' said Patrick with a smile.

'Just so,' said Andy. He continued, 'It's an address in a village called Martindell outside Exeter and the person advertising for help was a Colonel Bridger. He lives at the manor. If Maggie Peterson has gone there, it would seem that she won't be living in, but will have a cottage in the grounds.'

'Yes,' said Mu. 'I seem to remember that it said that in the ad. So are you going to arrest her?'

'Well, we can't go storming in unless we are certain that she's there,' Andy said. 'We have to keep our powder dry. I haven't even told Inspector Droy what I've discovered yet as I want to make a few more enquiries, and I certainly won't be telling Vera. If she builds up her hopes yet again and this turns out to be another dead end, well, better she doesn't know there was ever a chance.'

'So what happens next?' Patrick asked him.

'Well, you offered your help,' Andy said, turning back to him.

'We did, what do you want us to do?'

'What I'd like you to do is to go to Martindell and scout the place out.'

'You mean go and spy on her?' asked Mu.

'Not exactly,' replied Andy. 'I don't want to risk alerting her in any way. Now, am I right in thinking that neither of you have ever met her?'

'Well, I haven't,' said Mu firmly.

'And I certainly haven't,' replied Patrick. 'I've only just heard of the woman!'

'Good, that's what I thought. So if she did spot you, she wouldn't recognise you. Now, what I want you to do is to go to Martindell and have a look around, ask a few casual questions. When you're doing something like that it's a good idea to stick to the truth as much as possible. What I suggest is that you say you're looking for somewhere to spend your weekend leave, have a reason to be there looking round. There's sure to be an inn, or guest house, somewhere you could perhaps have a drink or a meal; and naturally chat to the barman or barmaid. Go for a walk and take a look at the manor. If possible, fall into conversation with someone who lives there, or a neighbour. I leave it up to you, but what we are trying to establish is that Maggie Peterson and the baby are both there and have been for some time. Once we're sure of that, we can go in and arrest her and bring her back to Plymouth for questioning.' Andy paused and then said to Mu, 'You would recognise the child, wouldn't you, Mrs Davenham?'

Mu considered. 'Yes, I think so. I haven't seen him for a while, I was working in Portsmouth, remember, before—' She broke off abruptly, and then said evenly, 'But I don't suppose he's changed all that much.'

'Then I shall ask you to identify him when the time comes.'

'Shouldn't Vera do that?'

'No, I don't want her to know anything about it until we're positive that he's there and he's hers. As I said before, I don't want her hopes built up only to have them dashed again.' He looked from one to the other and then said, 'Are you on?'

Patrick looked at Mu with a raised eyebrow. 'Are we on, Mu?'

'Definitely,' she replied.

'Then we'll go and have a look at Martindell tomorrow,' Patrick said.

'Let's meet up here again tomorrow evening, and you can tell me what you've discovered,' suggested Andy. 'And if for some reason you can't make tomorrow, well the next day.'

## 37

Maggie was finding life at Martindell easy and, if she were honest, a bit boring. Having got into a simple routine looking after Roger, especially with Josie as a helper, she found that the novelty of having a baby was beginning to wear off. He was adorable, of course, but as he was now on the move, he couldn't just be put in the pram to keep him safe. He was into everything and had to be watched all the time.

Bill Merton had become a friend. They met often when he came up to do the manor garden and it hadn't been long before she realised that he wanted something more. She knew he was lonely and in the evenings, when she was alone back in the cottage with Roger asleep upstairs, she could admit to herself, if not to anyone else, that she was too. One evening when she had got back from feeding them all at the manor and had put Roger to bed, she was sitting reading the paper when she was surprised by a knock on the door. When she opened it, she found Bill Merton standing on her doorstep.

'Thought you might like a bit of company,' he said with a smile. 'I brought some cards, an' I thought as we might have a game to pass the evening.'

Maggie smiled back at him. 'What a nice idea,' she said as she stood aside to let him come in.

Once inside he produced the cards and two bottles of beer. 'Thought we might do with a drink while we played,' he said.

While Maggie found them a glass each, Bill pulled the two upright chairs to the table and sat down. He seemed very much at home in her small kitchen, making it seem smaller than ever. He was a big man, tall, with broad shoulders from daily physical work, and had the countenance of a man who spent most of his time in the outdoors, tanned to leather with white crinkles at the corners of his eyes. He was not good-looking, but he had a friendly, lived-in face which was somehow attractive. As he poured the beer into the glasses, Maggie noticed his hands for the first time, a workman's hands, strong, with long fingers, and for an instant, she found herself imagining their touch on her face.

They spent a pleasant evening together, and when he finally got up to leave, he said, 'Hope you didn't mind me inviting myself.'

'Not at all,' replied Maggie and found that it was true. She had enjoyed the evening. He'd been good company, and she was sorry when he got up to go.

'That's all right, then. P'raps we can do it again. Lonely for you here all by yourself, I reckon.'

'Yes,' said Maggie, surprised at herself. 'I'd like to.'

When he'd disappeared into the darkness, Maggie went up to bed. She looked at Roger asleep in the ancient cot borrowed from the manor. He lay on his tummy, his nappied bottom a hump behind him, snuffling comfortably in his sleep.

As she undressed, she wondered what Bill Merton really wanted. Just friendship was all he'd offered so far, but she remembered the day when he'd mentioned that he might marry again sometime in the future. Surely he couldn't be thinking of her as a possible bride!

Over the following days, Bill visited her most evenings, and she found she looked forward to the knock at the door. He was a comfortable person to be with, making no demands on her, but with easy conversation about everyday things.

One afternoon, as he was about to leave the vegetable patch, he said, 'Why don't you come round to Hawthorn Farm when you're finished at the manor this evening? Have a bite with me?'

'Well, I can't really,' she said. 'I can't leave Roger in the cottage, can I?'

'No, course you can't,' he agreed, 'but Josie'll come round yours and sit with him while we have a nice quiet evening together.'

Maggie was hesitant. She had never been to Bill's farmhouse and she wanted to see it, but was it taking their friendship to another level? And did she want to? Not really. She had no intention of staying at Martindell once the war was over, but there was no need to tell Bill that. She would, however, miss his company if there were no more evenings of playing cards and drinking beer and so she agreed.

'All right,' she said. 'I'll come over when I get back. Just ask Josie to be at the cottage ready to put Roger to bed.'

The arrangement had worked well enough for them to do it again on another evening and both Bill and Maggie had been happy with the idea.

Josie was not. She watched the way Mrs Peterson had eased her way into Dad's affections, making him always dance to her tune, and she did not like it; not in the least. One evening, when Roger was safely asleep upstairs, Josie slipped out and left him alone in the cottage and went quietly to her own home. She climbed over the wall and crept up to the kitchen window. The blackout curtains prevented her from seeing inside, but the window was open a crack and she could hear what they were saying.

'You know, you're coming to Martindell was a miracle, Maggie,' her dad was saying. 'The memsahib has never been so calm, and the colonel knows he can rely on you to keep everything ticking over.'

'You do your share,' Maggie said. 'The colonel would never manage to produce any vegetables without your hard work in the garden.'

'Yes, we make a good team, Maggie.'

There was the clink of bottle on glass and then he said, 'We could make that permanent. Us? A good team? What do you think?'

'Permanent?' Maggie queried, as if she had not understood what he was asking.

'We could get married and you and young Roger could move in here with Josie and me, and...'

'Oh no they couldn't,' muttered Josie through clenched teeth. 'It's *our* home.'

'...we'd be a proper family. Josie's never had a family, only me. You could still work up at the manor, looking after the Bridgers, but your home would be here, with us.'

'Oh, Bill.' Maggie sighed regretfully. It was clear that

he'd got the idea all worked out. 'That's quite a question. My Colin's not long in his grave.'

'I know.' Bill sounded contrite. 'I'm sorry, Maggie. I shouldn't have mentioned it yet. It was too soon.'

'I'm not saying no; maybe one day in the future. Can't we go on as we are?'

'Of course we can.' There was relief in Bill's voice. 'Come on, it's your deal.'

'One more hand,' said Maggie, 'and then I must go back. We can't be too late for Josie.'

Josie stepped back from the window and scurried across the field to Maggie's cottage. As soon as she got in, she ran upstairs to check on Roger, before sitting down in the kitchen armchair and opening the book she had brought with her. But she didn't read a word. She fought tears of rage at the idea of Maggie Peterson marrying her dad, taking him away from her. Dad was hers and hers alone. She was fond of Roger and wouldn't mind him coming to live with them, but not *her*. She didn't belong in their home, and Josie knew that it wouldn't be theirs any more if she moved in. She was a managing sort of woman and Josie had seen the way she treated poor Mrs Bridger when no one was watching, ordering her about and speaking to her as if she was stupid. How long before she began to speak to Dad like that?

Hot tears squeezed from her eyes, and she dashed them away. Crying wouldn't help. If Dad really wanted to marry Mrs Peterson, there was nothing she, Josie, could do about it. She went to the sink to bathe her face and when Maggie opened the door ten minutes later, she was sitting calmly with her book in her lap.

'Everything all right upstairs?' Maggie asked.

'Yes, I haven't heard a peep out of him. I went up just now.'

'That's good,' said Maggie. 'Your dad walked me home. He's outside waiting for you. Off you go!'

# 38

Patrick and Mu arrived in Martindell just after twelve and, directed by the station master, headed straight for the pub, the Dog and Duck. Their way took them along a wide street lined with cottages, some of which opened their front doors onto the street itself, while others boasted front gardens, bright with summer flowers, and one or two that sheltered behind a wall or hedge, with a gate and a path to the front door, a sign of superiority. They passed several small shops, including a butcher's and a bakery, and on the corner of a narrow side street, a general store which also housed the post office.

The Dog and Duck was a long, low building on the edge of the village green. White painted, it had a tiny walled garden ablaze with colour at the front. Its oak door, flanked by tall hollyhocks, was welcomingly ajar, and Patrick led the way in. The doorway was low enough for him to have to duck going through, and inside the room was cool and dark, the bright summer sun outside only filtering fitfully through the small leaded windows.

Two elderly men were sitting at a table by one of the windows, a backgammon board between them. They glanced up as the couple came in, but then turned back to their game. Otherwise the room was empty.

Patrick crossed to the bar and rang the brass bell on the counter. A door at the back opened and a small woman, wiping her hands on a tea towel, came in answer to its summons.

'Good afternoon,' Patrick said. 'My wife and I have just come in on the train and we wondered if we could get something to eat.'

'Well, sir,' she said, 'I don't usually have any call to serve a midday meal, but I could do you a scratch lunch of bread and cheese and maybe some soup?'

'That would be perfect,' said Patrick and turning to Mu, added, 'Wouldn't it, darling?' He turned back to the landlady and said, 'Thank you, Mrs er...'

'Mrs Parker, Annie Parker,' supplied the woman.

'Thank you, Mrs Parker.'

'Can I get you a drink first, sir, to have while you're waiting?'

'I'll have a pint of Best,' replied Patrick. 'What about you, Mu?'

'Just a small glass of cider, please.'

While the landlady pulled Patrick's pint, she glanced across at them and said, 'We don't have many visitors here in Martindell. What's brought you here? Visiting someone locally, are you?'

It was the perfect opening and Patrick replied smoothly, 'No, I'm home on a couple of days' leave. We just wanted a day in the country before I have to go back to sea.'

'You in the navy, then?'

'Yes, for the duration.'

'My son Thomas, he's in the Merchant,' Annie said. 'Convoys from America. He says he wants to go and live there when the war's over.' She looked up at Patrick and went on, 'You ever been there?'

Patrick shook his head. 'No, but we'd like to one day, wouldn't we, darling?'

'I'd certainly like to visit,' Mu said.

'I wouldn't want to go,' Annie said. 'It'd be all different. I don't like change. Born and bred here in Martindell, I am.'

'It's a pretty village,' Mu said. 'We were admiring the cottage gardens as we walked from the station, and yours out front is beautiful. It must be a lovely place to live.'

'It suits me,' Annie said, 'but the youngsters can't wait to leave. Nothing to do here, they say.' She passed the drinks across the bar and said, 'Now, why don't you take those outside and sit in the sunshine. It's such a lovely day, and I'll bring your food out there.'

There was a table and a couple of benches in the little garden and once they were settled they looked about them. The silent peace of the place was only broken by bird song and the gentle hum of bees in the hollyhocks.

Mu took a sip of her cider and sighed. 'A bit different from Plymouth,' she said. 'Not a soul in sight!'

Across the green stood the church, a small grey stone building, surrounded by a sloping graveyard, with a large house next to it, probably the vicarage. Several other houses fronted the green, and a little way further along the road they could just see two old stone gateposts, the entrance to a driveway.

'D'you think that might be the way into the manor?' wondered Mu.

'Could be,' agreed Patrick. 'It's probably the drive of some large house, though it looks as if it's seen better days. Don't worry, Mu, we'll find out. I think Annie is going to be a fount of information if we get the chance to get chatting again. But we don't want to sound too inquisitive, do we?'

At that moment Annie reappeared carrying a tray with two bowls of soup, some bread and cheese, some tomatoes and a couple of apples.

'Here you are,' she said as she set it down on the table. 'Do you want a refill?' She nodded at their half-empty glasses.

'No, thank you,' replied Patrick. 'But before you go back in, we thought we'd go for a walk this afternoon. Can you suggest which way we should go? I see an entrance just down the road, is that a footpath out to the open countryside?'

'No, love you, that's the way into the manor. You can see gateposts are falling down and they aren't the only thing! The house is almost a ruin.'

'Sad when old houses can't be kept up,' remarked Patrick casually. 'Does someone still live there?'

'Oh yes, though they're the last of the Bridger family now. It was let for years, while the colonel was stationed in India. They came home a few years ago to find it hadn't been kept up. Far too big for them to look after, they rattle around in the place, but where else would they go?'

'But surely they have a housekeeper or a maid to look after them?' Mu said.

Annie suddenly seemed to think she'd said too much, and she picked up her tray. 'Well, I can't stand here gossiping all day,' she said briskly. 'If you want a good walk, you should go round to the back of the church. There's a footpath from there that loops round through the fields and brings you back to the other end of the village. It's got some lovely views across the moor.'

'Thank you,' Patrick said with a smile, 'that sounds just the sort of walk we enjoy. We'll certainly do that this afternoon.'

The soup Annie had brought was surprisingly good and with the bread, cheese and fruit made an excellent picnic lunch.

'Where shall we go first?' Patrick said when he came back out from paying the bill.

'Post office?' suggested Mu. 'We could go in and see if they've got any picture postcards and then I could write one to post while you have a chat with the owner.'

The village shop and post office was an everything shop. As they'd walked to the pub, they'd seen the butcher's shop and the bakery on the opposite side of the road, but the corner shop seemed to sell everything else. When they went inside they saw that the shelves were stacked with everything from reels of cotton to kitchen knives, children's clothes to garden tools. Fruit and vegetables were displayed in boxes along one wall, and on a cold slab in one corner there was a round of cheese. The post office was tucked away near the back, and next to the counter was a rack of postcards showing the beauties of Dartmoor, and some, slightly less scenic, of Exeter Cathedral.

While Mu was selecting her postcards, Patrick got into conversation with the proprietor, who, according to the licence name over the door, was one Peter Pomeroy.

'Visiting Martindell, are you?' he asked. 'Haven't seen you around here before, I don't think.'

'No, just here for the day,' Patrick said. 'I've a couple of days' leave and we wanted a little peace and quiet and some good country air.'

'Well, you'll certainly get that here,' replied Peter Pomeroy. 'What made you choose us, then?'

'Chance, really,' Patrick said. 'A friend in Exeter told us Martindell was a pretty village, very quiet, and that's what we wanted before we have to head back to Plymouth and the war.'

'The war's here too, you know,' retorted Pomeroy. 'And the last one. You only have to look in the churchyard to see that.'

At that moment Mu appeared at his side and having overheard this last remark said, 'I'd like to go into the church. It looks very old.'

'Part of it is Norman, but there was supposed to have been an even earlier one on the same site. You should go in, it's got a perfect Norman arch over the west door.'

Mu bought stamps for the card and just as they were preparing to leave, the shop door opened and a young girl came in carrying a basket.

'Afternoon, Mr Pomeroy,' she called.

'Afternoon, Josie. What are you after?'

'Dad's sent you some eggs and he wants some—' she began, and then suddenly realising there were strangers in the shop, she broke off.

Mu and Patrick smiled at her and saying goodbye to Mr Pomeroy, they walked out of the shop and closed the door behind them.

'Eggs for something else, I think, don't you?' asked Patrick with a grin, but Mu wasn't listening to him. She had stopped short on the pavement. Her way was blocked by a pram, and sitting up in the pram was Freddie.

'Patrick!' she hissed. 'Look!'

'What?' asked Patrick. 'Look at what?'

'The baby,' she whispered, though there was no one to hear her.

'The baby?' He looked at the pram and saw a large baby, sitting up and playing with its toes.

'It's Freddie,' muttered Mu. 'Look at his hair!'

Patrick looked and suddenly saw. The child in the pram had hair the same colour as Mu's, tiny curls of burnished auburn hair covering his head. Patrick glanced back into the shop where Josie was transacting whatever business she had come to do with Mr Pomeroy.

'But that's not Maggie Peterson.'

'No, of course it isn't, she must simply be looking after him, but it's definitely Freddie.'

'So what do you suggest we do? You can scarcely confront the girl. And anyway, Andy doesn't want to alert Maggie to the fact that we've found her.'

'We can admire the baby,' said Mu with a quick glance over her shoulder. 'Just start a conversation and see what she says.'

'All right,' agreed Patrick. 'I'll leave all the talking to you.'

At that moment the shop door opened and Josie came out again, a cloth covering whatever it was she had in her basket. She stopped abruptly as she saw the people who had been in the shop still standing by the pram. For a moment she felt a rush of panic. Were they the black market police she'd been warned about? They didn't look like police, but if they were looking for people using the black market, they wouldn't, would they? Then the lady spoke to her with a kind smile.

'What a lovely baby,' she said. 'Such pretty hair! Is she your baby sister?'

'It's a boy,' Josie corrected her. 'No, he's not my brother, I just look after him sometimes when his mother's busy.'

'How lucky she is to have you,' said the lady.

Seeing Josie back beside his pram, Freddie beamed at her, treating them all to the sight of his single tooth.

Josie placed the basket carefully in the carrier under the pram and grasping the handle said, 'Come on, Roger, Mummy will be wondering where you are.'

'She certainly is,' murmured Mu as the girl turned the pram and set off down the street. Slowly, arm in arm, Patrick and Mu followed her, watching until they saw her turn in between the old stone gateposts that guarded the manor driveway.

'I knew I was right!' cried Mu, clutching a tight hold on Patrick arm. 'I just knew it! You heard what she called him? She called him Roger.'

'And she went home to the manor.'

'We should go straight back to Plymouth,' Mu said. 'Now we know she's here and so is Freddie, we've got to tell Andy Sharpe. Suppose she moved on again! He must act at once.'

'D'you think she'll mention meeting two people she didn't know asking about the baby?' asked Patrick.

'No,' said Mu. 'I pretended I thought he was a girl, remember.'

'You don't want to take that footpath from behind the church?' asked Patrick. 'It looks as if it loops round behind the manor. We might be able to see into the garden. We might see her.'

'And she might see us,' returned Mu. 'No, Patrick, let's go back to the station.'

That evening, Mu and Patrick walked into the Anchor and found Andy Sharpe waiting for them as promised.

He could see that Mu was excited and said, 'Go and grab us a table, and I'll bring over some drinks. What's your tipple?'

Patrick asked for a pint and Mu a glass of cider.

'Well,' said Andy when they were settled at the table. 'What news?'

'We've seen Freddie,' Mu burst out. 'I saw him in the pram. He was being looked after by a girl called Josie, and she called him Roger. But I knew him at once. He hadn't changed that much, but his hair had grown, no longer just fluff, it's little curls all over his head and it's the same colour as mine. I know it was him. I have absolutely no doubt.'

'Well, you'll have to come to the station tomorrow and make a formal statement,' said Andy. 'Then we can go to Martindell and make proper enquiries. It's not our jurisdiction up there, but I think we'll be able to arrange things with the local force and keep hold of the case.'

'What do you mean, "proper enquiries"?' asked Mu. 'Can't you just arrest her? We know she stole Vera's baby, and you can prove it isn't hers.'

'We'll have grounds for bringing her back to Plymouth,' said Andy, 'but we'll have to make out a definite case against her before we can charge her with abduction.'

'Are you going to tell Vera?' asked Mu.

'No, not yet, there're too many things that have to be done

in the correct manner, and there could still be problems. I suggest we don't mention it to Vera until we've got Maggie and the baby safely back here in Plymouth.'

So far Patrick had taken no part in this conversation, but now he said, 'Andy's right, Mu. We have to be certain-sure before we say anything to Vera.'

The following morning Mu went to the police station and Inspector Droy took her statement himself. He had realised by now that Constable Sharpe had a personal interest in the outcome of the case and he did not want there to be any mishaps in its handling.

Mu described exactly what they had learned on their visit to Martindell; that the people who lived at the manor were indeed the people who had advertised for home help. That she had seen and identified the baby as her nephew, Freddie Shawbrook. That the young girl who was looking after the baby had confirmed that it was a boy and had addressed him as Roger, the name that Maggie Peterson had on the birth certificate of her own son, now deceased.

Droy spent some time conferring by telephone with his opposite number in Exeter, and it was agreed that a member of his force should be there when the Plymouth police arrived in Martindell for the arrest.

'And we'll take WPC Adams with us,' Droy said to Andy Sharpe. 'We'll need a woman officer with us if we're going to pick up the woman and the baby and bring them back here.'

# 39

'Why don't you come round our place this evening for some grub?' Bill suggested that afternoon when he gave Maggie a bag of potatoes and onions at the manor kitchen door.

Maggie hesitated. 'Well,' she replied, 'I don't know. I'm cooking here.'

'Come on,' coaxed Bill. 'Just feed them and then come and eat with Josie and me.'

'But what about Roger?'

'He's in his pram, isn't he?' said Bill. 'If you've fed him here, he can sleep at our house while we eat, and then Josie can take him home, while you and I have a quiet nightcap.'

'Sounds a lovely idea,' agreed Maggie.

It was very economical eating with the Bridgers every evening, making the most of their rations, but there were times when she thought that if she had to spend another mealtime with the memsahib, she would go mad. If she fed Roger quickly before she served them their dinner, she could get away afterwards and spend a sociable evening with Bill.

'All right,' she said with a smile. 'Thanks. I'll come straight round when I've finished here.'

As tended to happen, the meal took longer than Maggie hoped. Mrs Bridger was fretful, worried that Maggie wasn't eating with them.

'You must have some supper,' she insisted. 'It's not good to miss meals, especially for the little boy.'

Maggie had given up arguing with her when she got into one of these moods, and said resignedly, 'I fed Roger earlier, and I ate mine then.'

'Maggie will be quite all right, my dear,' soothed the colonel. 'You just eat up yours and then we can go into my room and listen to the wireless. It might be *ITMA* tonight. You like that programme, don't you?' He had no idea if his wife took in anything she heard on the wireless, but at least she was happy sitting beside him while he listened and he could enjoy the programme himself.

When Maggie finally reached Hawthorn Farm, there was a delicious aroma of hotpot wafting from the kitchen. Roger had fallen asleep in the pram as she'd walked over, and she left him outside in the yard in the last warmth of the mellow evening sun.

The three of them sat down at the table, and it was as they were eating their meal that Josie dropped her bombshell and said, 'There were some strangers in the village today.'

Maggie was immediately alert and said, 'Were there? Who were they, I wonder?'

Josie shrugged. 'I don't know, do I? A man and a lady. They were in the post office. Mr Pomeroy said they'd been asking questions.'

'Questions?' Maggie tried to keep her voice even, as if her interest was purely casual. 'What sort of questions?'

'Dunno. They stopped when I came in, but when I came

out again they were still standing by the pram admiring Roger.' She grinned. 'They thought he was a girl, cos of his hair, I s'pose. It was the same colour as hers.'

Hers. Did Josie mean the strange woman's? She must have done, but Maggie decided not to ask. She took a deep breath and said, 'His is getting a bit long, isn't it? I'll have to try and cut it. Can't have people thinking he's a girl. What else did they say?'

'Nothing really. Just asked if he was my baby sister and I told them no, that he was a boy and that I was looking after him for you.'

'For me,' Maggie said, her voice tense.

'Well,' answered Josie not picking up on the tension, 'I said for his mum... at least that's what I think I said, I can't remember now. Does it matter?'

'No, of course not,' said Maggie quickly. Then, anxious to change the subject, she said, 'This is delicious hotpot, Bill.' She mashed some potato into the last of the gravy on her plate and forked it into her mouth. 'What's the secret?'

'The secret? Ah well, can't tell you that, can I? Just let's say the hens have started laying again!' And they all laughed.

When the meal was over Josie took Roger, still asleep in the pram, back along the footpath to Maggie's house, leaving her father and Maggie together at the farmhouse kitchen table.

At least I won't have to do the washing up, Josie thought as she stumped along the path, pushing the pram.

She didn't mind looking after Roger, she quite enjoyed it. He was a lovely little chap, always greeting her with a gummy smile when she appeared, and she'd grown fond of him, but it irritated her the way her dad simply sent her off when he wanted to be alone with Mrs Peterson. Occasionally he gave her the odd half crown, telling her that it came from Mrs Peterson, but Josie knew it didn't. Mrs Peterson had never given her anything for her help, hardly even a thank you, but it was just like Dad to make sure she got what she'd earned.

Back in the farmhouse kitchen, Maggie agreed to a small glass of brandy from the bottle Bill kept hidden inside the grandfather clock, but she didn't want to stay long. She needed to get home and think about what Josie had said. About the strangers in the village, showing an interest in Roger. When Bill tried to refill her glass, she put her hand over the top.

'No, Bill,' she said, smiling to soften her refusal. 'I must get back, and anyway, we mustn't drink all your brandy in one evening, must we?'

'Plenty more where that came from,' Bill replied with a grin. 'Now that the hens are laying again!'

Still Maggie refused and five minutes later she was following the footpath home. When she got there she found Josie had already put Roger to bed in the manor cot and was quite ready to go home.

'Thank you, Josie,' Maggie said as she saw her out of the door. 'I don't know what I'd do without you sometimes.'

'Yeah, well, I do it to help Dad, not you!' retorted the girl. And with this riposte she disappeared into the warm darkness.

As soon as she'd gone, Maggie shut and locked the door behind her and flopped down on a chair. She had to think. Who were these people who had been in the village and looking at Roger? Why had they asked questions about him?

Was their interest in an attractive baby totally innocent? Perhaps the woman just loved babies, like Stella Todd did. Some women were like that, ready to coo over any baby that crossed their path. Josie said that the woman had thought he was a girl, and Maggie had to admit he was looking more girly as his newly grown hair spread into tiny curls all over his head, but then Josie had said that the woman had hair the same colour. Was that a coincidence? Lots of people must have auburn hair, it wasn't that unusual, was it? But Maggie didn't believe in coincidences, she couldn't afford to, not if she was going to keep at least one step ahead of anyone who might be looking for her. Looking for Roger. She sighed and went upstairs to look at Roger in his cot, and seeing him fast asleep, his auburn head on the pillow, his little hand crooked under his chin, she made her decision. It was time to move on.

This time it was much easier packing up their things. They only had what they'd come with, and as she'd managed to carry that with her before, she could do it again. She fetched her purse from her bag and counted her money. She hadn't spent much since she had arrived, living at the expense of the Bridgers and paid by the week, so she had enough for now, but knew that if she were to disappear again, she needed more. The cash in her purse would pay her fare back to Plymouth, and though that was the last place she wanted to go, she realised that she must go to the bank. It would be a small risk but it was one she knew she had to take.

Packed and ready, she went to bed, but only slept fitfully as she was afraid of oversleeping. She knew the milk train passed through Martindell at six o'clock each morning, and that was the train she wanted to be on. She was determined to be well away from the village before anyone realised she had gone. And, she decided, she must lay a false trail. When she bought her ticket, she would ask the time of the last train back from Exeter that evening, as if she were coming back after a day out. With luck that would give her an extra day's start just in case the strangers had been looking for her. And if they hadn't, well it didn't really matter, she'd probably stayed in the one place too long already. She certainly didn't want to live in Martindell with Bill Merton for the rest of her life.

As the sky lightened with the dawn, Maggie was up and getting Roger ready for the day, giving him his breakfast, and a final nappy change before they set out.

It was a beautiful summer morning, dew sparkling on the grass, the air filled with birdsong. For a moment she looked out across the fields touched with early sunlight. She had been happy enough here, she supposed, but it was time to move on. Closing the cottage door behind her, she locked it and pocketed the key and then, turning her back on it all, she walked away.

She took the longer way into the village so that she didn't have to pass Hawthorn Farm. It was such a lovely morning Bill might well be up himself and see her as she passed, and she was determined she was going to slip away without any questions from him.

She reached the station with ten minutes to spare. At the ticket office she bought a return. It cut into her small reserves of cash, but it would make anyone asking about her – the Bridgers, Bill, or anyone – assume that she was coming back.

'Can you tell me the time of the last train from Exeter this evening?' she asked. 'I'm visiting a friend there today and I don't want to miss it.'

'Nine thirty-seven,' came the reply. 'Gets in here at ten forty-one.'

'That's perfect,' Maggie said. 'I'll make sure I'm in plenty of time.'

'Well, you know what the trains are like just now,' said the man with a shrug. 'Could be later, but it won't go early, that's for sure.'

Maggie thanked him and pushed the pram onto the platform to wait. The train was ten minutes late, and those minutes seemed a lifetime to Maggie. She kept looking at the station entrance; suppose someone else turned up and recognised her and wondered why she was leaving? Moments before the train was due, an elderly woman carrying a large basket walked into the station. Maggie turned her back and rocked the pram as if she hadn't noticed her, but the woman remained at the other end of the platform, paying no attention to Maggie or the baby.

At last the train steamed round the corner, screeching to a halt beside them, enveloping them in a cloud of steam. The guard jumped down onto the platform, and when he saw Maggie approaching with the pram, he came forward to lift it into the van for her. She'd scooped Roger into her arms, and once she was sure the pram was safely aboard she got into an empty compartment and settled herself and Roger into a corner seat.

The stop was a short one and moments later the guard was blowing his whistle and waving his flag, and with another explosion of steam, the train pulled slowly out of the station. Maggie peered anxiously out of the window, but the platform was empty, no one arrived at the last minute looking for her, and with a sigh of relief she settled down to entertaining Roger on the journey to Exeter.

# 40

The train was a local, stopping at all the villages along the way. Several people boarded the train including two men who got into Maggie's compartment, but neither of them spoke except to say good morning before disappearing behind their newspapers. When the train finally pulled into Exeter, Maggie took her time collecting her things together, allowing the two men to disappear before she stepped out onto the platform. As soon as she had collected the pram from the guard's van she headed out of the station. She had accomplished the next step of her journey without question from anyone.

She had decided to wait for a while before buying her onward ticket to Plymouth, to let all those who'd been on the train disperse, and when she did approach the ticket office she left the pram a little way off so that no one would connect the purchase of a ticket to Plymouth with a woman with a baby – with her. She asked the time of the next train and left the station again. She had prepared some bottles for Roger and had some rusks and some stewed apple in a jam jar to give him later. To pass the time she sat on a park bench and gave him one of the bottles to keep him going. Her own sandwiches she saved. She waited until just five minutes before the train was due to depart, and she almost missed it. The guard grumbled as he put the pram into his van, and Maggie, carrying Roger, scrambled into a carriage as he blew his whistle. The train was packed with sailors returning to Plymouth from leave, but seeing her with a baby on her hip, Maggie was offered a seat which she accepted gratefully. The rocking of the train sent Roger to sleep in her arms, and no one spoke to her for fear of disturbing him.

As the train chugged its way to Plymouth, she considered her plans. Money was her first requirement. Once she had emptied her bank account, she would have plenty of cash to make good her escape. She considered her options. Should she go back to London, to Hackney, where she and Colin had lived before moving to Plymouth? No, that was too obvious, and there were people there who knew that her Roger had died. Better steer clear of that area, even if it was where she felt most at home. Where then? A city? Or back into the countryside where she could use the old excuse, that she was keeping her son safe from the bombing? And she must use a different name, something common. Maggie Wilson, her maiden name? No, if they were looking for her they'd think of that. What then? Meg Smith? Yes, that would do. She had been known as Meg at school, so she'd answer to that all right, and Smith could be anybody. From now, living on her wits she'd be Meg Smith. She would only use her real name when she absolutely had to.

When the train pulled into Plymouth station, she carried Roger to the guard's van and collected the pram. She thanked the guard, but he was busy unloading bicycles and a trunk and paid no attention to her as she put Roger into the pram and wheeled him away. He was grizzling as they went, uncomfortable and hungry. She looked down at him in frustration. She needed somewhere to take him to change and feed him. The bank was her priority, but she couldn't have him bellowing and drawing attention to them. In the end she went into the ladies' room and scooping him out of the pram, went into a cubicle and changed him on her knee. At least when he was clean and dry she could give him a bottle and hope that would keep him quiet for a bit.

As soon as she could she set off to the bank, but she was too late. The journey and Roger's needs had taken longer than she'd anticipated. The bank had closed at three thirty and now its doors were firmly locked. She could hear people inside, but they were not open to their customers. Maggie felt tears of frustration as she looked at the closed door. It meant, she realised, that she'd have to stay a night in Plymouth before she could withdraw her money. She turned away, pushing the pram along the pavement. The longer she stayed in the city the riskier it was. She needed to get off the street. She kept well away from Marden Road and found herself in an area of the city that she didn't know. Rounding a corner, she saw a pub standing on the edge of a bombsite. It looked tired and dirty with peeling paint and cracked windows, not the sort of place that Maggie would normally dream of entering, but perhaps, she thought, they might have a room for the night, no questions asked. The painted sign swinging above its door proclaimed it the Swan and that the licence was held by Mrs P. Dawkins.

Maggie pushed at the door, but it was closed. The pub wouldn't be opening for business until five thirty that evening, but Maggie wanted to be off the streets before then, so she hammered on the door with her fist. At first no one came in answer, but when she hammered again she heard the bolts being drawn back and the door creaked open.

'We're closed,' announced the woman who stared out at her. 'Don't open until half past five.' She began to push the door shut again, but Maggie said, 'Wait! Please!'

'What d'you want?' demanded the woman grumpily. 'Didn't you hear what I said? We're closed.'

'I'm looking for a room for the night,' Maggie said, adding quickly, 'I can pay, and it's only for one night. My husband's locked me out and I need somewhere for the baby.'

'What d'you mean, locked you out? Ain't you got a key to your own home?'

'Yes, usually, but I just popped out to the shops, didn't I? An' he's come home drunk and locked the door. Reckon he's passed out as usual. He won't come round till tomorrow if he's had the usual skinful.'

The woman eyed her thoughtfully, taking in the pram, the luggage tucked under it and the knapsack on Maggie's back.

'Well,' she said, 'as it happens, I have got a room, but it'll cost you. The man what uses it is away until Saturday. Just the one night, mind. Ten shillings. Pay in advance.'

'Ten shillings!' echoed Maggie in dismay. It was far too much.

'Take it or leave it,' said the woman, her hand raised to close the door again.

'I'll take it!' Maggie said hurriedly.

'Payment in advance,' said the woman holding out her hand as she opened the door wide enough to admit the pram. 'And you'll have to leave the pram in the backyard, Mrs er...'

'Smith,' said Maggie.

The woman nodded with a knowing smile. 'Mrs Smith.'

There was nothing for it, Maggie knew she had to get out of sight and have somewhere she could deal with Roger's needs. She pulled out her purse and four half crowns. She only had fifteen shillings left and she was handing over ten of them to Mrs P. Dawkins, the landlady of the Swan.

She parked the pram in the backyard and carried the holdall and the rucksack up to the room Mrs Dawkins showed her. It clearly belonged to somebody else, with a man's clothes in the narrow wardrobe, some underwear in a drawer, and a newspaper with a half-done crossword beside the single bed. The window was closed and the room smelt stale and stuffy. A bowl and ewer stood on the chest of drawers and the landlady told her that the bathroom was at the end of the landing.

'A shilling extra if you want a bath,' she had said as she turned to go back downstairs.

Maggie hated the room on sight, but beggars couldn't be choosers and it would only be for one night. As soon as the bank opened in the morning, she would withdraw all her money and be off, heading out of the city. She returned to the yard and lifted Roger out of the pram. He laid his face against her cheek, and she felt the last of his tears on her skin. But at least he had stopped crying. Once they were upstairs she filled the ewer from the bath tap and carried it back to the room. Stripping off Roger's clothes, which were damp and smelly, she washed him all over and dressed him in clean things from the skin out. She had one more bottle prepared and she gave it to him now, in the hope that with a full tummy he would go to sleep. Eventually, as she rocked him against her, he succumbed and fell asleep in her arms. She could hear sounds from downstairs and realised that it meant the pub was now open. She laid Roger on the bed and wedged him close against the wall with the pillow. She needed something to eat herself, but more importantly she needed milk for Roger. She still had the apple and the packet of rusks in her knapsack which she could crumble into the milk if necessary, but perhaps Mrs Dawkins had something more solid that she could mash up for him. She went downstairs and found Mrs Dawkins behind the bar, lining up pints for a group of sailors.

'And you'd like a little medicine in the top?' she was asking.

The sailors grinned and one of them answered, 'Of course, we always have to take our medicine, don't we, lads?'

There was a chorus of approval and Mrs Dawkins reached under the counter and producing a bottle of Haig, poured a liberal amount of whisky into each pint.

The landlady scooped up and counted the cash handed over by the sailors before putting it into the till and only then did she turn to Maggie.

'Anything I can get you, Mrs Smith? A noggin, too, perhaps?'

'No, thank you,' Maggie replied firmly. 'I wondered if you had a little milk to spare for the baby?'

'I expect I can find you some, for sixpence,' came the reply. 'And something for yourself? I've got a delicious hotpot on the stove, only a shilling a bowl.'

Maggie thought of the sandwich which would otherwise

be her supper. She could save that for the morning and so reluctantly she agreed to both. Having handed over another one and sixpence, she carried the food and the milk back up the stairs. When she got back to the room, Roger was still asleep. The portion of hotpot was not generous but she tipped some into the bowl she used for Roger, and mashed it with the fork. It would do as solid food for him if he woke and she could save the rusks and the apple for later. She ate a little of what was left herself, unidentified scraps of meat and vegetables floating in a mess of pale grey gravy. She thought with sudden longing of the hotpot she had shared with Bill and Josie only the night before, rich and full of flavour, and she had to fight back the tears that threatened.

As darkness fell outside her window, she pulled the blackout curtain across and turned on the light. The bulb was weak, giving only a dull yellow glow, casting shadows into the corners and making the room even more depressing than before. With nothing to do but to try and sleep, Maggie lay down beside Roger on the narrow bed. She did not undress, or turn back the sheets, the rank smell that emanated from the pillow warning her that they had not been changed for far too long.

What sort of man, she wondered, usually slept in this room, in this bed? What would happen if he came back unexpectedly? That dreadful thought was enough to make her get up again and check that she had locked the door.

Maggie slept fitfully and awoke unrested and gritty-eyed when Roger began to cry. She gave him the milk and some of the cold mashed hotpot. He took one mouthful and spat it out. She couldn't blame him, but she tried to coax him to eat a little more. Until she was able to go to the bank she couldn't buy him anything else. Roger simply closed his mouth and refused to open it. With a sigh she found one of the rusks and crumbling it into a little milk she fed him with that, saving the stewed apple, still in its jam jar, for later.

In the street below her window the city was beginning to stir. The clock on a nearby church struck seven and Maggie threw back the curtain to find bright sunshine gleaming on the windows of the building opposite. She unlocked the door and stepped out onto the landing. The pub was silent, no sound of Mrs Dawkins or anyone else astir. Quietly Maggie went along the passage and used the bathroom, splashing cold water on her face. There was no soap, so she made do with damping the corner of a towel and scrubbing her hands with that. She did not flush the lavatory for fear of waking the landlady. She owed Mrs Dawkins nothing, but she didn't want to encounter that lady ever again, and Maggie had decided that she was going to leave as quickly and as quietly as she could. She had absolutely no intention of parting with her last three shillings and sixpence. Back in the bedroom she hitched the knapsack onto her shoulders, picked up the holdall with one hand and hoisted Roger onto her hip with the other. Downstairs the bar was blackout-dark and smelt of tobacco and spilt beer. Maggie made her way through the kitchen to the door into the backyard. Putting down the holdall, she drew back the bolts and pulled on the door handle. The door opened grudgingly with a horrifying screech. For a moment Maggie froze. From upstairs there came the bang of a door followed by footsteps along the landing and Maggie realised that Mrs Dawkins must have heard her. She yanked the door wider and pushed her way into the yard. Thankfully, the pram was where she had left it. Hurriedly she dumped Roger and ran back for the holdall. As she grabbed it she heard footsteps on the stairs, and she ran back into the yard, dropping the holdall almost on top of Roger before pushing the pram out into the street. Behind there came an angry cry.

'Sneak out, would you? I'll have the law on you!'

Maggie gave one glance over her shoulder and saw Mrs Dawkins, barefoot, dressed in her nightie and with curling papers in her hair, standing at the kitchen door.

'You do that,' Maggie called back. 'And I'll tell them about the black market whisky you keep under the bar.'

It was a shot in the dark, she didn't know if it was black market, but it seemed to have hit home, as Mrs Dawkins went back indoors, slamming the door behind her.

Maggie set off down the street, relieved to be out and away from the Swan. She knew she had been cheated in every way, but she had achieved what she needed to, to be off the streets overnight. She had just under three hours before the bank would open its doors.

# 41

As Maggie left the Swan, the three police officers left Plymouth and drove to Exeter where they collected Constable Harris from the Devon force and then drove out to Martindell. The village seemed hardly awake when they arrived soon after nine. Constable Harris had done his homework and he guided them past the pub and in through the stone gateposts guarding the manor's drive. The drive itself curved through some trees and brought them onto a wide turning circle in front of the house.

'I'll go to the front door,' Droy said, 'you three cover the back and any side entrances. If Maggie Peterson is here, we don't want her making a break for it.'

They all got out of the car and Inspector Droy went up the front steps, waiting a few moments for the other three to take up positions round the outside of the house before he rang the bell.

The door was answered not by Maggie Peterson as he'd half expected, but by an elderly lady with a halo of white hair and a faraway look in her faded blue eyes.

'Not today, thank you,' she said and proceeded to try and close the door again. Droy put his boot in the way to prevent it and said, 'Mrs Bridger? I'm Inspector Droy of the City of Plymouth police. I've come all the way from Plymouth to see you. May I come in?' He held up his warrant card for her to see, but the old lady didn't even glance at it.

'I don't know you,' she said. 'I'll have to ask my husband.' And leaving Droy standing on the step and the front door open, she disappeared down a passage and out of sight. The inspector stepped indoors and waited in the hallway. He waited several minutes but when no one appeared he was about to follow the woman when an elderly gentleman emerged from the same passageway.

'Good morning, officer,' he said as he strode into the hallway. 'I am Colonel Bridger. Can I help you?'

'Good morning, sir. Inspector Droy, City of Plymouth police,' replied Droy, holding out his warrant card.

'City of Plymouth? Bit out of your area, aren't you? What do you want up here with us?'

'I am looking for a woman named Margaret Peterson, sir, whom I believe to be in your employ.'

'Margaret Peterson?' The colonel shook his head. 'No I don't...' Then his confused expression cleared. 'Oh,' he said, 'you mean Maggie, I'd forgotten her surname. I'm afraid she's not here any more.'

'She's left your employ?'

'It would seem so,' answered the colonel. 'She's left us in the lurch. Simply walked out without a word of explanation.'

'Can you think of a reason?' asked the inspector. 'A falling-out?'

'Certainly not,' retorted the colonel. 'She simply upped and left.' Then, with a sigh, he added, 'She's not the first to do that and she probably won't be the last. It isn't easy with the memsahib. But I thought Maggie was different.'

'In that case, sir, I wonder if there is somewhere we could go to talk. I have a few questions which you might be able to answer.'

'Questions? About Maggie?'

'Yes, sir. About Maggie.'

The colonel heaved another sigh and said, 'You'd better come through to my study.'

Inspector Droy followed the old man down the corridor and into a room that looked out over the garden. It was clearly where the colonel spent most of his time, furnished with a desk, some easy chairs and floor-to-ceiling bookshelves. The old lady who had answered the door was sitting in an armchair by the window.

She looked up with frightened eyes as they came in and said in a quavering voice, 'Colonel! There are strangers in the garden. What are they doing?'

Droy glanced out of the window and saw Andy Sharpe.

'I'm sorry, Colonel, madam, those are my men. We have come here to make enquiries about Maggie Peterson.'

'She's gone,' said Mrs Bridger. 'And I'm glad. I didn't like her. She had a fat baby.'

Ignoring this non-sequitur, Droy said, 'As I explained, sir, I had hoped to ask her some questions, but as she isn't here, perhaps I can ask you instead?' This last he addressed to the colonel who waved him to a seat and said, 'Of course, officer. How can we help?'

'Mrs Peterson. Does she live in this house?'

'No,' answered the colonel. 'She has a cottage on the estate. It's part of her remuneration.'

'I see. So at the end of the day she goes home.'

'Yes, that's right.'

'Please can you tell me in your own words when you last saw Mrs Peterson and how she was behaving.'

'Well,' the colonel replied after a moment's thought, 'she cooked us dinner on Tuesday as usual, though she didn't eat with us as she usually does. Normally she has her meals with us and feeds the baby over here too.'

'I see, and on Tuesday she didn't do that?'

'No, she left as soon as we'd finished.'

'With the baby?'

'Oh, yes,' answered the colonel. 'Certainly with the baby. She won't leave him with us, not since she found him in the dog basket.'

And she was right! Droy thought, but he did not voice his thought, he simply asked his next question. 'And where did she go?'

'Home, I imagine. There's nowhere else for her to go, really. Apart from the pub, of course, and she couldn't have gone there, not with the baby.'

'And this was definitely on Tuesday?'

'Yes, Tuesday evening.'

'The thing is, sir,' explained Droy, 'I have information that says Mrs Peterson's son Roger was seen in the village just two days ago, Tuesday.'

'Her son? I thought you were looking for Maggie.'

'Indeed I am, but I assumed that if her son was here, she would be also. He was being looked after by a young girl.'

'That would be Josie Merton,' said the colonel.

'And who is Josie Merton?' asked Droy.

'She's Bill Merton's daughter.'

Droy remained patient. 'And who's Bill Merton?'

He half expected the colonel to say, 'He's Josie's father,' but instead he said, 'He's a local farmer. Runs his sheep on one of our fields. Does our digging for victory!'

'So, the last time you actually saw Mrs Peterson was after dinner on Tuesday evening? And then she went home.' Droy paused but as the colonel seemed to have run out of steam, he prompted, 'And in the morning?'

'In the morning? She'd gone. At least, she didn't come here to do our breakfast, as she usually does.'

'You weren't worried about her?'

'No, not really. I thought she must have overslept, but when she still hadn't arrived by about ten o'clock, I walked over to the cottage just in case she was ill, or there had been an accident.'

'And she wasn't there?'

'No, there was no sign of her and the cottage was all locked up.'

'So you couldn't get inside. Haven't you got a spare key?'

'Yes, I have, but I didn't have it with me then.'

'So what did you do next?'

'I walked over to Hawthorn Farm to see if she was there for some reason. Perhaps taking the baby over to Josie.'

'But she wasn't?'

'No,' replied the old man testily, 'I've told you. I haven't seen hide nor hair of her since Tuesday evening.'

'Was Josie expecting to look after the baby yesterday morning?'

'I don't know. She wasn't there when I got to Hawthorn Farm and I haven't seen her or Bill Merton since Maggie disappeared.' He looked across at the inspector and asked,

'Why are you looking for Maggie, Inspector? What's she supposed to have done?'

'I need to ask her some questions,' replied Droy. 'She may be able to help us with our enquiries.'

'Well, I hope you find her soon,' sighed the old man. 'I need to know when she's coming back.'

'I think I can safely say, sir, that she won't be coming back. Not in the foreseeable future.' Droy got to his feet and smiled. 'Thank you, Colonel Bridger,' he said. 'You've been most helpful. Just one more thing – perhaps you could direct me to Hawthorn Farm.'

The colonel also rose and as they walked together to the hall he told Droy the way to Hawthorn Farm. The front door still stood open and as he stepped outside the inspector turned back and held out his hand. 'Thank you for your time, sir. I shan't trouble you again. There's nothing more for you to worry about.'

And with that the inspector left the old man standing in the hallway with absolutely *everything* to worry about and wondering how on earth he was going manage without Maggie.

# 42

It took just a few minutes to drive to Hawthorn Farm, and as they turned into the yard they were greeted by a cacophony of barking from three dogs that came out of an outhouse and capered excitedly around the car. Their noisy barking brought a young girl out of the house, and she stood staring as the four police officers got out of the car.

'Good morning,' said one of them as he stepped forward. 'My name's Inspector Droy. You must be Josie Merton.' When the girl nodded he went on, 'Is your father about?'

'He's up in the copse clearing the undergrowth,' she replied. 'What do you want him for?'

'I need to ask him some questions,' answered the inspector. 'Can you take me to him?'

'If you like.' The reply sounded grudging and Droy looked at her sharply, before saying, 'Perhaps *you* can help me. Do you know Mrs Maggie Peterson?'

'Yes, a bit.'

Her answer was still grudging, but Droy saw that the question had interested her and he asked, 'D'you know where she is now?'

'No.'

'When did you last see her?'

The girl shrugged. 'The other night?'

'Which night was that?'

'Tuesday. We had supper together...'

'Maggie had supper with you?'

'With me and Dad, yes. And then they sent me over to her place with Roger, so they could canoodle.' Josie sounded disgusted.

Droy raised an eyebrow at the word, but he made no comment, simply asked, 'And Roger is...?'

'Roger's her baby. I look after him sometimes.'

Inspector Droy nodded. 'I see. She must find that very helpful.'

'Dad does,' said the girl with a scowl. 'He's sweet on her.'

'Is that a bad thing?' asked Droy gently.

'I don't like her.'

'Why not?'

'I just don't. And I don't want her to marry Dad.'

'Is she likely to?'

'How should I know?' Josie answered rudely. 'You'll have to ask him.'

'But you're fond of the baby?'

Josie's expression softened. 'He is quite sweet. I enjoy looking after him.'

'Thank you, Josie,' Droy said. 'You've been most helpful. Shall we go and find your dad now?'

Leaving his colleagues at the farmhouse, Droy followed Josie out of the farmyard and across a field to a stand of trees, where they found Bill, coppicing tool in hand, clearing the spreading undergrowth. He stopped work as they approached and looked up enquiringly.

'Good morning, sir,' said Droy. 'I'm Inspector Droy of the City of Plymouth police.' He held out his warrant, but after a quick glance, Bill Merton shrugged and said, 'And how can I help you, officer?'

'I'm looking for a woman named Margaret Peterson,' replied Droy, 'and I understand from Colonel Bridger that you know her.'

'I know she works for the Bridgers,' said Bill carefully.

'Indeed, but I also understand that you and she have become friendly?'

'Who told you that?' demanded Bill.

'Your daughter mentioned that you'd all had supper together on Tuesday evening.'

'And…'

'And, so, sir, I wondered if you knew where she's gone.'

'What do you want her for?'

'Simply to answer some questions to help us with our enquiries.'

'You said City of Plymouth police. What enquiries are you making up here?'

'We are looking into the case of a missing child,' Droy said.

'A missing child? Whose child?'

'A baby that disappeared after an air raid in Plymouth. You may have read about it in the paper not long ago.'

'But what's that got to do with Maggie?'

'Until we find her, and the baby, we can only speculate, sir, but we do need to speak to her.'

'Are you suggesting that her Roger is this missing baby, Inspector?'

'We need to find Mrs Peterson as soon as possible to eliminate her from our enquiries.'

'I bet he is,' broke in Josie. 'I bet she's stolen him.'

'Josephine, be quiet,' snapped her father. 'You know nothing about the matter and nobody asked you.'

'He did,' answered Josie, pointing at Droy. 'He asked me about her.'

'That's enough from you, young lady,' retorted Bill. He turned to Inspector Droy and said, 'We can't discuss this out here. I think we'd better go back to the house and talk properly.'

'Certainly, sir,' answered Droy. 'Do please lead the way.'

When they reached the house Bill led them into the kitchen and they sat down at the table. Andy Sharpe came inside as well, but Droy asked the other two to keep an eye open outside. He wasn't expecting Maggie to put in an appearance, but he was determined they shouldn't miss her if she did.

'Now then, Inspector,' said Bill, taking the lead. 'What's this all about?'

Inspector Droy drew a deep breath and related all the information that was already in the public domain. 'And so it seems that Mrs Peterson may have information that will lead us to the baby.'

'But how could she?'

'It was her husband who rescued the child and no one has seen him since. The child, I mean. You may know that her husband, Colin, was killed in an air raid, and it would appear that he had not reported the rescue before he died.

Soon afterwards we asked Mrs Peterson about this, whether her husband had mentioned rescuing a baby, and she denied that he did, but almost immediately she disappeared from her home, taking her child with her.'

'And you think it's this missing baby?'

'Until we find both her and the baby we don't know anything for sure, but it is a definite possibility.'

'And how did you trace her here?' asked Bill. 'How did you know to come here?'

'Information received,' replied the inspector.

'I bet it was those people I saw in the village the other day, Dad,' cried Josie. 'She wanted to hear about them, didn't she? And in the morning she'd gone. When I went over to collect Roger, she wasn't there and I thought she must have taken him over to the manor.'

'Did you wonder where she was, sir?' asked Droy.

Bill shook his head. 'I didn't know she'd gone anywhere. I didn't go up to the manor yesterday, and all Josie told me was that Maggie had taken the baby with her. We both assumed that they were at the manor.'

'Well, they weren't. Poor Colonel Bridger has been left high and dry. He doesn't know which way to turn.'

For a moment silence descended on the room and then Droy said, 'So you have no idea where she might have gone?'

'No,' said Bill shortly.

'She never mentioned any family or friends that she might have gone to?'

'No. Maggie was a very private person. She didn't talk about herself. She came to work at the manor after her husband was killed. She said she wanted to keep the boy safely away from the bombs.' He paused for a long moment and then said, 'And you're telling me that the baby, Roger, wasn't hers?'

'Almost certainly,' said Droy. 'I'm sorry, sir, but the needs of that child are a priority.'

'I don't think you have to worry about his needs, hers or not, she looks after him properly, doesn't she, Josie?'

Josie sniffed. 'I s'pose,' she said grudgingly. 'But if he isn't hers, who is the mum?'

'That's a very good question, Josie,' answered Droy, 'and I have to repeat, until we find both Mrs Peterson and the boy we shan't know anything for certain.'

Bill Merton got to his feet and crossed to the window, staring out over the fields towards Maggie's cottage. It wasn't visible from here, but he knew now that she would never be coming back. His hopes of the four of them being a new family were in vain. He could hold out no hope of her coming back to him, and much as he hated the idea, he tended to believe what the inspector had told him; that Maggie had stolen a baby and was now on the run.

'If she should make contact with you, sir,' Droy said, 'please will you phone us and let us know? I'll write down the number, and then you simply ask for me.'

'She must have caught the milk train,' Bill said. 'They might know more at the station.'

'Thank you,' answered the inspector. 'We'll call in at the station and ask.'

As the four police officers drove away from Hawthorn Farm, Andy Sharpe looked back. Bill Merton and his daughter were still standing in the farmyard, staring after them.

'Poor bloke,' he said quietly. 'That woman seems to cause misery wherever she goes.'

# 43

When at last the heavy bank doors were pushed open, Maggie went straight inside. She had left Roger asleep in the pram just round the corner, pushed into the shade of an awning shading the window of a greengrocer's. The shop had been busy and she hoped that anyone who saw the pram would assume that the baby's mother was doing her shopping inside. Maggie wasn't expecting to take very long in the bank, just taking out money. She opened her bank book and was filling in the withdrawal form when she realised she wouldn't be able to draw on this account again until she came back to Plymouth after the war. When she reached the teller's window she showed the young man behind it, Ted Stokes, her bank book and asked to see an up-to-date statement.

'I seem to have mislaid the last one I had,' she said. 'So silly of me.'

'Not a problem, madam,' replied the teller. 'I'll just look it up for you.' He disappeared for a moment and then returned and handed Maggie a discreet piece of paper with the amount written on it.

'Thank you,' Maggie said when she had glanced at the

figure. Clearly the Shawbrooks and the Clays had been paying their rent in every week, and she was surprised how it had mounted up. Seventy-five pounds! She smiled up at the teller and said, 'Now I'd like to make a withdrawal please.'

'Certainly, madam, how much would you like?'

Maggie inserted the amount onto the withdrawal form, signed it with a flourish and passed it through to the man. He looked at it and his eyes widened.

'But that's almost every penny,' he said.

'Am I not entitled to withdraw my own money if I choose?' Maggie asked stiffly.

'Indeed you are, madam, of course, it's just that it's a great deal of money to carry out of the bank in your bag. Might I suggest a banker's draft, perhaps?'

'Cash,' answered Maggie firmly. 'In pound notes, and today please, not next week!'

'Yes, madam, certainly, madam. If you leave one pound in your account it will remain open.'

'I'm well aware of that, young man,' said Maggie, 'which is why I have done exactly that.'

The teller opened a drawer under the counter and lifted out a roll of notes. With practised ease he count off the seventy-four pound notes she'd asked for, and then putting them on the counter, counted them in front of her, so that she could count with him.

'Shall I put the cash in an envelope for you, madam?' he asked.

'You may as well,' agreed Maggie, and when he handed her the envelope he said, 'It's a lot of money, madam. Do take care if you're going to carry it about with you.'

'Don't worry,' she said as she tucked it into her bag. 'I will.' And with a cheerful smile she walked out of the bank.

She might not have been so cheerful had she looked back and seen Ted Stokes deep in conversation with Mr Dale, the bank manager.

'You should have referred her to me, Stokes,' Dale was saying. 'We can't have all and sundry just marching in and closing their accounts!'

'She hasn't actually closed the account sir,' Stokes reminded him. 'She has left a pound to keep it open.'

'It is still a great deal of money to withdraw at once,' insisted Mr Dale.

'She had her bank book, Mr Dale,' Ted Stokes said. 'I thought it was all in order.'

'And so it may be,' replied the manager, 'but with such a large withdrawal you should have referred her to me. Please remember that in future.'

Mr Stokes went back to his window, glad that Mr Dale had not asked him if he had compared the woman's signature with the specimen one held by the bank. A cold sweat broke out on his forehead. The woman might not even *be* Mrs Margaret Peterson.

Once clear of the bank Maggie walked back through the town. While she had been waiting for the bank to open its doors she had come to a momentous decision. If she wanted to start a new life away from Plymouth, she was going to have to go alone. If nothing else, last night at the Swan had taught her that. How easily the unscrupulous, like Mrs Dawkins, could take advantage of a woman on her own, especially with a baby. Despite the reasons she told herself that made Roger hers now, she knew that if the police caught up with her they would take him away and she would never see him again. It would be impossible to stay free if she took Roger with her now. She needed to find somewhere he could be left safely, until she was settled. Then perhaps she could come back and claim him. This way she might be able to keep him if she planned it carefully enough. Now she had money she could buy what she needed. She spent the day acquiring various items which would help her in her subterfuge, and as the afternoon drew to a close she made her move, her first step towards freedom.

## 44

David Shawbrook walked into the bank half an hour after Maggie had left. He had come to pay the rent on the flat. Vera had been angry that he was continuing to pay.

'Why should we?' she demanded. 'We don't owe her anything.'

'At present we are living in a property that she owns,' her father replied, 'which entitles her to the rent we agreed. If we default it puts us on a level with her.'

'No it doesn't,' maintained Vera. 'Stealing a baby and stealing ten shillings a week are two entirely different things.'

'They are both stealing,' answered David, 'it's just a question of degree.'

'Well, if you want to pay that Maggie, it's up to you. I wouldn't!'

'You couldn't anyway,' David pointed out. 'You haven't got any money!'

Vera pulled a face and he softened the comment with a smile, adding, 'Anyway, we move out next week, so this'll be the last payment.'

Vera and her father had continued to live together in the

Marden Road flat but neither of them wanted to stay there. It was too strange to be living in an apartment owned by Maggie Peterson and paying rent to the woman who, they were certain, had stolen Vera's child, so they'd decided to try and find somewhere else. Vera was managing to get around quite easily now and she took on the job of flat hunting. There was very little available since the heavy raids in the spring, but at last she found a flat in St Jude's. It was again the ground floor in a big old house. Larger than Marden Road, it would have plenty of room for Vera and her father, Freddie when they found him, and in the near future, Andy Sharpe as well; because Andy Sharpe was going to become a fixture in their lives.

As the investigation had continued, Constable Andy Sharpe had taken to dropping in to see Vera on his way home, ostensibly to keep her up to date with the investigation, but in truth because he found he couldn't stay away. She was a prickly character, easily roused to anger, but that bothered Andy not at all. He knew that she still blamed herself for the loss of Freddie and was eaten up with guilt, a guilt that would not be assuaged until Freddie was found. She had lost her mother and her siblings through no fault of her own, but the survivors' guilt was an added burden that she carried. The more he saw of her the more he admired her feistiness and determination, and a deeper relationship had been born.

One evening, when David was on duty at the wardens' post and they were alone, they were sitting together on the old sofa in the cellar and yet again Vera was complaining about how slowly the police were working on finding Maggie and Freddie.

'We're doing the best we can,' Andy told her. 'So, I'm afraid you'll just have to be patient.'

'I'm not a patient person,' she muttered.

'You don't have to tell me that,' grinned Andy. 'D'you think I haven't noticed?'

Vera punched his shoulder. 'Oh, you!' she said. 'You'll have to get used to it, cos I won't change!'

'I expect I'll learn to live with it,' Andy replied with a grin.

Vera looked up at him from under her lashes and said, 'Will you?'

'I'm gonna have to, aren't I?'

'Why? Why will you?'

'Well,' answered Andy, suddenly serious, 'I think we'd better get married, don't you?'

'Married!' squeaked Vera. 'You and me?'

'I don't see anyone else here, do you?'

'But s'pose I don't want to?'

'Then I'll just have to try and make you change your mind, won't I?'

'How you gonna do that, then?'

'Well,' Andy said slowly, 'I think I'll probably start like this.' And putting his arms round her he drew her close and, very gently, kissed her on the mouth.

For a moment Vera tried to pull away, but gradually Andy felt her relax against him, and his hold tightened a fraction before he broke away. Smiling down into her shining eyes, he said, 'Is that all right?'

'Mmm.'

'Is that yes?'

'I s'pose.' And so they kissed again.

'Good,' he said when they finally broke apart. 'That's settled then.'

'What about Freddie?' asked Vera, suddenly anxious.

'What about him?' Andy said. 'We're going to get him back and I'm going to be his dad, aren't I?'

Vera's smile lit her face, catching his heart, and he said the words he had not spoken before. 'I love you to bits, Vera. I'll look after you both, I promise.'

When Andy first approached David for his permission to marry Vera, who was still under age, her father had not been encouraging.

'She's far too young to be thinking of marrying and settling down,' he'd said.

But as he got to know Andy Sharpe better, he changed his mind. He came to realise that Andy was, in fact, just the husband for Vera. He was older than her by six years and was what David called, 'Steady.' It was clear he loved her and though he let her do much as she pleased, when he did say, 'No', there was no moving him and Vera, grudgingly, had come to accept the fact.

'She needs some stability in her life,' David said to Mu. 'Otherwise I'm afraid she'll just drift, and I think Andy Sharpe can provide that, don't you?'

'Someone to keep her in order?' Mu suggested with a smile.

David had agreed. 'Well,' he said, 'I reckon not many would put up with her nonsense. Andy's a good man, in both senses of the word, and Vera says he's up for promotion, which will mean he can afford to marry. And when young Freddie's back it'll give him a real father too,' David went on, 'not just borrowing me. I'll be quite happy to take my rightful place as Granddad – he needs a younger dad than me.'

'He won't remember anything else,' Mu said. 'You'll always be Granddad to him. So, will you give them your permission?'

'I already have,' answered David, 'even though I think they should wait a while. She's still very young.'

'Does that matter so very much, Dad? As long as they're both happy,' said Mu. 'In uncertain times like these you have to snatch your happiness where you can. She deserves some happiness after everything that's happened. We all do, if we're to survive this war.'

David was thinking about what Mu had said as he walked to the bank. She was right, he supposed. Nancy had been little older than Vera was now when they had married and neither of them had regretted a single day. Vera just seemed... well he wasn't sure what, but as her father, he wanted there to be a firm hand on the tiller, and Andy Sharpe seemed to be that.

Last payment, David thought as he pushed open the door to the bank, and he was glad. He understood Vera's reluctance to pay, and though money owed was money owed, he was glad they were moving elsewhere.

He was surprised to find he was the only customer in the bank. He could see the manager sitting in his glass box of an office at the back, but he didn't need to see him. He walked up to the young man at the teller's window.

'Good morning, Mr Stokes. I've come to pay my rent.'

The young man looked up and saw who it was. A regular, every week.

'Good morning, sir,' he replied.

'Where is everyone?' asked David, looking round. Very often he had to queue simply to pay in the money, but today the bank was empty.

'Not a very busy today, sir,' Stokes agreed. 'You're only my fifth customer this morning.'

David handed in the lodgement slip and the cash. Stokes looked at it and then looked up again. 'In fact,' he said as he stamped the slip, 'one of my customers was your Mrs Peterson.'

'What?' David stared at him in amazement. 'What did you say? This Mrs Peterson?' He pointed to the slip still in Stokes' hand.

Stokes looked startled at the reaction and flushing red, said, 'Of course I shouldn't have mentioned that to you. Private client business.'

'You say she was in here? In this bank? This morning?'

'Please don't repeat what I said, sir. I really shouldn't have mentioned it.'

'How long ago? Did she have a baby with her? Did you see which way she went?' The questions came tumbling out, and Mr Stokes looked more and more uncomfortable.

'I'm sorry, Mr Shawbrook, I should not have mentioned the matter. Please ignore what I said.'

'I'm afraid I can't, Mr Stokes. I really must speak to the manager.'

'Oh, please, don't trouble Mr Dale,' begged Stokes. 'I should not have spoken of another client. It won't happen again, I promise you.'

David could see that the young man was anxious about his job, but the piece of news he had imparted was so important to David, he couldn't let it go unexplored.

'It's nothing to do with breaking client confidentiality,' David assured him. 'But I do need to speak to Mr Dale, and I shall tell him you have been most helpful.'

Wringing his hands Stokes said, 'If you insist, sir,' and led the way to the manager's office. At his knock Dale looked up and seeing Stokes with a client in tow, came out to greet them.

'I would just like a private word with you, Mr Dale,' said David, and turning back to Stokes he added, 'Thank you very much for mentioning it, Mr Stokes, you have been most helpful.' Stokes gave him a baleful look and returned to his place where another client was now waiting to be served.

Dale led the way into his office and offering David a chair, sat down on the other side of his desk.

He steepled his hands and looked across at David. 'Now then, sir,' he said. 'How may I be of help? Opening an account, perhaps?'

'No, nothing like that,' replied David. 'Let me explain. I rent a flat from someone who has an account with your bank. A Mrs Margaret Peterson. Each week I come in and pay the rent as I have just done now. I understand from Mr Stokes that Mrs Peterson was in herself this morning, and this is a matter of great concern to me. I need to speak to her urgently, but had believed her to be out of town. I just needed to confirm with you that she was indeed here.'

Mr Dale looked at him stony-faced and said, 'I'm afraid I couldn't possibly comment on such a thing.'

But ignoring the bank manager's riposte, David went on, 'And if that is the case, please will you telephone the police and ask to speak to Inspector Droy, or if he isn't there, Sergeant Sharpe? Mrs Peterson is a person of great interest to them.'

'I have only your word for that,' returned Dale, 'And I couldn't—'

'If you don't a child may be at risk.'

'I don't see what that has to do with the bank, Mr... er?'

'Shawbrook. David Shawbrook.'

'Mr Shawbrook. We do not give out information of any sort about our clients.'

'In that case I shall go to the police myself and tell them where Mrs Peterson was this morning and I have no doubt they will want to question you about what her business was here today.'

'That is your prerogative, sir, but I can assure you, we shall be unable to help in the matter. And I can also assure you that Mr Stokes' indiscretion will be dealt with appropriately.'

'Mr Stokes may well have given us the information we need for the police to make an early arrest, and he will be commended for it,' said David. And with that he turned on his heel and stalked out of the manager's office. He paused as he passed Mr Stokes' window and said, 'I am sorry if you are reprimanded for telling me what you did, but please answer just one question, I beg of you. Did she have a baby with her?'

Stokes gave a quick glance to the glass walls of the manager's office, and seeing Mr Dale was on the telephone, murmured, 'No, sir,' before he too turned away and was busy behind his counter.

The moment he was out of the bank, David took a taxi to the police station, but when he got there it was to be told that Inspector Droy and Sergeant Sharpe were out of the station today.

'But where are they?' demanded David in frustration. 'I've some important information to tell them about the missing woman, Mrs Peterson.'

'I don't know, sir,' came the reply. 'But you can leave them a message and I'll see they gets it the moment they get in.'

It was the best David could do and he left a message to say that Maggie Peterson had been to the bank that morning but the manager was refusing to say what business she had transacted.

*If you get this message when you get in, come round to Marden Road and I'll explain. David Shawbrook.*

# 45

It was early on Thursday evening when Stella left the WVS post where she volunteered on Thursdays and Fridays. She had to wait some time for the bus, and it made her irritable. Her relief, Ann Phelps, had arrived at the post late, complaining that her bus had to detour because the bomb squad were dealing with an unexploded bomb. Stella knew it wasn't Ann's fault, things like that happened all the time, but today had been long and tiring and Stella couldn't wait to get home.

When the bus finally arrived she climbed aboard, only to hear from the conductor that they too had been diverted. She managed to get a window seat, and sat staring through the glass at the devastated streets through which they were passing. And that was when she saw her; Maggie Peterson, hurrying along the road, keeping abreast of the slow-moving bus. For a moment Stella stared at her. Was it really Maggie, or just someone who resembled her? No, she was sure it was Maggie. Well, almost. But what on earth would Maggie be doing in this area of Plymouth? Or in Plymouth at all? Surely she and Roger were safely settled in the country somewhere. She knew the police thought that Roger was not Maggie's baby, but she also knew that Maggie had always cared for him as if he were. The woman hurrying along the pavement didn't have a baby with her. No pram, no baby, just a knapsack on her back, and she seemed to be in a hurry.

As the bus came to a halt, Stella banged her fist on the window, and saw the woman give a quick glance in her direction. For a moment their eyes locked and Stella raised a hand to wave, and then as the bus jerked forward again, the woman, almost certainly Maggie Peterson, broke into a run, jogging along the pavement, outstripping the crawling bus, and disappearing down a side street. Stella half got to her feet, but sat back down again as the bus gathered a little speed. When they passed the entrance of the road down which Maggie had vanished, Stella peered along it, but there was no sign of her, or anyone running.

When the bus came to a halt at the next stop, Stella thought of getting off, but even as she got to her feet, she changed her mind. It would be pointless trying to find Maggie now. She had more than a head start, and even if she did see her again, Stella knew that the much younger Maggie could easily outrun her and lose her in the maze of broken streets. The bomb damage had left roads closed, blocked with rubble, but it had also opened new ways, pathways across bomb sites, linking streets, and offering hiding places in shattered buildings.

All the way home Stella kept staring out of the window, just in case she caught another glimpse of Maggie; for the more she thought about it, the more sure she was. Stella's certainty had been increased by the way the woman had reacted to seeing her. She had recognised her and immediately she'd made a run for it. Why would anyone do that if they hadn't known who it was rapping on the window? A stranger would have ignored her, or just waved and walked on. And where was Roger? Maggie certainly wasn't carrying him and there was no sign of the pram. What had she done with him?

When the bus finally dropped her, Stella was just ten minutes from home. As she walked up Marden Road she paused for a moment outside number thirty-four. Had Maggie come back to her own house? Ought she to go and knock on the door and see? But what would she say to the Shawbrooks? Say she'd seen Maggie from the window of the bus? Again, doubts assailed her. She had been certain it was Maggie, but she didn't have Roger with her, so perhaps it wasn't after all. And if she did go and tell them she'd seen her without the baby, it would certainly worry them even more.

Had she passed by a quarter of an hour later, she would have seen the police arriving at number thirty-four, and perhaps called in to mention what she had seen, but as it was she longed to get home and she walked on, up the road to her own house, and once inside, she put on the kettle and dropped into a chair, exhausted.

I'm too old for all this, she thought as she waited for the kettle to boil. Maggie Peterson is not my problem any more! I've already told them all I know, now it's up to the police.

She made her tea and carried it through to her little conservatory. The evening sun lay mellow on the garden, glowing on the frothy fronds of the goldenrod which grew in a clump out by the shed. John had planted it just before he died and though it was now straggly and well past its best, she'd not had the heart to dig it up, despite being encouraged to do so by Dick, her gardener.

There had been no post on the mat when she'd opened the front door and she had been disappointed. She had hoped there would be a letter from Harriet, just to know she was all right. Liverpool seemed so far away, and she ached to know how they all were. Liverpool, like Plymouth, had received the attentions of the Luftwaffe, and she lived for Harriet's letters for reassurance.

Looking out over the garden, she remembered Vera's visit when she had come to see if she, Stella, had any clue as to Maggie's whereabouts. Though not much more than a girl herself, Vera was still a mother, like Stella was, frantic to find her baby.

Suppose Harriet disappeared and I didn't know where she was? Stella thought now. I would be frantic too.

Of course she had helped the police as best she could when they came asking questions and they had convinced her that the baby Maggie was claiming as hers, was not.

Rather than go and tell the Shawbrooks that I've seen Maggie, Stella thought, I ought to go to the police. They'll know how to search her out. I could tell them whereabouts I saw her and then leave it to them.

She would go and see them in the morning, she decided. Inspector Droy. That had been the officer's name. Tomorrow morning on her way to the WVS for her Friday shift, she would stop into the police station and tell Inspector Droy about seeing Maggie.

It seemed it was the best she could do, and with this decision made, she returned to her kitchen, and switching on the wireless, prepared her supper.

As she was sitting at the table the sirens started to wail, signalling an alert, but Stella turned up the wireless and continued to eat her supper. She had decided months ago that she was not going to leave her home to take shelter every time the Moaning Minnies wailed.

'I'm too old to be running about in the cold and dark, and then sitting in a damp shelter,' she told Harriet when her daughter scolded her for taking such risks. 'I'll take my chances in the house. So don't worry about me!'

There was no raid that night but by the time the all-clear sounded, Stella was tucked up in bed, fast asleep.

It was early evening when the two police officers, back from Martindell, arrived on the Shawbrooks' doorstep. David and Vera were both there waiting for them and so were Patrick and Mu.

Vera greeted Andy with a hug and said excitedly, 'That Maggie's back in Plymouth. She's been to the bank.'

'First things first,' said David. 'Let's hear how they got on in Martindell. What did you discover up there?'

Andy left Droy to report on their day, which they decided had not been a waste of time as they had learned quite a lot about Maggie herself.

'It didn't take much to warn her that we might be on our way,' Droy said. 'I think you two must have worried her simply by speaking to the baby, Mrs Davenham. Josie mentioned the colour of your hair, that it was the same as the baby's. I think that's probably what made her run. She had certainly left Martindell before we arrived.'

'Anyone have any idea where she went?' asked Patrick. 'The people at the manor?'

No,' replied Droy. 'We interviewed the Bridgers at the manor and the farmer down the road, Bill Merton and his daughter Josie, but her disappearance was a shock to all of them. When we enquired at the station, the ticket clerk told us that she caught the first train out, yesterday. Apparently she bought a return ticket to Exeter and asked about the evening trains back, but needless to say, she didn't come back. She had told nobody she was leaving, she simply disappeared.'

'And now she's turned up here in Plymouth,' said David.

'But why on earth would she do that?' wondered Vera. 'You'd think it was the last place she'd go!'

'Because she needed money,' said David.

'But the bank won't tell us?' asked Mu.

'If necessary we can arrange that,' said Droy. 'But it may be too late to do anything about her now. With money in her pocket she's free to go wherever she likes, and I don't imagine she'll hang about in Plymouth, do you?'

'Well, we shan't be paying her any more,' Vera said firmly. 'Will we, Dad?' And her father agreed.

'What worries me,' said David to Mu, privately a little later, 'is that she didn't have Freddie with her.'

'But he was probably outside in the pram,' Mu pointed out.

'Possible, I suppose,' acknowledged David.

'Did you mention that to Vera?' Mu asked.

'No, and luckily she didn't ask me.'

'She'll think of it before very long, Dad.'

'I expect she will,' agreed her father, 'but time enough for that when she does, and as you say, he may have been left outside.'

# 46

Maggie walked briskly back towards the centre of the city. She was determined to leave Plymouth as quietly as she had arrived. She wouldn't go back to the station, that was too big a risk, but she could take a bus to one of the smaller stations and leave from there. Without Roger she was able to go wherever she liked and free to change her plans as the need arose. Her thoughts were interrupted by a knocking sound and looking round her, she suddenly realised it was coming from the stationary bus she was passing. She glanced up and to her horror, found herself looking straight at Stella Todd. Stella had banged on the window and was waving to her. Without further thought, Maggie looked away and began to run. She outpaced the slow-moving bus and coming to a junction, turned right and then immediately left. Once she was sure she was out of sight, she slowed to a walk. Running would make her more conspicuous. It had been stupid to run, she told herself, she could simply have ignored Stella as if she didn't recognise her, make her wonder if it really was her she was seeing. She didn't know if Stella knew about Roger now, perhaps she didn't, but that was another risk Maggie wasn't prepared to take. If Stella did know that the police were looking for her, she might get off the bus, go straight to the police station and report seeing her.

Now that she was on her own, with no Roger to hamper her, Maggie had planned an easy escape route from the city. She had discovered that a train from Saltash station would take her as far as Penzance, which seemed to her to be far enough away. She had bought some food for the journey and as she stashed the bread and cheese in her knapsack she couldn't help thinking how much easier life was without having to think of Roger and his needs any more. No nappies. No bottles. No mushy food. No broken nights.

The next train to Cornwall would pass through Saltash the following morning, but now she had been seen and recognised by Stella, she didn't dare wait in Plymouth for another night. If Stella reported that she had seen her, all the local stations might be watched.

Angry with Stella, angry with herself, she marched along trying to decide what to do next, and then she saw the queue at a special bus stop and she remembered the night buses.

When the Blitz was at its worst in the spring, there had been an exodus from the city every evening. Many people left homeless by the bombing, with no family elsewhere to offer refuge, with nowhere safe to sleep, and determined to leave the bombs and the city behind, sought the relative safety of outlying villages and the open countryside. They gathered at certain bus stops where they would be picked up by a 'night bus'; buses driven by volunteer drivers to take them out of the city. The driver and his passengers would sleep on the bus and return, unrested, the next morning in the illusory safety of daylight. It wasn't just buses either. Several of the big stores had offered their lorries as transport for those who were afraid to stay in their own homes, preferring escape to the country, seeking shelter in farmhouses, their outbuildings or under the stars, rather than risk being caught in another raid.

Now, Maggie thought, if she joined the queue waiting at the bus stop, she would be taken safely out of the city, and in the morning, before the driver took them back, she would quietly disappear and perhaps catch her train further down the line. She had no idea what time the bus would come, and so she asked a woman standing near the front.

The woman shrugged. 'Never know really. 'Bout half an hour I 'spect.'

Half an hour, Maggie thought. She was hungry and half an hour would give her time to get something to eat. She found a café that served her a meal of stew, potatoes and carrots for a shilling, and then returned to the bus stop. She was only just in time, people were already climbing onto the double decker that was waiting. It was clear to Maggie that they were not all going to get on. As she tried to push her way to the front of the queue, she wondered if there would be another bus from this stop. If not, she didn't know where else she could find one. Determined that it should not be she who was left behind, she gave an elderly woman a shove, causing her to stumble, and as she was trying to regain her feet Maggie edged in front of her.

'Oy, you,' cried a man's voice and a hand grabbed her from behind, holding onto her knapsack. 'Who d'you think you're shoving? Eh? My wife was ahead of you, and so was I. You wait your turn like the rest of us.'

'Take your hands off me!' exclaimed Maggie. 'Let me go!'

'Not till you stand aside and let my wife get on the bus,' growled the man.

The conductor who was overseeing the orderly boarding of the bus came forward and asked, 'What's going on here, then?'

Maggie was quick to speak. 'This man is stopping me getting on,' she cried. 'Tell him to let me go!'

'She was jumping the queue,' called another voice from behind and immediately there was a chorus of voices. 'Yes, she just walked up to the front.'

'We've been here half an hour!' called another.

'She pushed Mrs Hall out of the way,' added a third.

'We was *all* of us ahead of her in the queue,' said someone else.

'Please stand aside, madam,' said the conductor politely, 'and allow the rest of the queue to board.'

Maggie, red with rage, tried to pull free from the man who held her. 'I'm as entitled as any of these people to a place on the bus.'

'Certainly,' agreed the conductor, 'in your turn.'

The queue moved past her, and when at last the man who held her let go, he clambered up into the bus before her. As he stepped aboard, the conductor held up his hand and said, 'Full up. Sorry, madam, no room.'

'What!' Maggie shrieked. 'What do you mean, no room?'

'This bus is licensed to carry sixty-three passengers. And that's how many have just got on.'

'But I was here!' shouted Maggie, in fury.

'So you were,' the conductor said as he rang the bell. 'But you were too late.'

'I shall report you!' she called as the bus began to draw away.

'You do that,' replied the conductor. 'Won't get you very far, I'm a volunteer.'

Fuming with rage and humiliation, Maggie could only watch the bus disappear round the corner, carrying its passengers out of Plymouth. Angry with the man who had held her back, she was angry with herself too. How stupid of her to make an exhibition of herself. She should have simply asked if there would be another bus later. Still, it was unlikely anyone would remember what she looked like, indeed, who would be looking? All she had to do was to get out of the city as soon as she could and they could look till kingdom come.

She decide that even if Stella had gone straight to the police, it was unlikely that the police would have the manpower to watch all the possible stations. Maggie decided she would risk going to the mainline station and find out the time of the next train going north and then she would go south, heading for Penzance. Avoiding main roads she made her way to the station, but as she was less than two hundred yards away, the sirens began shrieking their alerts. Enemy aircraft were heading in towards the coast.

'Everyone into the shelter,' bellowed a voice, and she turned to see an air-raid warden herding people off the street and into a public shelter at the edge of Central Park. She began to turn away, but the warden crossed the road and grabbing her arm, said, 'Come on now, my dear, into the shelter with you.'

'I'm going home,' protested Maggie.

'Better not,' advised the warden. 'Safer in here. May not

be for long, could be on their way to Bristol, for all we know, but you need to get off the street.' This last was said firmly, brooking no argument, and conscious that she had made a spectacle of herself once already, Maggie allowed herself to be sent down the steps into the shelter. It was made up of several bays and she managed to find a place on one of the benches that lined the walls, and sat down. As more and more people poured in behind her, she realised that she was lucky to have found a place to sit, and that many of those still coming in would either have to stand or sit on the floor. She was crushed between a thin woman with a child on her knee and a burly man with unruly black hair and a heavy five o'clock shadow.

'Not much space down here, is there?' said the man conversationally. 'Sorry if you're feeling squashed.'

'Just glad to be sitting down,' Maggie said. They could still hear the wail of the sirens outside, and now the sound of planes overhead, but as yet no explosions. Perhaps it really was somewhere else's turn as the target tonight. It was hot and stuffy in the shelter with so many crammed in, and Maggie, who had slept very little the night before, found herself nodding. She dug her fingernails into her palms to try and stay awake, but within moments, unable to keep her eyes open, she had drifted off to sleep.

Looking down at her, the man smiled. Not often you have a young woman fall asleep on your shoulder, and this one's quite a looker. He put an arm round her to prevent her from falling off the bench as she slept, changing position a little to make her more comfortable. She slept like the dead, and when she woke up more than an hour later, she was embarrassed to find herself propped up by her neighbour. There was still no sound of the all-clear.

'I'm so sorry,' she stammered. 'How long have I been asleep?'

'An hour or so,' said the man. 'You must have been right tired, to sleep like that.'

'I didn't sleep very well last night,' Maggie admitted. 'Thank you for being my pillow!'

'Any time,' replied the man with a grin. Maggie looked at him properly for the first time. He reminded her of Bill Merton, a bear of a man, with an outdoor face, probably mid-forties, but with wide, expressive eyes, looking younger when he smiled. 'The name's Forest, Mike Forest.'

'Meg.' Maggie coughed in her effort to alter the Mag of Maggie to Meg. 'Meg Smith.'

'Well, Meg Smith, let's hope you feel better for your sleep. You were spark out.'

'Been a long day,' was the only explanation Maggie gave before saying, 'First I'm late going home and now I'm stuck in here for the night. Missed my train. What about you?'

'Come up by train from Cornwall,' said Mike. 'Got to pick up a lorry load of spares and drive down to Falmouth.'

'Falmouth!' Maggie's eyes brightened. 'Really?'

'Yeah, why?'

'You won't believe it,' Maggie improvised, 'but I was supposed to catch the train to Falmouth tomorrow to see my brother. He's got forty-eight hours' leave from his ship and I got time off special, to go and see him, but they just told me at the station that the train has been cancelled.'

This Meg had said, 'You won't believe it', and Mike didn't. He didn't know why she wanted to go to Falmouth, but he could guess. She was an attractive girl, so it probably wasn't a brother she was going to see.

'There isn't another one until Monday,' she was saying, 'and now I won't be able to see him before he goes back to sea.' She spoke sadly, an edge of misery in her voice.

'That's bad luck,' Mike said non-commitally. He could suggest he give her a lift. It was strictly against regulations, but it was a long drive and he'd be glad enough of the company.

At that moment the all-clear sounded and everyone began struggling to their feet, pushing their way out of the fetid shelter into the fresh summer air.

As they stood outside for a moment Mike looked at her. 'You can come with me if you like,' he offered 'I got stuff to sort out here tomorrow, but I'll be leaving for Falmouth about midday Saturday, if you want a ride.'

'Really?' Maggie treated him to her most dazzling smile. 'That would be wonderful. Yes, please. Where shall I meet you?'

'Might as well pick you up here at the park, by the gate into the cemetery,' Mike replied. 'Twelve o'clock, say? But if you're not there I shan't wait. All right?'

'Yes, all right,' Maggie agreed. 'I'll be waiting by the gate.'

'Got to go now,' Mike Forest said. 'Saturday, midday.'

With that he disappeared into the crowd still emerging from the air-raid shelter into the darkness.

Maggie was disappointed that she had another day to wait, but it seemed far safer to travel in the cab of a lorry than to use public transport. Surely, she thought, they won't be able to find me if I keep my head down and keep moving.

In the meantime she had to find somewhere to sleep. With no Roger to worry about, she made her way to one of the rescue centres offering a place for the newly homeless to lay their heads. She used the toilet and then wrapping herself in one of the rugs provided she lay down on the floor and fell into exhausted sleep.

# 47

The next morning Droy and Andy arrived at the bank at the same time as the manager. The inspector explained to Mr Dale why they needed to hear what transactions Mrs Peterson had made the previous day.

'I'm sorry, Inspector,' the manager said, 'but my hands are tied. I cannot divulge a client's business without a warrant from a magistrate.'

'Then that is what we shall get,' said Droy. 'I'll bid you good day, sir.'

Mr Stokes was not at his teller's window as Droy left the bank, but the inspector found him outside.

Out of sight of his boss, Stokes put a hand on the inspector's arm and said in a conversational tone, 'Seventy-four pounds is a great deal of money, isn't it? Especially if you're emptying your account and taking it all in one pound notes. But you'd be surprised how many people do these days.'

'Indeed,' said the inspector with a smile. 'Very risky, I'd say.'

Back at the station he found a message from Stella Todd. 'She said she had some information about your woman,

Maggie Peterson. Couldn't wait for you to come back and wouldn't tell me what it was. She insisted she would only tell you. She did say she'd be at the WVS post in Mutley Plain if you wanted to see her.'

'Right,' said the inspector. 'We'll go and see her straight away. With me, Andy.'

They found Stella at the WVS post. She was in a room at the back, sorting clothes, men's, women's and children's, into piles for future use.

She looked up as the two policeman came in, and greeted them rather nervously.

'Good morning, Inspector.'

Droy got straight to the point. 'Good morning, Mrs Todd,' he said. 'You left a message at the station saying you had some more information about Mrs Peterson.'

'Yes.' Stella hesitated, not quite sure where to begin. 'I think I should have come to the police station last night, I'm sorry.'

'Never mind,' replied the inspector, 'you're talking to us now. What have you go to tell us?'

'I was coming home from here last night and my bus got diverted. The driver said it was because of an unexploded bomb being removed, though he didn't say exactly where it was.'

'So were you on the bus?'

'Yes, yes. I didn't know about the diversion when I got on.'

'So, you were on the bus...'

'Yes, and we were going very slowly most of the time, sometimes stopping altogether. Anyway, I was looking out of the window and there she was, walking along beside us.

Maggie Peterson. I was amazed because I thought she and Roger were safely in the country somewhere.'

'Did she see you too?' asked Andy Sharpe.

'Oh yes,' replied Stella. 'I banged on the window, quite hard, actually, and she looked round. I waved and she saw me. Just a few seconds' eye contact, you know, and then she ran off.'

'As soon as she saw you in the bus she ran off?'

'Yes, Inspector. The bus had stopped at that time and she ran on down the road and turned into a side road.'

'And you're absolutely certain it was Maggie Peterson?'

'Well, I did wonder if I'd been mistaken, especially as she was on her own. She didn't have Roger with her, but the more I thought about it, the more convinced I became. I mean, if it wasn't Maggie, the woman wouldn't have recognised me, so why would she run?'

'And you say she didn't have the baby with her?' questioned Andy.

'No, but I expect she'd left him somewhere for a while and was going back to fetch him. Maybe she ran because she was late picking him up.'

Neither of the policemen thought that was likely, but they didn't say so. Instead Inspector Droy said, 'Where were you, exactly?'

'Mannamead,' replied Stella. 'That was another reason why I wasn't immediately sure it was Maggie. I mean, what would she be doing there?'

'And which street did she turn into?'

'I couldn't see a name,' said Stella. 'I don't know that area well. I was only there because the bus had to go a long way round.'

'I understand, Mrs Todd,' said Droy patiently. 'Can you tell us what she was wearing... or anything else about her that you think might be helpful.'

'Well, let me think now,' said Stella. 'She was wearing a blue summer skirt with a floral pattern, with a blue blouse and a cream jacket... oh, and she had a bag on her back, a big one.'

'You mean a haversack, like people take camping?'

'Yes,' agreed Stella. 'A sort of canvas bag on her back and a handbag. Yes, she had her arm through a handbag.'

'Thank you, Mrs Todd,' said Droy. 'It was good of you to come forward with this information.'

Stella looked a little sheepish and said, 'I should have come to you last night, then maybe you could have found her.'

Though the two policeman rather agreed with her, all the inspector said, was, 'Well, never mind that now, you've been very helpful. We must let you get back to what you were doing.' But as they walked away, Inspector Droy said, 'It's a pity she didn't come last night, but I doubt if we'd have found Maggie even if she had.'

'Where do you think she was heading?'

The inspector shrugged. 'She could have been cutting through Mutley to the station, I suppose. After all, we know she's got cash now. I imagine that's all she came back here for, and now she's leaving again. She could be going anywhere.'

'What worries me is, what has she done with Freddie?' said Andy Sharpe.

'I agree,' said Droy. 'Finding him must be our priority. Have we a photo of Maggie Peterson?'

'I seem to remember there was one on the mantelpiece in the flat,' replied Andy. 'But whether it's still there I don't know. It wasn't a particularly recent one. Why, what have you in mind?'

'Once we have a photograph we can check at the station and at the bus station and see if anyone's seen her. And I think it's time to enlist Keith Lane's help again. We promised him first shot at the story if and when it broke. We'll see if he can arrange something along the lines of, "Have you seen this woman?" with a picture on the front page of the *Morning News* and see what response we get, if any.'

'Sure to get some,' laughed Andy. 'Cranks, most of them, but you never know, someone might remember seeing her.'

'Right,' said Droy. 'You go round to Marden Road and find us a photo, I'll contact Keith, explain what we want, and see what he can organise. I'll see you back at the station with the picture.'

They went their separate ways, Andy heading straight for Marden Road and hoping that Vera would be in. She had dispensed with any walking aid now and though she still limped, she was out and about. When she opened the door to find him on the step, her face lit up and he gathered her into his arms.

'Any news?' she asked when she could speak at all.

'Your friend Stella Todd has contacted us,' answered Andy.

'She's not my friend,' retorted Vera, thinking of the last time she had seen her.

'I think you'll find she is now,' Andy told her. 'Stella was on a bus going home last night when she saw Maggie Peterson. She was in Mannamead, but perhaps heading for the station. Stella knocked on the window of the bus and as soon as she saw her, Maggie made a run for it.'

'Run?' Vera echoed. 'Pushing the pram?'

'No.' Andy took Vera's hands in his and said gently, 'She didn't have Freddie with her.'

'What? Where is he? What has she done with him?'

'Darling girl, we don't know, but finding him is our main priority now, I promise you.'

Vera sank down onto the sofa and buried her face in her hands. Andy sat down beside her and held her close. After a moment Vera pulled free and taking the handkerchief he offered, blew her nose.

'I can tell you this, Andy,' she said viciously, 'if she's harmed a hair of his head, I'll kill her.'

'I doubt if she's hurt him, Vera,' answered Andy, trying to sound reassuring. 'I know you don't accept this, but she clearly loves him, you know.'

'He's not hers to love,' said Vera bitterly.

'Well, we're doing all we can to find her so that she can tell us where Freddie is,' Andy said. 'And what we need now is a photograph of her. I seem to remember…' He looked up at the mantelpiece. 'Oh dammit, it's gone.'

'There are some photos in the trunk,' Vera said and pulled at his hand. 'Come on, it's still down in the cellar, let's go and have a look.'

As the lock was already broken it was the work of moments to open the trunk and pull out the contents.

'Here we are,' cried Vera triumphantly as she picked up a framed picture of Maggie and Colin Peterson on their wedding day. 'We can soon cut him out,' she said.

'Here's another one that might be better,' Andy said and

showed her the photo of the pregnant Maggie. 'It's quite good of her and we can simply cut it down to head and shoulders, so it doesn't show that she's expecting.' He opened the frames and removed the pictures, saying, 'I'll take them both and leave it to the experts to decide.'

'I'll come with you,' Vera said as she closed the trunk again.

'Better not,' said Andy. 'I've got to make official enquiries, and you're a member of the public.'

'But it's my baby we're trying to find.'

'And it will be better, I promise you, love, to leave it to us.' He pulled her into his arms again and kissed her. 'I'll come back and tell you as soon as I know anything, I promise.'

When he had gone Vera picked up her bag and walked up the road to see Stella Todd. She wanted to hear exactly what she'd seen the previous evening, but in that she was going to be unlucky. Number fifty-three was quiet, and though she rang the doorbell loud and long, several times, there was no reply.

Inspector Droy was pleased with their morning's work. Though the bank manager had refused to tell them what Maggie Peterson's business had been at the bank, thanks to Mr Stokes, they now knew that she had emptied her bank account which clearly indicated that she wasn't coming back in the foreseeable future. She still owned the house in Marden Road, but if she ever wanted to realise her capital and sell the place, she would have to come back to Plymouth, and when she did, they would be waiting for her. They had also learned that Maggie no longer had baby Freddie with her, which made it essential that they find her as soon as possible, so that she could tell them where he was. They had all the proof they needed that he was not hers and they hoped family identification would be enough to convince the court that he was indeed Vera Shawbrook's child.

When he got back to the police station he phoned Keith Lane at the *Western Morning News* and explained what he would like him to do, and once he had convinced Keith that he would have the drop on all the other newspapers, he agreed to set things in motion the minute he had the photograph.

'Might even get the paper to offer a reward,' Keith said, 'but can't promise.'

Andy Sharpe arrived soon after, with two photos in his pocket. They both agreed that the one of Maggie alone cut down to head and shoulders would be the better one to use, and Droy arranged for several copies to be made.


It was the final day of Patrick's leave. The last few days had flown by and all too soon it was his last day, the day before he had to take the train north. His new posting turned out to be Campbeltown on the Kintyre peninsula in Scotland. His promotion to lieutenant had just come through and though she didn't want him to go, Mu was immensely proud of him. When the posting was official they had decided to keep their room at Mrs Dunbar's. In the few days they had been there it had become their home. As a married woman, Mu would normally have had to give up nursing, but an interview with Matron had assured her that the hospital were so short of staff that if she returned to work she would be a very welcome Nurse Davenham on the ward, and would be allowed to live out, no longer in the nurses' home. And now that day was close. She would be starting back at the hospital in two days' time. Patrick would be catching the train north tomorrow and Mu was determined they should not waste a minute of today. When Patrick asked her if she wanted to go round to Marden Road she shook her head.

'No,' she replied firmly. 'There's nothing we can do there, and I want you to myself today.'

'But don't you want to know how Andy and the inspector got on at the bank?'

'No,' said Mu. 'No doubt I shall hear soon enough. Today is our day, not Vera's. Whether we're there to hear what they discovered or not, will make no difference to what happens next. What would you like to do?'

'Go back to bed,' Patrick replied promptly.

Mu laughed. 'After we've done that!'

'A day in the country?'

'Sounds lovely,' replied Mu, 'but a day to ourselves. No sleuthing this time.'

'Agreed,' said Patrick. 'Where do you suggest?'

'What about Plym Forest?' said Mu. 'It's not that far, we can catch a bus and have a picnic.'

'Sounds perfect,' agreed Patrick, 'for later.' And they returned to bed.

When they finally got up, Mu packed a picnic and they caught the bus out of the city. Dressed in all its summer glory, the woods were alive with birdsong and the warm summer sun struck through the leaves, dappling the ground with dancing shadows. They wandered hand in hand, following narrow pathways through the trees until they came to a clearing, an oasis of sunlight. A fallen tree offered a perfect backrest and they sat down on the soft moss that covered the ground to eat their picnic.

I shall always remember today, Mu thought when they'd eaten their sandwiches and she lay back to gaze up at the clear azure sky. I'll never forget the peace and the quiet and Patrick.

'We should go dancing this evening,' Patrick said suddenly. He raised himself on his elbow and looked down at her. 'What do you think?'

'Dancing?' Mu was surprised but she loved to dance. 'Where?'

'On the Hoe,' Patrick said. 'Mrs Dunbar told me about it. People have been coming from all over the place, just to dance. We should too, don't you think?'

'Sounds wonderful,' said Mu.

Patrick and Mu had never danced together before, and when they reached the Hoe they were amazed to find it crowded with people, dancing in the evening sunshine. Men in uniform, soldiers, sailors, airmen; housewives, office workers and sales girls on their way home from work, youngsters joining in with parents and friends, elderly gentlemen pirouetting their wives. All the world was there, and the air was filled with music and laughter, for a blissful hour the war forgotten.

As they joined the dancers, Patrick pulled Mu into his arms and with his lips against her hair murmured, 'Happy, Mrs Davenham?'

Mu looked up into his face and smiled. 'With you, Lieutenant Davenham? Always.' And as they danced with all the others on the Hoe, they knew they were part of something more important than a simple dance in the evening sun. It was a collective act of defiance.

Later they went into a restaurant and had dinner, but both of them were aware of how fast the time was flying, and they didn't linger. Neither of them wanted to share their last precious hours together with anyone else and they returned to Elm Road and their room at Mrs Dunbar's. In the few days they'd been back in Plymouth it had become their private refuge, their marital home.

'I shall be able to picture you sitting in our room, writing to me!' Patrick teased, as they lay side by side on the bed, adding with a smile, 'You are going to write to me while I'm away this time, aren't you?'

'Every day,' promised Mu. 'You're everything to me, Patrick.' She looked so serious that he gathered her into his arms and held her against him, kissing her fiercely and delighting in her response. Tomorrow he'd have to catch the train to Scotland, and he could sleep on the train, but tonight neither of them wanted to waste time sleeping.

With the dawn he was gone and Mu ached for him to return the moment he had walked out of the door. She had not gone with him to the station, she preferred to say her goodbyes in private. Determined not to cry, not to make it more difficult for him to leave her, she held him close for a long moment, for one final kiss, and then released him. When he walked through the front door he didn't look back, he simply climbed into the taxi and instructed the driver to take him to the station. Mu watched the taxi disappear round the corner before she closed the door and returned to their room, not knowing when, or if, she would see him again.

# 48

Keith Lane had done them proud. When Droy bought a paper early next day, there she was. Maggie Peterson, under the headline, **HAVE YOU SEEN HER?** in large, bold type. Underneath her picture was the story.

The police are looking for Maggie Peterson (27), in connection with the abduction of a baby boy, Freddie Shawbrook, now aged eleven months. Mrs Peterson was last seen in Plymouth the day before yesterday, and the police are anxious to find her so that she can help them with their enquiries into the missing baby's whereabouts. It is probable that Mrs Peterson has already left the city, but if you have seen her in the past three days, the police would ask you to call the number below, and ask for Inspector Droy, so that they can trace her movements and discover where she might have gone.

There is a reward of £50 for information leading to the arrest of Mrs Peterson.

Droy took the paper to the police station and showed it to Andy Sharpe.

'Pity about the mention of a reward,' he said. 'It'll bring out all the cranks, and the phone will be ringing non-stop.'

'Worth it though,' said Andy, 'if it also produces someone with real information.'

Droy was right. The phone was soon ringing, and Andy was fielding calls from people who thought they'd seen Maggie in all different areas of the city. A Mrs Dawkins insisted that she had stayed at her pub for a night and had had the baby with her, and asked how she claimed the £50. Another, a man ringing from a call box, asserted that two nights ago Maggie had tried to get on one of the night buses at the top of Alexandra Road.

'Pushed my wife out of the way, she did, so's she could get on first. Definitely the woman in the paper. Tall, with dark hair and a haversack on her back. The conductor made her wait and she didn't get on in the end.' Andy thought this sounded hopeful and made a note of the man's name and address to follow up in the hope of more information.

'It's where she might have been, after Stella Todd saw her,' he said when he told Droy about the call. 'If she cut back down from Mannamead.'

'Better go and see him and see if he knows anything else,' said Droy.

At that moment the phone rang again and was picked up by the desk sergeant.

'Inspector, sir,' he called. 'Someone for you. About the newspaper?'

'I'll just take this one and then we'll go and see him.' He took the receiver and said, 'Inspector Droy speaking.'

He listened for several minutes and then said, 'Thank you, sir. You've been most helpful.'

★★★

Maggie had arrived at the cemetery almost an hour before noon but, not wanting to be seen waiting around, she passed the time locked in a cubicle in the ladies' public convenience in the station opposite. When her watch showed ten minutes to twelve, she emerged and headed out to the street. As she did so she passed the news stand by the entrance, and almost cried out in horror as she saw the headline, **HAVE YOU SEEN HER?** with her own face prominently displayed below on the front page, and as a smaller headline the offer of a fifty-pound reward. For a moment she stood stock-still, before gathering her wits together, turning her face away and scuttling hurriedly out of the station. Had the news vendor seen her? Where was her lift? She looked at her watch again. He wasn't due for another five minutes. She scanned the street, but as yet there was no sign of Mike Forest and his lorry.

She had slept at a rescue centre again and passed the daylight hours in the park. No one had paid any attention to her, but now, with her face plastered across the news stand, she was even more desperate to get out of the city to the anonymity of the countryside.

What if he doesn't come? she thought in panic. She needed him more than ever. Anyone might see her, it wasn't just the police who would be on the lookout for her now. With a fifty-pound reward being offered, it could be anyone, anyone at all. She stared along the road, but there was still no sign of the man with the lorry.

I'll wait the by the cemetery gates, she decided, that way I can easily duck inside if I see anything or anyone suspicious.

She thought of the row she'd had with the man at the bus stop. He might see the picture and recognise her. Thank goodness she hadn't got on that bus, or they might have been able to pick up her trail there. Or the dreadful Mrs Dawkins at the Swan. If she saw the paper, she'd certainly be after the reward, whether she'd seen her or not!

Maggie looked along the road again, but there was still no sign of a lorry, then suddenly, it came round the corner. She hurried across the road and waved to make sure he'd seen her. He'd said he wouldn't wait if she wasn't there and she didn't want him to drive past.

No, thank goodness, she could see him slowing down. He pulled up at the kerb and jumped down from the cab.

'All right, Meg?' he said.

'Yes, I'm ready, shall I get in?'

'I think not, Mrs Peterson,' came a voice from behind her and she spun round to find herself face to face with Constable Andy Sharpe. 'I'm arresting you on suspicion of abducting a child, Frederick Shawbrook...' She stared at him blankly for a moment as he cautioned her and then she said, 'My son Roger is my son. He is not Freddie Whoever-you-said.'

'We shall be taking you back to the police station to be interviewed under the caution you've just heard...' A different voice.

Maggie turned again and found Inspector Droy standing the other side of her holding a pair of handcuffs. There was no escape. Maggie turned on Mike Forest, fury in her eyes.

'You set me up for this,' she blazed as Droy put on the handcuffs.

'I certainly phoned the police,' agreed Mike equably.

'You have no idea what you've done, you interfering bastard! They're trying to take my son away from me, but I won't let them!'

'If it's a mistake,' Mike said reasonably, 'it'll soon be sorted out. But if it isn't, well, I've got a lad that age and if you'd abducted *my* baby, I wouldn't be responsible for my actions. I'd want you caught, locked away, and the key thrown in the Tamar.'

'Thank you for your help, Mr Forest,' Droy said. 'When will you next be in Plymouth?'

'Day after tomorrow,' came the reply.

'That's fine. Perhaps you'd come into the station then, and make a formal statement.'

As Inspector Droy was speaking to Mike Forest, Andy Sharpe turned cold eyes onto Maggie. 'Where's the baby, Maggie?' he demanded. 'Where's Freddie?'

Maggie returned his look with a raised chin and a smirk, but remained mute, her lips pressed tightly together as if to prevent the answer escaping.

'Where is the baby, Maggie?' Andy asked again. 'What have you done with him?' When Maggie still remained silent, Andy exclaimed, a note of anger rising in his voice, 'For goodness' sake, Maggie! Why make things worse for yourself? Tell us where Freddie is!'

She held his gaze for several moments before she said, 'Who's Freddie? I know where Roger is... and he's quite safe.'

'So, where *is* Roger?'

'Wouldn't you like to know?'

'Yes,' replied Andy, 'I would.'

'Well,' she answered in a voice from the playground, 'I'm not going to tell you, so there!'

'Leave her be,' said Droy. 'We'll deal with her at the station.'

Reluctantly Andy said no more, but he was determined to get the truth once they had her in the interview room.

They led Maggie back to the police car. Andy sat beside her in the back and Droy drove them to the police station.

Once the paperwork had been done, and Maggie had picked at, and left, the lunch that arrived in her cell on a tin tray, she was taken to an interview room. Asked if she would like to have a lawyer present, she said no.

'I don't need one, I've done nothing wrong.'

'We can provide you with one if you want one,' Inspector Droy told her. 'It would be in your best interests.'

But Maggie remained adamant. 'I don't need anyone.'

'Then please sit down.' The inspector waved her to a chair across the table and took his seat on the other side. 'You see WPC Adams is here in the room but she will take no part in this interview. And you understand that Constable Dawes will be recording the interview in shorthand? He will write down my questions and your answers and you will be asked to sign it as a true and accurate account of this interview, today. Are you quite sure you do not want to have a solicitor with you while you are being questioned?'

'I will answer your questions,' Maggie replied. 'If I find I need someone later I will tell you.'

'Please note that in your record, Dawes,' instructed the inspector.

He laid a folder on the table in front of him and then

looked up, holding Maggie's eye for a long moment before he looked down at his papers and continued.

'For the record…' he said and he named the other people in the interview room and then asked Maggie to confirm her name, address and date of birth. Then he sat back and folding his arms said, 'The first thing I need to ask you, Mrs Peterson, is where is the child you call Roger Peterson?'

'I'm not saying.'

'And is the child you call Roger Peterson in fact your son?'

'Of course he is.' Maggie's gaze was unflinching.

'And what proof have you?'

'If you really need me to prove it,' answered Maggie, 'I have this.' And she drew Roger's birth certificate out of her pocket.

'I see that this is indeed the birth certificate for a boy, born to you and Colin Peterson on the twenty-ninth July 1940.'

'So, you have the proof that he is my son,' she replied, before adding in a low, sad voice, 'He's all I have left of Colin.'

'Well, I'm afraid there is a problem here,' Droy told her. 'If he is your son, how do you explain this?' He took a document from the folder in front of him and laid it before her. Maggie picked it up and looked at it and the colour drained from her face. She saw at once that it was a copy of her Roger's death certificate. She stared at it for a long moment and then, rallying, demanded, 'Where did you get this?'

'It's a matter of public record, madam,' replied the inspector. 'Your son died when he was only a few hours old.

The thirtieth July 1940 to be exact. The baby you claim is your son, is not. We have reason to believe that he is the son of Vera Shawbrook, of 21 Suffolk Place. Have you anything to say to that?'

'No,' replied Maggie.

'We believe that the child was inadvertently left in the house during the air raid on the twenty-first of April this year. A witness heard him crying the next morning and informed a nearby police officer, your husband, Sergeant Colin Peterson. Sergeant Peterson risked his life to enter the damaged house, 21 Suffolk Place, and carried the baby out to safety.' The inspector paused again, waiting for a response, but Maggie made none.

'We think that Sergeant Peterson brought the baby home to you. Before he reported finding the baby to the correct authorities, he, himself, was killed, and you decided to keep the child to replace the one you lost nine months earlier.'

Maggie glowered at him across the table. 'If Colin hadn't rescued him,' she retorted, 'he'd be dead. Colin saved his life and brought him home to me, because the whole city was in turmoil. Of course he reported finding the baby,' she said defiantly, 'he did that the very next day and we were waiting to hear if they had found his family, when Colin was killed. I still expected to hear from the authorities about the child, but in the meantime I took care of him. I looked after him, a damn sight better than his own family had. They left him to die by himself in an air raid!' She looked round the room as if she expected someone to commend what she had done. When no one said anything she went on, 'Every day I expected someone to call and say they had found his family, but nobody came, so I assumed they must be dead, killed in the raid that had destroyed his home.' Maggie glared round the room, before continuing angrily, 'That baby would have had no chance in life if Colin had taken him straight to a rescue centre. He'd have been dumped in some children's home, with other waifs and strays. Colin knew that and that was why he brought him home to me, to be looked after properly until somebody claimed him. I've looked after him for these last weeks as best I could. He's my son now, whatever you say.'

'I say he is not,' replied the inspector. He glanced at the police constable, seated in the corner of the room, taking down in shorthand, verbatim, all that was being said. 'You have all this, Dawes?'

'Yes, sir,' came the quick reply.

'I believe you took great trouble to conceal the fact that the child was not yours. You made up a story about him being looked after by one of his grandmothers... you seemed confused yourself about which one, but we have checked and as both had died before the date on your true son's birth certificate, that confusion doesn't matter. In either case the story was a lie.'

The inspector paused again, but Maggie said nothing.

'I have here the statement of a lady named Stella Todd...' he glanced again at Maggie, but she remained expressionless, so he continued, 'who has confirmed that she had to lend you a pram and some other items of baby equipment, as you seemed to have none. Officers who worked with your husband had a collection to provide you with a little extra cash to help tide you over the first few days after Colin was killed. I came to visit you myself to break the news of his death. I saw the child and you told me that he was your son.

You took none of the opportunities that occurred to report his rescue to me or to the proper authorities, indeed you did everything you could to convince those who saw you with the baby that he was yours. When Constable Sharpe came to your home and asked if you knew whether Colin had rescued a child from a particular house, you said no. You even went as far as to commiserate with the family who were desperately trying to find their baby.'

'They left him in a house all by himself during an air raid!' Maggie spoke slowly as if she were trying to explain something simple to a dullard. 'By himself! They don't deserve to have him. He'll be far better with me. I shall look after him properly. I shan't leave him alone anywhere.'

'And then,' the inspector continued, ignoring her sudden outburst, 'you simply took your chance and carried him off to the country, taking great care not to let anyone know where you were going.'

'I did what any sensible mother would do,' snapped Maggie. 'I took him away from a city which was a prime target for the Luftwaffe. I took him into the country where they weren't being bombed.'

'You told Mrs Todd that was what you were going to do, but you lied to her. You told her that you were going to work and live-in, in a pub.'

'So, I changed my mind. I had a better offer. I went to Martindell instead and worked for the Bridgers who live in the manor. That was a far better job than the one in the pub. And I had my own house. Which would you have chosen?'

'But you didn't think to mention that to Mrs Todd, who'd been so kind to you?'

'She's a gossip,' shrugged Maggie. 'I didn't want the whole street to know my business.'

'She respected your confidence and told no one even the little she did know. It was through her reticence that you didn't realise that the man and his daughter who have rented your flat are the child's true mother and grandfather.'

For a moment Maggie stared at him. 'Those people, the Shawbrooks? That wasn't the name in the paper. They're nothing to do with him.'

'So you did see the appeal in the paper? You did know that the baby's family were actively looking for him?' Maggie made no reply, simply turned her head and looked up at the window.

Inspector Droy paused again before going on, 'I know there was a misprint in the paper, but it would have been clear to you that it was the same child. The name may have been wrong, but the address and the date were right.

'Perhaps if Mrs Todd had been more of a gossip, she would have told you their sad story, but she thought you were struggling to come to terms with Colin's death, and so she didn't mention it, just told you they were looking for somewhere to live as they'd been bombed out. She thought she was helping both them and you.' He paused and then said, 'You left in a bit of hurry, didn't you? You didn't wait for the Shawbrooks to collect the keys. Mrs Todd has said in her statement that you asked her to hand them over, but that when she went in that morning the flat wasn't really ready to receive them. Always ready to help you, she tidied it up. But one of the things you had not taken with you in your hurry to pack was the little panda bear that your husband had brought home with the baby.'

'That dirty little thing? I gave him the lovely teddy that belonged—' She broke off and changed what she'd been going to say. 'I thought I'd thrown that thing away. It was disgusting.'

'I have a witness that says the child had the panda when your husband saved him from the house in Suffolk Place. A panda with a purple ribbon round its neck. That panda was found in your flat. It was recognised by the child's mother and our enquiries stem from there.'

'There must be hundreds of pandas like that,' scoffed Maggie.

'Quite possibly,' agreed the inspector, 'but Freddie Shawbrook's panda had a mended ear, and so did the one in your flat. It was the first lead we had that you were the person who had taken Freddie Shawbrook.'

'I didn't take him,' Maggie flashed back. 'Colin brought him home and I was left with him. I've looked after him ever since. He's mine now, and I want him back.'

'And where is he now, Mrs Peterson?'

Maggie gave him a crafty smile and said, 'That's for me to know and you to find out.'

'And I assure you we will,' Droy told her. 'But things would go better for you in court for you to tell us where he is.'

'So that he can be given back to that trollop? She doesn't deserve him.'

'Whatever you think of her, she's his mother, and once that has been proved to be so, he will be returned to her and to the other members of his family.'

'But what about me?' cried Maggie. 'I've taken care of him all this time! He'd be dead if Colin hadn't rescued him.'

'I'm sure that a judge will take that into consideration at your trial,' said Inspector Droy, closing the folder in front of him.

'My trial?' Maggie stared at him.

'You will be charged with abducting a baby, and keeping him hidden when you knew that his family were actively searching for him.' He turned to WPC Adams who had been present in the room for the entire interview. 'Take her back to her cell,' he said. 'We'll charge her and she'll be up before the magistrates in the next couple of days. We shall object to bail. Take her down.'

The WPC stepped forward and laying a hand on Maggie's shoulder, said, 'Please come with me Mrs Peterson.'

Slowly Maggie got to her feet and the policewoman led her to the door. As she reached it, Maggie turned back, staring at Inspector Droy she said, 'My husband Colin was a far better man than you. He saved that baby's life. Roger would be dead by now if I hadn't looked after him.'

When the door closed behind her Inspector Droy sighed. 'She knows he isn't her Roger,' he said, 'but she truly believes she has the right to keep him.'

'If she had reported what she'd been doing as soon as she knew the family were alive and looking for him, they'd probably have greeted her with open arms and thanked her for keeping him safe. Whether she knew if Colin had reported the rescue or not. But all her subterfuge will go against her. Her intent was to keep the child, and that intent was clear.'

'But we still don't know where Freddie is,' Andy pointed out. 'What can she have done with him? We need to find him before we tell Vera we've got Maggie.'

'I don't think she will have harmed him,' Droy said. 'Whatever she's done, she seems to have loved the child. I imagine she's left him with someone. Do we know who her friends are?'

'I don't think she has any here in Plymouth,' replied Andy. 'I would have said Mrs Todd, but I think that friendship is over. Anyway, we know he isn't there.'

'In that case you'd better ring round the hospitals and children's homes and see if anyone has taken in a baby boy with auburn hair.'

'I'll get on to that straight away,' said Andy, getting to his feet. 'There can't be that many.'

'We can, of course, ask her again,' said Droy, 'but I doubt if she'll tell us. I'm beginning to think she's a little unhinged. In the meantime, if you do decide to tell the Shawbrooks that we have Maggie in custody, please remember you may not disclose anything that was said here in interview.'

'No, sir, I do know that,' replied Sharpe. But even as he said it he knew Vera would do her utmost to get it out of him.

# 49

Mrs Leason, matron of the St Crispin's children's home in Laira, sat down in her own sitting room and poured herself a cup of tea. The day, as always, had been a busy one. It was seldom anything else, with thirty children whose ages ranged from six months to thirteen years old, to care for. She was always tired by the evening these days and was beginning to wonder if she were too old for the job and ought to retire. Her staff were excellent, but they too were stretched. Still, she always looked forward to her cup of tea before she made her evening rounds. She reached for the paper which lay folded on the small table beside her and shook it open at the front page. She stared at the headline, **HAVE YOU SEEN HER?** with its photograph underneath. Quickly she skimmed through the story and knew that she had to make a phone call. First, however, taking the newspaper with her, she went back to her office and found the day book in which they recorded everything that happened in the home, however trivial. Beside it was the official ledger in which was listed every child, sex, name, date of birth if known, estimate of age if not. She turned to the official record first and saw the latest addition to their number. A boy, Roger Smith, date of birth 29th July 1940. Known parent Margaret Smith, no fixed abode. In brackets, as with so many, *(Bombed out)*. Just the barest of facts then. She reached for the day book to see if anyone had written any comments. Roger's arrival was recorded in there as well, with the additional information that his mother was moving out of the city to live with her sister and her family, and that she would be back to fetch him as soon as she was settled in the new household.

Mrs Leason sighed. There were far too many such children, left by their parents because there was nowhere else for them to live. She remembered Mrs Smith quite well. She had seemed particularly nervous when she was registering him, asking why they needed so many details when the child was only going to be there for a few weeks.

'Because, God forbid, Mrs Smith, that something should happen to you, we need to know, if possible, who the next of kin is.'

Mrs Smith had looked flustered at this and said, 'Well, I suppose there isn't one really. But don't worry, Mrs Leason, I will come back and fetch him, just as soon as I'm able.'

Clearly, thought Mrs Leason, Mrs Smith is a single mother. Perhaps a widow, but more likely left with a bun in the oven when some sailor returned to his ship, and she had found that she couldn't cope. She didn't doubt that Mrs Smith fully intended to come back for her son, but she didn't really believe she would.

Now she picked up the paper again and looked at Mrs Smith's face. Mrs Leason had no doubts that Mrs Smith was the woman they were looking for, and she was not the mother of little Roger, asleep upstairs in his cot. Whether she had actually abducted the child, she didn't know. That wasn't her problem, but she knew she must ring the police station and tell them that she had Roger – or more probably Freddie – safe and sound in her care.

Inspector Droy was just leaving the station when the call came in.

'For you, sir,' called the desk sergeant and passed Droy the phone. He nearly instructed the sergeant to say that he was unavailable. After all, they had done all they could today. Indeed, he'd been about to send Andy Sharpe home, telling him he'd be better able to hunt for Freddie when he was fresh in the morning, but he took the call first. You never knew, someone had asked for him by name, and it could be important, so he held out his hand for the receiver.

'Inspector Droy,' he said briskly.

'Ah, Inspector, good evening. This is Mrs Leason, the matron at St Crispin's children's home in Laira.'

'Good evening, madam,' Droy replied. 'How can I help you?'

'I'm hoping I can help *you*,' answered Mrs Leason. 'I've just read the piece in the paper, about the woman you're looking for in connection with an abduction.'

'Oh, yes?' Droy certainly wasn't going to say that they had already found her, not until they had found the child and she'd been up before the magistrate.

'A woman resembling your Mrs Peterson came here two days ago, and asked us to look after her son. She told me she had been bombed out and was at present homeless. She said she was going to stay with her sister and family and when she was settled she would come and fetch Roger away.'

'Definitely Roger?' Droy couldn't keep the excitement out of his voice.

'Oh yes, Inspector, and definitely Mrs Peterson.'

'And she left the child with you?'

'She did indeed. He's asleep upstairs this very minute.'

'Mrs Leason,' Droy cried, 'that's absolutely wonderful news. I shall be able to break it to his real mother tomorrow. Of course she won't be able to claim him until the courts are satisfied that he is truly her son, but that shouldn't take too long. Can you keep him for now?'

'Well, I can,' agreed Mrs Leason, 'but what do I do if Mrs Peterson should come back before then?'

'Don't worry about that, Mrs Leason, I can assure you she won't.'

'Ah, I see,' said Mrs Leason. 'Thank you, you've set my mind at rest. Roger can certainly stay here for now.'

'Please can you amend your records? He has to get used to his own name again, and that's Freddie Shawbrook. I will come and see you tomorrow morning, if that is convenient, so that we can sort some of the inevitable paperwork.'

'Of course,' agreed the matron. 'I'll look forward to seeing you. Say about ten thirty?'

'Ten thirty it is,' said Inspector Droy and rang off. 'Sharpe!' he called. 'Come on! We're going to Marden Road!'

When the two policemen arrived at the flat they found Vera and her father had just finished their evening meal.

'Did that picture in the paper work?' Vera cried as she grabbed Andy's hand and pulled him into the flat. 'Have you caught her?'

'Yes, we have,' Andy said, beaming at her. 'She's in a cell at the police station.'

'Good,' said Vera with satisfaction. 'I hope she's very uncomfortable and miserable and—' Suddenly she broke off and asked, 'But where's Freddie?'

'He's safe and well,' answered Droy. 'He's in St Crispin's children's home in Laira.'

'But why have you put him there?' demanded Vera. 'Why haven't you brought him straight here to me?'

'We didn't put him there,' said Andy. 'She did. Maggie Peterson left him there a couple of days ago.'

'Why?'

'We don't know,' replied Andy, 'but that doesn't matter for now. At least we know he's safe.'

'But how did you find him?' Vera asked.

'The matron at the children's home saw Maggie's picture in the paper this evening,' explained Droy. 'She recognised her as the woman who had recently left a baby with them. She'd read that we were looking for him and so she phoned the police station to tell us. She told me that she's certain it's your Freddie even though she registered him as Roger Smith.'

Vera jumped to her feet. 'Come on then, let's go and get him.'

'Vera, I'm sorry, but we can't, not tonight,' said Droy. 'I've arranged to go and see the matron tomorrow morning. Even then I doubt if you'll be free to take him away from the home.'

'But he's mine!' Vera almost shouted.

'I know, love,' Andy said taking her hand, 'but you have to be patient. It's all going to take time.'

'We should let Mu know he's been found,' her father said, deftly changing the subject. 'She spent a lot of time trying to find him.'

'She's back at the hospital from today,' said Vera. 'She won't be off duty until later.'

'Don't worry,' Andy said. 'If she doesn't come here when she comes off duty, I'll drop in to see her at Mrs Dunbar's on my way home.'

'Well, I must be going,' said Inspector Droy. 'Just thought I'd bring you the good news. I'll go and see Mrs Leason tomorrow and I'll let you know what happens next.'

'Well, I'm coming with you,' stated Vera. 'I want to see my Freddie.'

The following morning they all went with Inspector Droy to St Crispin's. The others had to wait in a separate room while Droy and Mrs Leason spoke together in the matron's office. David and Andy sat waiting patiently, but Vera was unable to sit still. She paced the room, putting her ear to the door and listening, then coming back again to the window to look out into the garden. Then back to the door again.

'For goodness' sake, Vera,' David cried, 'sit down!'

She sat for a moment and then she was up on her feet again. 'I can't, Dad. I really can't. What are they talking about in there? Why can't I just go and see Freddie? I just want to see him!'

'I know, love,' Andy said soothingly. 'I know. They probably won't be much longer.'

'I'm sorry, Miss Shawbrook,' Mrs Leason said when they finally emerged. 'I can't release the baby left here by Mrs Margaret Smith until a judge has confirmed that he is indeed your child.'

'But surely I can see him?' cried Vera in anguish.

'I think that would be all right,' Mrs Leason said cautiously. 'I'll take you up to the nursery.'

She led the way through the house and up some stairs to a large room on the top floor. When she opened the door they could see several cots lined up against the wall, and a large playpen in the middle of the room. Sitting on the floor, banging a tin drum with a wooden spoon, was a baby boy with a cap of auburn curls.

Vera paused in the doorway and then with tears in her eyes, she turned to Andy and whispered, 'It's Freddie.' Slowly she walked across to the playpen and as she approached the child looked up at her and smiled. Mrs Leason, David and the two policemen watched as Vera knelt down beside him and passed a tired-looking panda with a purple bow around its neck through the bars of the playpen. For a moment or two the little boy looked at it and then his face creased into a huge beam of delight as he reached for it, and stroking the tip of the mended ear with his thumb, said, 'Pan!'

# Epilogue

## August 1941

Vera and Mu sat in the waiting room of St Crispin's children's home. Vera was on the edge of her chair with excitement. During the weeks before the judgement in her favour, Vera been visiting the home almost every day, letting Freddie get to know her again, but now, today, she was going to be taking him home.

On that first visit to St Crispin's Vera had turned to Inspector Droy and demanded, 'So, now can I take Freddie home with me?'

'Not for a while yet,' the inspector answered. 'Officially he's not yours until the judge says so.'

'Judge?' squeaked Vera. 'What judge?'

'You'll have to show that he really is your son,' explained Andy. 'There may be a court hearing to decide. You may all have to give evidence, or swear affidavits. To be honest, I'm not quite sure how it works, but you'll be told.'

Vera had been disappointed, for despite what Andy had

told her she had hoped Freddie would be returned to her at once, but she had to accept that the authorities needed to be sure he was truly hers. She wanted no challenges from Maggie Peterson, or anyone else, in the future.

The first time after that, when she had been allowed to visit, Freddie had been brought in by the matron. Vera had immediately got to her feet and reached for him, but the little boy turned his head away and buried his face in Mrs Leason's shoulder.

Vera had been devastated, crying out, 'He doesn't know me any more!'

'You have to give him time,' soothed Mrs Leason. 'A lot of things have happened to him in his short life, especially these last few months. He'll get to know you again in time. He won't be able to tell you, though he does say several words now, but the link with you will be re-established if you don't rush him. It's amazing the connections that a small baby makes with its mother, her distinctive smell, the sound of her voice, the feel of her skin. Freddie will have established those with you before he was removed. Somewhere deep inside he will gradually recognise you again.'

'But will he forget *her*?' Vera asked. 'I don't want him to be remembering *her* voice.' Adding fiercely, 'And certainly not her smell.'

'They may have been superimposed for a while,' replied Mrs Leason, 'but they won't have been imprinted from birth.'

The new flat had been inspected by Mrs Leason, a stipulation made by the judge, and it had been passed as an acceptable home for Freddie when he returned to his family.

With this final requirement now fulfilled, today was the day he would leave St Crispin's and come home.

'I believe you're getting married,' Miss Leason said to Vera with a smile. 'I hope you'll be very happy. Freddie's a lucky little boy to have such a loving and supportive family.'

When he was brought into the waiting room, he was dressed and ready for outdoors, and seeing Vera he staggered across the room on uncertain legs and lifted his arms to be picked up.

'Hello, Freddie,' said Vera softly as he snuggled against her shoulder. 'I've come to take you home.'

Mrs Leason smiled. She was pleased there had been such a happy outcome to what might have been such a tragic story, and she knew that young Freddie Shawbrook was none the worse for his experiences with Maggie Peterson.

She handed Vera his identity card and a new ration book and Mu picked up a carrier bag containing his few clothes.

'As you were bombed out, you may be able to apply for more coupons if necessary,' Mrs Leason said. She turned to Mu and asked, 'Are you going to be living with them as well?'

Mu shook her head. 'No,' she said. 'My husband is in Scotland with the navy. I've been nursing while he's been away, but I've just discovered that I'm expecting, and now the hospital won't employ me any more. We've decided that I should move to Campbeltown where he's stationed so that I'm close by when he has shore leave.'

Patrick had been over the moon when Mu had written to tell him that they were having a baby.

*My darling heart, I couldn't be more thrilled and excited. A whole new person! If you're not allowed to work at the hospital any more, why don't you come up here to live? I'll be able to see you whenever I'm ashore. I've found you a decent room in the town, with a Mrs Gulliver. I've seen my parents several times, and they can't wait to meet you. They are so excited about having a grandchild. Look after yourself, darling, and remember I love you more than anyone in the world! All my love to you and our bump!*

*Patrick xx*

Mu's reply had been immediate.

*Vera has Freddie safely back again and she and Andy are to be married next Saturday. They will be living with Dad in the new flat, so nobody needs me now except you and Bump. I'll be on the train to Glasgow on Monday, after their wedding, so tell Mrs Gulliver I'll be there in about ten days. I can't wait!*

*Bump and I send our love. Mu. xx*

# Acknowledgements

Much of this book was written during the difficult times of the 2020 summer lockdown. I would like to thank all those who kept me going when I seemed to be running out of steam, particularly Rosie de Courcy, my editor, and her team at Head of Zeus and Judith Murdoch, my agent. They were, as always, unfailingly supportive, ready with advice and encouragement when I needed it most.

Also my thanks go to my good friends, Commander John McCombe RN (retired) and Dermot Flynn, 'a former naval person', both of whom allowed me to pick their brains when I was aboard HMS *Cumbria* in the Western Approaches. Their help was invaluable – any mistakes are my own.

Finally, I would like to thank Alan and Maggie Peterson for their generous donation to the Cure Parkinson's Trust, the charity that helps fund research to find a cure for this debilitating disease, and thus lending me Maggie's name for my main character.

This year has been difficult for everyone and I am full of gratitude for anyone who has helped in the production of this book. Thank you all.